THE LADY OF ASHES MYSTERIES

Lady of Ashes
Stolen Remains
A Virtuous Death
The Mourning Bells
Death at the Abbey
A Grave Celebration

ALSO BY CHRISTINE TRENT

By the King's Design
A Royal Likeness
The Queen's Dollmaker

A GRAVE CELEBRATION

A Lady of Ashes Mystery

CHRISTINE TRENT

TWOPENCE PRESS

www.twopencepress.com

TWOPENCE PRESS books are published by
Twopence Press, LLC
P.O. Box 1753
Leonardtown, Maryland 20650

All Twopence Press titles are available at special quantity discounts for bulk purchases for sales promotion, premiums, fund-raising, educational, or institutional use.

eISBN-13: 978-1-944745-01-1
eISBN-10: 1-944745-01-7
First Twopence Press Electronic Edition: November 2016

ISBN-13: 978-1-944745-00-4
ISBN-10: 1-944745-00-9
First Twopence Press Trade Paperback Printing: November 2016

10 9 8 7 6 5 4 3 2 1

Printed in the United States of America

Cover Design and Interior Format by

In memory of
Georgia Carpenter
March 30, 1945–October 24, 2015
*Mother, voracious mystery reader, and my irreplaceable
grammar editor*

CAST OF CHARACTERS

THE BRITISH
Violet Harper—undertaker
Sir Henry Elliot—British ambassador to Constantinople
Asa Brooks—Elliot's man of affairs
Commander George Nares—captain of HMS Newport

THE FRENCH
Ferdinand de Lesseps—mastermind behind the Suez Canal
Louise-Hélène Autard de Bragard—de Lesseps's much younger fiancée
Isabelle Dumont—lady's maid to Louise-Hélène
Eugénie de Montijo—empress of France
Julie Lesage—lady's maid to Eugénie
Théophile Gautier—poet, dramatist, novelist, journalist, and art and literary critic
Auguste Mariette—director of the Museum of Cairo

THE EGYPTIANS
Isma'il Pasha—khedive (viceroy) of Egypt
Tewfik Pasha—Isma'il's eldest son and heir
Hassan Salib—cultural attaché to the khedive
Rashad Salib—Hassan's brother; porter to the khedive
Samir Basara—archaeologist working at the Museum of Cairo

THE AMERICANS
Samuel Harper—Violet's husband and a Civil War veteran
Thaddeus Mott—adventurer, sailor, soldier of fortune
Ross Keating—Civil War veteran
Owen Morris—Civil War veteran
Caleb Purdy—Civil War veteran

THE AUSTRIANS
Franz-Josef—emperor of Austria and king of Hungary
Karl Dorn—Franz-Josef's chamberlain

THE RUSSIANS
Grand Duke Michael—brother of Tsar Alexander II of Russia
Count Nikolay Pavlovich Ignatiev—Russian ambassador to
  Constantinople

THE PRUSSIANS
Crown Prince Frederick—heir to the throne of Prussia
Richard Lepsius—Prussian Egyptologist

The names of the Egyptian sovereigns who erected the Pyramids, those useless monuments of human pride, will be ignored. The name of the Prince who will have opened the grand canal through Suez will be blessed from century to century down to the most distant posterity.
— Ferdinand de Lesseps to Egyptian ruler Muhammad Sa'id, ca. 1854

chapter 1

November 10, 1869
Cairo, Egypt

THE HANDWRITTEN LETTER WAS QUICK, to the point, and left Auguste Mariette blustering in a rage he hadn't known since he'd caught an employee snoring inside a fragile Eleventh Dynasty limestone sarcophagus. He scanned the note again in disbelief.

> *You are hereby notified that crates being shipped to Cairo along the Nile have been intercepted and are now en route to Port Said for my inspection. This inspection will be conducted aboard* El Mahrousa *as it sails the Suez Canal toward the opening ceremonies in Port Ismailia. From there, items in the shipment that I do not select will be forwarded on to you in Cairo via the Fresh Water Canal for inclusion in the museum's collection.*
>
> *Isma'il Pasha*
> *Khedive of Egypt*

Impossible, Mariette thought. *Damn the khedive and his shameful arrogance.*

The museum director crumpled the letter with both hands and threw it, grimacing when it barely cleared the other side of his desk and dropped to the floor with an unsatisfying *smack*. He was itching to summon a servant just to have someone to vent his rage on. How *dare* the khedive once again intercept a precious shipment of antiquities, treating them not as if they were to be preserved for Egyptian posterity, but as if they belonged in his own personal curio cabinet?

Bile rose in Mariette's throat, and he hawked a ball of phlegm into a nearby spittoon of carved bronze. A reproduction, of course. He would never dream of sullying a genuine antique article.

After everything Mariette had done to celebrate the opening of the Suez Canal, including writing the scenario for an opera, *Aida*, for which the khedive had professed great admiration, this was how he was to be treated.

This had all started a decade ago, after Mariette had established the Museum of Egyptian Antiquities. For the love of Anubis, the Egyptian government had practically *begged* him to take the role of director, especially given his success in conserving no fewer than thirty-five important dig sites around the country— including the necropolis at Memphis, no less. Supposedly they wanted all of these precious items brought together and kept out of the hands of other countries, which were constantly attempting to spirit them out of Egypt and sell them into private hands.

Especially the British. *Bon sang*, but they made an avocation out of stealing everything from everybody under the auspices of preservation. The Elgin Marbles from the Greeks, imperial relics from China's Old Summer Palace, and they had been rapaciously excavating Egypt's pyramids and temples for decades. Ironically, the British Museum contained more precious Egyptian artifacts than Mariette had been able to gather since the inception of Egypt's national museum in 1858.

As if it weren't enough to battle foreign governments, he was forced to do battle with the Egyptians themselves. What was he supposed to do to keep the khedive—formally elevated from governor to his new position of khedive, or viceroy, by the Ottoman sultan—from perpetually confiscating his own country's valuables? The man was incorrigible, Mariette concluded, as ten years ago the khedive had intercepted a boatload of antiquities from the tomb of Queen Ahhotep I, on its journey from Thebes to Cairo, forcing Mariette to race out, crossing the khedive's orders to rescue the cargo. Mariette had periodically intervened to save treasures ever since, but it was most upsetting when the culprit was the very authority who had granted his position to protect Egyptian treasures.

So was this what it meant to be the director of antiquities? To perpetually pluck valuables out of the grasping, thieving hands of the very people who should most respect the antiquities as possessions of the Egyptians? It was *scandaleux*, an outrage.

Mariette spat again, but it wasn't particularly satisfying, especially when he reached up and realized there was a bit of dribble in his beard. Several epithets came to mind, and he pounded his fist on the desk as he uttered each one with as much venom as he could muster. Spent from that, he sat down heavily in his tufted leather chair. His nearly fifty years were catching up with both his patience and his girth.

Had he wasted his entire career in this double-dealing country, despite all of his magnificent discoveries? Of what use was it if the artifacts would all end up in private collections? Should he have simply stayed in Boulogne and never come here?

Perhaps his wife wouldn't have died if she hadn't been brought here. He laughed hollowly, recalling how she routinely complained that he was becoming an Egyptian, with his dense, curling chin-curtain beard and his propensity for Egyptian-style dress. He could have made no such claim of her, given that she received shipments of the latest French fashions, books, and outdated magazines on nearly every boat docking in Cairo from their home country until she was carried away by fever five years ago.

He sat with his elbow on the polished sycamore desk, specially crafted for him with locally harvested trees after he had become the director of antiquities. He smoothed his mustache with a thumb and forefinger as he thoughtfully regarded the artifacts and wood crates lining the shelves and floor of his office. Normally, this activity would have calmed him, reminding him of the importance of his life's mission. Today, however, there seemed to be more heat billowing from within Mariette than could be seen emanating from the funnel of an Atlantic steamer ship. He had to do something about this intolerable situation. He knew that he could not fight the British single-handedly, but surely there was a solution to the khedive's endless plundering of Egypt's treasures. Mariette's ego and pride simply could *not* bear the thought of leaving behind a legacy that wasn't positively sterling.

The director continued compulsively smoothing his facial hair as he picked up a canopic jar from the corner of his desk. He ran his thumb over the smooth base of the jar as he looked into the blank, carved eyes of Duamutef, the jackal-headed god representing the east. Inside the jar was a dried-up stomach, but Mariette respected ancient Egypt's burial practices enough not to open the jar to gawk sacrilegiously at its contents, even if he did keep the jar sitting on his desk as decoration.

As he deliberated his options over the next two hours, he ignored several raps on his door. He even barked at a servant who had arrived with his ritual afternoon coffee, sending the frightened man scurrying back into the hallway. Finally, though, Mariette's good humor returned, almost as if Duamutef of the canopic jar had reminded him of the importance of protecting the organs of the dead. He knew what he had to do. The khedive might not believe Egypt's precious antiquities rightfully belonged in a museum, but that didn't mean the man couldn't be . . . *persuaded*.

chapter 2

November 16, 1869
Port Said, Egypt

THE MAN WHO HAD JUST been stabbed stared in horrified disbelief at his attacker, then pulled a calloused hand away from his chest. His palm was smeared in dark red mixed with the fine wood shavings that habitually covered him like a tightly fitted glove.

The thrust of the blade had been so sudden and so deep that he had hardly realized what had happened, so quickly had the conversation gone from casual inquiry at the lumberyard to violent argument with his attacker, whom he didn't even recognize.

The attacker stood over him now, leering wolfishly over what had been done, as the victim sank to his knees. He tasted the nauseating, metallic tang of his own blood.

Not just an attacker, a murderer.

The man gazed beyond his attacker at the magnificent ships pulling into the port—yachts, corvettes, gunboats, and other gleaming white vessels—all flying colors of their respective countries.

Tonight was supposed to be the gateway to a week of celebrations fit for the royalty who traveled aboard the ships, and especially for the glory of Monsieur de Lesseps, who had spent so much time in Egypt that he was practically accepted as a native.

More blood gushing up caused the man to cough and gurgle involuntarily, and he immediately thought that he was shaming himself by responding so weakly. He should be able to die bravely, without fear or panic.

He attempted to fix a steely glare at his murderer, but black spots danced before him, obstructing his vision. He struggled to both spit out and swallow his own blood in an attempt to clear his throat, and he found that he was becoming light-headed and dizzy.

Before he toppled completely over onto the rough, dusty ground, an incongruous thought struck him. How disappointing it was that he would not get to revel in all the important people aboard the ships now docking who all held the polluted secrets that important people tended to keep, amassing them like curiosities in a cabinet, to be pulled out and inspected on occasion before being placed back on their orderly shelves.

The man heard a mingling of voices around him, but he was pitching forward now and could see no one, not even his murderer.

He felt nothing as he hit the ground, neither his nose breaking nor the jagged stone opening a gash in his forehead. He wasn't even aware of the small cloud of dust that enveloped him as his body made contact with the hard earth. His last thought was of the indignity of being flipped over by someone's foot, as the murderer laughed at him with malevolent amusement. But the man's eyes had glassed over, and he could no longer attach a face to the raucous merriment above him.

chapter 3

I T WAS A RELIEF TO be on terra firma again, Violet thought. They had been nearly two weeks at sea, and although the journey had been uneventful, there was only so much sea air and salt spray she could take. Not to mention the fact that their quarters, while not uncomfortable, had given her some serious bouts of stomach roiling as she tried to sleep while they tossed to and fro in the water.

Her gladness that they were docked, though, was nothing compared to how overwhelmed she was by what awaited them on shore. She knew that a major international event would attract a great deal of attention and fanfare, and the port didn't disappoint her expectations. It looked like an enormous, glittering festival, dominated by two stages that faced each other, one flying the French colors and one flying the Egyptian flag. Throngs of people surged around every available square inch of space.

The stages were simply the largest edifices in a sweeping vista of striped tents, garland-festooned buildings, and people of every imaginable nationality. Rows of buildings had signs in multiple languages identifying them as jewelry makers, butchers, gold sellers, and coffee shops, and there were others selling candies, vegetables, pigeons, and eggs. There was even a lumberyard, full of cut logs and sawn planks, as well as a place to hire out camels.

Violet glanced down at her dress, a pale blue frock edged in black, unadorned except for a black bow with its ribbons trailing down the skirt. Was it stylish enough for such an international exposition?

As she disembarked into the afternoon sunshine with Sam's hand lightly, but protectively, at her back, she felt like a piece of glass in a necklace full of priceless gemstones. Heavens, why did she care about such a thing all of a sudden? She was a woman who wore mourning dress as a raven wears its black feathers—a natural part of her being, her raison d'être. What difference did it make if she wasn't clad in a rich scarlet shawl over a royal blue tunic like that flawlessly complected woman welcoming newcomers? Or if she didn't have the ability to carry off the rich burgundy-and-silver ensemble of that laughing woman standing next to a man in matching colors?

As if sensing her sudden insecurity, Sam lifted his hand from her back, crooked his arm, and offered it to her as he smiled down at her. "I hope this country is prepared. The legends of Cleopatra have nothing on my wife." He tapped his cane twice on the gangplank for emphasis. "Their scribes might have to start creating new mythology."

"Oh, Sam." Violet knew it was foolish to feel so ridiculously pleased, as though she were a giddy young girl receiving her first compliment from a beau, yet she briefly leaned her head against his arm in appreciation. That arm was clad in a Union infantry shell jacket, with its single row of bright brass buttons running up the front and adorning the wrists. Their ship's captain had initially expressed disapproval that a member of the British delegation would wear a foreign uniform, but he eventually just shrugged and said, "Americans," before piloting back to Great Britain.

The Harpers' belongings were being transferred to HMS *Newport*, a vessel that carried the Prince of Wales and the ambassador to Constantinople. *Newport* had been part of a flotilla of foreign dignitaries sailing down the Nile for the past several weeks to tour Egyptian sites as guests of the khedive.

Violet had only been invited to the opening ceremonies, not the luxurious sightseeing trip, and so she and Sam were now joining the British delegation's ship.

It was just as well that she hadn't been invited on the exotic trip down the Nile, since at the time she was completing a murder investigation on a remote estate in Nottinghamshire for a very peculiar duke. If she had abruptly left for Egypt, a devious criminal might have gotten away with more than one murder.

At Sam's waist was a leather scabbard containing a saber given to him by a superior officer as a personal gift for brave service at Marye's Heights during the battle at Fredericksburg, Virginia. Sam had been wounded in that battle, hence his limp that was either worse or better depending on the weather. Today, though, the jacket seemed to have the effect of making him as tall and erect and proud as she had ever seen him. Violet hadn't been sure about his selection of clothing for the evening, but now she realized that it was perfect, given the number of men on shore ostentatiously adorned in epaulets, ribbons, and medals.

Violet took a deep breath as they reached the end of the gangplank. There they were greeted by the woman in the scarlet shawl, whom Violet could now see held a basket and was offering up what appeared to be filled cookies to the disembarking passengers. Next to the woman was a man in a formal black suit who held out a hand in greeting. He was tall and thin, with leathery sunburnt skin and hair the color of storm clouds. It all suggested someone whose disposition didn't quite agree with his task, but then he smiled at them, and the impending doom parted and decades washed away from his face.

"Mr. and Mrs. Harper?" he asked. "I am Sir Henry Elliot, the ambassador to Constantinople. I received a telegraph that I was to meet your ship and see that you made it onto HMS *Newport* with the rest of the delegation. First, though, you must try one of these," he said, indicating the proffered basket.

Violet hesitated, so the ambassador reached in himself. "Ah, yes, my favorite," he said, happily taking two of the rich little golden treats and popping one in his mouth, immediately followed by the other. He took approximately two chews before swallowing. "Fig rolls, Mrs. Harper. Trust me, the cuisine here is just as exotic as the landscape."

The ambassador flicked away crumbs, then pointed to an area near the stage that was flying French colors. "Kindly join us over there at dusk." He inclined his head and moved away quickly, a man undoubtedly on many missions this afternoon.

Violet tentatively took a cookie from the woman and bit into it. The sweet and heady tastes of honey and cardamom burst inside her mouth as no sticky Chelsea bun back home could ever hope to accomplish. "Mmmm," she said as Sam reached for a serving and made his own appreciative noises.

They moved farther along, slowly making their way to where the stages were. There were throngs of people milling about in anticipation of the forthcoming ceremonies. All around them was a whirlwind of spicy cooking smells, brightly clad people, and the chattering of an endless number of languages.

"Is this the opening of the Suez Canal or the Tower of Babel?" Sam asked as he waved away a young boy who was attempting to sell them a caged pair of doves. Violet saw that her husband surreptitiously handed the boy a coin, causing the child to frown in confusion when Sam still shook his head no at accepting the cage. The boy gleefully darted off to the next set of Europeans he saw.

"Laborers for the canal came from many countries," Violet said. "Until recently, much of the labor was conscripted in some way. Monsieur de Lesseps was blackmailed over it, remember?" Violet had nearly been killed in solving a problem related to the canal for the queen, but it had resulted in Her Majesty's invitation for the Harpers to attend the ceremonies.

"Of course." Sam frowned at the memory, a time when he'd been off in Sweden working with Mr. Nobel. He had been very angry with himself at the time for having no notion of his wife's distress, and Violet now regretted bringing it up.

They were completely distracted from the topic, though, by the blast of trumpets coming from one of the delegation ships. Violet and Sam turned, as did thousands of others, and nearly everything hushed in response to the heralding of something—

or someone—important. Six liveried trumpeters stood on one end of a ship's deck, blowing as mightily as if they were playing Jewish shofars inside a temple.

The impressive ship's sails had been furled out of the way, as if to part for the great esteem and illustriousness of whoever was about to emerge. Now that they had the attention of everyone ashore, the trumpeters marched in a precise row toward the center of the ship, where three each lined up on either side of the gangplank.

Sam put a hand up to shield his eyes from the glaring sun. "Can't tell what nationality the flag is," he said.

Violet squinted up, too. "Austrian, I think?"

The trumpeters blew again, but this time it was not simply a blast but a tune, presumably an anthem. As it rose in crescendo, a figure in military uniform, gleaming medals across his chest, appeared on deck and waved solemnly to the crowds before exiting along the gangplank. He carried himself stiffly and with remarkable precision, almost as if he knew how to maintain an exact distance between his feet with each step he took. A well-dressed servant followed the royal figure at a considerable distance.

Violet remarked, "Sam, I believe that's the emperor of Austria!"

Off to her right, Violet noticed a woman clad in an officer's cap with her skirt looped up to reveal bright yellow leggings making her way to the bottom of the Austrian ship's gangplank, where she gazed up at the man with a smile on her lips. The emperor looked straight ahead until he reached the shore, and as the trumpeters made a closing blast, he bowed for far too long over the woman's hand and kissed it, then offered his elbow as Sam had done to Violet earlier. Who was this woman? She couldn't possibly be his wife, for obviously she would have been on the same ship with him.

Curious . . .

After the man rose from the woman's hand, he greeted others who now surrounded the woman, among them an older, mustachioed man, solidly built with a mane of white hair. Standing meekly behind him was a young slip of a girl, certainly no older than Susanna, whose attending maid seemed more confident than her mistress. His granddaughter, perhaps? The murmur of indistinguishable voices floated over to Violet. Maybe it was the warm sunshine relaxing her, or maybe it was the ambrosial fig rolls settling contentedly in her stomach, but despite the fact that she felt like a reporter for a society magazine, or maybe even the *Illustrated Police News*, her great curiosity caused Violet to be less concerned about her appearance. Now she wondered more about the members of the various other delegations with whom they would be sharing time and space for the next week.

When the excitement of the emperor had subsided, and the throngs went about their business, Violet and Sam continued to wander. In the midst of the crowds, they came upon two children playing a sprightly game of leapfrog. Finding a bench in a nearby shady spot under an empty market awning, they amused themselves watching the children play. After a half hour of entertainment, they made their way to the spot the ambassador had previously indicated. It would seem that each delegation had received the same instructions, for the area was teeming with Europeans, including a man Violet knew well: Albert Edward, the Prince of Wales, nicknamed Bertie by Queen Victoria.

Before Ambassador Elliot—who had just joined them, out of breath as if he had just run from England itself—could begin introductions, the prince approached Violet and Sam.

"It would seem I am never to be rid of the undertaker," he said. The words seemed harsh, but his tone held no malice. "At least you do not look the part, Mrs. Harper, and you are indeed quite fetching in your gown. A decided improvement on old Lord Raybourn."

Raybourn had accompanied the prince on his previous trip to Egypt back in March. Raybourn's murder had sparked an investigation that had placed Violet in the unenviable position of irritating the pleasure-loving prince.

Violet curtsied, finding the self-confidence she had briefly lost when initially leaving the safety of the ship. "Your Highness, fear not, as although I do not look the part, my undertaking bag is being transferred to your ship as we speak, in case there is an emergency embalming I need to perform."

She tilted her head and offered him a challenging gaze. The prince had caused her no end of trouble during one of her investigations for the queen, and she would permit no one—not even the heir to the throne—to cause her a disturbance on this pleasure trip.

At first she thought she would be sharply reprimanded, so horrified were the expressions on the faces of everyone else around them, but the prince simply laughed. "You all must be very careful," he instructed the assembled group. "Mrs. Harper will discover your darkest secrets and drain them out of you with needle and tube."

The others followed his lead, laughing politely, but the prince's endorsement clearly hadn't relieved them of their discomfort.

Violet smiled politely, too. It wasn't the first time Violet had earned aristocratic reproach, and she doubted this would be her final moment in doing so, either. At least her profession was out in the open before everyone already, and she wouldn't have to endure a protracted series of disapproving clucks and grimaces. The disapproval surrounded Violet now like hornets from a hive that had just been poked, buzzing about, not sure what they were venturing out for.

Violet had been nearly bludgeoned, stabbed, and scalded to death before, so an assembly of bejeweled and beribboned noteworthies scowling at her could be dispatched simply by ignoring their imagined or real disapproval, whereupon the hornets would return to the nest.

The meek girl, though, did not seem repulsed by Violet. In fact, her intense gaze was one of open curiosity. That curiosity appeared to be genuine, not that of a hornet contemplating a juicy grasshopper.

The young woman staring at Violet made her way past the woman in the outlandish yellow dress, a maid close on her heels.

"Madame," she said haltingly, "I remember your name. Were you not responsible for assisting de Lesseps in a peculiar situation a few months ago? I am Louise-Hélène Autard de Bragard, and we are to be married back in Paris after the ceremonies are concluded." The young woman, whose mouse-brown hair was an uncontrolled mass despite a plethora of pins protruding from beneath her hat, stuck out a hand and shook Violet's. Louise-Hélène's other hand clutched a necklace that she quickly shoved into her dress pocket. Violet caught the flash of a cross as the beaded item disappeared into the gown.

Was there a hint of trembling in the girl's hand? She couldn't possibly be twenty years old, and yet here she was, surrounded by the most illustrious, powerful leaders of the civilized world—her fiancé included. Perhaps she felt as out of place at the moment as Violet did.

"Pleased to meet you, mademoiselle," Violet said as she held the girl's hand. "Warmest felicitations on your upcoming nuptials. It was my honor to assist Monsieur de Lesseps," Violet replied as the much older, mustachioed man joined them and put a possessive hand to the girl's elbow.

"I am de Lesseps," he announced. De Lesseps wore his name with the confidence of a man who was used to great success in his life, as if "de Lesseps" were a title of grandeur, which Violet supposed that in some ways it was.

The Prince of Wales stepped forward and introduced Violet to de Lesseps. The older man's eyes twinkled. "You cannot mean to say that I was rescued from blackmail by a *belle femme* who buries dead bodies?"

"Sadly, yes," the prince said. "She seems to appear at the oddest times. But you will become accustomed to her apparent omnipresence, monsieur. We all have."

De Lesseps's mustache broadened with his smile at the prince's remark.

Again, there was no malice in the prince's tone, and he even took it upon himself to introduce Violet to the other delegation members milling about nearby.

The elegant woman in the nautical-themed clothing was Eugénie de Montijo, the empress of France, who was in attendance without her husband, Emperor Napoléon III, who had pressing affairs of state keeping him back in his home country.

Violet recognized the man who had been accompanied by the earlier ceremonial trumpet fanfare as he disembarked from the ship, and the prince introduced Austrian emperor Franz-Josef, who had left behind his own empress, Elisabeth. Standing near Franz-Josef, Eugénie, and Louise-Hélène were people Violet assumed to be a valet and two maids, given their lesser dress and deferential posture, plus the fact that they were not made part of the introductions.

A stout olive-complected man in yet another military uniform and a pail-shaped burgundy hat now joined them. "Monsieur de Lesseps, my men will be ready to start fireworks at seven o'clock," he said. His manner was deferential to the Frenchman, so much so that Violet was surprised to learn that this was Isma'il Pasha, the khedive of Egypt.

"Yes, I expect a stunning show, Pasha," de Lesseps said, almost offhandedly. Was de Lesseps's reputation and stature such that he could speak in such a manner to the sovereign head of Egypt?

"It will be perfect, monsieur," Pasha said, nodding his head rapidly, his hands folded in front of him.

As Pasha moved off, presumably to ensure that the volatile fireworks understood their responsibility for perfection, the Prince of Wales shook his head. "A shame, that is," he said, drawing a cigar from inside his jacket. "Why the viceroy of Egypt kowtows to a Frenchman is beyond me. Now if it were an Englishman . . ."

Franz-Josef's man appeared promptly at his side with a glass cylinder. The man flicked a metal lever on the jar, and a jet flame hissed from a nozzle on it.

Bertie drew deeply, and Violet thought he might expound on his sardonic comment after exhaling a long plume of smoke, but he merely said, "Looks like the Russians are entertaining themselves elsewhere, Mrs. Harper, so I'll introduce you later."

He inclined his head at her and signaled to Sam to join him as he moved into conversation with de Lesseps and Franz-Josef.

Louise-Hélène engaged Violet in animated chattering while the men stood about talking inanities with their chests puffed out as far as possible. It was as though verbal battle lines had been drawn across Austria, France, and Great Britain, with the United States observing.

In heavily accented English, de Lesseps's fiancée talked about everything from the shopping at Port Said to the mummy-unwrapping parties she had attended along the Nile. It struck Violet that the girl was nervous and her ebullience seemed to mask some sort of dislike, maybe even fear. Louise-Hélène frequently cut looks in Eugénie's direction, but the poor girl was neither sophisticated enough to conceal her feelings nor nearly as discreet as she might have thought she was. What was the source of her animosity? For her part, Eugénie seemed not to notice that the girl was even there, going over to cling to Franz-Josef's arm and concentrate her attention on the men's conversation.

Louise-Hélène's prattling was rudely interrupted by Eugénie's maid, whom Louise-Hélène introduced as Julie Lesage. She was a haughty woman dressed in far more expensive clothes than either Violet or Louise-Hélène. Of course, she was probably wearing her mistress's cast-off and altered clothing. Violet estimated she was in her midtwenties. Julie would have been an attractive woman with her fair hair and skin, and large green eyes, but her expression was hard and embittered, thus shattering her beauty.

"I noticed you purchased a little alabaster pyramid today, Mademoiselle de Bragard. I'm surprised you didn't also pick up a toy camel to complete your ancient pyramid tableau to play with in your cabin." The young woman smirked at her own joke.

Violet was aghast at the maid's treatment of Louise-Hélène. De Lesseps's betrothed had good standing to verbally smack the maid into the crowded waters of the canal, but instead seemed as apprehensive of the maid as she was of Eugénie. Louise-Hélène's maid bit her lip as though pinching back a retort. The animosity between the women was palpable.

Violet felt an unexpected rush of affection, or perhaps it was solicitude, for this Louise-Hélène, who reminded Violet of her own dear daughter, Susanna, who was seven thousand miles away in Colorado with her husband.

"I should love to see your acquisitions," Violet said warmly. "Perhaps there will be an opportunity this week. Actually, I would be grateful for your recommendations for shopping here at Port Said since we only have this evening here before heading to Port Ismailia in the morning."

Louise-Hélène blushed, bringing attractive color to her face beneath that wild mane of hair barely subdued by her hat. "I am happy to give you recommendations. Isabelle, take my parasol, please," she said, handing her own maid her umbrella and now using her free hands to gesture around at the shore. "Do you see the tall green tent in the distance? That marks the entrance to the Arab shopping district. That is where you can find the artifacts *anciens*."

"Or the most amateurish fakes," Julie murmured derisively. Isabelle responded in a whispered stream of furious French that Violet couldn't follow.

Obviously pretending not to hear, Louise-Hélène swung her hand around and pointed off to another tent top, closer and more readily visible over the heads of the crowds. "That red tent is where the European district begins. My fiancé has ensured that not only are goods from the delegation countries well represented, but that there are stalls from all of the countries that have provided workers for the canal. It is quite magnificent."

"Thank you," Violet said. "I shall have to pry my husband away from what is surely talk about tonnage and sail plans to have him escort me shopping. I would very much like to try the Arab district first." She was about to signal for Sam's attention, but Julie opened her mouth first.

"So you are the best the British queen can send here to represent her country? A handler of dead bodies? Is your husband the grave digger?" She exuded mockery and disdain.

Violet's first instinct was to snarl a retort, but instead she took a deep breath. "I am but a minor member of Her Majesty's delegation. She has bestowed a great honor upon us, and I will not see her disparaged," she said evenly, but Julie's expression told Violet that the other woman realized she had scored a point. What hold did this maid have on Louise-Hélène?

By this point, Eugénie must have been bored by the men's talk, for she had rejoined the women. The empress was even more elegant up close than she had been from a distance. It was a wonder that Franz-Josef was the only man fawning over her. From her perfectly coiffed hair to her graceful hand movements, Eugénie exuded grace from even the very threads of her couturier-made clothing, despite how flamboyant it was.

"Did someone mention shopping?" she asked. "I was stuck on board during this afternoon's shopping expedition while Julie fussed with my hair. *Ma chérie*," she said, addressing Louise-Hélène, "you don't know how fortunate you are that your hair has such . . . fullness so that you do not need to be consumed with endless hours of primping and smartening."

Louise-Hélène went red once more at the apparent insult. "Yes, Your Highness," she said through gritted teeth. Violet was certain the girl would have broken down in tears if her pride hadn't been a firmly erected wall around her emotions. "Madame Harper is planning to go to the Arab district for souvenirs. Perhaps you would like to join her. There is also the European district—"

Eugénie, though, didn't seem to notice Louise-Hélène's discomfort. "Ah, yes, I will certainly visit the European district. I must see if the emperor will escort me." She merely had to flutter her eyelashes in Franz-Josef's direction and the emperor was upon her, his servant in his wake. Eugénie laughingly told the emperor of her desire to shop, and he immediately offered an arm to her. It wasn't difficult to see how he could be besotted with her, her tiny nose wrinkling when she smiled, her teeth like perfectly shaped pearls, radiant against the sun's rays.

Poor Louise-Hélène. She must feel like an utter wallflower against Eugénie's charms. Not to mention that Eugénie was the empress of France.

Violet was distracted by this line of thought as Franz-Josef entered into a heated discussion with his servant, eventually snapping, "You *vill* do as you are told!" before turning on his heel with Eugénie and leaving the rest of them behind.

Violet approached the man, who was standing near Sam. "Good evening," she said to him.

"Good evening," he replied, respectfully snapping his heels together with a loud click. Sam stepped in. "Violet, this is the emperor's manservant, Karl Dorn."

Dorn nodded precisely. "Frau Harper, a pleasure. I beg leave to tell you that I am His Imperial Highness's chamberlain, not his manservant." Strangely, large droplets of sweat appeared on Dorn's brow and upper lip. Perhaps his livery was made of wool, or perhaps he was reeling under the lash from his master's tongue.

Whatever it was, Violet was not about to intrude on his private misery. Besides, she wanted to visit the Arab shopping district for whatever interesting finds might be there before the evening festivities started. Hadn't Sam mentioned purchasing a new undertaking bag for her?

They took their leave of Dorn and strolled toward the green tent. However, they were stopped near the entrance to the shopping district by an almost-familiar face.

"Frau Harper?" asked a man with an intense gaze, whom Violet guessed to be a little older than she was. He was clad in the typical military uniform that almost all of the Europeans were wearing, but this one had a black cross at the collar.

"Yes, how do you do?" she said as Sam rustled protectively next to her.

The man broke into a smile that breached his powerful scrutiny, like the moon emerging from behind clouds. "I recognize you from the letters my mother-in-law has sent to my wife."

"Sir? Do I know your mother-in-law?" How could she possibly know any of the important foreign members of this gathering?

The man bowed. "I should be very surprised to hear that you do not. I am married to Vicky. I am Frederick, the crown prince of Prussia, at your service."

Vicky? Oh, of course! Queen Victoria's daughter. "Your Highness, I am honored to meet you." Violet sank into a curtsy and rose again. "The queen is happy to have an alliance with your country."

He brushed the compliment aside. "I am most happy to be married to the princess. In fact, it is because of Vicky that I wished to meet you. You were not on the Nile trip, but I understood that you would be in attendance once the festivities began. You see, I wish for you to deliver a letter to Her Majesty from Vicky." He glanced around as if to be sure no one was watching before pulling a letter from an outer coat pocket and handing it to Violet.

Violet could hardly believe she was being entrusted with such a thing. She stared down at the sealed envelope without taking it. "Your Highness, do you not wish to have a servant carry it to Osborne?"

The Prussian prince's expression clouded again, and Violet realized that he was not used to having his orders even remotely disobeyed. Her stomach clenched over her terrible etiquette. "I mean, sir, Your Highness," she said, stumbling over her words, "that I have not couriered anything before, and am not sure I am worthy of your trust in such a matter."

"Ah." The moonlight returned. "Actually, Mrs. Harper, I prefer to have the letter transmitted as privately as possible, hence I have sought you out. You see, my wife did not accompany me because she suspects she may be *schwanger*. You understand?"

Violet didn't.

"*Fruchtbar*," the prince repeated. "Heavy. Laden. Fecund?"

Now it was Violet's turn for understanding. "Ah, she is with child."

"*Ja*, yes. She did not want to risk the dangers of travel, and I also could not see that the canal opening was reason to risk her health or that of my heir. However, Herr de Lesseps believes this to be a slap in his face by the British royal family, that the queen instructed my wife to stay home while deliberately sending someone less, shall we say, impressive, as part of the delegation. You, Frau Harper."

It was becoming a familiar refrain, this constant reminder of how unworthy she was of being present on this trip.

"I do not replace your wife, Your Highness. My presence is merely incidental, particularly considering that the Prince of Wales is here. Have you not informed Monsieur de Lesseps of the truth?"

"*Nein.* We have not even revealed our happy news to our families yet, as she is not far along in her time. It is better that de Lesseps is *böse* at Prussia and Great Britain than that we should give away our secret too soon. You will take the letter?" He pushed it at her again.

Violet reached out her hand to take the letter. "I will not be carrying state secrets, will I?" she said with a weak laugh. "I don't wish to be attacked by French spies."

Frederick smiled. "I would not entrust state secrets to you, *liebe Frau.* It is just a letter from a loving daughter to her mother."

"Your Highness," Sam said, "we will not be traveling straight home, as I intend to take a brief holiday in Pompeii with my wife on our return to London."

Frederick blinked at Sam's unexpectedly American accent but did not comment upon it. "I trust that you will not stop for too long when Her Majesty will be anxiously awaiting to hear from her beloved daughter."

This was the limitless arrogance Violet was used to from her titled, wealthy funerary customers. And, of course, she knew that she wasn't capable of denying a sovereign's wishes, even if he was from another country.

Violet tucked the letter inside her reticule, hoping it wasn't a mistake to be traveling with what could be a very important missive on her person.

The Arab shopping district, known as Gemalia, was set inside an area of streets containing relatively new buildings that looked like a haphazard stirring together of French and Moorish architecture, all done in wood painted to look like stone. Presumably the entire district had not existed more than a few years ago, only springing up once de Lesseps had set his mind to dredging a canal through here.

In the streets were stalls set in buildings with overhanging floors, making Violet feel as though she were in a medieval market street. The shop stalls were bursting with cotton fabrics of scarlet, cerulean, plum, and celadon along with fringed shawls and head coverings. Other stalls offered a dizzying array of goods including inlaid backgammon sets and gleaming and intricately worked bangle bracelets of gold, as well as finely hammered copper and brassware stacked in piles on wood shelves.

Most prevalent were stalls featuring burlap sacks heaped with coriander, peppers, and fennel, along with other exotic spices of impossible colors and overwhelming fragrances. Sweet aromas blended with savory bouquets, creating a veil of perfume that clung to Violet's clothing and released its scent with every rustle of her skirts.

It didn't take long to realize that it had been a mistake to come without an escort conversant in at least one of the plethora of languages here, each clamoring to be heard over the other. Presumably the European district wasn't much better, although English or French might be predominant over there.

Sam, though, didn't seem intimidated at all as they wandered down the cobblestones of the main throughway, headlong against children, dogs, turbaned men pushing carts, and veiled women with trays of steaming bread balanced on their heads.

Not even Piccadilly Circus was this chaotic.

They stopped before a stall containing an upright loom at least eight feet tall. On a low bench in front of it sat a woman flanked by two boys. All three of them held in their laps bundles of colored yarn, which they were feeding into the loom that the woman operated by a foot pedal. Violet watched, mesmerized, as a pattern in shades of red, black, brown, and yellow came alive before her eyes. Stacked around the stall in random piles taller than Violet were carpets of varying sizes and patterns.

A short, narrow loom sat nearby, an unfinished tapestry waiting to be brought to life on it.

The man who was running the stall—presumably husband to the woman and father to the children—put on a sales smile, and began animatedly chattering at them. Sam held up a hand and shook his head no, then grabbed Violet's hand. "Look, in the back here."

He led her behind the small loom and into the building, where there was a table full of tapestried pillows, wall hangings, and an array of bags, from a tiny coin purse to one so large one might hide a camel in it. "I'm sure we can find your new undertaker's bag here," Sam suggested.

Violet was entranced by the creations, which were like magnificent artwork when compared to her own leather bag. It had serviced her for years, but was worn and old now. She eyed a bag on the table that was roughly the same size as her own, thinking she would happily throw the old one overboard in exchange for this bag, with its sturdy leather handles and stunning pattern. The design was a black background with a row of crosslike symbols repeated horizontally across the center of the bag in gold and crimson.

"This is an ankh," she said, pointing out one of the crosses on the bag to Sam. "The Egyptian symbol of life, if I recall the travel guide correctly. It seems appropriate."

Sam took the bag and went to the man behind the table, and before Violet even realized what was happening, the man's eager smile had turned into an argument between the two men, the seller's voice rising in pitch and Sam gesturing with his fingers, with feigned incredulity on his face. As quickly as the tempest started, though, it dissipated out to sea. Sam pulled a few coins from his pocket and handed them to the man, who smiled broadly and nodded.

Sam returned with the bag. "Ready to purchase something else? Maybe a pretty fan?"

She needed nothing else now that she had this superb new bag. She planned to transfer all of her cutting tools and cosmetic massages to this new bag as soon as they returned to the ship. Poor Sam had been aghast when she decided to bring all the tools of her trade except for her breakable embalming solution bottles on this pleasure trip, but she had learned long ago that Death tended to be impatient of other people's plans, and barged in whenever he pleased. It was always best to be prepared.

Sam had certainly seemed to be prepared for his encounter with the vendor.

Violet clutched his arm as they walked away. "How did you do that? You don't speak Arabic."

Sam grinned, thoroughly pleased with himself. "Sweetheart, my father used to negotiate prices for Holsteins and hens all the time. That was my initiation into the art. And my stint working for Charles Francis Adams only served to hone my skills."

Violet had first met Sam while he was doing secret work for Charles Francis Adams, the US ambassador to Great Britain until last year. Sam's work had helped end the building in England of commerce-raiding ships that were destroying the Northern blockade back in his home country, although she hadn't known that until long afterward.

"To think that all of your aptitude would eventually result in your most daring deed, that of procuring the handsomest undertaker's bag ever woven," Violet said, looking up at her husband, who returned her appreciative gaze with one of his own and laughed.

"My love, you are—as you British say—quite cheeky. I will remember your sauciness."

They continued through the swarming crowds, stopping to purchase some sliced mango, a twist full of dates, and a few handfuls of almonds, all of which they ate while browsing stalls. Sam seemed exhilarated by it all, so Violet tried not to be intimidated by all of the shouting vendors.

To demonstrate her newfound bravery, she pulled on Sam's arm so they could stop at a stall whose owner was particularly thundering in his demands that they stop. He held up a lidded jar made of marble, or perhaps it was alabaster. Violet could only assume it was an example of the ancient artifacts that Egypt was famous for selling.

"*Ahlan wa sahlan*," the man said, addressing Sam, who shook his head to indicate that he didn't understand him. The vendor cocked his head to one side and appraised Sam. "You are the English?" he said with a heavy Arabic accent.

"Nearly," Sam replied. "My wife is English. I am American."

The man smiled broadly, his teeth noticeably yellow against his dark skin. "I am Yahir. I speak the English. I welcome you like my family, and may you tread an easy path. You will like to buy one of my precious antiques? They are all fresh from a dig in Luxor, the temple founded by Amenophis III. These are very old, more than three thousand years, sir." The dealer held out a statue to Sam, who glanced at it and handed it to Violet.

It was about a foot tall and easily fit in her hand. Carved of red granite, it appeared to be someone very important, sitting regally in a chair with his hands laid flat on his knees.

"Amenophis was very great, very important. This shows him on his throne. Very rare, a very valuable piece." Yahir continued smiling in encouragement.

Sam ignored him. "What do you think, sweetheart?"

"It's lovely," Violet said quietly, cradling it in one hand as she appraised it, and stroking the smooth granite with the other.

"How much?" Sam asked Yahir, who spread his hands out expansively.

"Ah, a bargain, sir, at eight of your sterling pounds."

Violet had never held such a piece of art in her hands before. Her mind easily transported itself back to what she imagined to have been a time of astounding funeral customs. What might it have been like to have been an undertaker in ancient Egypt? To have preserved organs and gently wrapped bodies to protect them from the elements? The visions were practically transferring themselves from the statuette directly to her mind. Wouldn't it make a fascinating display piece inside the shop back in—

A hand clamped around her wrist. "Mrs. Harper, I don't advise this," came a familiar voice from beside her.

Nearly squealing in fright, Violet turned to see the British ambassador standing there with another, younger man behind him. "Sir Henry, I didn't expect to see you here."

Sam was frowning at the ambassador's hand, which still clamped Violet's wrist. "My apologies, Mrs. Harper," the ambassador said, hastily letting go of her arm under Sam's visibly incensed scrutiny. "This is my secretary, Asa Brooks," Sir Henry said, presenting the man behind him. "He came highly recommended by the queen."

That was curious. Since when did the queen recommend people for ambassadorial assistant posts?

Brushing aside her misgivings, Violet joined Sam in shaking hands with Brooks. "I see you have discovered one of Egypt's many artifact dealers," Brooks said.

"Yes, he is offering us this statuette of Amenophis III. Isn't it beautiful?" She held it aloft for his and Sir Henry's inspection.

The ambassador nodded. "Yes, he was also known as Amenhotep the Magnificent. He was the ninth pharaoh of the Eighteenth Dynasty. More important for you to know, the Luxor temple—which is part of Auguste Mariette's dig at Karnak—is one of the temples whose artifacts are most commonly replicated. Statuettes, scarabs, and stelae are frequently imitated with a skill that deceives many experts. If I might?" He held out a hand to Violet, and she handed him the statue, over the vociferous objections of the shopkeeper, who insisted with a reddening face that his goods were of the most perfect provenance.

"We are familiar with Mariette's name," Sam said, his expression much calmer now that his wife's arm wasn't in the other man's clutches. "He has a rather important role for a Frenchman, doesn't he?" Behind Sam, Yahir was becoming agitated at the discussion.

Elliot smiled. "You do remember that a Frenchman named de

Lesseps has cut a hundred-mile canal through Egypt, don't you? There is little the French seem incapable of cajoling, herding, or forcing through this country."

There was little to argue in that.

"Well," Elliot said, dismissively handing the statuette back to Yahir, "I am sorry to say that this is one of the country's many, many fakes, and not worth a shilling of your money." Yahir let out a howl of outrage, but Elliot continued on as if the man weren't there. "Do not look so glum, Mrs. Harper. Selling fakes to tourists is a major form of commerce in countries with ancient sites, especially at ports that tourists frequent. I'm sure that Yahir here was duped into selling this statue," he said drily, resulting in great protests by the shopkeeper.

"I'm grateful to you, ambassador," Sam said, shaking the man's hand. The four of them walked away from the outraged Yahir, and the ambassador generously shared his knowledge about Egyptian customs with them as they continued making their way through the district. Brooks purchased a curved snuff box and immediately put it to use, while Violet purchased a fan painted with a sunset pyramid scene using gold and copper leaf and accented with an unusually brilliant orange carnelian stone surrounded by pearls in the handle. Sam skillfully negotiated at another stall for a scarab brooch for Violet made of smoky red garnet, the base of which popped open to reveal solid gold wings.

The jeweler who sold them the brooch made no pretension that it was an antique, instead telling them that the scarab was a choice purchase as it was considered a good luck charm by both the rich and the poor, and was even believed by some to hold strong magical powers. Violet smiled politely at this. Undertakers encountered too much dark reality to hope that a bejeweled bug would offer any respite from the malevolent deeds of men.

Elliot nodded sage approval at all of the purchases, then indicated to Brooks that it was time to take their leave of the couple. Elliot urged Sam and Violet to return to the stage area soon for the fireworks.

Violet and Sam walked a little farther, purchasing trinkets for Violet's parents and her closest friend, Mary, as well as their daughter, Susanna, before nearly reaching the end of the entire bazaar area. As they turned around to return to where the rest of the delegation would be gathered, Violet experienced another shock when a hand appeared out of nowhere and yanked her fan away from her.

chapter 4

IT HAPPENED WITH SUCH SPEED and ferocity that for a moment Violet's mind was stunned into inactivity. Her head cleared at Sam's explosion of "Little guttersnipe!" as instantly her old burn injury flared to painful life.

Her right arm had just been brutally wrenched by the thief, and now stabbing pain knifed its way up to her shoulder. She had to ignore it, though, as Sam had already grabbed her hand and was urging her to run with him after the dark-haired urchin who had Violet's fan clutched in his grubby fist.

How comical they must look, Violet being dragged along by her husband, who was managing both her new undertaking bag and his cane in his other hand even as he tried to overcome his slight limp with muscular movements. It was almost impossible to keep the boy in sight, so adept was he at ducking under people's arms and darting around animals and carts.

Sam was determined, though. "That little wretch is not going to steal from us," he muttered heavily while plowing forward. The boy continued to run without even looking backward, as if he knew instinctively that his victims were pursuing him. He abruptly scampered down an alleyway full of vendors. Sam and Violet continued to give chase, as the stalls containing papyrus paintings, perfume bottles, and brass boxes inlaid with mother-of-pearl all flashed past them in a blur.

This particular alleyway opened suddenly onto a wide, busy street full of human, horse, and camel traffic moving in no discernibly logical pattern. They managed to keep track of the boy until they reached the other side of the road. With nothing in his way, he launched himself in another direction behind a tiny grove of mulberry trees that practically shuddered with the profusion of silkworms feeding on their fruit. To Violet's utter dismay, the young imp seemed to have vanished like a wisp of smoke.

Violet and Sam halted, panting and perspiring heavily from the unexpected activity. The burning sensation in her arm had subsided, and it was the burn in her lungs that affected her now. "Where did he go?" Violet asked haltingly between breaths.

Sam shook his head as he bent down, hands on his knees as he dropped both the bag and his cane. "I don't know. He moved like a rabbit being pursued by a bobcat. I'm afraid we will have to buy you a new fan."

But at this point, Violet was too distracted to care about the fan, despite its expense. Next to the grove of trees was a small building, perhaps ten feet square, painted white and elaborately decorated in sapphire-blue tiles, including a faux window outlined on the front of it. Two steps led up to a heavy wood door inlaid with swirls of brass, and the entire top of the building was crenelated by star formations. It was completely unlike any other structure around it, like a little windowless dollhouse set apart from the other shops and warehouses nearby.

Violet was entranced by the charming little building, which couldn't possibly be a home or shop, given that it had no actual windows. It was so intriguing that she wondered if perhaps she could explore it. With Sam behind her, she climbed the two steps and knocked on the door, even though she didn't believe it possible that there was anyone inside. Her raps echoed heavily behind the door, but there was no answer. She rapped again, then gently tried the round brass knob, which was locked.

"What do you think you are doing here?" a voice demanded in English that, while accented, was more cultured than that of Yahir, the artifact seller. Violet turned. That voice belonged to a middle-aged man with dark hair curling over his forehead and behind his ears. His brown eyes flashed with irritation.

Sam stepped protectively in front of Violet and addressed him. "Pardon us, we are tourists. We did not mean to disrupt your home."

"Home? That is an interesting way to phrase it. This mausoleum belongs to my family. It is good fortune that I have come to check on a recent burial or I wouldn't have caught you. Why are you intruding here?" The man stood belligerently, his fists on either side of his waist, crumpling the sides of his butter-yellow robe worn over a white tunic.

Sam didn't say anything for several moments, and Violet knew her husband was debating whether to apologize or to offer the man a voluble piece of his mind. She herself was torn between embarrassment at having invaded such a private space and sheer fascination over the fact that this was a burial place. She knew nothing about Egyptian funerary practices other than what every schoolchild knew about ancient mummy wrappings. If she could only spend just a few minutes inside this mausoleum . . .

She held her breath over what Sam might do, and exhaled slowly in relief when he obviously decided on the better part of valor. "We meant no harm to you or your family. We are with the British delegation attending the canal ceremonies. I escorted my wife for some shopping in Gemalia, and an urchin stole one of my wife's purchases. We gave chase, but lost him here."

At this, the man softened toward Sam. "Ah, it must have been one of the *fellah* rats." His expression reflected the disparagement in his voice. "The peasant class have no manners. They work the fields all day and rob their betters at night." He failed to note that it was not quite dark yet, but Violet wasn't about to point that out, as he was finally settling down from his ire. "Whatever it was, you will never see it again, as I guarantee the rat has already sold it back to a dealer in one of the stalls. I pray it was not valuable."

Sam shook his head and put a hand to Violet's elbow as he brought her forward. "I am Samuel Harper. This is my wife, Violet. You speak English very well."

The man shook Sam's hand and nodded at Violet. "I am Samir Basara. I am an archaeologist for the Museum of Antiquities, and have had cause to learn English and French, and am also acquainted with several other languages. I, too, am attending the festivities, although not in an official capacity. I live in Cairo, but my family lives here, so it was advantageous for me to be the one to attend and report back on the ceremonies. I wished to check on my family before the flotilla starts out tomorrow."

Basara must be an employee of Monsieur Mariette, the director whom Sir Henry had mentioned. "Are you traveling with the khedive?" Violet asked, speaking for the first time.

"No, I travel on my own, by land," he said. "I suffer the sickness of *al-bihar*. Even though it is just a canal, I do not like the motion. I much prefer trains and caravans."

"I'm afraid I have quite the opposite problem," Violet said. "Trains hold a special terror for me." She self-consciously reached over and touched her right arm. A faint twinge was now all that remained from the painful yanking of minutes ago.

Basara spread his hands. "Every human has his individual fear, but we all fear the most merciful Allah, do we not?"

Violet nodded as Sam spoke up again. "My wife is an undertaker, and I'm sure she would be very honored to visit your family's mausoleum, if it is not too rude for us to make this request."

Basara's response was not what Violet would have expected. "You say you are with the British delegation? In what respect?"

Sam also seemed thrown by the question. "Pardon? We were invited by Queen Victoria to attend on her behalf."

Basara smiled then. "You are associated with the royal family, then?" Sam started to explain, but Basara ignored him. "My family would be pleased to know that the royalty of a foreign land, even if English, were here to pay respects. Come." Basara pulled a large brass key from a chain around his neck.

"This actually used to be the edge of the town before the port was ever completely developed. Now, my family's resting place is on a main thoroughfare."

"Why do you not move the mausoleum?" Violet asked, thinking it would be better off inside a cemetery.

Basara looked at her as if she'd sprouted a second nose. "You do not move the dead," he told her firmly. "My family members have been buried here for the past two hundred years, and one day I, my wife, and our children will be buried here. The living must work around the dead."

Violet couldn't argue with that logic.

"Most families own mausoleums, whether they be rich or poor. They are usually built in remote places, but then the city builds up and they end up like mine, engulfed by life."

They entered the mausoleum, and Violet was immediately struck by how still and quiet it was inside, though there was a rush of people and animals just steps outside. Despite the lack of windows, light filtered in through slats in the ceiling and illuminated the limestone walls. The floor was no floor at all, but a thick layer of sand that supported cactus gardens in each of its four corners, with brightly tiled benches lining all four walls. On one bench sat several lanterns and a tinderbox.

Violet was puzzled. There were no wall niches above the benches. Where were the bodies buried? Surely not directly under the sand?

Basara cleared his throat and began speaking. "I do not know your English customs, but in Egypt we have a distinct way of burying our dead, different from our neighboring countries. You must know that the ancient pharaohs were buried in crypts surrounded with food, implements, wealth, and servants so that when resurrected they would find their lives much as they had left them. When Egypt adopted Islam nine hundred years ago, we were told that dead bodies must be buried in unmarked graves, but this concept was not completely embraced."

Basara's tone and inflection demonstrated his archaeological training as he showed them around as a guide would through a pharaonic tomb. He crouched down near the center of the room and began sweeping away sand with his hand while he continued to speak. "So we have our small mausoleums, which remind us of our pyramids, and yet we bury our dead in a simple way inside them."

Beneath the sand lay black earth, which Basara continued to sweep away with his hand. "It is Islamic custom for a person to be buried before sundown the day of his death, or, at most, within three days. We have a funeral in a mosque, where special prayers, the *janazah*, are said. The coffin is then borne by male relatives to the mausoleum, with mourners following behind. Some mausoleums are in cemeteries; some, like that of my family, are old enough that they were never in specially made cemeteries, and now find themselves as relics in the middle of towns and cities."

With the dirt cleared away, an iron ring became visible. Basara pulled on it and, with a great creaking noise, the panel that it was attached to pulled up, revealing a staircase leading belowground. The archaeologist indicated that Violet and Sam should proceed down.

Violet exchanged a quick glance with Sam in the dimness, silently asking if Basara could be trusted. Sam nodded, put down the purchases, and motioned for Violet to descend.

Violet cursed her own heavy skirts as she gingerly made her way down the narrow staircase into the pitch-black of the crypt, thankful that Basara was soon behind them with two glowing lanterns. Except for the breathing of the three living persons, the crypt was utterly silent. Violet couldn't help herself: she found herself smiling at the serenity of it, noting that a crypt was a crypt no matter where it was in the world, except the floor of this one was covered in sand, as it was upstairs, making it awkward for her to balance properly on her booted feet.

Basara moved in front of them to light the way, continuing to explain Egyptian customs. As if he sensed Violet's peace here underground, he stopped and said, "Knowing that most of my ancestors have been down here, both in death and while alive as mourners, gives me great peace. I spend time here to think and pray and imagine the day that I will join my family here."

He resumed walking toward one of the two openings placed

across from each other in the small hallway they were in. Chiseled stones were piled outside each entrance. "The women are buried in here." He silently handed Violet a lantern before saying to Sam, "You may follow me to where my male relatives are buried."

With a glance of uncertainty at Violet, Sam followed Basara through the door across from Violet, leaving her alone to take a large hop down into what was apparently a separate crypt for female relatives. She held up the lantern and gasped at what she saw. It was as if there were giant molehills in the sand. Women had been laid to rest in here, with handfuls of sand cast around and over their bodies. Violet put a hand to her mouth, startled by how very different from Western practice this was, and yet her fascination with the Egyptian practice would not permit her to look away. What was the purpose of this?

She knelt down next to the nearest body, a slim figure shrouded in creamy linen. The face was, of course, decomposing, but her hair was still dark, and the woman's hands were not covered. Violet held the lantern close to one of the hands, and estimated the woman to be in her early twenties. She wondered what had happened to the young woman. Childbirth? Illness? Disease? An accident? Violet sighed. She would never know unless she asked Basara, and that seemed too intrusive.

She rose again, holding the lantern up high as she steadied herself once more on the easily shifting sand. This was so different from the services she performed in England. The bodies were entombed here, but they weren't really buried. Moreover, Violet estimated there were about twenty bodies in the room, but surely more women than that had been buried since the mausoleum was erected. Were there more crypt rooms farther down the hall?

She brushed loose sand away from her skirts, and was glad to see Basara and Sam already waiting for her, as she needed assistance to make her inelegant climb out of the crypt.

"Men and women are never buried together," Basara said, resuming his talk as if there had been no interruption.

Violet nodded. "May I inquire as to what the piles of bricks outside each crypt are for?"

"Yes, my lady, they are used to seal off the crypts after burial, and are dismantled each time the crypt must be opened up to add new bodies. My family has buried two distant cousins of mine recently, and the walls have not been put back again. Very tragic. The woman died shortly after producing a stillborn son, and her husband became crazed and deliberately drowned himself in a public fountain."

"How terrible," Violet whispered.

"*Insha'Allah*, our family will recover from this tragedy, which has brought disgrace upon our name. It is especially difficult because the fountain in question was built in honor of Isma'il Pasha, our khedive, and it was inscribed as a fountain intended for healing." Basara shook his head, as though to erase the shameful memory of it all. In a sterner tone he said, "The khedive is not aware of the polluting of the fountain, you understand."

Sam nodded. "It is a private thing for your family, and we are honored by your trust."

Violet was impressed by her husband's innate understanding and diplomatic response. His experiences working for the American ambassador had certainly not gone to waste. Basara's response was to nod curtly. "Now, you may wonder about all of the sand?"

"Yes, I'm very curious about how it is involved in your burials," Violet said without thinking. Heavens, hadn't she just thought to herself that it would be rude to ask about it?

But Basara seemed to take no offense, shifting into archaeologist mode. "The sand reminds us of our ancient tombs in the desert, but more practically, it also helps to preserve bodies. You noticed how far your leap was into the crypt?"

Violet nodded. Who could overlook such a drop?

"There are several layers of bodies in each of the two crypts. Some sand is placed inside when each body is buried, but once the crypt is full, a thick layer of sand is placed over the bodies, and then we begin placing more bodies over them. I suspect we can do two or three more layers before we will either have to expand the crypt or build an additional mausoleum."

Violet hoped that no alarm showed on her face. Had she landed upon layers of bodies when she dropped into the crypt? The thought was frightful. But surely there was an open area where family members could stand without humiliating the dead by standing upon them.

Basara turned back toward the stairs, and the Harpers followed him. Once back up in the square of benches and cacti, Basara took Violet's lantern, extinguished both of them, and began scooping earth back over the trap door in the ground. "After the body is buried, there is an official forty-day mourning period for the deceased that includes special prayers and rituals, and the family is surrounded by others come to pay their respects. For my cousins, of course, we did not receive many visitors." He shrugged. "We buried both of my cousins more quickly than normal, within two hours of his drowning, just to avoid the prying eyes and nosy questions."

Violet had to assume, then, that the woman she had examined was the wife. Had her infant son been buried with her husband?

Surely I am the only person in the world who concerns herself with such thoughts.

"But they would have been buried before sundown in any case?" Violet asked.

"If at all possible, everyone is buried by sundown. It is unseemly to wait unless there are reasons to do so."

The archaeologist had replaced the dirt, then spread sand over it so that it was impossible to tell that the area had been disturbed. With their tour concluded, Violet and Sam gathered their purchases, thanked Basara, and stepped back out into the bright Egyptian street, the noise of which was overwhelming as compared to the solitude and tranquility inside. They stood and observed the street traffic for several minutes while getting their bearings.

"Well," Sam said, breaking Violet's reverie, "should I be surprised that my wife managed to stumble into some sort of undertaking-related thing all this way from home? I reckon I should be pleased that it's all just an observation for you and that we don't have any actual bodies to deal with, eh?"

Violet smiled. "It was worth losing the fan to stumble upon this."

Violet and Sam walked back into the shopping district to purchase a replacement fan before heading back to the port to witness the fireworks. By the time they had returned to the bustling area of people, animals, and ships rocking lazily in the water, they had nearly forgotten the excitement of Violet's fan being stolen. Not that Violet would ever forget the elation of having been able to visit a mausoleum.

Perhaps when they reached Pompeii she should also see about visiting an ancient Roman mausoleum. Wouldn't it be interesting to visit burial places in countries around the—

"Excuse me, are you Mr. and Mrs. Harper?" A tall man with a thick and finely groomed dark beard appeared from nowhere. "Sir Henry requested that I keep an eye out for you upon your return from Gemalia. I trust your shopping time was pleasurable?"

Without waiting for an answer, he continued. "I am Commander George Nares, captain of *Newport*. Fireworks will begin shortly, so I want you to be aware of where HMS *Newport* is now, for your ease in boarding later." He directed Violet's attention to the canal. "First is the French ship, *L'Aigle*, carrying de Lesseps, the Empress Eugénie, and her entourage. Next is the khedive's yacht, *El Mahrousa*. An impressive beast, she is, five floors tall and over four hundred feet long." He shook his head, as though the thought were inconceivable. "*Newport* is third in line, as I'm sure you can see by her colors. We will spend the night aboard her and sail to Ismailia once it is light, with people lining the banks to cheer us on," Nares said. "The khedive has thought of everything," he added drily.

As he spoke and gestured, the captain's glossy beard sparkled in the dwindling sunlight, and Violet wondered what kind of pomade gave it such a sheen. Unfortunately, his balding pate also had a sheen, but from sweat, not applied ingredients. The captain also had a long, regal nose and a very serious countenance, all of which she supposed inspired confidence in those who relied upon his navigation skills.

"My wife and I will board immediately after the fireworks," Sam said.

Nares nodded at Sam. "And now if you will join the other members of the delegation . . . ?" He held out a hand to guide them over to the area between the two enormous platforms. Already she could see that de Lesseps and the French entourage were climbing the French side, while Isma'il Pasha was mounting the steps directly opposite onto the Egyptian stage.

By the time she and Sam reached their viewing spot, de Lesseps stood with Louise-Hélène a few steps behind him, while Eugénie was planted directly next to de Lesseps, smiling radiantly and holding up a regal arm to the now-cheering crowd of thousands. Other Frenchmen, mostly uniformed, occupied spots on the stage, while the royal delegates stood at places between the military men and the great de Lesseps. Less important delegates, like Violet and Sam Harper, stood on the ground below.

The khedive had also reached the top of his own platform, surrounded by all manner of Egyptians, Persians, and other Easterners, but the eyes from below were on de Lesseps, not on the viceroy.

De Lesseps used both hands to encourage the crowds to silence before he spoke. "I welcome you to Port Said, zee start of our magnificent journey," he said, his salutation booming over the crowd with far more clarity than Violet would have thought possible. "Tonight we prepare for what the world has never seen before, the joining of two great seas, the Mediterranean and the Red Sea, thus allowing cargo ships to cross from the Continent to the East and back again without having to go around Cape of Good Hope. Imagine the time saved. Imagine the reduced threat of pirates to peaceful carriers. Imagine ordering porcelain from China and having it in a mere week. Not even Napoléon Bonaparte was able to accomplish *zees* feat, may the great God rest his soul. *Non*, none but Ferdinand de Lesseps could have done it."

There was polite clapping on the stage around de Lesseps, but from the corner of her eye, Violet caught the khedive signaling down to the crowds, who erupted into cheers and began chanting, "De Lesseps! De Lesseps!"

The Frenchman smiled broadly at the enthusiasm. The sun was sinking quickly, and torchères flared magically around the entire port area, but most particularly around the two stages, so that it was almost as if they were bathed in heavenly light.

As the chanting died down, de Lesseps resumed his speech. "It has been ten years since I gave the first symbolic swing of the pickax to signal the start of construction for what you see before you. *Zees* evening, and for several days hence, the most distinguished heads of state and their beautiful wives"— he paused to acknowledge Eugénie, who nodded graciously at him—"will witness for themselves how the future of shipping; *non*, the future of Franco-Egyptian relations; *non*, I say to you, the entire future of world cooperation and harmony has been seeded here today. Right here, in this harbor, there *ees* no France. There *ees* no Egypt. There *ees* no Austria, Prussia, Russia, or Great Britain. There *ees* only the Suez Canal!"

De Lesseps! De Lesseps!

His voice grew stronger, and Violet realized that the unearthly glow surrounding the man, combined with the temperate breezes and the swell of humanity here, was mesmerizing. It was no wonder that the khedive no longer had to encourage the crowd; it had taken on a fantastical life of its own.

"Even during times of war, countries will cooperatively use the Suez Canal, laying aside their differences in order to transport their goods to their citizens, to their colonies, and to their allies. In fact, I say to you today, *mes amis*, that war itself might lay itself aside in the better interest of the Suez Canal."

De Lesseps! De Lesseps! De Lesseps!

"Grandiose old man, isn't he?" Sam whispered in her ear from behind her.

"Indeed, but he is effective. You can almost believe there will be no more armed conflict in the world because of this canal," Violet replied, leaning back against her husband. She felt his tender kiss on the top of her head. Despite the energy and furor around her, she felt a yawn beginning. "I feel strangely hypnotized and drawn in."

De Lesseps wrapped up his speech with his benevolent request that everyone enjoy the evening's reception and fireworks and surprise entertainments. The crowd went wild once more, as the last sliver of persimmon-colored sun sank below the distant sand dunes.

From behind de Lesseps, Louise-Hélène poked her face out to scan the crowd and, seeing Violet, waved shyly from above. Violet lifted a hand in return. There was something quite touching about the girl, and once again the undertaker wondered if Louise-Hélène was truly prepared for the life on which she was about to embark.

Now it was the khedive's turn, and heads swiveled his way. He was less confident than de Lesseps but just as happy, his grin threatening to split his ruddy face in half. "There are thousands of people here, as far as the eye can see and the ear can hear, all come to celebrate the greatest innovation in history."

The khedive made an exaggerated sweeping gesture over the crowds. "I see members of all races and nations here. The Persian brushes against the man of Morocco and the man of Zanzibar, while the inhabitant of Arabia has put up his multicolored tent next to the striped one of the Indian. All come together in harmony. Tonight the emperor of Austria will dance with the empress of France, while the prince of Russia pours a glass of wine for the princess of the Netherlands."

There were cheers, but Violet felt an emerging rumble of discontent in some of the people because of his words. Why? The khedive either didn't notice or ignored the subtlety, as he continued with his effusions.

"Today you see Egypt in glory, a glory that has not been seen since Rameses the Great ruled the land over three thousand years ago. No other country but Egypt could provide such a gift to the world, that of the Suez Canal, a hundred-mile passage that will not only revise maps, but will revive the nation that once ruled the world, and put it at the same table as the European states!"

The khedive pumped up a fist for emphasis and once again received his share of cheers, although they weren't as strong as they had been for de Lesseps. Odd, given that many of the people surrounding Violet were dressed in typical Egyptian tunics and robes, and so would presumably exult in his patriotic talk.

"Tomorrow we will be reunited in Ismailia, with games and entertainments that will display the customs and historical traditions of Egypt. I urge you to sample the feasts and amusements that will be presented in a manner recalling the great European fairs, for Egypt now joins Europe in progress and modernity."

There were calls for the khedive—*Pasha! Pasha!*—but they were still subdued.

"I thank Ferdinand de Lesseps, who is not just the friend of Egypt, but the friend of the world, and express my special regard for the beauteous Empress Eugénie of France, who has graced us with her loveliness these past few weeks."

More cheers, but Violet ignored them, searching again for Louise-Helene's face. Ah, there she was, her expression stony as she, too, lightly clapped gloved hands together for the empress.

"Now the sun has completely disappeared in the sky, a sign that it is time for the fireworks to begin. I invite everyone to direct their attention to the north, at the mouth of the port, where in moments we will have glorious starbursts in the air, a mere prelude to the dazzling, breathtaking diversions that will delight you along the canal."

That earned genuine cries of approval from the audience. It occurred to Violet that both acclamation and denunciation were spoken in universal languages.

Every head moved as one, like an obedient audience under the masterful spell of an accomplished magician. Violet and Sam also turned willingly toward the horizon and looked up, as the first burst of red, yellow, and blue exploded above them in a shower of light, then dissipated toward the wide expanse of water.

While nearly everyone else was distracted by the fireworks, Violet noticed that flaming torches had been set up to keep the area lit and elegantly robed servers had magically appeared. They bore expensive silver trays laden with food and drink, threading effortlessly through the crowds to present them to the guests.

It was as if the entire port area had turned into an endless outdoor ballroom, with the ships' sails serving as rustic tent coverings in the background.

"A fresh glass of *karkadé*, my lady?" A deferential server in a billowing periwinkle-and-white-striped gown proffered a tray of tall glasses filled with cherry-colored liquid with red flower petals floating on top.

"What is it?" Violet asked as she and Sam both took glasses.

"Hibiscus flowers, sugar, and a bit of mint made into a tea. Very popular here in Egypt, my lady. The preferred drink of the pharaohs."

Violet soon understood why. Despite the floral leaves brushing oddly against her upper lip, the drink was cool and sweet, and very refreshing. Clearly Sam didn't agree, as he frowned at the glass after merely sniffing the contents.

Against the booms and illumination of the fireworks, a band struck up somewhere in the distance, and soon the delegates on the pavilions were dancing to Austrian waltzes, Bohemian polkas, and French quadrilles. Laughter from the dance participants, whose jewels and medals twinkled in the firelight as they spun and cavorted, meshed with the booming fireworks and the musical instruments to create a symphony of festive sound. Violet turned back to observe the dancers, and noticed that even Louise-Hélène was gasping with the joy of being handed down the line by her fiancé and the Austrian emperor, with Eugénie close on her heels.

Violet returned her attention to the fireworks and leaned her head against Sam's arm. He kissed the top of her head once more, and she wondered if there was anyplace else on earth as melodic and effervescent as this single spot on which she stood right now. The theft of her fan already forgotten, she merely wanted to soak in all of this extraordinary—

Violet's tranquility fell to ashes as terrified screams pierced the air, causing the band to come to a disjointed halt and paralyzing the dancers onstage. Within seconds she understood why. At the lumberyard, flames had suddenly appeared, and were climbing farther and farther upward, their power increasing as they greedily devoured the crackling and popping wood in their path.

The fire moved outward, too, seeking more air to fuel its insatiable need to consume everything around it.

Violet's heart sank at the ominous realization that the fireworks building lay next door.

chapter 5

"OH NO," VIOLET BREATHED, MOMENTARILY paralyzed herself. The revelers who had just been laughing and pointing up at the fireworks now had expressions of abject terror as they stampeded in dozens of directions around Violet and Sam. Some fled to ships, and others ran to points like Gemalia and the European district, while yet others followed the rough path beyond the platforms that ran parallel to the canal.

"What in the name of . . . ?" Sam demanded, as puzzled as Violet was, but quickly gaining command. "Wife, I have to see if I can help. Wait here for me, where you'll be safe." He stepped away from her, but she grabbed his hand.

"I will *not* wait here," Violet insisted sharply. "I am coming with you."

Sam shook his head, but led her against the tide of human salmon furiously making its way upriver from the fire, with Sam forging a path through them. Violet was jostled and shoved, and her hem made contact with many feet. She wondered if her dress would even be salvageable by the time they reached the lumberyard.

The crowds were far behind them by the time they reached the source of the fire, which was now leaping and writhing with far more enthusiasm than the dancers on the platforms had. The khedive must have been prepared for just such an occurrence, for there were already hundreds of uniformed soldiers there, hauling buckets of water from the canal's edge to the fire. If they could not extinguish it before it consumed the fireworks, the result would be an apocalyptic inferno.

"Look!" Sam said, pointing at a particular line of soldiers passing buckets. Their faces were grimy and sweaty as they shouted unintelligibly to one another, their voices drowned out by the roar of the fire. As each bucket was splashed onto the fire, there was a great hissing noise, as though the fire were an evil spirit being brought to heel and protesting in rage over it. The hissing was also accompanied by plumes of black smoke, the remnants of which were soon hovering over them. The heat was considerable, but easily ignored in the tension of the moment.

Violet had no idea what he meant. "What do you see?" she asked, coughing against the acrid taste and smell in her throat.

"Those men, sweetheart. See the yellow corded tassels at the base of their hats? Some of these men are Union cavalry. They're all *Americans*. What are they doing here?"

Violet took her new undertaking case from Sam's other hand. It had somehow managed to come through the melee much more successfully than Violet's dress. She didn't even dare look down to assess her bedraggled condition. "Go and see what you can do to help them," she urged her husband, knowing that was what he yearned to do.

"I can't leave you here alone in this chaos," he protested, his expression wavering.

"I will be fine," Violet assured her husband. "Besides, I see Monsieur de Lesseps and his fiancée, as well as Sir Henry. I will go to them." The two men were poking around in an area of the lumberyard that had been extinguished, with Louise-Hélène and her maid, Isabelle, in their wake.

Grinning like a boy granted permission to go to the pond and catch toads, Sam took off toward his fellow soldiers, once more seeming to forget that he had an injured leg. Violet smiled and shook her head at her husband's retreating back as she once more coughed and waved her free hand in front of her face in a useless attempt to clear the smoke.

Small pockets of the fire were already being brought under control as Sam reached the line of men. A group of them stopped to converse with him, and there were shouts, handshakes, and back slaps as they realized he was one of their own and quickly incorporated him into the line of water movers.

Violet's attention was diverted, though, by the sound of angry voices. To her surprise, Isma'il Pasha and Ferdinand de Lesseps were in a heated argument, with de Lesseps gesturing angrily at something in or near a heap of charred wood, the fire gone but the ebony planks still emitting curling plumes of drifting smoke and ashy bits that floated into the air like the smuts that hung in the London air every winter.

She started to approach them, but was stopped by a wild-eyed man in Egyptian garb. His hair was gray, but whether that was its natural look or a coating of ash was impossible to discern. "My lady, have you seen my son Yusef Halabi? I cannot find him anywhere," he said, desperation lacing his words.

"Your son?" Violet replied, confused but sympathetic to his plight. "I don't believe I know your boy. How old is he? What does he look like?"

"How old?" the man parroted. "Let me see, he turned thirty last month. He left earlier today to purchase some nails for me, as the crew of one of the delegation ships needed them, and I haven't seen him since. Now my lumberyard is . . . is . . . ." The man shook his head, unable to form a description of what had happened. "And I don't know where Yusef is."

Now Violet understood. "Sir, I am sorry to say that I do not know your son," she said softly. Surely the shock of losing his business—for there was certainly nothing left to recover—was making him anxious for a son who had merely skipped out with friends. Or had perhaps returned without his father's awareness and then fled with the sea of humanity that had rushed away from the fire. Violet suggested both of these possibilities to him, concluding, "I am certain he will return as soon as he is able."

The man cradled his head in both hands, rocking back and forth. "*La*, my lady, no. My son he is very reliable, very devoted to his father. He would never do either of these things you suggest." He dropped his hands in resignation. "I must keep looking," he muttered, and walked away, shoulders slumped.

Violet suspected that following him to offer further condolences would not be appreciated, and so she turned once more to where de Lesseps and Pasha were still arguing, but in lower tones. Louise-Hélène looked in Violet's direction and held up a hand to stop Violet's approach. She whispered something to de Lesseps; then she and Isabelle picked up their skirts and made their way to Violet.

Louise-Hélène's expression was anxious and worried, and that distress had transferred over to the maid, who rubbed her hands together without ceasing.

"Mrs. Harper, I'm glad I found you," Louise-Hélène said breathlessly. Like that of the man Violet had just encountered, Louise-Hélène's wild hair was coated in ash, so Violet could only imagine what her own visage was.

"May I be of service to you, mademoiselle?" she replied.

"It is terrible, just terrible, what has happened. What has the world come to? Poor de Lesseps," Louise-Hélène said, her voice cracking and tears welling up in her eyes. There was no answer to be had, and Violet recognized in the girl a hysterical mourner who needed to be soothed.

"Yes, mademoiselle, the fire is a great tragedy, and de Lesseps's entertainments for the evening were rui— had to be ceased, but tomorrow is a fresh day and by sunrise everyone will have forgotten what has happened. In fact, they might consider it the most thrilling part of the festivities."

"Madame Harper," Louise-Hélène said, looking strangely at Violet as though the undertaker were ready for the lunatic asylum, "the fire is not the great tragedy; the calamity is the dead body caused by the fire."

Violet was not often stunned into silence, but this was an exception. She shook her head. "Are you saying someone burned to death here tonight?" she asked incredulously.

Louise-Hélène nodded. "Yes, he was found over there." The

girl pointed to where de Lesseps and Pasha were still in heated conversation. "I believe my fiancé and the khedive each blame each other for the fire and the man's death."

Suddenly, Violet had a very sick feeling in her stomach about whose body lay there.

She breathed deeply and removed all thought of being a tourist. Mentally donning her undertaker's hat with its long black tails of crepe, she said firmly to the girl, "You must take me to him at once."

Louise-Hélène's eyes widened. "You wish to talk to de Lesseps?"

"No, I wish to see this man who was burned."

Isabelle gasped from behind her mistress, and Louise-Hélène said, "*Non*, madame, I could not possibly do so. I did not see the *cadavre* myself—de Lesseps would not permit it. I only know it—he—is there, behind the wood pile where de Lesseps and the khedive now stand."

Violet smoothed her skirts and wished that the empty tapestry bag in her hand were filled with the undertaking supplies still aboard *Newport*. "Very well, I shall find the body myself."

"Madame Harper, you cannot—" But Violet did not stop to hear Louise-Hélène's admonishments, and soon heard the two women scurrying after her. Violet walked deliberately past the two arguing men, catching snippets of their conversation, which by now was mostly de Lesseps lecturing and Pasha pleading.

"I have provided two thousand men to take care of this, as well as the Americans, de Lesseps. You have not—"

"You were responsible for the evening's entertainments, Isma'il. You cannot expect me to import Frenchmen to solve every problem for you." De Lesseps was remarkable in his placid disregard.

"There are limits to what I can do, *sahbi*. Limits." Pasha's words were threatening, but his tone was apprehensive.

Violet was determined not to listen to this private conversation and ignored it as she rushed by, but the khedive noticed her and the other two women, and halted her with a "Where are you going, *madaam*?" For the moment, the argument ceased between him and the Frenchman.

"I understand there is a body here," she replied calmly.

"This is none of your concern. Find your husband and return to your ship." The khedive flicked his fingers out toward the water in dismissal.

But Violet Harper had not become a highly regarded undertaker over the past sixteen years by permitting herself to be intimidated by brutes, fools, and nincompoops.

She drew herself up and stared steadily at the khedive. "It is indeed my concern, sir. I am an undertaker, and as I do not see another one on the premises, I will tend to this body."

The khedive looked at her incredulously. "What do you mean you are an undertaker? Do you mean to tell me you are a preparer of the dead? Impossible. Besides, you are not only a woman, you are English. You know nothing of our customs."

Violet smiled. "Ah, but I do know. I know that we are already too late to bury him before sundown the day of his death. I also know that we need to find out who he is quickly so that he can be buried in his family mausoleum."

Unable to contradict her, the khedive harrumphed loudly, but Violet noticed a burgeoning look of respect residing in de Lesseps's eyes. The Frenchman intervened. "Perhaps the lady might be of assistance, Pasha. Neither of us wishes that any notice be brought to the situation."

"I can have my own men take care of—"

"*Oui*, you can, but this woman is not Egyptian, and so will not spread it about to your countrymen, and she is only a very minor member of the British delegation with no authority whatsoever in her home country. Let her see to the body and let's be done with it right away."

Violet knew she was being insulted, but her primary concern was the corpse lying nearby in complete indignity. She resisted the urge to tap a foot impatiently while the khedive wavered. Finally, he threw up his hands. "As you wish, *sahbi*," he said, and walked away without another word.

De Lesseps seemed to take no notice of the khedive's petulance. "*Zees* way—Madame Harper, isn't it?" He led her back behind the great pile of burnt lumber, where she immediately saw the poor man, who lay sprawled, almost as if he had tripped, fallen, and been unable to get up before the fire consumed him.

As she rushed forward and knelt next to the body, she heard de Lesseps, Louise-Hélène, and Isabelle behind her, their shoes scuffling in the dirt and shavings as they backed away. Louise-Hélène made retching noises as the other two attempted to comfort her, but the young woman's distress was of no interest to Violet now.

Only this dead man was.

She gently reached under him and turned him over, finding his body a little lighter than a typical man of his size. The man's mouth hung open in an eerie expression of his horror over his own death, his lips peeled and his burnt-over teeth so crowded it was almost as if he had two sets of them.

She had never seen such a traumatized body before. The thin outer layers of his skin had partially peeled off, and what remained was mottled in black, red, and purple. Parts of the thicker dermal layer of skin had shrunk and split, so the underlying fat had leaked out in streaks that looked like runny egg yolks. If Violet were not so accustomed to death, she might have been gasping as loudly as the people standing twenty feet away from her were.

His hair was mostly gone, and his clothing—what was left of it—had melted into his skin. The unmistakable scent of charred muscle and innards filled her nostrils.

Why was it that lamb made a delightful fragrance as it roasted, but a human being's flesh was noxious? Violet figured it was the Almighty's way of reminding people that humans were not to be used as a source of food.

However, the man had not been consumed by fire; it had been extinguished quickly enough that he was not completely roasted. As gently as she could, she put a hand on his chest. "Sir, I am very sorry for what has happened to you, but I promise to make it right for you. I will see you reunited with your ancestors in your family crypt, and I will improve your looks as best I can, although I admit it will not be easy."

Drat, all she had was her new tapestry bag, not her regular undertaking bag. She considered asking Isabelle to retrieve it from *Newport*, but decided against it. All that would serve to do at the moment was stir up rumors and gossip as to why Violet needed the tools of her macabre trade. However, the least she could do was—

"Isabelle," she said, keeping her hand resting on the body's chest but turning to look back where the trio was standing, with de Lesseps acting the protector over the two women. "I am going to need some sort of sheet or blanket. This man needs to be covered up before he is removed."

Isabelle nodded wordlessly and left.

Violet turned back to concentrate on the corpse under her care. "Forgive my impertinence, sir, but I must inspect you a bit." She gently touched him in various places, careful not to press too hard against his skin, fearful that it might erupt.

His nose was disjointed. It seemed strange that it would have broken as he fell. If he had been overcome by the smoke, he would have slowly collapsed to the ground.

As she considered his body further, it occurred to her that the man couldn't possibly have been here for the duration of the fire, for surely he would have— Well, not to put too fine a point on it, but surely more of his flesh would have burned away by now. There was a lot of him left for having been in the epicenter of a blazing-hot fire, even if most fires were incapable of reducing a man to ash. It seemed to Violet that—

Wait. What was this?

Violet held her breath against the repulsive smell and bent down to look closer. Why, that looked like a—

She sat up straight. Impossible! Her heart began hammering erratically inside her chest. How could this be? Swallowing to maintain control and to avoid alarming de Lesseps and his fiancée, she slowly bent over to examine the area again, lightly pressing two fingers against the troubling spot.

There was no doubt.

There was a gash in this man's midsection most definitely caused by a large knife. Violet's mind raced. He couldn't have been stabbed after the fire, for it was only recently put out and he had been discovered shortly thereafter. Besides, who would stab an already-dead person?

But if he had been stabbed prior to the fire, well, that provided a horrifying explanation as to why his body was not more ravaged. His dead body must have been dragged to this place so that the crime would be covered up by the fire in progress. Which might also mean that—dear God in heaven—the fire was intentionally set, specifically to disguise this murder.

Thousands upon thousands of people had descended upon Port Said. How was it possible to discover who had wished this poor man harm and why?

Well, for the moment, Violet knew of one man who was missing. Hopefully, the lumberyard owner would return soon, although she did not relish the idea of presenting the body to him, if this was indeed his son.

At that moment, Isabelle returned with a long length of cotton in bold stripes of magenta, white, and charcoal, her hand shaking as she held it out to Violet. "I bought this from the nearest merchant I could find who hadn't fled the area," she said breathlessly.

It wasn't exactly a snowy white winding sheet, but Violet couldn't fault the girl's quick resolution of the problem. Before she had time to decide whether it was more important to enrobe the man in respectful coverings or report to de Lesseps what she had ascertained, two Egyptian men approached. Their clothing was grime-free, suggesting they had not been members of the chaotic fire brigade.

"*Madaam* Harper?" the taller one asked, flashing a charming smile as he spoke in nearly flawless English. Both were probably in their early thirties, although the second one was stockier and seemed ill at ease.

Violet did not answer as she spread the cloth over the body, covering him from the shoulders down. She then rose up and said, "I am she. You are . . . ?"

He executed a neat bow. "I am Hassan Salib, the khedive's cultural attaché. This is Rashad, one of the khedive's porters." Rashad simply stared in response to Violet's greeting.

"We were sent by our employer to take care of a most unfortunate occurrence," Hassan said. He nodded down at the covered body. "I believe this must be the man who has suffered the terrible tragedy?"

At this point, de Lesseps abandoned his role of female protector and marched over to get involved in what the khedive's man was saying. "What do you mean you are here to take care of it?" he demanded. "I told Pasha the undertaker here would be sufficient for what had to be done. He dares undermine my authority?"

Hassan bowed again, and this time spoke English with a French accent. "Thank you for your thoughts, Monsieur de Lesseps. As you know, it is customary that the dead be—"

"*Oui, oui,* I know. They must be buried by sundown the day of death. It is too late for that, and I won't have you parading him through the streets and wailing over him, attracting the people's interest like bees to *pots de crème.*"

Violet hardly thought that description apt, given that the body before them was quite the opposite of a sweet custard dessert. However, there were much more important items to address, and so she spoke up with brisk determination: "Monsieur de Lesseps, I must inform you that—"

But she was ignored. Hassan, not intimidated in the least by de Lesseps, replied to the man politely but firmly, "There is no intent to make a spectacle of the man, but the khedive insists that we take him away from this place ourselves. It is not right for a Briton, a woman"—he flicked an apologetic glance at Violet—"to have an Egyptian body in her charge. I apologize, monsieur, but I must obey my orders."

"Where is Pasha?" de Lesseps said incredulously. "Was he too much of a coward to come with you? He obviously knows he is conducting himself like a frightened, nose-twitching little *lapin!*"

Perhaps he is digging a burrow aboard *El Mahrousa* at this very moment."

Violet could see that the fire was nearly extinguished, with some of the soldiers on the fire brigades tending to the smoking embers, and other men relighting torchères that had been extinguished, thus starting to bathe the area in peaceful light again. Sam was lingering with several of his Civil War comrades, no doubt sharing tales of their exploits. Looking off in the opposite direction, she saw that people were trickling back to the area surrounding the pavilions. Something had to be done with this poor man soon, and the khedive needed to know that his countryman had been murdered.

She tried again. "Monsieur Salib." What title did one give a high-ranking Egyptian employee? "Before the body is moved, the khedive must be made aware that—"

Another interruption, this time a commotion from where Louise-Hélène and Isabelle still stood. It was the lumberyard owner, returned from his tormented wanderings. Violet quickly stepped over to meet him, hoping to prevent him from seeing what she was now sure was his son lying there.

It was no use, for his gaze was instantly drawn to the brightly dyed cloth covering the lower half of the body. "Who—who is that?" he asked, his voice quavering as he slowly raised a finger to point, like a ghost in Mr. Dickens's novel about Mr. Scrooge.

She replied as soothingly as she could. "We aren't quite sure. Perhaps you should—"

Once more Violet felt as if she were barreled over and splattered like a heap of dung in the path of a runaway carriage. "Someone died here," de Lesseps said gracelessly, almost as if he had given up on the idea of keeping it quiet.

The lumberyard owner stepped to the body, recoiled once in horror, then bent down again. Everyone collectively held their breaths as he examined the body. It wasn't long before the man began to shake in his grief, the shaking soon turning to a loud keening as he rose and beat his breast. Tearing at his hair, he called out miserably in English, "Yusef, Yusef, my son."

His sorrowful refrain soon exploded into a torrent of curses. Grief, like bargaining in shopping stalls, knew no language barrier, and everyone present bowed their heads instinctively in the face of the man's wild-eyed anguish.

This was becoming a dreadful scenario for Violet, who still had the unenviable task of telling not only de Lesseps and Hassan Salib but now this son's heartbroken father, too, of how the man had been murdered. The father's loud demonstrations were attracting the attention of people gathering again in the hopes of the festivities starting once more.

Something had to be done. De Lesseps was practically the king over the entire canal affair, so she had to tell him. Violet signaled to him, and together they walked away to where Louise-Hélène and her maid stood, both still wide-eyed over the entire experience of the past hour.

"Monsieur," Violet said in a low voice, barely hearing herself over the sound of the father's grieving, "I regret to inform you that the man is Yusef Halabi, the son of the lumberyard owner, and he did not die in the fire."

"What do you mean? That he died from the smoke, not the flame?"

"No, not at all," Violet said, steeling herself for the reaction to come after her next words. "He has a deep stab wound in his midsection. His father said he disappeared earlier in the day. I believe he was murdered elsewhere and then dragged here. It may even be that the fire was deliberately set to cover up his murder."

Louise-Hélène brought a gloved hand to her mouth, her eyes welling with tears of empathy. De Lesseps, though, did not respond at all as Violet might have anticipated.

He merely shrugged.

Now it was Violet who wanted to bring a hand to her mouth at the callousness of the response. "Monsieur, did you not hear me? I say the man has been murdered. We must find who killed him."

But it was as if Violet had told him some food was spoiled and could not be served. He merely turned up his nose. "No, the only thing we must do is get rid of the *cadavre* now. The father is beginning to embarrass me. I cannot have the most important event in the history of the world ruined because some savage attacked and killed another one."

"Monsieur de Lesseps, I take great umbrage and exception to such a callous—"

"That is all very well, Madame Harper, and you may lecture me and poke me with your parasol later. For now, though, we must see that the father removes his son *immédiatement*. I must salvage the evening so that all *ees* forgotten by the time we set sail in the morning. You will refrain from saying anything to anyone about what may—or may not—have happened, and we will once again have harmony over the Suez Canal."

De Lesseps smoothed his mustache for emphasis and turned on his heel. The other two women followed him, but not before Louise-Hélène turned back and once more shyly waved to Violet. This time, the undertaker's blood was boiling too turbulently beneath her skin for her to respond.

What a hideous encounter. Well, there was nothing to be done but to ensure the man's body was cared for. Realizing that the father's wailing had finally ceased, she turned back to comfort him once more.

Except he was no longer there. In fact, the father, his son's corpse, Hassan, Rashad, and the cloth were all gone. She couldn't see them anywhere. Had de Lesseps signaled them without Violet's awareness?

Were they properly handling Halabi's body? Had they securely wrapped him? His burnt condition made him so fragile. If she discovered that his body had been dropped and broken up in the street . . .

Violet was now so furious that she saw black spots before her eyes. "Here is something else de Lesseps should know about Egypt's funeral customs," she muttered fiercely under her breath. "It is not good luck to disregard the dead."

Trying to shake off her anger, Violet sought out Sam, who was happily covered in soot and soaked in canal water as he talked with two of the Americans. "Men, this is my lovely English bride, Violet. Sweetheart, this is First Sergeant Caleb Purdy. He was a cavalry scout in the war."

Violet shook hands with a man whose hair was too scraggly, his beard unkempt, and his clothing rumpled, but he was exceedingly polite to Violet. He greeted her with an unexpected gallantry, even as he joked about Sam.

"Your husband was infantry, ma'am? A shame. Everyone knows the infantry is made up of mangy critters unable to sit astride a horse properly."

Sam laughed aloud. "What my friend here means to say is that the cavalry are good for scouting missions and leading raids, but never have the nerve for anything truly dangerous, like the infantry boldly head toward. After all, who ever saw a dead cavalryman?"

Purdy pretended to shoot Sam with his thumb and forefinger, but accepted the good-natured insult with aplomb.

"And this is Sergeant Ross Keating," Sam said, introducing another man. "I knew this worthless little mongrel from Fredericksburg. We did some reconnaissance together."

Keating was surely in his late twenties but appeared to be no more than a boy, with his clear blue eyes seemingly unspoiled by the horrors of war and his smile containing no hint of sadness. Most of the Civil War veterans Violet had met in her time in America—Sam included—carried a faint melancholia about them, even in their happy times. But with Keating, the only clue of the difficult life he'd experienced lay in the scar that stretched from the end of one eyebrow back into the hairline above his ear. A bullet grazing, perhaps?

Violet smiled and chatted pleasantly with them, hoping her agitation did not show through. It was easy enough to let her mind drift as the three continued reminiscing about leaking tents, maggot-filled hardtack, and harmless pranks played on fellow soldiers.

Violet, meanwhile, considered all that had happened tonight. The shopping expedition, the theft of her fan, the mausoleum tour, the showering fireworks . . . all culminating in the tragedy of the lumberyard fire and the discovery of a body stabbed to death.

And de Lesseps would not permit her to report it, to save his grand opening. But what of the indignity served to poor Yusef Halabi? And to his father? That man deserved to know what had happened. He probably blamed himself for the fire, which meant he would also view himself as responsible for his son's death. He shouldn't have that guilt shrouding him the rest of his life.

How could de Lesseps refuse to clear up the doubts?

The situation was most intolerable.

Well, he was not going to prevent her from telling her husband about it, for certain. Perhaps Sam and his friends would have an idea about the fire's origins.

The men were joined by yet another soldier, this one introduced as Thaddeus Mott. A hardened, middle-aged man whose leathered skin had done nothing to wear down his handsomeness, Mott bent over Violet's hand and introduced himself. "Mrs. Harper, a pleasure. I confess to you here and now that I am an adventurer, a sailor, and a soldier of fortune, in no particular order." He removed his dark blue hat and swept it out with a grand flourish, as though he were a romantic cavalier from another century.

Sam and the others laughed uproariously, with Sam telling her, "He's a former Union officer. He also took part in wars in Mexico, Italy, and Turkey. A man among men."

Mott nodded his acceptance of the flattery. "And as such, here I am in Egypt, with the sorrowful task of whipping a few Americans into whipping quite a few more Egyptians into something resembling an army."

That statement completely shook Violet out of her reverie. "Pardon? You are creating an army?"

"Yes, dear lady. The viceroy, Isma'il Pasha, wishes to modernize Egypt and return her to greatness, much as Ferdinand de Lesseps wants preeminence for France. It is a wonder the two men get along so well, although I suppose the Suez Canal is a mutual interest in each obtaining glory and grandeur.

"The Suez Canal is only one part of Pasha's plan, though. He has built thousands of miles of railroads, started enormous cotton plantations, and reduced slave trading. After fighting for four years to end slavery in the United States, I could hardly say no to a man who wants to end it here, could I?" He grinned at Violet, as though his years of deprivation and slaughter were no more than a pleasant holiday at the seashore.

The other men's respect and admiration for Mott was palpable.

"No, I suppose it would have been ungentlemanly to do otherwise," Violet replied lightly.

Mott raised an eyebrow at Sam. "You didn't adequately describe what a vision she is, Harper. Perhaps I need my own English bride." He turned back to Violet. "Could you find an equally lovely lady for me, Mrs. Harper? Someone who might ignore my face but instead be dazzled by a lieutenant colonel who seeks international fame and great wealth?"

The man obviously knew his own magnetism and his self-deprecation was false, but it was done with such charm that Violet could only smile in return. "Surely no woman is equal to the task of being your helpmeet, sir."

He shrugged. "Perhaps not. I suppose, then, that I shall stay married to my Emily." Mott grinned at Violet. "For now, though, I am busy enough with the boatload of boys I brought with me to help the khedive with his army. I am thoroughly surprised by how undisciplined and unwilling to be led they are. This fire was a good exercise for training recruits in unexpected situations."

Violet was again taken aback. "Are you saying that you deliberately set this fire during the speeches as a training aid?"

Mott tapped his hat against his thigh, having never replaced it on his head. "Dash it, no, Mrs. Harper. It was simply a gloriously convenient coincidence."

"Glorious" wasn't exactly the term Violet would have used,

but "convenient coincidence" was. She was beginning to think that something very sinister was occurring at Port Said behind the facade of laughing faces, brightly colored apparel, and extravagant entertainment.

What it was, she had no idea, but she was determined to provide that dead man an answer. The dead deserved no less.

Before Violet could get Sam alone to tell him what had happened, she felt a tap on her shoulder. "Undertaker lady?" asked a man's urbane voice.

She turned, leaving the Civil War comrades on their own again.

His face was shadowy in the torchlight, but Violet recognized Samir Basara, the owner of the mausoleum. Gads, that felt like days ago, although only mere hours had passed since she had toured his family's crypt.

He nodded at her. "Yes, I thought I recognized your clothing. You and your husband are enjoying Egyptian hospitality, despite the fire? I suspect the khedive will launch fireworks again as soon as everyone returns. The joy must proceed, eh?"

"It has certainly been an exciting evening," Violet replied noncommittally. Then an idea struck her. "May I speak with you privately?"

He frowned at her request. "We must have your husband's permission."

Violet sighed. Sam was still surrounded by Purdy, Keating, Mott, and now some other men. One of them had produced a banjo—that peculiarly twangy instrument beloved in America—and they were singing patriotic songs, enthusiastically if not especially on key. Purdy had even broken out into some kind of stumbling jig. Clearly the army was not a place for learning the social refinements.

With Basara behind her, Violet sought out Sam, who instantly recognized the archaeologist. Basara asked in an almost courtly way permission to speak with Violet, which Sam granted, adding, "You misunderstand my wife if you think she will not do as she wishes."

Basara frowned again. "Perhaps your wife needs a firmer hand."

Sam winked in Violet's direction. "I have learned that I can no more put a firm hand to my wife than I could put one to the wind to stop it."

Basara grunted in disapproval, but did not refuse to speak with Violet. They made their way through the crowd, which had grown in size almost to what it was before, as she led him back toward the charred remnants of the lumberyard. As they walked, Violet wondered how she would ask her questions while trying to accommodate de Lesseps's desires.

She took Basara directly to the spot where the dead man had lain, thinking it was as private an area as any, given that most of the revelers were avoiding the spot where the extinguished fire still released intermittent wisps of woodsy smoke. The acrid odor was overwhelming, and smothered the pleasant smells she had carried with her from the spice stalls. Basara looked distinctly uncomfortable, but Violet wasn't sure if it was because of the location, or for being alone with her here.

However, back in the spot where she had so recently been outraged, Violet was overcome with calm, as the right questions implanted themselves in her head. "Mr. Basara, do you know the owner of this lumberyard?"

He looked at her quizzically. "Old Halabi? He has been here for decades. Everyone knows his family."

"So he has a family?" she pursued.

"Of course. Does not every man strive to have a family? Why these ridiculous questions about a simple merchant?" There was a hint of irritation in his voice.

Violet was not about to be deterred. "He has a wife? Children? Sons, perhaps?"

"Yes to all of this. A wife, Hagar. A chattering magpie of a girl, Ati. And two sons, Nebi and Yusef. Yusef works with his father, while Nebi, the younger son, decided to seek his fortune in antiquities, stealing and then selling them to foreigners. Nebi should be seized and hanged in the public square, but he seems to have friends who protect him."

An interesting note about Nebi, but Violet was not interested right now in the brother's illegal enterprises, so she bore down gently on what she wanted to know. "Did Yusef and his father get along well? Was there any trouble between them?"

"Trouble? What sort of trouble do you mean? Yusef was very obedient, unlike his brother. Nebi tried to convince him to join in his criminal acts, but Yusef never did so." Basara shook his head at the perfidious actions of the errant younger son.

It was a sure sign that Violet had been involved in far too many crimes that her mind immediately leapt to the conclusion that perhaps Yusef's brother had killed him for not participating in his misdeeds. She shook her head at the suspicions running rampant through her mind.

As her thoughts cleared, another question occurred to her. "Does the family have a mausoleum? Do you know where it is?" Perhaps she could convince the family to permit her to see the body once more before it was buried. Unlikely, but she was at least willing to try.

"As I said before, most families have them. I do not make it my business to map them out. Where it is depends on how old his family is, though. A newer family will have one in a cemetery, unlike my family, which is old enough that the town has grown around the mausoleum."

Violet could not mistake the note of extreme pride in his voice about that fact. "Another question, sir. Do you know if anyone had a grudge against Halabi the father? Has he ever wronged anyone?"

Basara spread his hands as if fending off an assault. "Why do you ask such questions? Are they not better placed directly to him? Anyone could have been angry with him. A dissatisfied builder, a log shipper, a ship's captain. But I know of no specific instance. Is that all?"

Violet realized that Basara was becoming irritated with her, and she had no desire to alienate him. Perhaps a friendly overture was in order. "Not quite. I am interested in your archaeological work."

At that, Basara's defensiveness softened perceptibly. "You are? What are you interested in?"

"You said that you work for the Museum of Antiquities. Do you help to uncover ancient burial grounds? I am, of course, most interested in such things." Violet held up her empty tapestry bag, hoping he would understand it to represent an undertaker's accoutrements.

"Yes." Basara quickly warmed to the subject. "I am currently working for Monsieur Mariette near the Temple of Seti. This is the first temple one visits on a tour of Upper Egypt. I am primarily responsible for finding suitable workers. It is difficult, for Monsieur de Lesseps consumed most labor sources for the canal and the khedive does not hold the special interest for discovering the past that his father did but, rather, seems to be focused on the future. There is no more corvée labor to be had, thanks to your country's— Well, because that practice was ended, so our efforts to find men who are not the pestilent *fellahin* have doubled in recent years. With the canal finished, we should be able to accelerate the digging. Many precious artifacts have been placed into the museum, but they are just a single grain of sand as compared to the desert of items that exists. Provided we can work faster than thieves like Nebi Halabi." His face darkened.

Violet thanked him for speaking with her, convinced that any more questions would only serve to further provoke him. As he left, she, too, started walking back to where Sam and his friends were. A waiter reappeared with glasses of *karkad*é, and she happily took one, stopping to enjoy its singular sweetness. As she drank, the fireworks began popping again, and a collective *ohhhh* floated up from the regathered crowds.

Violet rejoined Sam with his comrades, and they watched the spectacle of the fireworks, although she found herself detached from the festivities. It was as though the fire had never occurred, a body had never been found, and nothing untoward had ever happened in bustling, humming Port Said. Who, she mused, wandered about pleased to see that his crime had been effectively incinerated away?

chapter 6

A S VIOLET SIPPED THE LAST of her drink, even swallowing the hibiscus leaves, she was approached by two more men in uniform. To think that she had humored Sam when he opted to wear his uniform! The port was now a sea of vivid Egyptian tunics and sharply uniformed Europeans.

One of the men was clearly the other's superior, walking slightly in front with the careless swagger that comes with knowing there is always someone behind you to catch your cloak.

This was confirmed for Violet when the second man, larger and more imposing but less regal, spoke to make introductions.

"Excuse me, you are British *devushka*?" he asked. His luxurious and full, dark, drooping mustache was a contrast to his thinning hair. His gaze upon Violet was intent to the point of ferocity.

"I am Violet Harper with the British delegation," she replied cautiously, handing her glass back to another server who passed by, his tray full of glasses drained by others who apparently loved hibiscus tea as much as she did.

"Please you tell me your patronymic," he said.

"Pardon me, my what?"

"He wishes to know your middle name. It is a sign of respect." Once more, Sir Henry Elliot had appeared from nowhere with Asa Brooks trailing silently in his wake. It was as though the ambassador had a secret assistant telegraphing him every few minutes of Violet's whereabouts.

"Oh." Violet held out a hand politely. "I am Violet Rose

Harper," she said.

The mustachioed man placed a palm under hers without touching her and said, "Violet Rose, I am Count Nikolay Pavlovich Ignatiev of Russian delegation. I am ambassador to Constantinople. This"—he stepped back so that the other man filled her view—"is Grand Duke Michael Nikolaevich, brother of Tsar Alexander. The duke is governor of Caucasus, while his brother is now Alexander II."

Was Violet supposed to offer this man her hand? Curtsy? And wherever was the Caucasus? She hadn't realized how badly she would need international etiquette lessons before departing Dover. She figured it was best now to go overboard on flattery, though, and curtsied as though she didn't look and feel like human wreckage.

The grand duke was courteous enough to ignore her ashy appearance, as well. He muttered something unintelligible to Ignatiev, who responded in equally harsh Russian. Ignatiev stepped forward once more and said, "His Highness was here earlier. He wishes you will say more."

What was the man talking about? She looked to Sir Henry for help, but he seemed baffled, as well. "His Highness wishes me to say more about what, General?"

Ignatiev frowned and spoke respectfully to the grand duke again, who gestured toward the lumberyard. Ignatiev appeared to disagree—politely, of course—but when he received a stern look he turned back to Violet. "He would know more about body, Violet Rose."

Violet gasped. "How does His Highness know about this?"

Ignatiev offered what might have been a smile but looked for all the world like a grimace. "Not everyone runs like mountain hare in face of danger. Some confront it, like wild boar against brown bear." He pounded his fist against his chest for emphasis. "We moved *toward* fire. And we found you, Violet Rose, with dead body, while Ferdinand Marie watched you."

"What is this?" Sir Henry said, aghast. He turned to face Violet. "Did you kill someone, Mrs. Harper?"

"What? Don't be ridiculous," she snapped, angry to have been so accused and distressed that already de Lesseps's secret was out and he would likely blame her. "I am an undertaker. I preserve the dead, I don't create them." Once more, she found herself holding up her empty tapestry bag, as if it were some ubiquitous symbol of her profession.

Ignatiev spoke in Russian once more to the grand duke, whose face registered shock. Perhaps an undertaker was more frightening than either a boar or a bear.

Unfortunately, Sir Henry was just as interested in the situation as the Russians. "Do you mean to say that someone perished in the fire? Tragic! I hadn't heard. Who was it?"

"I . . . I am not—" What was Violet to say? To vindicate herself was to ignore de Lesseps's orders.

"Surely it wasn't a delegation member, or de Lesseps would have sent word," Sir Henry said, urging Violet to say something. Ignatiev and the grand duke also waited intently for her to reveal who the mysterious body was.

Sir Henry tried one final gambit. "Where has the body been taken?"

Violet lashed out in frustration. "That's just it, I don't know! De Lesseps asked me to take care of him, but he was spirited away."

Ignatiev chuckled, and it was disturbingly throaty, like the growl of a wolf in a children's tale. "Ah! So you tell us about him, Violet Rose."

How had Violet managed to get herself snared so easily? Before she could respond, Franz-Josef strolled by, Eugénie on his arm. Both of them looked as fresh as cream, another artifice suggesting that the fire had never occurred and all was well. Violet swiped a hand across her face and felt the grime that had encrusted itself on her. She needed to get to a washbowl soon.

More intriguing, though, was the expression on Ignatiev's face as he watched them disappearing into the crowd together. The man swallowed several times as his eyes hardened and glittered malevolently, and Violet wouldn't have been surprised to see bile spewing from his throat at any moment.

Interesting.

Ignatiev fixed his features once more, and although he still looked ferocious, he at least didn't seem to be wishing to snap bones with his teeth. "So you tell us about dead man?"

What else was Violet to do? They already knew that someone had died. She capitulated. "It was Yusef Halabi, one of the sons of the lumberyard owner. He worked here with his father," she said.

Ignatiev nodded thoughtfully and spoke to the grand duke once more in Russian, while Sir Henry expressed his shock. "How could he have possibly died in the fire? The lumberyard is completely exposed, so he wouldn't have been trapped by smoke, and the fire didn't spread so quickly that he couldn't have run from it."

Violet didn't like where the conversation was going, as she had already gone against de Lesseps's orders, and the British ambassador was so near the truth that he would soon have it figured out. "I cannot say," she simply and truthfully replied.

Seemingly satisfied with her vague answer, Ignatiev cut off Sir Henry's next question with, "You are unusual woman, an undertaker. I have met only one other woman as strange as you. She was nurse in Crimea. Very forceful and bold about care for injured men. Only Briton not notoriously incompetent, nor worried about interfering with Russian rights over Ottomans." He bared his yellowed teeth in a smile. Sir Henry responded with a strangled sound, although he maintained a diplomatic expression.

"I know Miss Nightingale," Violet said. "I have served her family as undertaker for many years."

Ignatiev shook his head. "Both of you very strange," he said, as if that explained everything.

Grand Duke Michael spoke to the general and then crooked a finger to instruct the military man to follow him. Before he turned away, though, Ignatiev said softly to Violet, "You be careful of Ottomans, Violet Rose. They do not respect others."

He strode off before she could ask him what that meant.

Baffled, she stared after the general, trying to understand his cryptic words. Sir Henry was quick to offer his own opinion. "Ignatiev is not very forgiving, you must understand. Great Britain has embarrassed him on two occasions, causing enormous damage to his pride."

"But he offered caution about the Ottomans—"

"Yes, but it was a veiled complaint about us. You see, the immediate cause of the Crimean War involved the rights of Christian minorities in the Holy Land, which the Ottoman Empire controls. Egypt conquered the area in 1832, but their rule was chaotic and turbulent. In 1840, Great Britain ensured that control was returned to the Ottomans, which seemed a fitting solution at the time. But Christians were not well treated by the Ottomans. France was enraged by offenses made against Catholics, while Russia was equally incensed over injustices served Eastern Orthodox Christians."

"But surely the general doesn't blame Great Britain for the sultan's actions?" Violet asked, still confused.

"Not exactly. He is actually angrier that Great Britain thwarted his country's ambitions. In the confused mission of the war, Russia decided to take territory and power at Ottoman expense, leading to further bloodshed and butchery. Great Britain— along with France, Sardinia, and, of course, the Ottomans—was ranged against Russia's lust for land. Ignatiev was involved in postwar negotiations over the demarcation of the Russo-Ottoman frontier, a great humiliation for his homeland."

Ignatiev had made his national pride quite clear, so Violet could imagine how painful it was for him to sit at a table and sign away territory he believed rightfully belonged to Russia. "You said, Sir Henry, that the general was embarrassed twice by our country?"

"Yes." Sir Henry brushed away an insect that had discovered his curling, wiry eyebrow hair. "After the Crimea, he was appointed military attaché at the Russian embassy in London. He wasn't there long when he was discovered to have pocketed a newly developed cartridge while inspecting the ordnance works of the British Army. He claimed he had done so inadvertently, but no one believed him. After all, ammunition cartridges do not exactly fall into one's clothing, do they?"

Violet was also hard-pressed to imagine how that could have happened accidentally. "Was he arrested?" she asked.

He shook his head, once more sending the buzzing insect on its way. "No, but to avoid diplomatic embarrassment, Russia summoned him home. I will admit that he has had great political successes since then, particularly in annexing Outer Manchuria from the Chinese, and forcing the emirate of Bukhara into a vassal state. It was these achievements that led to his posting as ambassador to Constantinople, a position he has held for about five years now. His quarters are in the same district as mine, but as you might imagine, we do not have much occasion for socializing."

No, these two men assuredly did not share port and cigars together. And, good heavens, there seemed to be more posturing on this spit of land called Port Said than in a park full of peacocks. "May I ask, why do you think Russia is in attendance at the canal's ceremonies? After all, they feel humiliated by Great Britain and France through the Crimean War results, then again by Britain after the diplomatic incident in London, and they have no love for the Ottoman Empire, of which Egypt is a part. Why, then, attend a spectacle in which you are a nonentity?"

The insect made for Elliot's eyebrows once more. This time he reached up and grabbed it, crushing it and then rubbing his fingers together so that the remains scattered to the ground. "That is an excellent observation, my dear Mrs. Harper. Why indeed *are* they here?"

Later, though, Violet arrived at another observation. How was it that Sir Henry always seemed to arrive just in time to rescue Violet from delicate situations? First in the shopping district, then with the Russians. Was he keeping an eye on her?

∞

Violet was exhausted. Much had occurred since she landed in port, and she was not only filthy but hungry, too. Her boots were rubbing at her heels, and her new bag seemed to be heavier by the moment even though it was empty. In the darkness she had lost sight of Sam, who was no doubt having a rollicking time with his friends, even though they had spent hours in a dangerous situation together.

She couldn't fault him. Sam had given up much to live with her in England. She was actually glad that he had found some fellow Americans for comradeship. Perhaps she could return to the ship to clean up and have word sent to him that she was there before collapsing in bed. She could tell him about everything that had happened tomorrow morning as they were sailing for Ismailia.

The idea blossomed quickly in Violet's mind, and she started to make her way to where *Newport* was berthed. She dreamed along the way about scenting the washbowl with lavender and snuggling into her underfilled pillow, which smelled overly of sea air and mustiness, but which right now appealed to her more than the riches of Midas.

Once again, she was intercepted before she had gotten far. This time it was Louise-Hélène, who was without her maid for the first time. Even without fireworks bursting in the air to add light to the unevenly spaced torches, Violet could see that the girl was nervous, looking around furtively and licking her lips. Several pins must have given up on their futile task of taming her hair, for strands of it had escaped their loose confines and trailed down the side of her face. It was actually a rather charming look, far more so than her efforts to look as polished as the older women around her.

"Mademoiselle, may I be of assistance to you?" Violet asked, hoping that it was something she could quickly answer for de Lesseps's fiancée.

"*Oui*, Madame Harper, I was hoping I might find you before the evening's activities were over. Have you noticed my maid, Isabelle, anywhere?"

"No, I have never seen her other than at your side. Do you fear she is lost? I'm sure she has simply found a tent of interest and forgotten herself in the middle of all the excitement."

Louise-Hélène frowned, as if seriously considering Violet's placating statement. "Perhaps that is so. But it is fortunate that I have found you alone, madame, as I wish to apologize to you."

What could this meek girl have to express regret about? "I see no reason for you to do so, but whatever it is, consider yourself forgiven as if it had never happened."

Violet's assurance confused Louise-Hélène even further, if the look of disbelief on her face was any indication.

"But you do not know what it is for which I crave your forgiveness," she said indignantly. "Perhaps it is for something grievous."

Looking at the future Madame de Lesseps, with her unmanageable locks and bewildered expression, Violet could hardly countenance such a thing.

"Very well," she said gently. "Tell me, mademoiselle, why I should forgive you."

"Because I am about to speak ill of my future husband, and I know I shall have to confess all to Monsignor Bauer to cleanse my soul." Louise-Hélène sighed, and another wisp of hair came loose.

The girl was truly lovely. In Violet's opinion, slander against others was practically a sport, with a person's reputation the ball that the disparaging cricket bat sent flying across the field.

Violet took Louise-Hélène's hand in her own. "Mademoiselle, perhaps it is not my forgiveness you need, but a confidential ear?"

The girl's eyes filled with tears but she blinked them back. "*Oui*, perhaps it is as you say. Madame Harper, I am most worried about my fiancé. Today's most"—Louise-Hélène looked upward, reaching for a word—"*unfortunate* events have left Ferdinand almost insensible, may the Sacred Heart comfort him."

"How so?" Violet said, wondering if anxiety was giving the older man heart palpitations or something that required a doctor.

Was there even a physician among all of the delegation members?

"He is so very . . . angry," Louise-Hélène replied, seeming to struggle again for what she wished to say.

"Angry over what?" Violet clasped the girl's hand tighter.

"The fire. He believes it to have been deliberately set."

On that point, Violet and de Lesseps were in agreement.

"Perhaps, then, it is time for your fiancé to ask the khedive to bring in whatever sort of police force exists in Egypt."

Louise-Hélène looked at Violet sadly. "I'm afraid that is impossible."

"Why? Are there no police? We have only had professional police in Britain since—"

"No, that is not it, madame. The problem is that Ferdinand believes the fire was started by the khedive himself. Or ordered by him."

Violet's mind reeled, trying to grasp what the young Frenchwoman was saying. "But . . . that makes no sense. Isma'il Pasha is as committed to the success of the opening ceremonies as de Lesseps. Why would he commit such an atrocity against himself and his own interests?"

"I believe there is much we don't understand about Egypt's politics, madame. If I understand Ferdinand correctly, though, the khedive's first loyalty is to Ferdinand. But he must also obey the sultan, who is not as forgiving about transgressions as my fiancé."

Louise-Hélène was speaking in riddles. "What transgressions has he committed?" Violet asked, dropping the girl's hand.

Louise-Hélène shook her head. "I do not know. I have simply heard Ferdinand say that the khedive will have to pay more tribute to the sultan to alleviate the Ottoman ruler's concerns, or Ferdinand will have to fix the situation himself."

Violet was still confused. What did the Ottoman sultan and his misgivings have to do with de Lesseps's suspicion that the khedive had deliberately set the lumberyard fire? How would such an act be in either the khedive's or the sultan's interests?

She opened her mouth to voice these questions, but Isabelle

had appeared from nowhere, breathless and flushed.

"*Je m'excuse*, mademoiselle, for my absence. I got caught up watching a performance of trained weasels and lost track of the time. Such tricks they could do!"

Isabelle was lying about her disappearance, Violet was sure, but Louise-Hélène just smiled at her maid and said, "All is well. But now I need to return to my cabin and remove these hideous stays."

Bidding Violet adieu, Louise-Hélène abruptly strolled back to where *L'Aigle* sat docked, with Isabelle following closely behind her, as if Louise-Hélène had completely forgotten her concerns about de Lesseps. It was almost as if the young woman had been an actor in a Greek tragedy who had delivered lines and walked offstage.

Standing alone in the dark, staring at their retreating backs, Violet wondered upon whom, exactly, her growing suspicions should rest.

chapter 7

IN ANY CASE, VIOLET DECIDED that Louise-Hélène's idea
of getting out of her corseted dress was a good one, and so
the undertaker made her way to *Newport*, determined not to let
another soul interfere with that goal.

It was not to be, though, for in her path was a cluster of men,
including Sam, Thaddeus Mott, de Lesseps, the khedive, and a
handful of Egyptians, fiercely intent in a discussion.

Violet approached Sam, who was frowning and shaking his
head while the khedive spoke. "I shall send men with axes to
quickly destroy it," Pasha was saying, making a chopping motion
with his hand.

"*Mon Dieu*, that will take days," de Lesseps said. "We should
set it afire, then send men overnight to collect the flotsam."

Violet touched Sam's arm. "What is wrong?" she whispered.

He turned to her while de Lesseps and the khedive continued
their discussion. "De Lesseps has a telegram that a ship has run
aground in El Qantarah, about fifteen miles down the canal
from here. Apparently, the captain was in his cups and passed
out at the wheel."

"Good heavens," Violet murmured. "Is the poor man all
right?"

Sam shook his head. "Don't know. The primary concern is
moving the hulk. She's lodged in the bank, and no one will be
able to get past her tomorrow morning."

More disaster for the opening ceremonies.

Discussion ensued, with de Lesseps and Pasha volleying back and forth ideas for eliminating the problem as quickly as possible. The word "dynamite" was uttered.

"Monsieur de Lesseps," Sam interrupted, "I have some experience with dynamite and have performed several blasts under the tutelage of Alfred Nobel himself. I would like to offer my services to you."

"Nobel, you say, Monsieur Harper?" De Lesseps appeared impressed, and said in an aside to the puzzled khedive, "Nobel invented dynamite. If what he says *ees* true, then Harper is probably quite skilled with it."

With de Lesseps's approval, the khedive readily agreed to Sam's assistance. In short order, it was agreed that Sam and Mott would accompany de Lesseps and Pasha, along with several servants, down to where the ship was lodged in the bank.

All thoughts of bath and bed faded. Violet took Sam's arm, fully intending to accompany her husband to the wreck site to check on the poor captain, whom no one seemed to care about, but de Lesseps frowned at her.

"Madame Harper, you may be more comfortable resting aboard *Newport* while your husband assists us."

While the man had no idea how true his statement was, Violet was determined otherwise. "I would not, monsieur, but thank you for your concern."

The Frenchman adopted the tone of a parent talking to a child. "It may seem very exciting what we are to do, madame, but it is work *dangereux*, not fit for your delicate sensibilities."

Violet had faced this same patronizing attitude in many situations many times over, yet it still rankled.

"Monsieur," she said, adopting the same air of exaggerated patience, "you may recall that I have just examined a burnt body, that of a man who was unfortunately taken away before I could properly attend to him." She flashed a look of irritation at Pasha. "I have also witnessed my husband's use of dynamite and can assure you it holds no terror for me."

"Nevertheless, I do believe—"

Sam held up a hand. "Monsieur de Lesseps, my wife will stay with me."

With that finality, they boarded a small boat with two sails in an odd V-shape, which was quickly loaded with the necessary tools and explosives. Would that Violet's hearse could be loaded up with a coffin, flowers, and draperies in such quick order.

They quickly sailed the fifteen miles to the scene where the ship was lodged. Workers had already arrived there, traveling by land along the canal's shoreline, and brightly burning torches illuminated the ship, a brig. It listed to one side like a drunken sailor, its sails dangling unhappily in the water.

"Interesting," Sam said quietly to her. "Brigs are a favorite of pirates."

After disembarking, the men sloshed their way onto the hull of the ship, scrambling onto it like half-drowned monkeys. Violet couldn't argue that she should be allowed to follow them, as drenched skirts would have been lead weights on her. She paced nervously while the men thumped around on the ship, wondering how they would decide to break the ship away from where it was.

Several Egyptians remained on shore with Violet, their eyes downcast and avoiding contact with hers.

The air was chilly now, making Violet wish she had gone aboard *Newport* first to retrieve her wrap, but there was little to do about it now. She continued pacing and rubbing her arms, much to the obvious discomfort of the khedive's workers, who were nervously avoiding her as though she were plague-ridden.

Sudden shouts in Arabic from aboard the ship captured both Violet's attention and that of the workers. The khedive's figure appeared as he stood on the hull, barking instructions and pointing at the two men nearest Violet. They reacted instantly, and she realized they were Hassan and Rashad, the ones who had probably carried off the lumberyard owner's son earlier.

The two men scrambled into the water and onto the ship, and soon disappeared as they followed the khedive belowdecks.

To Violet's great dismay, the two servants soon emerged,

struggling with a body that was clearly not that of just a drunken sailor.

Not again.

Gritting her teeth against the jostling indignity being served to the corpse, Violet was about to shout her own admonishment at the men when—*splash!*—the body left their grip and tumbled into the water, sinking below the surface.

Muttering oaths, Violet instinctively ran to the edge of the embankment, frustrated that she could find no way to easily enter the water shy of diving in, soaking her heavy skirts, and possibly drowning herself.

The other workers, realizing what she was doing, were now yelling at her, their Arabic clearly expressing their displeasure. One even approached her, angry and red-faced enough that he forgot to avoid eye contact.

"Lady, shore. Shore!" This was followed by a string of Arabic Violet couldn't understand but, combined with his insistent hand gestures, took to mean that he would forcibly restrain her if necessary.

She backed away, having no desire to cause an international incident, but paced and fretted as the men clumsily dragged the body out of the water and shoved it up the embankment. Gritting her teeth, she ran to the body, ignoring the outraged chattering of the men behind her.

"Mr. Salib?" Violet asked of the man who had spoken English to her earlier at the lumberyard. He flashed his smile again. Good Lord, the man was handsome, Violet thought, then was immediately stricken with guilt over such a disloyal idea.

"Please, my lady, you will call me Hassan."

"Very well. Hassan, did you not tell me you are the khedive's cultural attaché? Why are you here, doing such work?" She knelt down before the body, knowing instinctively she wouldn't like whatever it was she would find.

Hassan's expression was suddenly pained. "The khedive is a very, er, mistrustful master. He trusts me, and therefore asks me to do things of a . . . politically sensitive nature . . . that he would not ask of others. That is why I am here now. You can imagine the inferno of gossip that ordinary servants would start over this. As it is, I will have to sternly rebuke and threaten all the men standing here before returning to Port Said."

"I see," she said, flicking a glance at Rashad.

Hassan responded immediately to her unspoken question. "He is merely a porter, but he is also my brother, so the khedive extends trust to him, as well. It is good that he doesn't speak much English, you understand."

Violet nodded and turned her attention to the second body she had encountered in mere hours. "What happened to him?"

"We do not know, my lady. We found him curled around the wheel on the quarterdeck. The ship's mates have run off, I imagine to avoid any blame in the situation."

"But if the captain was inebriated, why would they be incriminated?" Violet asked.

Hassan smiled grimly. "There must always be someone to blame, my lady, and my master is quick to blame the wrong people when something goes wrong. It is wise not to be in Pasha's sight when blame is assigned. May I assist you in what you are doing?"

"Not yet." How poetic was it that the first body had been burned and this one was now drenched? She ran expert hands over the man, obviously the captain by the look of his jacket, with its shoulder epaulets containing an anchor design. Presumably this was meant to imitate a naval uniform. He was a middle-aged man with a full head of dark hair, sodden and disarrayed, and also a very full paunch, so certainly a man who enjoyed his beer. Violet gently ran her fingers through the man's waterlogged hair, feeling his scalp. Hmm, there were several lumps on his head. She knew he had fallen while drunk, so they were probably from his head hitting the deck, combined with more injury when the ship ran aground.

Still . . .

"Hassan, will you have a torch brought over here so I can examine this man more closely?" she said.

The man frowned and looked back at the ship, where the khedive and the others still worked. "My lady, please, this man must be removed as quickly as possible. You understand?"

Violet was beginning to understand too well. "Yes. But I must finish what I am doing first. This man deserves to be properly prepared for burial."

"The khedive, he—he does not necessarily care about this man's disposition. He wishes to please de Lesseps. Besides, you do not know Egyptian burial customs . . ." Hassan's words faltered as he glanced nervously at the ship again.

"Actually, I have visited a mausoleum since my arrival and I know—"

"That may be, my lady, but I cannot impress upon you urgently enough that Pasha will have his way in all things. You know nothing of our culture, my lady, and I must insist that we—"

"Enough, sir," Violet snapped, determined to finish her examination. "I realize the khedive is the most important man in your country, and I will be most happy to explain to him why this second man was not immediately whisked away for anonymous burial. But for the moment, I will be left alone to my task."

The khedive's man opened his mouth to say something else, then bowed his head and stepped away, taking his brother with him. He issued instructions in Arabic to a man standing nearby, and in moments Violet had two torches flaring nearby.

The illumination from the torches was, well, most illuminating.

The captain had an expansive and protuberant bruise on his face, covering half of one side of it. Violet placed her hands on either side of his face. Yes, the lump was very large and mottled. "You took a terrible tumble, sir. A most unfortunate outcome of your activities."

She quickly unbuttoned the brass buttons of his jacket, hoping the others were too focused on the khedive's movements to observe her own actions too closely. The jacket was heavy from its soaking, but she pushed the sides apart and pulled up his loosely constructed shirt over his considerable girth.

What Violet saw caused her to immediately sit back up as she suppressed a gasp. The captain's chest was a mass of blue and purple bruising, too.

So he had fallen, striking both the side of his face and his chest prior to actual death. Except that his stomach showed no signs of bruising at all. And wouldn't his protruding midsection have hit the decking first?

In fact, wasn't his stomach large enough that his chest wouldn't have struck the decking at all?

Greatly disturbed by the conclusion to which she was leaping, Violet quickly closed the captain's shirt and jacket. There had to be a logical explanation for this, she thought, returning again to her knees and playing out his accident in her mind. Could he have fallen unconscious against the wheel, then dropped to the ground and hit his head? If so, the bruising on his chest would be minimal, and there was still the man's paunch in the way.

Could he have fallen to the ground and hit his head, thus being killed, and then been struck in the chest as the ship ran aground? Hassan and Rashad had found him wrapped around the wheel's shaft, which was surely constructed of a sturdy wood like teak or mahogany.

She shook her head. If he had been hit in the chest after death, he wouldn't have bruised. No, there was only one logical conclusion to be reached.

The captain might have been in his cups, but he had been violently struck prior to death, and Violet was quite sure it was this attack that had killed him.

Was it merely a coincidence that she had discovered two bodies in a few short hours that both had met horrific ends? She prayed it was so, but years of undertaking experience whispered to her that suspicion was better than optimism in this case. She had to report her conclusions, although she wasn't sure whether the khedive or de Lesseps would be willing to take any actions. Perhaps she should—

Her thoughts were interrupted by a loud screeching noise coming from the grounded ship. She scrambled up, her heart pounding erratically. What on earth had just happened?

chapter 8

I T WAS CLEAR SOON ENOUGH that the men had somehow managed to dislodge the ship from the embankment and the piercing noise had been made as the hulk had been mostly righted. She was still bedraggled and listing, though, and Violet saw that workers were carrying familiar packaged bundles onto the ship.

They were planning to blow up the ship rather than try to sail her.

Violet knew her husband was probably as happy as a lark doing this work. His efforts at bringing dynamite to British coal mining had not gone well, partly because of the location he had chosen for it, but also because of the government's—particularly Queen Victoria's—horrified view of the substance. No one seemed to understand what Sam had, that very first time he witnessed dynamite in action. It was powerful but could be controlled more effectively than other explosives.

Dynamite was still not in common use, so Violet had to give credit to the khedive for actually employing it this time. But perhaps de Lesseps had used it for dredging the canal and so deserved the credit. Either way—

"Clear! Clear!" Sam was shouting, having emerged onto the deck. He gestured with his hands for everyone to get out of the way as he himself left the ship, which brought Violet back to her own issue at hand, the ship's captain.

"Hassan, we must move the captain farther ashore," she called out blindly, not seeing him among the men moving away from the area near the ship.

The khedive's cultural attaché did not respond. Violet glanced at the ground and immediately understood why.

Once again, a body had been spirited off from right under her nose.

∞

The earsplitting cacophony and brilliant light display of the dynamite put the evening's earlier fireworks to shame, but could hardly be compared to the fury about to erupt from Violet Harper. Whereas she once had been deafened and startled to near insensibility by a dynamite explosion she witnessed at Cumberland Lodge in Windsor, today she merely reached both arms out to keep steady despite the rocking ground beneath her. The noise couldn't overcome the blood pounding through her ears, and the sight didn't obliterate her own vision of personally boxing Hassan's ears, for surely he was the one who had removed the captain's body.

When she next saw him, she would—

Sam had materialized next to her, proud as a prince. "Did you see it? It was a beauty! They'll need to dredge the flotsam, but it shouldn't take long. The canal should be fixed as fast as greased lightning."

Violet opened her mouth to tell her husband what had happened and how infuriated she was, but the joy on his face stopped her. Why tarnish his success? She would simply confront the khedive or de Lesseps—or, by heavens, both of them—herself regarding their insensitive treatment of these poor dead men. It was not to be tolerated.

The return trip was mostly dark and silent: just a few oil lanterns illuminated their way back to Port Said, and the only sounds around Violet were those of breathing, coughing, and the occasional flaring of a pungent cigar. Sam fairly hummed with satisfaction at her side, while she steamed like a Colchester oyster in a pot of scalding water.

As they neared the port, Violet knew she had to say something, lest her shell burst open. "Monsieur de Lesseps, may I speak with you privately?" she said, approaching the Frenchman, whose cigar smoke was engulfing the khedive's head as the two spoke of something concerning the next day's events.

De Lesseps graciously nodded his head and followed her several steps away from everyone else. Unfortunately, the khedive seemed to think the invitation included him, and was right on their heels. Well, there was no help for it, and perhaps it was better for the khedive to hear what she had to say.

"Monsieur, I would like you to know that I inspected the captain's body when it was brought ashore," Violet began. "I believe—"

"This is a peculiarity of yours, Madame Harper," de Lesseps said, not unkindly. "Inspecting dead bodies. For what, I cannot imagine. How can this work possibly be of interest to a woman?"

So much time wasted in her life perpetually explaining to people why the dead deserved the living's utmost respect. Violet started the speech she had uttered so many times before. "We are all destined to be one of those lifeless bodies. It is my sacred duty to ensure that the deceased, who can no longer care for themselves, make their way to their final resting places in a respectful manner. We would all wish to be treated thusly when we die."

De Lesseps looked unconvinced. "You are idealistic, Madame Harper. I would wager to say that most people in the world are tossed into anonymous graves, with no ceremony and no lamentation."

Violet drew herself up as tall as she could. "That may well be, but bodies under my care will always be buried with dignity."

"I see." De Lesseps's expression was inscrutable.

Violet realized that the man had successfully changed the subject. Refusing to be put off, she said, "And because of my interest in the proper care of the dead, I must inform you that I do not believe that the captain died of a fall from being in his cups. He had bruising that was not consistent with falling. I think—"

Now de Lesseps's expression was perfectly readable. "This again, Madame Harper? You have a decidedly suspicious mind. Pasha here says the man was known to love beer, although how he could tolerate the swill these Egyptians make, I don't know."

Next to him, the khedive made a rumbling noise in his throat, but did not add comment.

Violet was becoming greatly irritated with de Lesseps's cavalier attitude toward the dead men. "It is not 'this again,' " she protested angrily. "I tell you that neither of these men died by accident. Each of them was murdered, although why and by whom I cannot begin to fathom. Unfortunately, both bodies were whisked away before I was able to properly inspect them. Whether or not this is deliberate or coincidental, I also cannot say. But these men deserved more than just—how did you put it, monsieur?—anonymous graves and a lack of lamentation. I will see that they have it."

Violet huffed as she completed her impassioned speech, and realized that her fists were tightly clenched at her sides. She slowly relaxed them. There was no sense in causing her own apoplexy.

De Lesseps was quiet for several moments, studying her. She refused to break his gaze, yet was aware that the khedive was waiting anxiously for the Frenchman's response.

"Very well, Madame Harper," he said slowly. "I can see that you are a determined woman. Although I doubt there *ees* this sinister plot afoot, these deaths do put the festivities at risk. And since you were once helpful to me in my unfortunate blackmail situation, you may quietly—how did you put it?—see that they have more than anonymity. But if your little investigation interferes with the events in Ismailia over the next few days, I'll have you scuttled back home on the first steamer I can find."

The khedive cleared his throat. "My friend, both of these men will be buried by now. What investigation will the lady perform?"

De Lesseps shrugged in apparent dismissal. "We will allow her to play at this until she realizes that sometimes the most obvious answer *ees* truly the answer—that men frequently die by accident or through their own stupidity."

De Lesseps's ringing endorsement was as genuine as the imaginary pull of a coffin safety bell, but Violet wasn't going to argue any further.

"Thank you, monsieur, for your graciousness," she said. "It is not my intent to cause you distress, nor to ruin your plans."

"Ah, no, it *ees* I who should thank you, madame, for such a pretty and heated display of temper. It was most entertaining, even more so than tonight's fireworks and dynamite explosion."

He was being condescending, of course, but already Violet's mind was racing forward on how to investigate the deaths of both the lumberyard owner's son and the ship's captain, even without having their bodies present. De Lesseps's tepid response was of no more import.

What was curious, though, was Pasha's reaction. The khedive seemed deeply disturbed by what had transpired between Violet and de Lesseps.

Violet turned to leave the men to their cigars and conversation, but de Lesseps stopped her.

"Madame Harper, perhaps you and your husband would like to be seated with the writing dignitaries at tomorrow evening's dinner."

"We will be happy to sit wherever you would have us." She accepted the invitation with a gracious nod.

Before she could once more walk away, de Lesseps nodded at both her and the khedive, offering his good night. Violet was left alone with Isma'il Pasha, who looked like a chubby specter, as enveloped as he was in cigar smoke in the moonlight.

Acutely aware of the fact that she was standing alone in the presence of the leader—effectively the king—of Egypt, whom she had probably insulted countless times already in the few hours she had been in the country, Violet struggled for polite conversation. Or at least a polite statement about the night's weather, even though the air had become chilled.

She needn't have worried about it, for Pasha opened up a

discussion with her.

"I do not trust you, Mrs. Harper," he said blandly, drawing in on the cigar, whose flaring orange tip made for a demonic punctuation point to his words.

It wasn't an observation, exactly, but rather a pointed accusation. Violet sensed that the khedive was waiting intently for her reaction, which would then determine the outcome of the rest of the trip.

"No one has ever said that to me before, Your Highness. But then, my customers are in no position for insolence and cheek."

The khedive choked and spluttered on his cigar smoke. "And who are *you* to believe *me* to be inso—" He stopped, straightened, and stared at Violet, then burst into rough, barking laughter. "Very amusing, *madaam*, very amusing. You are—what do the English say?—you are entrancing." He grew serious again. "But I find it curious that a woman of no noble or political connection has managed her way into the canal festivities, and in fact you are poking about in these unfortunate accidents. Could your queen not send someone of more importance? Why is she not here herself?"

Feeling the heat rush to her cheeks at the disrespect shown her sovereign, Violet said, "I would remind Your Highness that the Prince of Wales is here."

"Yes, yes, the little boy who plays with his women as he waits for the day the diamond circle will be dropped on his head." He snorted his contempt. "Very impressive. The queen sent him in order to get him out of her sight, no doubt. But then she sends a commoner of no count in her own stead." He shook his head as though the thought were impossible for any rational person to fathom.

Violet cast about for a suitable excuse. "I'm sure it is very difficult for Her Majesty to make long journeys. Her responsibilities at home—"

"Great princes of Europe are here to pay homage to Egypt, and have been here for weeks."

"Her responsibilities can be overwhelming for a widow, and

the prince is training for the throne." The words sounded hollow even in her own ears. How had she managed to put herself in the position of defending the royal House of Hanover?

"Is Great Britain of such importance that its monarch—over all other kings of Europe—cannot be bothered to celebrate the most far-reaching technological advancement in history?"

Violet tried once more. "Your Highness, I do not think that the queen would ever mean to imply that you—"

The khedive still wasn't finished. "And you are by some coincidence an undertaker, a most unseemly activity for a comely woman who would do well at managing her own little vegetable stand. But here you are, at hand for two regrettable deaths. It is as if your mere presence means doom for someone."

"Now that is something that I believe my customers would agree with," Violet said.

"Hah!" the khedive barked again. "Yes, yes, they would. Well, I suppose no harm can possibly come to *me* by your presence, which I admit is an agreeable one."

Violet breathed a silent sigh of relief. "Your Highness is kind to me when I have perhaps been a bit abrupt. You must understand that the care of the deceased must always come first with me."

Pasha nodded blandly. "And you must also understand that the glory of Egypt must always come first with me. There are those who believe that Egypt belongs to dusty museums and even grubbier public servants. When our two goals conflict, then Egypt will be preeminent. We have an accord, Mrs. Harper?"

Violet thought he might spit on his hand and hold it out for her to shake in a trader's pact. But she was no trader, and she wasn't sure she could hold to the bargain anyway. "I comprehend you perfectly, Your Highness," she said without actually accepting what she believed to be his insistence that taking Egypt's ancient treasures was his birthright.

Pasha seemed satisfied with her response. "De Lesseps invited you to dine with the art and writing dignitaries tomorrow evening. That will be a good place for you."

Had she just been complimented or insulted?

"Monsieur de Lesseps is a man of detailed plans," she said. "I'm sure he has personally decided where every potted plant should be set."

"No!" Pasha said, mercurially reverting back to anger. "Egypt and all of the celebrations are mine, *madaam*. I have spent almost two million pounds sterling for these festivities, depleting my own treasury and borrowing everywhere to ensure the canal and its opening are the most awe-inspiring attractions ever beheld. De Lesseps spends, but never his own money. Egypt's grandeur is due to no one else but me. Never forget this."

"Of course, Your Highness, of course," she said, soothing him as she would a widower outraged that his wife had died and left him saddled with their children. "You command a great nation, clear to everyone."

The storm passed, and a much-mollified Pasha spoke. "At least you realize this. I have brought many modern reforms to Egypt. There are more railroad lines in my country now than there are wrinkles on an old woman's face. We have greater opera and theater than the Italians. The city of Cairo today reminds every visitor of Paris in its magnificence. I have worked tirelessly for the past six years to bring these things about, and my name will be in children's history books as the greatest king—I mean, viceroy—that Egypt has ever known."

Violet hardly knew how to respond, but was saved from doing so by Sam's opportune arrival. "We will arrive in a few moments to transfer back to *Newport*. Your Highness," he said, bowing to Pasha, who nodded absentmindedly at Violet's husband.

She took Sam's arm and excused herself from the khedive's presence, grateful that her audience with him had come to a merciful close. In just a few minutes she would be rinsing soot and filth from her skin.

"Mrs. Harper." Pasha raised his voice, causing her to turn around to face him once more. "I still do not trust you."

Violet made no response, but turned back and continued walking with Sam.

I do not trust you, either, Your Highness.

CHAPTER 9

BY THE TIME THEY ARRIVED back at Port Said, the flotilla had been arranged with the French ship, *L'Aigle*, at the front, followed by Pasha's *El Mahrousa*, then *Newport*, followed by the remaining delegation ships, all in a neatly ordered line for the morning's procession.

Back aboard *Newport*, Violet was relieved to cleanse herself with the washbowl and pitcher provided. She changed into her nightgown and slipped into bed next to Sam, who was already snoring softly after the strenuous activity of putting out the fire and dynamiting the ship. Whether it was her husband's snoring or just agitation over everything she had seen and heard that day, Violet wasn't sure what was keeping her awake. But after more than an hour of restlessness, she climbed back out of their creaking bed, donned a clean dress, and went topside for some fresh air to clear her mind.

Lanterns glowed from posts at various points along the rail, and the ship was almost completely motionless in the canal water. A breeze blew gently across the deck, as if lulling all of the ship's passengers to sleep but her. Violet heard raucous laughter in the distance, and in the direction of the noise saw light emitting from what she thought might be the Russian ship. Apparently they weren't sleeping, either.

She spotted another figure on deck, staring out at the dying lanterns and torches scattered along the shore. The winking and sputtering lights made it seem as if the star-filled sky was also blanketing the ground. It was peaceful and unnerving at the same time.

Violet approached the figure standing along the rail, which turned out to be the captain himself, staring distractedly out to shore while stroking his very luxurious dark beard. He resembled a great sage contemplating life's greatest questions.

"Commander Nares?" she asked, standing next to him. "I see you are having trouble sleeping, as well." She reached for the ship's rail to steady herself, even though there was little movement beneath her.

"Ah, Mrs. Harper. Good evening. I am frequently up at all hours. Whenever I am out to sea—even if it is just a small canal—I feel an overwhelming sense of . . . responsibility . . . for my men and ship. I doubt I sleep more than two hours a night when aboard. My poor wife must believe I transform into Rip Van Winkle when I am home, though." Nares chuckled softly at his own joke. "Does the sea air bother you? Is that why you cannot sleep? I trust that none of my men have distressed you."

"No, nothing of the sort. I am just a bit troubled in my mind over what has happened this evening." Violet hardly knew how to sort out what had been the most disturbing aspect of her short time in Port Said.

"You mean the death of the lumberyard owner's son? Or that of the Egyptian captain?" Nares said gently. "I understand de Lesseps was in quite a turmoil over it, although I suspect for different reasons than you were, madam."

"Yes, it's hard to know whether Monsieur de Lesseps is genuinely concerned or if he is merely—" Violet bit her lip. She shouldn't be speaking of this to anyone else, despite the captain's kindness, and she faced out to shore once more to avoid him.

The captain chuckled again. "You mean to say, 'If de Lesseps is merely concerned with his own grandeur.' He will one day soon have his comeuppance, I assure you, Mrs. Harper."

She turned sharply toward Nares. "What do you mean?"

"I mean nothing at all. It's just that when ordinary men set themselves up as kings, others find the crown is ill-fitting."

Nares, then seemingly wanting to leave the topic of de Lesseps entirely, said, "Are you and your husband looking forward to the real festivities, which will start tomorrow in Ismailia?"

With all of the commotion that had already occurred, Violet could hardly think about more festivities. She chose a more diplomatic route. "I understand there is to be a special dinner tomorrow evening. Will you be in attendance, Commander?"

"Me? No, I leave the merrymaking to you and your husband, the prince, and Sir Henry. I shall remain behind with my duties aboard the ship while you are at the Dinner of the Sovereigns."

"Is that what tomorrow night's dinner is called? Monsieur de Lesseps did not tell me this."

"It is intended to laud all of the countries participating in the ceremonies, get them fantastically stupefied on Egyptian beer and French wine, and leave each delegation member feeling as though he were personally responsible for all of the greatness, even though very few of the sovereigns here had anything whatsoever to do with the project. I expect it to be quite the lavish affair."

"But I am of no moment to such a cause."

"No, but you are British, and so you will have to do since you do have some personal connection to the queen, and beyond that de Lesseps was only able to secure the prince from the royal family."

Violet wondered what the source of Nares's chagrin was. "You imply that this dinner will help France. Or Egypt."

"Undoubtedly de Lesseps and Pasha believe that everyone will command all of their shipping concerns to immediately begin using the Suez Canal and pay whatever exorbitant passage fees that the Ditchdigger and Pasha conjure up. De Lesseps will allow each country to believe he is giving it the absolute best rate, while in reality he will swindle them all." Nares grunted his displeasure. "I presume you will spend tomorrow night ashore?"

Perhaps she needed to pay more attention to the program in her cabin. "Why? Will other guests be doing so?"

"I'm fairly certain everyone has lodgings assigned to them.

The khedive has had them constructed—rather hastily, I'm afraid—to house all of the delegation in Ismailia. What sort of condition they will be in, I can only imagine." Nares shook his head. "I'm glad I will remain upon *Newport* with my crew while we are there."

Yet something else for Violet to worry about. "Do you know, Commander, why no one else from the royal family other than the Prince of Wales is present, since their absence seems to agitate the khedive?"

Nares tapped the rail and stepped away, offering his arm to Violet for a promenade around the deck. "You see, Mrs. Harper," he said as they strolled, "the British government has a very complicated relationship with Egypt. British merchants have worked diligently to find trading opportunities in the Nile Valley, while Her Majesty's government has worked just as hard to ensure that this entire region stays stabilized. To that end, our government openly supports Sultan Abdülaziz, who controls the entire Ottoman Empire."

Should Violet expose her own ignorance? "I'm afraid I'm not sure what the empire encompasses, Commander. Egypt, for one, I presume."

Nares paused to consider Violet's question. "Albania, Cyprus, Bulgaria, Libya, Iraq . . . there are more, but they don't come to me at the moment. Despite the number of countries under its auspices, the empire has been in decline since the Crimean War, having taken on far too much debt in that conflict than it could ever hope to repay. Great Britain is trying to help it along, although between us, Mrs. Harper, I don't see a great future for it. The empire will fall apart, and the individual nations will begin warring with one another, as they always do. They are not as gifted at empire building as we British are."

Violet was glad Sam wasn't privy to that comment, as he would have reminded the commander of the American colonies' break from Britain. She couldn't help but wonder if Great Britain's "help" was resented by Egypt. "The khedive—he is aware of our country's support of the sultan?"

At that moment, Nares stumbled but quickly righted himself, then grabbed a lantern that was burning nearby on a large metal chest. Kneeling down, he held it over the decking. "What the deuce, how did this board come loose? Well," he said, rising up, "that will not do. Someone will have to fix this at first light. But for now, I believe it would be beneficial if we walked with our light." The ship captain was on constant alert as they walked now, almost as if the ship were his own skin that he needed to protect from any abrasion or disfigurement.

"As you were saying, Commander . . ." Violet prompted.

"What? Oh, yes, Pasha is clever. He has managed a much higher position for himself than what is granted to the rulers of other empire states. They are mere governors, but he is now viceroy. The other states rely on the sultan to guide them, but Pasha is forging his own way. He knows that Great Britain will support whoever will provide the most stable environment for us to have flourishing trade. Right now that is the sultan, but I believe Pasha is elevating himself so that he will be on equal footing with the sultan. Or, at the least, will be able to operate without the sultan's interference."

Violet and Nares were now walking along the portion of *Newport's* rail where Violet had first seen the commander. He paused to hang the lantern, then resumed his original position, his elbows on the rail as he gazed into the dark. "If that happens," he continued, "Great Britain would be forced into dealing directly with Pasha, at the risk of alienating the sultan. This canal not only elevates Pasha's position, it weakens ours, as Great Britain's domination of shipping could be crippled by our dependence on it. Worse, it gives glory, as well as stronger claims to the Mediterranean, to France."

Did the man just actually shudder at the thought? Regardless, Violet was beginning to understand the situation. "So for the queen to attend would suggest that she is supporting the khedive's rise to power instead of the sultan's?" she asked.

"Precisely, madam. To send the prince leaves the impression that it is more of an honorary visit. What offense could the sultan have at the royal son visiting one of his nations?"

And a royal prince should be enough to satisfy the khedive, Violet concluded mentally.

"Our ambassador walks a fine line, does he not?" she asked.

"More than you know. Pasha is very enthralled with de Lesseps at the moment, for obvious reasons. Such slavish devotion causes him to forget that Great Britain was instrumental in helping Egypt's national building projects long before the Ditchdigger came along."

Violet smiled. "Building projects? I know you aren't referring to the pyramids or the temples."

Nares shared her wry amusement. "Nor has Great Britain participated in erecting the Great Sphinx. No, what we have done is far more important. Pasha brags that he has laid thousands of miles of track, but he neglects to say that it was the Robert Stephenson Company that came here from Newcastle in 1851 to build Egypt's first standard gauge railway. In fact, it was the first railway inside the entire Ottoman Empire. Stephenson even built Pasha his own specially appointed carriage, something that even the sultan does not have."

Violet now understood even more. "So Great Britain has participated in Pasha's self-aggrandizement. Yet we must be seen to support the sultan. But our country's true goal is to ensure that British shipping interests remain intact."

"The politics at play are very complicated, Mrs. Harper, and complicated politics are usually quite dangerous for those who play heavily in them. The ambassador enjoys such intrigues; I personally do not. I suppose that is why I am a mere ship's captain."

How dangerous was the situation, though? Enough to result in two murders? Worse, would there be more?

For the life of her, though, Violet couldn't understand how in the world the two dead men could possibly have anything to do with the complex foreign intrigues at hand. What was she missing?

CΘ

November 17, 1869

Violet was awakened not by bells on deck, or by a steam whistle, or even by an off-key rendition of a sea shanty by Nares's men. No, it was a deep, guttural howling, like that of a wounded gray wolf, an animal she had listened to many a night while in the Colorado Territory with her husband.

Sam launched himself out of bed at the sound, nearly knocking himself out on a support beam. "Good God Almighty," he exclaimed as he fished around for his trousers. "Do you know what that sounds like?"

"Yes," she said, tossing aside the bedcovers and joining her husband in frantically getting dressed. "I was hoping I had heard the last of such sounds when we boarded the train for New York."

Once presentable, they dashed up to the main deck, and were stunned by what greeted them.

The morning was strikingly gorgeous, with the sun already bathing everything in warmth, eradicating all memory of last night's distress. Pasha must have sent workers out like little nocturnal dung beetles, scooping up all of the evidence of the fire, the murder, and the stampeding fear, then rolling it away out of sight. In fact, both the fireworks stand and the lumberyard were gone and the sand raked over both places.

However, *Newport* was now leading the flotilla down the canal, with *L'Aigle* and the other ships behind it. The howling emanated from de Lesseps, who stood on his deck screaming epithets at Commander Nares, Sir Henry, the Prince of Wales, and even Violet and Sam. Running out of those insults, he added the queen, all of her children, her children's children, the prime minister, and Parliament to his invective against those who should be cooked slowly on a spit in hell for impudence, arrogance, and duplicity.

Violet was as shocked as de Lesseps.

Newport's captain came up from behind them. "Good morning, Mr. and Mrs. Harper. Truly a fine morning, is it not?" he said, his face threatening to split in two from the mischievous grin spread across it. "Appears we accidentally drifted into the lead," he said with a wink of the eye.

Violet was at a complete loss for words. "Sir, you did not tell me you intended to insult Monsieur de Lesseps in this way. It does not seem politically astute."

Nares took no offense. "I did tell you he would receive his comeuppance, though, Mrs. Harper. No doubt I will be in grave trouble with the Lord High Admiral, not to mention Prime Minister Gladstone, but I deem it thoroughly worth it to witness the Ditchdigger's reaction. Ten years of work behind him and Pasha, and Great Britain is the first to sail the canal. This calls for a special celebration, does it not?"

Violet noticed that Nares and his men were all standing around, highly amused, but the Prince of Wales and Sir Henry were conspicuously absent. "Are His Highness and the ambassador aware of this action, Commander?"

"Not officially. And they will undoubtedly reprimand me, as well." Nares was perfectly cheerful about it.

"I imagine, sir, that the khedive will be equally as angry about our taking the flotilla lead," Violet insisted, in disbelief that the ship's captain was so cavalier about what he had done.

"Eh, I do not believe that Pasha adores de Lesseps as much as people would believe him to. Pasha has reason to be in our good graces, too, and you won't see him protest too loudly over this." He walked off, whistling jauntily, with de Lesseps's voice growing weaker in the background as his voice gave out from bellowing.

"When did Commander Nares talk to you about de Lesseps having a comeuppance?" Sam asked Violet, his face grave. "Is there something treasonous going on here?"

Violet told Sam of her conversation with Nares in the middle of the night. He nodded. "So the Prince of Wales and Sir Henry knew of it and approved of it, and are hiding in their cabins so that they can claim they knew nothing of it."

Violet was still surprised that Nares had so easily hidden his intentions from her last night, and was trying to prevent that surprise from twisting itself into anger over what any thinking person would realize was a usurpation of de Lesseps's role in the Suez Canal celebrations. However, she was merely an observing delegate here, not a member of the political process, so the wisest course was to remain silent.

But that was only as long as there were no further corpses presenting themselves.

People lined the embankment of the canal as far as the eye could see, waving flags and cheering as the flotilla got truly under way on its eight-hour journey to Ismailia. As was true when they docked last night, the crowds were made up of every nationality and style of clothing imaginable, and the enthusiasm was almost drowned out by the snapping of flags and banners waving from poles, tent tops, and outstretched arms. Did they realize that Great Britain had made itself the first to achieve transit between the Mediterranean and Ismailia?

From somewhere behind them, the musicians on the Austrian ship had started up the same anthem from last night, which was received happily by the crowds. De Lesseps had seemingly washed down his anger. Violet saw him at the prow, Eugénie next to him and Louise-Hélène a couple of steps behind the two popular French citizens. De Lesseps and Eugénie both soaked in the adoration of the crowds, turning to one side and then the other, waving to the throngs.

It was more difficult to see what was happening on ships farther down the line, but she presumed the same sort of sovereign-to-commoner greeting was occurring. Violet knew she and Sam looked like cats rumpled by a romp in forest undergrowth, but there was no help for it at this point. Shrugging at each other philosophically, they also lifted hands of greeting to everyone along the shore.

More cheers rose up as the Prince of Wales and Sir Henry Elliot finally emerged from below decks. They were dressed in their finest silk top hats and velvet-collared coats, their hands encased in golden-brown doeskin gloves as they also waved down to the embankment.

Violet felt even more disheveled in her appearance.

But no one was paying attention to the undertaker and her husband, for there was simply too much to behold in the procession to worry about a woman who had had only about thirty seconds of ablutions a short while ago.

Not only were there throngs lining both sides of the canal for their journey, but also, at strategic intervals along the shore, were examples of the dredges and elevators de Lesseps had employed for constructing the canal. She was especially amazed by one of the gargantuan dredges, which to Violet looked like a pregnant spider upon its back, its huge metal arms attached to retaining lines like an arachnid's legs clinging to strands of web.

Reading her mind, Sam remarked simply, "Impressive. I heard that they were the brainchild of the Greek workers."

They would be entering Ismailia soon enough, so Violet proposed that they go down and get ready properly. Despite her lack of sleep after the previous night's events, followed by this morning's shock, it was hard not to be excited and carried away by the sheer magnificence of the flotilla. The joy expressed by the international well-wishers on either side of the canal was truly an experience that could not be described.

If only Violet Harper weren't so mindful that there were two dead men who needed justice.

chapter 10

Aboard the French yacht L'Aigle
along the Suez Canal

LOUISE-HÉLÈNE AUTARD DE BRAGARD, KNOWN fondly
as "*ma louloute*," or "my darling," by her fiancé, Ferdinand de
Lesseps, was fully aware of her tendency to scowl too much. It
gave others the impression that she was bitter and angry most of
the time, when the opposite was true. In fact, she was inexpressibly
overjoyed at the favorable hand that God and the Blessed Mother
had dealt her.

Here she stood on the deck of the French yacht *L'Aigle*, named
for both the bird of prey and the symbol of Bonaparte's First
French Empire. It was gloriously luxurious, and her private
cabin—for use only by her and her lady's maid, Isabelle—had
every comfort possible. Bottles of wine, feathery bedcoverings,
and exotic culinary delicacies were always presented before she
even realized she had a desire for them. Ferdinand even somehow
ensured that fresh flowers were delivered each day.

She might be only twenty-one and her fiancé forty years
her senior, but he had the energy of a man half his age. He
had a vitality that consumed everyone around him. Men did
his bidding without questions, as if he were able to imbue the
importance of his canal project into their very souls. Louise-
Hélène hoped that Ferdinand's vigor would extend to their

private bedchamber once they were married, and immediately blushed inwardly that she had such improper thoughts.

She must stay focused on making him proud during the next few days of diplomatic relations so that he would be glad of his decision to pluck up the granddaughter of a former magistrate on the island of Mauritius. Well, it had been known as Isle de France until the British—or *les rosbifs*, as they were disparagingly called—had invaded the French colony in 1810. The Roast Beefs had then proceeded to make the profitable island of sugar plantations part of its never-ending, never-satisfied realm, just one of many indignities the French had suffered.

Her grandfather was one of the few French permitted to remain in his position, since the de Bragards were part of the Franco-Mauritius elites, but his health was broken and Louise-Hélène only remembered him as a stooped man, kind but vacant-eyed. Her father, Gustave, took over the magistrate position, but ensured that Louise-Hélène and her sisters were sent to France for education. She had a chance meeting with the great de Lesseps two years ago when he made one of his many trips to tout the Suez Canal's progress. He was invited to a music recital in which many young men and women were playing. For some reason, he became enamored of Louise-Hélène's fingering of "La Marseillaise" on the trumpet and insisted upon meeting her. He later claimed not only that he was entranced by a woman playing the trumpet, but also that her rendition of the French national anthem had brought tears to an old widower's eyes.

Two years of infrequent visits by de Lesseps back to Paris, a flurry of letters to her parents back in Mauritius, and now here she stood on the deck of *L'Aigle*, cruising to Ismailia for more canal-opening festivities. By her side was Isabelle Dumont, her lady's maid and now her chaperone, although de Lesseps had proved himself such a gentleman that Louise-Hélène doubted he would have ever pressed an advantage, even in the close quarters of the sailing yacht.

He was kind, strong, educated, and one of the most important men in France—no, in the entire world. His age was easy to overlook. No, she could have done much worse than to fold her hand into Ferdinand de Lesseps's.

A strong breeze blew across the bow of the ship. Louise-Hélène hoped that her floppy white hat, edged in white ostrich feathers and secured firmly under her chin by silk ribbons, successfully tamed the mass of dark curls pinned atop her head. Her coiffure was frequently as uncontrollable as her expression. All of a sudden, though, another manner of wind circled around Louise-Hélène, in the form of Eugénie de Montijo, a former Spanish countess and the current empress of France. Louise-Hélène found Eugénie to be impossibly beautiful, cultured, and intellectual, all of which was emphasized by smoky dark eyes and understated, elegant clothing.

Louise-Hélène felt like a dowdy imposter next to the empress, whose husband, Napoléon III, had sent her as his representative at the canal opening while he dealt with domestic opposition to his policies. Something about Republicanism and growing Prussian power, Louise-Hélène recalled. She had no head for politics and could never pretend to have one. Ferdinand didn't seem to mind that she was an uncomplicated girl, but it didn't make her any less uncomfortable when Eugénie strolled into her path.

Eugénie sauntered over to her now, a walking cream confection, with her own lady's maid following an appropriate distance behind. The empress's tailored ivory jacket with wide lapels and side pockets suggested a gentleman's cut, but of course on the empress it looked dainty. Beneath the jacket was a matching waistcoat with shell buttons so numerous as to create an effect of a train track from stomach to neck. Her skirt was of the same material. Eugénie wore no jewelry, letting the stark contrast of her dark coloring against the ivory fabric speak for itself.

Louise-Hélène didn't have to look down at her lace-ruffled copper skirt with the hem band of brown to know that she looked positively frumpy and out-of-date by comparison. Why, even Eugénie's maid, Julie, looked more stylish from within the shadow of her grand mistress.

All during the earlier trip down the Nile to Cairo and back to the northern coast—which had been interesting enough, what with the views of swaying palm trees, round-domed mosques, and all manner of ancient structures along the way—Eugénie had been the undisputed center of attention. Her tinkling laugh, her pretty wit, and her seemingly effortless ability to make every man from the lowliest porter to the khedive of Egypt himself fall half in love with her filled Louise-Hélène with inexplicable jealousy. She could hardly believe that Eugénie was reputed to be very devout and presumably would never act on her flirtations.

For all of Ferdinand's chivalry toward his own betrothed, he also seemed impressed by the empress's charms, and Louise-Hélène had even once caught him gazing at Eugénie's back with something akin to hunger. Was it just the natural state of being a woman to feel intimidated by her betters? Or perhaps it was only the natural state of an unsophisticated soul like Louise-Hélène? Her stomach fluttered in dismay to think that perhaps she wasn't up to being Ferdinand's consort.

As if understanding her mistress's thoughts, Isabelle discreetly put a hand to Louise-Hélène's back, as though to steady her. Louise-Hélène nodded, and Isabelle dropped her hand away as the empress approached.

"Your Majesty," Louise-Hélène murmured deferentially, dropping into a curtsy as she had done so many times over the past few weeks. Behind her, Isabelle dropped even lower in homage. The empress always smiled sweetly in her direction, but looked just past Louise-Hélène, as if perpetually searching for someone else. As far as Louise-Hélène could tell, that someone was Franz-Josef, the Austro-Hungarian emperor, who was also part of the flotilla on the Nile. He was as dashing as Eugénie was beautiful, and they looked like two darkly exotic heavenly orbs dancing around each other when in each other's company. Eugénie frequently took Franz-Josef's arm when they all disembarked their respective ships for touring the latest Egyptian ruin. Eugénie knew how to glide along lightly, playfully tapping Franz-Josef with her fan or pursing her lips enchantingly to convince him to purchase a souvenir for her. All Louise-Hélène was capable of doing was clutching onto Ferdinand's arm and hoping she didn't trip along the unevenly gapped slats on the dock.

She tried not to continuously wonder what indiscretions might be occurring, what with both Eugénie's and Franz-Josef's regal spouses sitting a world away. It was sinful for Louise-Hélène to speculate on the transgressions of others. She pressed discreetly against her skirt, on the pocket that lay hidden beneath, and took comfort in feeling the beads of her rosary there.

"*Ma louloute*," replied Eugénie, the only other person in the world who took the liberty of calling her by Ferdinand's pet nickname, which was not only an endearment but also a play on the name Louise. It made Louise-Hélène's stomach roil that the empress used the term, but the empress was, after all, royalty— and of the great nation of France—making awe a clashing emotion with jealousy in Louise-Hélène's breast. Maybe it was the competition between the two that kept her in constant need of fennel seeds to chew to settle her stomach.

"Your Majesty," Louise-Hélène repeated as Eugénie motioned for her to rise. "The breezes blow *doucement* today, do they not?" Isabelle came from a good family, and had been able to advise Louise-Hélène on the nuances of idle chatter, something she had missed while absorbed in music lessons. What Isabelle lacked in hairdressing talent, she more than made up for in comportment and conduct skills.

"*Oui*, but they are not gentle enough to avoid sending my hair into complete disarray." Eugénie's laugh tinkled across the deck, and more than one sailor stopped his work to gaze her way. Louise-Hélène wasn't sure if Eugénie was making a sly stab at her own hair, which was in disarray in the best of times.

"Why do you look so glum, *ma louloute*?" Eugénie asked. Was there an air of fake concern in her query? "You frown too much. Happiness improves the digestion and the disposition. I do recommend it."

Her stomach churned, but Louise-Hélène forced herself to smile as Isabelle had taught her to do in many private sessions in her cabin. "Your dress is charming, Majesty. Your *couturière* is to be commended."

"Do you think so?" Eugénie replied absently, brushing an invisible piece of lint from her arm. "The emperor says he likes this color, but I feel like I am an old medieval French queen donned in mourning. I certainly hope he appreciates the trouble I took with it. Your dress is quite lovely, too, my dear."

Louise-Hélène felt the heat creeping up her neck, knowing that the empress was surely patronizing her. Now Isabelle's hand was at her back again. "Thank you, Your Majesty. You are most kind. My fiancé says we should be in Ismailia soon." Maybe reminding the empress that Louise-Hélène did possess status as de Lesseps's betrothed would make her feel less inferior.

No such luck.

"Yes, won't it be *sensationnel*? I was talking to him earlier, and he described for me the grand platforms that will be there, along with the music and fireworks. I just hope it will not be too chilly. Why, there he is now. Monsieur de Lesseps!" Eugénie called out, taking her leave of Louise-Hélène and gliding to where Ferdinand stood, arguing with the ship's captain about something, probably the timing of their entry into Ismailia. Ferdinand was very precise in all that he did.

In moments, Eugénie was on Ferdinand's arm, having whisked him away from the captain, and was chatting animatedly with him about whatever it was monarchs chattered about, while Julie followed respectfully in their wake. No doubt Eugénie was commiserating with him about the British arrogance in sneaking their ship to the front of the flotilla. In that internal warring of factions, Louise-Hélène was swelled with pride that the empress of France thought so much of her husband-to-be, yet she also wanted to take scissors to the woman's dress and scatter the pieces in the canal.

Perhaps just this once Louise-Hélène's scowl really was the result of annoyance.

"Look, madame," Isabelle said, pointing and drawing Louise-Hélène's attention away from Ferdinand's and Eugénie's close conversation. "I believe we are almost there."

Isabelle was another provision made for her by God. Seven years older than Louise-Hélène, she had been lady's maid to the *directrice* of Louise-Hélène's school. When Isabelle discovered that Louise-Hélène was to be married to Ferdinand, the maid had come to her in secret, begging to be taken into the new de Lesseps household. Isabelle desperately needed an opportunity to shed her old existence, and Louise-Hélène was in serious need of assistance in many areas. The fact that Isabelle had dangerous secrets didn't bother Louise-Hélène in the least, as long as Isabelle remained her friend and confidante.

The ship slowed and, within minutes, Ismailia came into sight. Despite her desire to seem sophisticated, Louise-Hélène let out an awestruck "Ohhhh." For even at this distance, two great platforms were visible on shore, with wide steps leading to a massive stage on each. Poles had been erected on the four corners of each platform, and red draperies were artfully hung so that the structures resembled elevated theaters. The French flag was hoisted over one platform, the Egyptian flag over the other.

Other, smaller platforms surrounded the two main stages, presumably for the delegation or entertainments, but they were lower and not as richly decorated. It was easy to see off in the distance that much of the embankment next to the canal was still rugged and disheveled, as though equipment had been hastily moved out a few minutes prior. For all she knew, it had.

There were also throngs of people in brightly patterned robes and headwear gathering along the rough embankments as they had in Port Said. No doubt the European flotilla would garner even more adulation here than it had along the Nile, where it seemed people came out at all hours to wave and cheer at the ships sailing past them.

As *L'Aigle* slowed, sailors began scrambling around her and Isabelle. Ropes were unwound and sails were furled as the men shouted furious instructions to one another. Louise-Hélène grasped the smooth, polished oak rail that ran along the edge of the deck. It was funny how she needed nothing to balance her while they were sailing at top speed, but once they slowed, the waters began slapping up against the boat and rocking it mercilessly.

"Shall I retrieve your fennel seeds, mademoiselle?" Isabelle said quietly.

"*Non*, I will be well," Louise-Hélène said. She turned her gaze from the fascinating activity on shore to Isabelle, and noticed out of the corner of her eye that Eugénie had disappeared but Ferdinand remained, smiling and waving to people on the ground.

Surely, she thought, *this country is a second home to him.*

And just as surely she hoped he would not expect her to make her home anywhere but France. She reached into her dress pocket and rubbed her rosary beads again for comfort.

Isabelle nodded. "If you will permit me, mademoiselle, I should like to carry the fennel with us as a precaution."

Louise-Hélène nodded and her maid disappeared as Ferdinand caught her eye. She smiled and walked toward him, her hand continuing to clutch the rail. He greeted her enthusiastically. "Is it not *fantastique*? I told the khedive to put on the finest celebrations imaginable. He has done well."

"He has," Louise-Hélène agreed, blushing when Ferdinand took her hand, undid the top button of her glove, and laid a gentle kiss on the underside of her wrist before squeezing her hand and releasing it. The sensation of his mustache and lips against her skin left her breathless.

"This *ees* nothing, though," Ferdinand said, returning his gaze to the shore, as if unaware of how dazed Louise-Hélène had become in just a few seconds. "Tomorrow there will be speeches and prayers, a picnic, and a grand ball at the khedive's palace. You will find your rooms inside my villa spacious and comfortable. After five years of planning and ten years of building, this *ees* the recognition I have waited for. The recognition of France as a mighty country, and of the great possibilities that exist for all of Europe. This canal changes everything, *ma louloute*, everything. The world will never be the same. Perhaps the canal opening can close the wounds of the Prussians and the Austrians after so much war between them. I just hope nothing else foolish happens beyond the obvious British chicanery."

"Foolish? What do you mean? Are you concerned about an accident of some sort?"

He shook his head. "I'm sure it *ees* just the unsteady nerves of an old man."

"You aren't old!" she cried. "You are most young to me. In your kind heart, and in your spirit."

Ferdinand smiled down on her. There was appreciation in his eyes, but something else, too. Fear? Hesitancy? The future Madame de Lesseps realized that she didn't know her betrothed very well at all.

He changed the subject entirely. "*Ma louloute*, where is your parasol?" Ferdinand asked. "All of the ladies will be carrying them. I believe it will be a most sunny day."

Naturally, Eugénie reappeared on deck with Julie, carrying an elegant ivory-colored parasol with what looked to be a bone handle. And yet, as if her own maid had heard Ferdinand, Isabelle emerged from below carrying Louise-Hélène's umbrella. Louise-Hélène almost teared up in gratitude, silently whispering more thanks to Him above for her friend here below.

Louise-Hélène's greatest hope was that it would not be *she* committing the foolish act that Ferdinand so dreaded.

chapter 11

Aboard the Russian ship Alexandrite

NIKOLAY PAVLOVICH IGNATIEV SAT BELOWDECKS, arms crossed in irritation as he waited endlessly for his chess partner to make a move. Ignatiev was tired of much that was happening around him.

He was tired of sailing on this frigate, beautiful though she was. Russians proudly named many of their ships after precious gems, and this one was no different. He especially liked that the particular gem in question was named for their revered tsar, Alexander II, and that it was a stone that flashed unusual shades of red and blue, two of Russia's national colors. The *Alexandrite* herself was a beauty, too. His Imperial Majesty must have thought the trip important, hence his decision to send such a luxurious ship for the delegation. Surely many in the flotilla had been impressed by Russia's presence.

That pleasure over his floating quarters and its impact had lasted mere days. Ignatiev, a general in the Imperial Russian army before starting his diplomatic career, preferred action to all of this pomp and frippery. However, his position as a negotiator at the Congress of Paris after the Crimean War, then his service in dealing firmly with the Orientals during the Second Opium War, and now his role as ambassador to Constantinople had taught him to tamp down his ever-present irritation when talks stalled or when petty functionaries made petty demands.

Or when a player spent all of his time with his finger on a bishop without ever moving it. An hour playing chess with the Grand Duke Michael Nikolaevich was as slow as a year in Siberian exile.

Even more so, he was tired of pretending to lose at chess, draughts, and dominoes to the duke, his fellow delegation member. Of course, Ignatiev valued his own life and would never say so aloud. One did not insult the son of the old tsar, Nicholas, even if he was only a fourth son who held no hope of ever inheriting the throne from his brother. The consolation prize for a man like the duke was to be governor general of the Caucasus, a territory that Russia had been conquering and annexing in pieces for decades. Michael lived there with his children and his wife, who had just calved a sixth child for him. It would seem that the duke missed his wife and squalling offspring, for he spoke of little else but returning to them. Just another week left of this theatrical display and the duke could scurry back and cling to Olga's skirts.

Ignatiev was also tired of the atrocious vodka that had been brought aboard. Had he known, he would have brought along bottles of his own *vino dvoynoe*. He thought longingly of the special icehouse he had had built in Constantinople, which was currently packed with pregnant casks of the finest— and strongest—vodka made in his home country. Perhaps de Lesseps would suggest a binge at some point during the opening ceremonies. To drink to excess with a group of his newly made acquaintances would at last make the interminable past two weeks worthwhile. As his father always proclaimed, "It is good to drink; not to drink is a sin."

Finally, Ignatiev was fatigued from the constant touring and stopping on this foolish Nile trip. Smiling did not come easily to a man with chapped, thick lips that he attempted to disguise with an even thicker mustache that spread across his face like an unruly waterfall. The mustache was also designed to draw attention away from his badly receded hairline, which had caused his forehead to take a great blistering during the past two weeks of sauntering down the Nile. His temper had grown even shorter than it normally was, despite the relative mildness of the weather.

There was such futility in all of the hand shaking and cheek kissing and cheering that occurred at every stop. Ignatiev had a very specific mission to accomplish here in Egypt; then he wanted to return to his ambassadorial post. And his vodka casks. At this rate, they would still be here next year.

Ignatiev snapped to attention at the faint sound of wood scraping against wood. Was the duke actually completing a move? He unconsciously held his breath as he watched Michael move his bishop three diagonal spaces to the left, thus committing an amateurish blunder. Ignatiev realized instantly that the duke only saw two moves ahead, and believed he had the general's queen on the run, but Ignatiev was poised to crush him.

Once again, Ignatiev would have to make a move even more colossally stupid than the duke's, and then they could end this game. Afterward, he could slip down to his cabin for a cup of putrid liquor before they performed the day's back thumping, cheering, and gasping over every magnificence the khedive and de Lesseps had provided.

Ignatiev expelled his breath and slumped back in his chair again. The duke had pulled his bishop back, removed his hand, and was now contemplating the board all over again. Dear God, if Ignatiev had his Baby Dragoon in his palm right now, he wasn't sure if he would shoot Michael or himself.

"I find it hard to concentrate under such difficult conditions, don't you, General?" the duke said without looking up from the board. The duke was the same age as Ignatiev, thirty-seven, but the general had to admit that the duke wore his age much better. Of course, the duke had been blessed with dark good looks and a slim build. Even his mustache, worn in the same style as Ignatiev's, seemed to be less about disguising an unfortunate upper lip and more about making him look exotic. The man could probably snap his fingers at any courtesan he wanted, but instead pined away for the sharp-tongued Olga Feodorovna, who ruled her family with an iron petticoat.

"Pardon me, Your Highness, what conditions are those?" Ignatiev said with as much patience as he could muster.

The duke looked up in surprise, as if it simply weren't possible that Ignatiev didn't know. "Without our wives and families with us. Trapped away at sea, just a couple of old warriors with no company but servants and each other."

Bah, the duke dared to call himself a warrior? In the *spalnya* with his wife, perhaps. As if Ignatiev needed to be reminded that even with his exalted position as both a general and an ambassador, few women wished to share his bed permanently. Instead, he was forced to seek company where it could be paid for in rubles or drink.

"Yes, terrible," Ignatiev responded shortly.

The duke didn't notice Ignatiev's dour expression, as he was still gazing down at the board. "My brother insisted I come down to the canal opening. He did not care that Olga just bore my son a month ago and needs me desperately. She suffers without me. The Suez Canal ceremonies could have been easily managed by you, General, and did not require my esteemed presence." A finger stretched out again and tapped the top of a rook, but Ignatiev was under no illusion that the piece was going anywhere.

"No, Your Highness." It was all Ignatiev could do to maintain civility. While he agreed that the trip would have been easier without the mooning and carping of his fellow traveler, it did seem important that a member of the imperial family, even a lowly member, be present. And at least Michael was innocuous enough not to interfere with any of Ignatiev's activities.

"I have my responsibilities, too, as governor general. I cannot allow neglect of my territory to go on much longer." The finger left the rook and swirled over a pawn like a sea eagle that had caught sight of a lamprey in shallow waters.

"Yes, Your Highness." Ignatiev finally reached a conclusion. Given a choice, he would definitely shoot the duke.

Fortunately, shouts from the upper deck diverted them both, and presently the duke's manservant picked his way down the stairs carefully, as he was clad in the impractical heels of his livery at all times. "Your Highness, we are *arrivés*," he said.

French was the language of the Russian court, and Michael insisted that his servants speak it to him, as well, to bolster a cultured image. Ignatiev himself spoke French and a smattering of German and English, but had never bothered to pick up the Turkish language. The former three had served him well in any situation he had ever found himself, although what he had to accomplish before leaving Egypt made him think that perhaps a bit of Arabic wouldn't have been out of order.

Once on deck with the duke, Ignatiev took in the great cheering along the docks, as well as the scarlet-draped pavilions and throngs of brightly clad Egyptians. There was de Lesseps's yacht, the French flag snapping smartly on her mast, behind the British ship *Newport*, which had managed an arrogant usurpation of *L'Aigle*'s place in the flotilla line. Ah, and there were the British colors flying above a gunboat, with two escorting ships. They had not been in attendance during the Nile trip. Was this just a coincidence, or were the British making a statement?

Ignatiev well knew the sorts of statements the British were capable of making, refusing to dwell upon his time as military attaché at the Russian embassy in London and the near disaster that had occurred there.

Well then, it was time not only for the festivities to begin, but also for Ignatiev's plans to commence. For too long, there had been an imbalance of power in a particular situation, and Ignatiev would see that the scales were brought back to level. If the khedive proved to be too intractable, well, Russia was a mighty nation and had other, less courteous means of getting her way.

Ignatiev shrugged to himself. Diplomacy or brute force—it mattered little to him which method he had to use to bring Russia back to her rightful station. She deserved it, and the general would see that it happened.

chapter 12

Aboard the Austrian ship SMS Viribus Unitis

FRANZ-JOSEF, EMPEROR OF AUSTRIA AND king of Hungary, stood—darkly handsome, slim, and erect—with almost military precision as he waited for his chamberlain, Karl Dorn, to arrive to take his instructions regarding the disembarking ceremony at Ismailia in the afternoon. Many referred to the emperor as the "red-trousered lieutenant" for his deep fondness for the military, and although he was aware of this moniker, he also knew no one would dare speak it in his presence, lest the *Vollkoffer* be cast permanently from attending court.

Franz-Josef was most comfortable in this rigid, upright position. His mind operated best when he stood with hands clasped behind his back. Sometimes he might add in a clipped, precise pacing back and forth, but only when he was seriously agitated. This was infrequent. Not even the death of his infant daughter Sophie had caused him to pace.

His mind navigated now through a flood of thoughts. Franz-Josef had discovered in his thirty-nine years that too many thoughts at one time made one befuddled, so he always tried to narrow the turmoil down to the two most important topics at hand. In the last twenty minutes on his feet, he compressed it all down to two people: Ferdinand de Lesseps and Eugénie de Montijo.

Both French. Neither one fathomable.

He sighed in relief at having determined what he needed to be focused on today, as today would start all of the official diplomatic functions and he would have to be fully attentive for them. Ceremony and ritual marked the essence of the House of Habsburg, and Franz-Josef had never yet let his country down in this regard. This devotion to propriety was what made de Lesseps and Eugénie so damnably frustrating.

Franz-Josef allowed his gaze to wander around his stateroom inside the steam-powered corvette. *Viribus Unitis* was the most diminutive of his warships, with only one gun deck—with most of the cannons removed for this trip. She was just the right vessel to ply the relatively narrow waters of both the Nile and the Suez Canal, and also to demonstrate Austro-Hungarian might to all who had gathered here in Egypt. The ship might have a screw-driven propeller beneath her ironclad frame, but she also maintained the glory of a full sail plan, and the massive sheets made a glorious noise while they were under way, befitting the precious cargo she carried in the form of an emperor and king. The interior was a miniature re-creation of several of the staterooms at Hofburg Palace. Small, but just as well adorned with crystal chandeliers, painted ceilings, and intricate wall moldings.

The ship had been named for Franz-Josef's personal motto, "With United Forces." He laughed mirthlessly to himself. The motto once had been resplendently appropriate, but since Prussia's ascendancy two years ago, it was now almost a mocking epithet. Despite the splendor of the floating imperial court that was this ship, very few diplomats in the multinational flotilla seemed impressed.

He allowed his mind to temporarily veer off to what he had determined was *not* a primary focus for today, that of the *blöd idiotisch* Prussians. How had his generals permitted such a defeat, and in only seven weeks? He shook his head. It should have proved a simple effort to solve the complex problem of German reunification.

For centuries, the German world had been largely overshadowed by two powers, Catholic Austria and Protestant Prussia, while the rest of Germany was split into a variety of smaller duchies and states, including the sizable kingdoms of Hanover, Saxony, and Bavaria.

Austria and Prussia had fought together against France in the Napoleonic Wars. After their conclusion, the German states had been reorganized into thirty-seven more unified states, known as the German Confederation. Austria, however, was the truly dominant power across the confederation, as she should have been.

But Prussia was jealous. The execrable Otto von Bismarck believed that Prussia should be dominant, and hadn't the Protestants been attempting to assert themselves in such a manner since Martin Luther?

So Bismarck had deliberately challenged Franz-Josef for control of the confederation, just as Luther had challenged Mother Church for control of the hearts and minds of Christendom. The first scuffle had occurred in 1864, when Austria and Prussia both invaded the Schleswig duchy, a much-disputed territory. The two countries reached a truce, which was of course quickly broken by the Prussians. The French, British, and Russians all got involved along the way, but it was Eugénie's husband, Napoléon III, who was most important to the cause. In response to Bismarck's pleading, Napoléon III had convinced the Italians to side with the Prussians, with the Prussians agreeing to give Venetia to Italy if they won.

In turn, Franz-Josef tried to win Napoléon III over by offering to surrender Venetia to him if he would simply remain neutral in the conflict. He was unsuccessful, and so he was forced to lead a war. Franz-Josef still seethed when he considered the poor performance of the German states allied with him. Except for the Saxons. Wild men, they were. Austria should have handily won this conflict, but it was not so.

And what was the result for the House of Habsburg for all of her trouble? A humiliating peace treaty, with Austria agreeing to all of Prussia's terms. Austria excluded from all German affairs. The formation of a new Prussian-led North German Confederation. Venetia given over to the Italians. States south of the River Main permitted to remain independent. Franz-Josef had attempted to negotiate terms that would leave Saxony independent, as payment for her good service to the House of Habsburg, but he wasn't able to achieve even that tiny victory. Just thinking about it made him want to pace back and forth until he excavated down into the ship's hold.

Then Napoléon III once more stuck his colossal *Schnauze* into the entire affair, attempting to extract even more territorial concessions. Thank *Gott* he wasn't able to add any further shame in the end, but his interference in what was already a brutal debacle for Austria still stung.

Franz-Josef shook his head, clearing the memory of treachery and betrayal. He must remember to focus on what was important today. What was it? Oh, yes, de Lesseps and Eugénie. How could two people aboard the same ship drive the emperor to such wildly divergent emotions, when he prided himself on complete self-control?

Franz-Josef had been hesitant when a French messenger had come to court bearing a gilded invitation to the Suez Canal opening ceremonies. But the Frenchman had followed the etiquette of the Viennese court flawlessly, giving the emperor no room for complaint and thus making Franz-Josef feel compelled to attend. He had briefly considered sending someone else in his stead, but if de Lesseps had gone to this much trouble to entice Franz-Josef to come, perhaps it might be of benefit to Austria.

Even if there would be Prussian representatives there.

Besides, Elisabeth had been overly irritable and testy as of late. In the fifteen years that they had been married, Franz-Josef had loved his wife with a passion that bordered on infatuation. His mother had chastised him that he was a *Dummkopf* at times, unable to have two things in his brain at once without one falling out, and that his fixation on his wife prevented him from attending to matters of state.

Mutter had never liked Elisabeth, though, not since Franz-Josef had stood up to her for once in his entire life. He had insisted that he would not marry Elisabeth's sister, as had been planned in excruciating detail for him, but that he would have Elisabeth or no one. She had been an ethereal, graceful sixteen-year-old when he met her—seven years his junior—with long, blonde hair that would later darken, and skin so flawless it was if he had been introduced to a Mengs painting of an angel. Or of the Virgin herself.

As if the angel had an agreement with the devil, though, Elisabeth—or Sisi, as she had become known—had not aged at all in the sixteen years of their marriage. She had doubled in years, but was just as slender, just as exquisite, as she had been the day he was first introduced to her and had opened his chest, pulled out his own heart, and given it to her for safekeeping.

His affection had rarely been returned, although they had managed to produce four children, including the ill-fated Sophie. At first, Franz-Josef was convinced that Sisi was shy and would learn to love him, as he was, after all, the emperor.

But the more time that went on, the more distant Sisi became, as if she were emotionally floating off on wings. She became more and more obsessed with maintaining that delicate beauty that made others gasp in awe, as if they were perpetually witnessing a perfect golden butterfly testing out her wings after breaking out of the confines of a cocoon. Franz-Josef counted himself among the numerous spectators.

Without turning his head, he glanced at the portrait of Sisi that hung on the wall of his cabin. Normally kept across from his desk in his private study, away from any prying eyes, the painting was his favorite, and he had insisted that it be wrapped up carefully and brought along on this trip. It was an intimate portrait of his wife displaying her long, curled hair in two sections, crossed almost provocatively across her chest, with one arm atop the other beneath her breasts and the tresses, creating a mystery for the gazer as to whether it was her hair or her breasts her arms supported. Franz-Josef was consumed with desire every time he laid eyes on the image, even though he knew the desire would have to be slaked elsewhere. Sisi wore a flowing white gown in the portrait, once more reinforcing the idea of virginal beauty.

Maintaining that beauty, though, apparently required that most of her time be spent with her ladies behind locked doors, experimenting with all manner of potions and preparations he could not begin to understand. And why should he? He was the emperor.

Franz-Josef had been willing to endure anything for his beloved Sisi, even when she became interested in traveling without him. Eventually, though, she suggested that perhaps he would be *happier* if he found some appropriate *companionship* during the times she was away.

So besotted was he with his wife that he obeyed the suggestion, not because of his grand desire for a mistress but to please her. And it worked. He and Sisi had worked out a kind of friendship with each other, and they had even managed to produce their fourth child last year, little Marie Valerie. Mother had once again proclaimed him ignorant of the situation, stating that Sisi had only come to his bed as a reward for his having done her bidding in the compromise with Hungary. It had concluded in 1867, and gave that country more autonomy than it had had in the past, an idea that Sisi had fervently supported.

Franz-Josef ignored his mother, concluding that Sisi had simply had a soft, weak moment for her husband, although it occasionally gave him pause that Sisi referred to Marie Valerie as her "Hungarian child." Rumors had wafted over to him that she was only speaking Hungarian with their youngest daughter, intending it to be the child's native tongue.

The Hungarians, though, were not the important issue at hand. The French were. Especially Eugénie, who was the first woman who had stirred genuine desire in him since he met Sisi all those years ago. The women were similar in that they both had beautiful, arresting features, but whereas Sisi maintained an aura of innocence, Eugénie flirted with him outrageously. Sisi fanatically protected her image, whereas Eugénie wore her elegant looks carelessly, as if she were supremely confident that they would never dare abandon her. How in the vault of heaven had a woman like that been pledged to Napoléon III, he a *Wurm* if ever there was one?

Perhaps it was enrobing himself in the exotic headiness of Egypt that was causing him to forget himself with Eugénie. Or maybe it was simply that he hadn't seen Sisi in so long, as consumed as she was in Hungary with their new daughter.

The thought crept into his mind that he might be falling in love with the bewitching Eugénie, but he swept that thought away immediately. The emperor of Austria did not succumb to schoolboy crushes. Besides, France presented a different problem than just his secret attachment to the empress.

It was de Lesseps who frustrated him, in an opposite manner to how Eugénie did. Ever since arriving in Egypt, Franz-Josef had attempted to have de Lesseps pay court to him aboard *Viribus Unitis*, to demonstrate Austria's stature to the rest of the delegation, despite Prussia's winning chess move on the European board. Prussia might have temporarily eclipsed Franz-Josef's country, but the emperor would regain the resplendent glory the House of Habsburg once enjoyed and was famous for . . . even if he must do it single-handedly. It was his duty to maintain his family's honor. Fortunately, there were others to help him with the recalcitrant de Lesseps. The Frenchman had responded to Franz-Josef's letters throughout the Nile voyage with vague and unsatisfying answers. Not once had de Lesseps boarded *Viribus Unitis* to pay homage to the floating Viennese court.

Speaking of which, there was a telltale scratching at the door to his spacious cabin. "*Eintreten*," Franz-Josef barked as he checked his own fixed positioning, ensuring both of his black-booted feet were pointing directly forward and that his back was ramrod straight.

As expected, it was Karl Dorn, his chamberlain, who gently opened just one side of the two doors. Both doors could be opened at once if, and only if, a guest of appropriate stature were entering. A chamberlain was accorded no such respect. "Your

Highness," Dorn said, bowing and scraping in appropriate court ritual and finally rising, his eyes modestly downcast. "I have just spoken with the captain, and we will be in Ismailia in approximately an hour."

"Approximately?" Franz-Josef demanded. "Or exactly?" Punctuality was important. Without punctuality, there was no order. Without order, there could be no protocol. Without protocol, there could be no court ceremony. Without court ceremony, the grandeur of the House of Habsburg would be tarnished, and a tarnished house was sure to fall. Therefore, punctuality meant the very survival of his family.

Dorn bowed again. "I believe that I can initiate our disembarking ceremony now, which will have Your Highness ready to step off at the precise moment that all of the other flotilla ships have finished disgorging their less illustrious passengers, thus enabling Your Highness to make an entrance with all eyes upon you."

The emperor noted that Dorn hadn't quite answered the question, but if the chamberlain could ensure Franz-Josef made an impression, it was forgivable. "Prince Frederick will have already disembarked?" he asked.

"I am sure of it, Your Highness." Dorn bowed again. "The Prussian ship is ahead of ours and will be berthed much sooner."

Franz-Josef almost permitted himself an unplanned smile. Frederick had been opposed to the war between Prussia and Austria, and argued bitterly against it with Bismarck. Because of Frederick's dissent, Franz-Josef should have been willing to extend the man some grace, but Frederick still had that cursed Prussian blood coursing through his veins. Prussian insults ran as deep as the Danube, no matter the conciliatory attitude that the prince had taken in the recent past.

"My cloak has been pressed?" he inquired. It was his favorite cloak, of black wool with a thin edge of stoat fur and a scarlet underside, kept firmly attached to him by the military-type braids crisscrossing his chest. When draped over his matching red jacket with its gold medals, the emperor made an imposing and formidable presence.

"Of course, Your Highness. It shall be brought to you at once."

Franz-Josef nodded, satisfied that he would be intimidating to all concerned . . . except to the lovely Eugénie. It was his hope that she would see him as dashing . . . romantic . . . even godlike. He imagined her eyes shining with tears at the sight of him, proud and tall and erect as he descended the gangplank, surrounded by impeccably liveried servants. So confident would he be in his footing, she would see that he had no need to watch his step as other mere mortals did. Franz-Josef's contemplation of what might happen was causing that uncomfortable, primal stirring again.

There were many ways in which Eugénie could be useful, but for today, he was a man and she was a woman, and together they would be resplendent. Political vengeance was best accomplished under the cover of night when no one could witness it. Which reminded the emperor of something important.

"I *vish* to have this letter delivered." Franz-Josef relaxed enough to withdraw a sealed missive from the inside of his jacket and extend it toward the chamberlain, who offered both hands, palms up, for Franz-Josef to drop it onto as though Dorn's hands formed a salver.

Dorn glanced at the name of the addressee. "I shall have this rowed over immediately, Your Highness." He bowed, beginning his departure, but Franz-Josef interrupted him.

"*Nein*. I do not *vish* for anyone other than you to know about this letter, which is a private matter. You will deliver it personally."

The color drained from Dorn's face and he visibly winced. "But I must— There are the disembarking ceremonies and I—" But Franz-Josef stopped the protests with a glare. "Of course, Your Highness, I will do this right away."

Dorn bowed his way back out the door, taking the proper amount of time to push the door closed—not so quickly that he would give the impression of leaving in a huff and not so slowly that he could be accused of eavesdropping—and ensuring it latched with a nearly inaudible click. Franz-Josef was alone once more until the formalities of his arrival into Ismailia could be conducted. He fully expected Dorn to fulfill his new task and return in time to ensure everything went off without a single disruption.

The earlier casual Nile River cruise was over, they had survived the little turmoil at Port Said, and now the formal affairs would begin. Franz-Josef was a master of formal ritual, and this was his moment to show the British, the Russians, the Egyptians, the French, and especially the Prussians that Austria was not finished yet.

If someone else would have to be finished in order to prove it, so be it.

chapter 13

Aboard the Egyptian ship El Mahrousa

ISMA'IL PASHA HAD HAD QUITE enough for one day. As hard as he was trying to impress the European nations, it seemed that none of them would comply with respect. Pasha was on very delicate ground already with the sultan, what with his own efforts to modernize Egypt and the sultan's desire to keep foreign influences out of the Ottoman Empire and thus maintain his own stature with little regard for Pasha's.

And now his servants were giving him trouble.

"I have told you a hundred—no, a thousand—times, no! It is *my* right, not Mariette's! I am no longer just the governor, I am the *khedive*! He is a mere director of a museum, and French at that, so how can he claim to appreciate Egyptian antiquities more than I!?" he shouted to his cultural attaché as the two men sat on brightly colored cushions, unwrapping artifacts from the chests that sat before them, once tightly bound and now nearly destroyed by ham-handed servants rushing to do Pasha's bidding.

It was taking days for Pasha to finish his inspection of the crates. He had been working under the cover of night aboard *El Mahrousa*, but now he was hastily finishing the task so that his portion could be installed in his palace when they arrived in Ismailia.

Pasha both admired and loathed Hassan, his cultural attaché, who had been trained in Europe and spoke several languages fluently. Hassan also understood antiquities, a very valuable asset in Pasha's mind. But the man was frustratingly prim and moral. It was difficult to drag Egypt into the modern world when the very man who should support Europeanizing the country was behaving like a rebellious child.

Not that Hassan was actually rebellious about Egypt's modernization, but he certainly seemed to be taking the side of the French where this cache of goods was concerned.

"Your Highness, is it wise to make an enemy of the director of antiquities?"

Without hesitation, Pasha instinctively reached out and slapped the man across the face for his insolence. "How dare you question my actions? Mariette is paid out of my treasury and is my creature—he does not think to become my enemy."

Pasha was rewarded with a studiously blank look from Hassan as the attaché disrobed an Eye of Horus amulet from its layers of sheeting, but Pasha heard the sigh behind the man's next words. "Yes, Your Highness, I understand that it elevates your stature to keep precious relics in your possession, much as European kings do, and may your magnificence awe them and humble them. However, does it not add to your glory that you generously allow this entire shipment to go to Cairo for inclusion in a permanent memorial to Egypt's greatness?"

Pasha frowned. Was that true? Would it add to his family's glory? He had already accomplished a great deal. After inheriting the governorship of Egypt from his uncle in 1863, he had burned with an ambition like the sun across the Western Desert—except that the ambition had not been to adorn himself with wives, homes, or servants, although he certainly had plenty of each. No, he wanted to be known as the man who elevated Egypt to her former glory as in the ancient days.

Naturally, all Egyptians wanted that glory, but only Pasha realized that it could be accomplished solely through large-scale cultural and industrial reforms that would put his country in line with the European powers that dominated the world. To this end, he had reformed the postal system, created a sugar industry, built theaters, and even launched a vast railroad-building project.

In addition, fully one-fourth of Cairo had been remodeled to resemble that most cosmopolitan of cities, Paris. The Parisian section of Cairo and the railroad extravaganza were developed in no small part because of Pasha's desire to please and impress Ferdinand de Lesseps.

The canal project had been de Lesseps's brilliant creation. But it had been Pasha's now deceased uncle Sa'id who had granted a concession to de Lesseps's Suez Canal Company, permitting it to construct and operate the canal for ninety-nine years. Excavation had started a decade ago, and when Pasha became *wāli*, or governor, of Egypt, in 1863, he had immediately recognized the importance of moving the canal project forward.

Pasha and de Lesseps had been of one mind on the project for a long time. The opening of the canal connected the Mediterranean and the Red Sea, eliminating thousands of miles of travel around Africa for ships carrying goods to and from the East. And those ships would have to pay tribute to Isma'il Pasha—soon to be called Isma'il the Magnificent if he had anything to do with it—in order to travel through the canal.

Not that everything had gone smoothly. Pasha and his uncle had been so enamored of de Lesseps's talents and plans that they had readily agreed to provisions that put Egypt at a disadvantage, although admittedly the worst of them hadn't really been de Lesseps's fault. The canal developer had been short on funds for labor, and so Egypt had generously agreed to provide the necessary men, all of whom would work under de Lesseps's total authority. It was of little cost to Pasha since Egypt had always made use of corvée labor for its national building projects. That was where all the trouble had started.

Pasha signaled to Hassan that he didn't want the mirror case that had just been unpacked. Too crude. Hassan nodded and began rewrapping the object so that it once again resembled a mummy. "Crude" well described what had temporarily happened to relations between Egypt and France. The use of corvée labor, whereby men were conscripted for a specific period of time with no wages as a service to their nation, was perfectly legitimate. Many nations did it. Even the French had used this sort of labor, abolishing it in their revolution but reviving it later and calling it *prestation*, a requirement of three days of a man's labor before he was permitted to vote.

And so things had progressed well for several years until those *ghabi* British had become so imperious. They had been utterly opposed to the canal project, viewing themselves as masters of the sea, and had made constant diplomatic moves against the project, especially since it was led by the French. Even worse, the British had abolished slavery decades ago, and had no understanding whatsoever of the corvée system. Full of pride and stupidity, they condemned the use of what they considered to be "slave labor," and then armed the Bedouin, sending them in to make trouble by initiating a revolt by the workers.

The project could not endure the revolt, so de Lesseps had been forced to abandon corvée labor. Of course, the British had had no such outrage when workers had died in similar forced labor conditions during the building of the British railway in Egypt, had they?

In his anger at remembering Great Britain's interference, he pounded his fist against the crate from which he was pulling items. A board cracked loudly, causing Hassan to snap his head up. "Your Highness, are you injured? Is all well?"

Pasha flicked his hand at him, irritated with his cultural attaché even though he knew he probably shouldn't be. The problems had erupted after Great Britain—which neither contributed a dime to the project nor was in any way responsible for it—took away a source of labor that had only cost food, transportation, and minimal shelter.

Now the labor would be an enormous cost. He had gone calmly to de Lesseps to discuss how they would resolve the matter. To his shock, the great man had no compromise in mind.

"This is your problem, Pasha, not mine. You promised me

labor, and labor is what you shall provide," de Lesseps had declared, barely looking at him.

Pasha had hardly believed his ears. Did de Lesseps not understand how much he had already raised, borrowed, and stolen to help fund the project? "Monsieur de Lesseps, surely you must realize that it is inconceivable that I would pay for labor for the remainder of the project? It will bankrupt my country."

But de Lesseps, the man who had eagerly shared dishes of *kushari*, kebabs, and sheep's brains with him, had merely shrugged in that irritatingly French manner, which suggested condescension over a trivial matter. "You have agreed to it. It is not my fault that the British were able to squeeze you like a dead pigeon. You must own up to your problem yourself, and not expect France to rescue you."

Spots of red had clouded Pasha's field of vision. In one clever sentence, de Lesseps had called him weak, a dupe of the British, and of little consequence to the French. "You are suggesting that I should now come up with the funds to pay for the million and a half??? Egyptian workers on the project, not to mention the number of Italians, Greeks, and Syrians that *you* have imported? I have built a vast railroad system so that bringing that labor to you is simple and of little cost. I have permitted you to dig wherever you choose, with no regard for what artifacts might lie beneath. I have allowed you to bask in undue glory for the sacrifices I have made. You return my generosity by refusing to help? By refusing to stand up to the British? Who is the rescuer and who is the helpless woman?"

His angry barb must have found some tiny target, for the Frenchman had altered his tone. "*Sahbi*, my beloved friend, you take this too personally," de Lesseps had replied, grabbing Pasha's shoulders and kissing both cheeks. "Remember that what we are doing represents the most important advancement ever known in the world. It is more important than Egypt's pyramids and more important than France's revolution, and certainly more meaningful than Britain's domination of the seas. You must remember that when the canal is finished, we will crush Britain's power at the same time that we elevate your renown and fame. What does 'pharaoh' mean when compared to the name Isma'il the Magnificent?"

The thought had calmed Pasha at the time. De Lesseps was dangling a glittering prize in front of Egypt's khedive, and the Frenchman knew it. Pasha had sighed, unwilling to continue this argument—the only one he and de Lesseps had ever had—any further. Of course, Pasha then had to fetch workers from whatever country he could, not only housing them in camps and feeding them but paying them wages, as well. It had nearly snapped the treasury in half to scrape together the monies to finish the project, but he had done it. He, Isma'il Pasha. No other.

At least de Lesseps had so far been proved correct that Pasha's standing would be elevated through the building of the canal. Despite everything Great Britain had done to thwart him, the queen's government had invited him on an honorary visit two years ago. Surely that was proof that Great Britain recognized him as a formidable ruler in the world, even if he had only gotten as far as meeting the Earl of Derby, the country's prime minister, and never actually entered the queen's palace to meet her. Something about her being occupied with laying a foundation stone to a monument dedicated to her dead husband.

At the same time, he had persuaded Sultan Abdülaziz to recognize him as khedive—viceroy—of Egypt. Pasha had had to agree to an increase in tribute to the sultan in exchange, but it was a small price to pay. It was especially small given how much the canal had cost him.

"Your Highness?" Hassan said again, a frown furrowing his face. Pasha realized that he had been laughing aloud at his own thoughts.

"I wish to keep these three mummy masks," he said, pointing into the crate. "Ensure they are placed in Tewfik's chambers at my villa. He will appreciate them." Pasha's seventeen-year-old son was fond of his father's growing collection of *cartonnage* masks. Many of these masks, made of layers of linen or papyrus, were covered with plaster, then painted and gilded in very realistic depictions of whatever mummified face they covered, and these three were no exception.

It was at least one thing he could admire in his eldest son and heir, given that the boy had not been Pasha's first choice to take over Egypt. Pasha had successfully changed the order of succession of the khedivate of Egypt so that the title no longer passed to the eldest living male descendant of Muhammad Ali, but would now descend from father to son. Pasha's successful maneuvering had not lasted.

European powers in the form of Britain, Austria, Prussia, and even the sultan had interpreted this to mean the khedivate would pass to the eldest son, when Pasha had had another son in mind entirely, but now they all recognized only Tewfik as heir. Once again, Pasha had been outwitted and outflanked. Unfortunately, because Tewfik had never been intended to rule, he had not been sent to Europe for education like his younger brothers, but had grown up in Egypt. Tewfik did not have Hassan's sophistication, nor de Lesseps's diplomatic skills. Truthfully, the boy concerned Pasha. He was too quiet, too sullen, too inexperienced in practical matters. He was like a piece of milky quartz, too dense and cloudy for much use as a brilliant gem. But what could be done? He was stuck with Tewfik and must carve and polish him as best he could so that one day he would prove to be at least an acceptable ruler, even if he couldn't be a dazzling one.

Hassan had solemnly rewrapped the masks and laid them aside for Pasha's collection. Now he withdrew another object from the crate he was working in and presented it to Pasha for inspection. It was a Senet game box, with an elongated board on top printed in hieroglyphics and a drawer running beneath that contained the game's playing pieces. The box had not been wrapped like the other items in the crate for some reason. Pasha signaled for Hassan to turn the box to one side. Bah, the hieroglyphic markings were obscured, almost as if someone had attempted to scrape them off, especially when the airless tomb environment should have kept the item pristine in its resting place for whomever it was intended to entertain in the beyond. Mariette was a fool if he thought whatever dig site he had unearthed had revealed virgin treasure, for this box had obviously been gone over by some tomb raider long ago. The French weren't always as shrewd as they thought they were.

Pasha shook his head, and Hassan took the offending artifact away from the khedive.

Eventually, though, there was a tidy pile of exquisitely carved, painted, and decorated items for his villa, including a finely wrought gold mirror case in the shape of an ankh. Pasha thought that piece might be the best find of the lot. "Have Rashad take these ahead tonight to my palace," he instructed his cultural attaché. Rashad was Pasha's porter, as well as Hassan's brother. To the extent that Hassan was cultured, Rashad was a clod, but a strong and obedient clod who never cast subtle looks of disapproval toward his master. "The rest can be returned to Mariette."

That pained look passed over Hassan's face for a mere moment. Then his voice was as bland as his schooled countenance. "You wish for Rashad to remove them from the ship while all of the delegation is there, Your Highness? Are you sure?"

"Do not question my orders," Pasha growled, unwilling to admit that it probably was risky for anyone to witness the unloaded crates, especially someone who might report back to Mariette. If Mariette had de Lesseps's ear, he would pour in poison about Pasha's activities and de Lesseps would probably be angered yet again. However, it was the khedive of Egypt's right to rule his nation as he saw fit, was it not?

As Hassan bowed with elegant submission and left the cabin, Pasha rang a bell for a servant to come and wipe his hands of the dust and grime collected from the artifacts.

Pasha's main intent might be to modernize Egypt, but a little personal grandeur from the glorious past was not such a bad thing. His crowning glory, though, was directly beneath his feet, in the form of both his magnificent sailing yacht and the canal. Just hours ago the yacht had woven its way effortlessly into these new waters, and the marriage of ship to water represented an immortal coupling of Pasha with Egypt's greatness.

Let the Mariettes of the world complain. Pasha would brook no interference in insignificant matters like a simple objet d'art for his residence. He was answerable to no one except the sultan. Besides, the artifacts belonged to Egypt, and Isma'il Pasha was Egypt; therefore he had an absolute right to them. He was the master of Egypt, and no one in Egypt would dare cross him during the next several days of celebrations.

He would see to it.

cḥapṭep 14

Aboard the British warship HMS Newport

AFTER A FINAL BITE OF nutmeg-rich potted shrimp in the captain's dining room, Violet Harper patted her mouth with a linen napkin. It was much finer than any she had ever expected to use aboard a military ship like *Newport*. Commander Nares had described *Newport* as a *Philomel*-class wooden-hulled screw-driven gun vessel, which meant absolutely nothing to Violet but had fascinated her husband, Sam. All Violet knew was that the ship had both a steam stack and three sets of sails, that her cannon had been removed from the middle section . . . and that she was wily enough to pull into first place in the flotilla line.

The ship's captain had told her and Sam that removing the cannon not only provided space for makeshift cabins to be constructed for the British delegation, but also symbolized the British intent for peace on this trip, especially with the French. Nares laughed at his own little joke.

To Violet's great surprise, though, the British delegation was surprisingly . . . light. Besides the captain and crew, it was simply herself, Sam, the Prince of Wales, Sir Henry Elliot, and Asa Brooks. Two other small gunboats accompanied them, but their cannons, too, had either been left behind or moved into less conspicuous spaces.

They all ate luncheon together to fortify themselves prior to docking in Ismailia. All except the prince, who had chosen to eat privately in his cabin and stay there until their arrival.

Violet learned much about her new fellow passengers as they sat around the table, full and content.

Elliot was the ambassador at Constantinople, and as such had spent considerable time in the Ottoman Empire. He had held diplomatic postings in St. Petersburg, the Hague, Copenhagen, and Naples before his appointment to Constantinople, making him one of those interesting creatures whose stories entrance others as the sight of fish in a parlor aquarium hypnotizes visitors to a home. Time flew by when he embarked on lengthy, spun-out stories of participating in a Russian sweat bath, of mistakenly eating veal brain fritters and rabbit intestines in Italy, and of nearly coming to blows with a man who attempted a three-kisses-on-the-cheek greeting on an unsuspecting Elliot.

Asa Brooks was more enigmatic, in Violet's mind. Elliot seemed confused about him, as well, sometimes referring to the younger man as his man of affairs and sometimes as his secretary. Brooks was his employer's opposite in nearly every way: a handsome and unlined face, broad shoulders, and a propensity toward reserve bordering on isolation. Elliot's stories elicited no more from Brooks than polite smiles and barely concealed yawns.

"What is our docking time?" Sam asked Commander Nares, who had just pushed away from his place and signaled for sherry to be poured for everyone.

As the sweet amber liquid was splashed into glasses by nattily dressed footmen whom Violet had seen testing the ship's tackle in bare feet just a short while ago, the captain unhooked his pocket watch and gave it a glance. "About another two hours, I'd say."

With full bellies, the conversation turned to the mundane topics common among strangers—weather, roundly unpopular political news, and the greatness of the British Empire. As that dwindled, Ambassador Elliot finally pushed away from the table, suggesting that he might take a walk around the upper deck for some fresh air and inviting Violet and Sam to join him.

They climbed the steep main stairway up to the deck, and

Violet was never quite sure whether it was more important to clutch her skirts to keep from getting tangled up in them or to clutch the rope handrail to keep from losing balance. She popped into the open, feeling like a badger emerging from its burrow, blinking against the bright sunlight. She touched the hair exposed beneath her hat. Why, she was even developing the silvery stripes against black that denoted a badger's head.

Enough of that exaggeration, she told herself sternly. *Thirty-six years of age is an eternity away from being a Chelsea pensioner.* She tucked her hand in Elliot's proffered elbow, and Sam followed behind them on their stroll around the deck. Had it just been last night that she had done this with Commander Nares? The deck was swarming with sailors like a colony of ants on a hill, each man with his own task, communicating with the others by signals and sounds not decipherable by the average passerby.

The frenetic activity never stopped on a ship. Sweeping, swabbing, painting, cargo-securing, and rig-checking work seemed to have a constancy to it, as if the ship herself were the queen ant, to be served with reverent, self-sacrificing devotion by all of the other members of the colony. Sam eventually stopped to ask questions of a seaman tarring ropes. The sailor looked very much like one of the men who had been serving them at table just a short while ago, except now he wore the customary naval uniform of baggy blue trousers and shirt, that color cheap to produce since Britain's acquisition of India gave it access to indigo plants.

Violet continued her promenade with the ambassador, gazing out at the Egyptian landscape as they neared Ismailia. Despite the hum of naval activity, Violet began to relax—even becoming sleepy as the effect of the food and the sherry combined with the smooth movement of the ship and the unexpectedly balmy weather of Egypt to lull her into a nearly insensible state.

Violet had anticipated the Egyptian climate would be brutally hot and oppressive. But in November, at least, it was quite pleasant. Beyond the edges of the canal was a mesmerizing landscape of sandy dunes, which were probably inhospitable and fit only for camels and scorpions, accented with a backdrop of lush green hills. Tall minarets were faintly visible in the distance, resembling lighthouses planted in the earth to beckon people to them.

From her vantage point, caressed by luscious breezes, it all seemed romantic and exotic, and it was easy to push aside the horror from last night. She must have sighed aloud, for Elliot paused. "Is anything wrong, Mrs. Harper?"

"What?" She shook her head to clear it. "No, no, I'm quite all right. Just enjoying . . . this." She spread her free hand out, indicating the scenery.

"Yes, this country has a way of slowly folding you into itself like quicksand, except you voluntarily step into it and allow it to cover you. What impresses me the most is the Egyptian sunset. You believe yourself to be transported back to a time of pyramids, mummies, and hieroglyphics. I have been in this region for two years, and it never ceases to take my breath."

The ambassador shook his head as if also coming out of reverie. He glanced behind them, causing Violet to do the same, and she saw that Sam was once again joining them. Elliot quickly bent his head and whispered to her in low tones, "Careful, Mrs. Harper, that you don't permit Egypt to become your quicksand."

Karl Dorn grunted in pain as the rowboat was dropped the last few feet into the water. He clutched his side, pressing in against the pain that had been plaguing him for so long. It was remarkable how very concrete liquid became when hit directly. Water splashed onto the floor of the rowboat, soaking his polished boots. Emperor Franz-Josef would be furious if he noticed Dorn appearing anything but fastidious, but there was no help for it now.

The boatman quietly dipped oars into the water to maneuver them away from *Viribus Unitis* and on to their destination. Fortunately, His Highness had yet to notice Dorn's discomfort, which had been an ever-present enemy since the day he fought in the Battle of Königgrätz in the unfortunately but accurately named Seven Weeks' War. Dorn had enthusiastically joined to fight on behalf of the emperor. There was such pride in it, to know that he was willing to lay down his life for the House of Habsburg, that glorious ruling house to whom all Austrians owed allegiance. So in June 1866, Dorn had kissed his mother and sister good-bye, bowed to his father and older brother, both of whom ran the family *Apotheker* shop. He was heading off, a young man of twenty-five, to do his duty with joy and resolve.

He had been a handsome young man, with light hair, a closely cropped beard, and a smile that went straight to his eyes that he knew had a certain effect on young women his age. He planned to cause more of the *Mädchen* to swoon upon his return, with tales of remarkable bravery and valor.

The only thing remarkable was how quickly he dropped weight from his tall, sturdy frame, and how he had found his first gray hair while shaving in the dim reflection of his metal dining plate. The first time a sniper shot at him, he realized that the leaner he was, the more quickly he could run, and gray hair was completely unnoticeable beneath mud and dust and blood, so Dorn welcomed his new lankiness and premature signs of aging.

Within two weeks he was already battle-weary. The worst was yet to come when he was sent with his cohort to Bohemia, where General Moltke had rapidly mobilized the Prussian army, led by Wilhelm I, and the two sides met at Königgrätz in July. The Austrian officers had boasted to all of the troops about their numerical superiority, claiming with confidence that this would end the war and Prussia's overreach.

It was certainly the end, but for Austria. Dorn's country—even with troops from all over the confederation, including the ferocious Saxons—was no match for Prussia, whose soldiers were equipped with Dreyse's breech-loading needle guns. Austria's muzzle-loaders couldn't compete with them, and her battle deaths were seven times that of Prussia. It might have been even more deaths, but Dorn had been able to save a group of nearly a dozen injured men by fending off Prussian troops while *der Sanitäter* carried them off the battlefield.

The flotilla ships, once in a single-file line, were now clustered together as they sought out docking berths. As he was rowed past the ship flying the British colors, he noticed a dark-haired woman on deck, her silhouette framed in lantern light as she gazed down at his tiny boat slicing through the water.

As if embarrassed to be caught staring at him, the woman lifted her hand in greeting, and despite all of the formality drilled into him, he waved a hand in return, silently frowning at his own casual behavior. The emperor would not like to know that he was being familiar with foreigners, even if it was just a universal sign of salutation. He and the woman dropped their hands almost simultaneously as Dorn was rowed out of sight.

"Almost there, Herr Dorn," the boatman said as he lifted the oars out of the water to let the tiny craft slow on its own as they approached the larger ship. Dorn nodded at the man.

He contemplated how easy it would be for the ship they were approaching to simply turn toward them and capsize them. Dorn didn't swim, and he would surely drown. Of course, the Austrian army was enormous and should have also been able to overturn the Prussians, but nothing about the brief war had happened the way it should have. Including the aftermath of Königgrätz.

He had been picked up by Prussian soldiers and taken to their officer, who became convinced that Dorn was a significant officer in the Austrian army disguising himself as a common foot soldier. Apparently Dorn resembled this unknown *Oberstleutnant*, and no amount of talking would convince the man that he was a mere junior *Rekrut*, and thus the officer decided to force battle-plan information from Dorn himself.

While Austria was quickly capitulating after Königgrätz, Dorn was imprisoned in an underground cell, enduring merciless beatings day and night. He hadn't even realized that Austria had already sued for peace terms and the Prussian was simply persisting in torturing him out of spite. Or perhaps vicious cruelty.

With peace finally settled, the officer was forced to let Dorn go. He limped his way back to his family, malnutrition and a nearly full head of gray hair the least of his problems. His mother and sister could have filled the Bodensee with their tears at the sight of him, but his father and brother went to work straightaway to fix him. Dorn had supreme confidence that they could do so, but months later, he seemed to have made little progress, and *mein Gott*, how his side hurt. The pain frequently knifed through him as if he were being attacked by a saber over and over again.

Eventually, his father had shaken his head over Dorn, claiming he could fathom no cure for whatever mysterious ailment or injury he had. Multiple doctors had looked at him, as well, and Dorn had become used to men peering over him with sympathetic looks and then huddling in the corner with his father to whisper condolences. None of the girls he had once flirted with came to visit him, and he had prepared himself for the wretched life of an invalid.

Until the messenger from Hofburg Palace arrived.

Just as quickly as his life had become one of misery, so did his fortune spin around on the head of a pin again. Suddenly with everything to live for, Dorn had dragged himself from his sickbed and taught himself to ignore pain, no matter how weak and exhausted it left him by the end of the day. He had gathered up every pill, root, powder, and draught that had been brought to his bedside and packed it in his luggage, for the emperor himself had invited Dorn to come to Hofburg Palace. He had been granted a minor court post as a reward for his bravery and endurance against the Prussians.

Dorn had had no idea how word had traveled to the court about him, but he had known a divine event when it happened. That good fortune had spread over him like a cloak, for he had soon been elevated to chamberlain. He had been one of many in this position, whose role was to coordinate all of the court's rituals, but he had served in it well. The rest of the court had despised Dorn as an upstart, and he had gained few friends there, but that was of little relevance to him. More important was the idea that as he had gathered stature. He would be able to secure a proper marriage with a woman who might not mind that he was wreckage, much like the flotsam he had watched float by helplessly during the trip along the Nile. This could only happen while Dorn continued to remain secure in His Highness's esteem, and there was nothing Dorn would not do to maintain that regard, no matter the cost. No matter the sacrifice.

When His Highness had declared his intentions to attend the Suez Canal opening ceremonies, Dorn had angled to be the chamberlain selected for the trip. He'd heard that Islamic doctors had special powers, and he was determined to visit one or more of them while in Egypt, in hopes that he could finally have his pain treated. Meanwhile, he was chewing and swallowing his way through any substance that promised relief.

Dorn patted his chest once more, where the emperor's sealed letter lay in a secret pocket sewn inside his jacket. Although this was simply a quick rowing across the port waters, he felt as if he were on a secret mission, a spy furtively carrying a coded message into the enemy camp. He knew what typically happened to spies, but this wasn't really a time of war, was it?

The rowboat bumped up against the larger ship, and Dorn unintentionally let out a muttered "Oof." His insides were jumbled around by even the slightest impact or disturbance these days.

"Apologies, Herr Dorn," the boatman offered, touching the edge of his cap.

Dorn nodded wordlessly at the man, his attention distracted by the commotion on the deck of the ship above them. Ropes with sharp metal hooks on the ends were lowered down to attach to rings along the edge of the rowboat. The boatman attached them all while Dorn sat motionless, a hand discreetly pressing against his right side.

As the boat was reeled up, water sluicing off her sides and splashing back down into the canal, Dorn realized he was willingly entering a veritable lion's den on his master's behalf. He must conduct himself with decorum and bravery, just as if this ship were the fields of Königgrätz. Except that this might prove to be even more dangerous.

chapter 15

Port Ismailia

ONCE MORE, VIOLET AND SAM disembarked *Newport*, this time to another glittering array of brightly colored tents and three enormous stages. These were surrounded by potted plants, trellises, and painted wood fencing, most likely to hide the mass of preparation materials behind them. Set back a small distance from this main activity area was a palace with its own lake that would rival any British ducal estate. Nearby was a sprawling villa of cream with a red-tiled roof and unusual red designs across the front of it. Other imposing buildings in the town suggested that Ismailia was less a port and more an official location for canal business. Every structure, though, appeared to be new, as if carefully constructed just for this very event.

Also dotting the landscape were triumphal arches, statues, and other ceremonial creations echoing that of Napoléon's Paris. Perhaps yet another nod to de Lesseps, or perhaps they were intended to associate the khedive with the great emperors of ancient Rome.

A long, wide scarlet carpet made a trail from the disembarkation point to the three stages, and, as expected, Violet and Sam were not guided that way, but were encouraged to mingle with the other minor delegation members. Louise-Hélène was conspicuously absent from the French entourage. Also absent was de Lesseps's bitterness about *Newport's* duplicity, which Violet had no doubt still raged privately inside him.

Also as expected, de Lesseps, Eugénie, Pasha, and the other heads of state clustered together to greet people. Admirers cheered them on and handed Eugénie white jasmine flowers, whose sweet fragrances permeated the air. The same flowers were woven into garlands adorning the stages, tents, and fencing, and were even festooning posts topped with various international flags.

There were also smaller stages set up with entertainments. On one, men dressed all in white, with white undershirts, short jackets, and long, tulip-shaped skirts over white trousers, twirled across the stage in tempo to hypnotic music involving guitars, bells, and drums. Male singers in the background performed an eerie combination of wailing and chanting.

The dancers looked like a sea of jasmine floating across the stage.

On another stage were fire eaters. Violet held her breath as men in emerald green costumes lowered slim, flaming torches toward their mouths in unison, parting their lips and magically seeming to swallow the fire before pulling the extinguished sticks from their mouths.

On yet another stage Sam's Civil War mates were now preparing for a demonstration. Sam pulled Violet along to where they were standing at the base of the platform. Thaddeus Mott was instructing his uniformed comrades on drills with their gleaming steel sabers and their bayoneted rifles as examples of American military might and discipline.

Sam's longing to be onstage was palpable.

The parade of dignitaries must have concluded, for Violet now saw the various sovereigns wandering about, nodding graciously at those who chattered pleasantries at them and clapping politely at entertainers who left stages, only to be replaced by even faster, louder, and more amazing spectacles.

There were also servants rushing to and fro, not only attending to the royal guests but continuously engaged with

the never-ending setup of the festivities, as well. Like busy
ants they frenetically carried chairs, musical instruments, bolts
of fabric, torchères, and stalks of greenery, dropping this item
here, picking up that item over there. It seemed as though they
would surely crash into one another, but Pasha's workers were
well disciplined.

Even the khedive's cultural attaché, Hassan, was involved,
calling out instructions Violet couldn't understand to the
plethora of workers around him, even as he himself was moving
what seemed to be a very heavy trunk with his brother, Rashad.

Violet noticed Louise-Hélène standing nearby, plucking a
delicacy off a silver salver being offered to her, then sharing
it with her maid. De Lesseps's fiancée appeared quite serene,
considering the mood he himself must be in and the fact that she
had been excluded from the earlier procession. She and Isabelle
chatted and pointed at the soldiers' activities onstage.

Sam squeezed her shoulder absentmindedly when Violet told
him that she intended to join the two women, so intent was he
on the firing demonstration.

"*Bonjour*, mademoiselle," Violet greeted Louise-Hélène as the
young Frenchwoman stood, hands outstretched, while Isabelle
rebuttoned one of her mistress's gloves. Although her gown today
was much more fashionable, the poor girl would never be able
to compete with Eugénie. "Are you enjoying the entertainments
thus far?"

Louise-Hélène visibly jumped, startled by Violet's presence.
"Oh, Madame Harper, I did not expect . . . you. My fiancé is
most unhappy with you, you know. That trick with *Newport* was
most unbecoming of a supposedly *cultivé* and dignified people."

"Surely he cannot believe that I personally had anything to do
with that. I was as surprised by it as everyone else."

"*Oui*, I told him this, but he has no forgiveness in him right
now. Assuredly, he will stay quite angry until he is convinced that
his reputation has not been damaged." Louise-Hélène clasped
her gloved hands together now that Isabelle was finished with
them. She gazed at Violet expectantly, while Isabelle studiously

avoided them by moving closer to the stage, ostensibly for a closer vantage point.

How had Violet managed to get herself into the position of diplomatic negotiations? The trouble with *Newport* was none of her affair. "I believe that Commander Nares will be officially reprimanded once we return to England, mademoiselle. It may be that the ship's captain acted out of masculine competitiveness, and I do not think that a diplomatic incident was desired." Perhaps that was true.

Louise-Hélène nodded and dropped her guard. "I do so fear for de Lesseps's good health. So much anxiety he has experienced. Every little thing that goes wrong with the ceremonies makes him so . . . so . . . *dérangé*. These festivities should please him, not send him to the asylum for lunatics. I am on my knees every morning, praying for him."

Violet was saved from further defense of British actions by Eugénie's arrival in an all-cream ensemble that highlighted her dark hair to perfection. The empress was breathless. "I see you are enjoying the little American demonstration, *mes chéries*. It is all so . . . exhilarating . . . here, is it not?"

"I suppose it must be true if you say it, Your Highness," Louise-Hélène replied. Violet was shocked at her overtly snide tone, but Eugénie seemed to take no notice.

"Monsignor Bauer will have a speaking role during the opening speeches. Wasn't it thoughtful of de Lesseps to include my confessor? I sent a telegram to the emperor when we arrived in Port Said, telling him of the palace along the Nile that the khedive had built for me, the one with the replica of my private apartments in the Tuileries. Did you see it, *ma louloute?*"

"No," Louise-Hélène answered flatly.

"You must have been preoccupied with the villa Pasha had built for de Lesseps. Weren't the miniature pyramids in the gardens just divinity itself? I told Napoléon that our reception in Egypt has been magnificent; there has been nothing like it in my lifetime. Oh, and did you know that there are future roads here in Ismailia to be named after us? Avenue of the Prince of Prussia, Avenue of Franz-Josef, and, of course, Avenue of Empress Eugénie. How delightful!"

"Delightful," Louise-Hélène repeated, almost physically ignoring the empress by turning to watch the stage with her maid.

Julie came scurrying to join her mistress, immediately popping open a parasol over Eugénie's head before making a fuss over whether Eugénie's dress was still perfectly arranged. She did it quite skillfully, but not so slyly that Violet didn't notice Julie handing her mistress a note folded into a tiny square. Eugénie turned around to open it privately, and when she turned back to them once more, the note was no longer visible, either tucked into some hidden pocket of her ensemble or handed back to Julie for safekeeping.

"What do you think of the dervishes over there, Madame Harper?" Eugénie asked distractedly, nodding over to where the skirt-clad male dancers continued their routine. Her face was flushed, and Violet wasn't sure if it was from embarrassment or anxiety over the missive she'd just read. Or perhaps it was just heightened excitement from the carnival-like atmosphere.

"Is that what they are called? It is very impressive. There is no such equivalent in England."

"I am a Spanish countess, and thought nothing could match my beloved Granada. Then I traveled to Paris to be educated, then married, and believed there was nothing to equal the splendor of the Tuileries and Fontainebleau. Now I see that the desert can be opened up to offer unparalleled delights of ancient buildings, divine delicacies, and unusual animals. Have you noticed the camels, Madame Harper? What strange creatures! My senses have been assailed for weeks now. I wonder if I shall ever recover." Eugénie stared past Violet, her thoughts having obviously drifted elsewhere.

She then tilted her head at Violet, as though realizing the undertaker was still there. "Later this afternoon I will be giving the khedive my own special gift," Eugénie said, that flush creeping up her face again.

"What is that, Your Highness?" Violet asked, knowing that asking the question was what was expected of her.

Eugénie brought her hands together. "I must tell someone—it is too much for me to keep to myself. I have had a piano most *spectaculaire* shipped here. It is for the khedive's yacht. It is made of Macassar ebony harvested in the Dutch East Indies and dried for ten years, and the keys are made from an African forest elephant from the Kongo Kingdom. I am assured there is nothing like it in the world. A small gift in return for what we have experienced here the past few weeks."

Was it a notice of the delivery that had excited the empress?

"That is indeed a unique gift, Your Majesty. The khedive will have the joy of hearing it played whenever he is aboard."

"Yes. Joy is an important thing, Madame Harper. There is so little of it these days, is it not so? One must find it wherever possible." She motioned to Julie, who instantly produced a fan. It was far larger than the one Violet had purchased, and heavily embellished with black lace that showcased a sharply colored and evocative scene of a medieval wedding painted across the blades. So well-done was it that it might have been painted by Rossetti himself.

However, Violet became distracted by what was happening onstage with Mott and his crew. The colonel was berating Caleb Purdy mercilessly, and even cuffed him on the ear, as near as Violet could tell for a misfiring of the soldier's weapon. Mott was no longer the happy, carefree man she had met the previous day, but an intent and driven taskmaster. He must have been as worried about the opening ceremonies as Pasha and de Lesseps.

The other soldiers stared ahead, intentionally ignoring Mott and his victim. The target of Mott's wrath spoke inaudibly in response to his superior's shouted rhetorical questions. Violet turned away, unable to watch any more of it.

As she did so, she realized that Louise-Hélène and her maid were gone, but Eugénie and her own maid still remained. She laughed softly and offered an elegant French shrug. "Are you offended by it, madame?" the empress asked.

Was she speaking of Mott's tirade or Louise-Hélène's disappearance?

Surely the empress meant the tirade, and although Violet had certainly seen far worse in her time, it still made her uncomfortable to witness the man's punishment. "I suppose no more than how much Monsieur de Lesseps is offended by the British delegation right now, Your Majesty."

Eugénie's sophisticated, amused laugh tinkled above Mott's voice. The scolding ceased at last, and Violet and Eugénie watched as the ex-Union officer ordered his men back into formation and they began their round of drills again. This time the thrust of their weapons and their marching were done in perfect unison together. "Ah, yes, he is most *en colère* over it. For myself, I found it amusing. However, you may find that little *ma louloute* is more outraged than her fiancé. She believes she is clever, you know, but I see inside, beneath the perfectly unmanageable mane of hair, and I know her for what she is. She is devoted to de Lesseps, and there is nothing she would not do to protect him."

Was that a casual observation or a warning?

Unfortunately, there was no warning whatsoever to the *Crack! Boom!* that split through their conversation. Violet flinched as the soldiers fired their weapons simultaneously in the air. Once more, she was temporarily deafened by the sound. It was such a strange sensation, as though her ears were filled with cotton, and she could hear noise but couldn't discern voices. The rifle firings were followed by the acrid odor of burnt gunpowder.

How horrible war must be, yet how devoted men were to it, she thought, observing her husband's enthusiastic—if inaudible—clapping. As her hearing slowly returned, Violet noticed that she was alone. Eugénie and her maid had disappeared the moment the shots were fired. Or had the empress really disappeared the moment she had delivered her warning?

The long, low bellowing of horns, which sounded like an

ancient call to temple and reminded Violet of the trumpeters aboard Franz-Josef's ship, secured everyone's attention from the entertainment. The crowds moved in droves to where the three elevated wood pavilions stood. Violet and Sam moved with the sea of people who wished to observe whatever was to come next.

Up close, Violet now realized that the largest pavilion was dedicated to the khedive and all of his distinguished guests and their attendants; the second was for the Catholic church, recognizable by the heraldic Jerusalem cross hanging inside of it; the third, with what appeared to be Qur'anic inscriptions on the pulpit, was clearly for the Muslim scholars. All of the pavilions contained broad stairways lined with carpets and adorned with more flowers and the flags of guest nations. Golden crescents rose from the corners of each pavilion, and palm fronds covered the posts that supported the drapery-swathed trellises over the platforms. Marie Antoinette could not have done better to transform her own gardens into such enchanting delights. No wonder Eugénie was rapturous.

Violet and Sam watched as all of the khedive's special dignitaries made the procession up the stairway of his pavilion to greet him. Naturally, de Lesseps and Eugénie were first, with Franz-Josef close behind, then the Prussian, Russian, British, Dutch, and other royalty climbing the treads to join Pasha. Egyptian servants were onstage, guiding the guests to designated places to stand. Naturally, de Lesseps was to one side of the khedive, while Eugénie was on his other. Louise-Hélène was buried somewhere inside the platform throng.

The fragrance from the jasmine flowers was heady, and, if possible, this setting was even more intoxicating than last night had been before the fire. Pasha was going to incredible lengths to impress this delegation.

"Act one, scene one," came a rumbling baritone from behind Violet. "Elaborate stages are set for the crown princes and priests of the world to bestow *bénédictions* upon the poor starving peasants, while extending *vénération* to themselves. Enter the king of all, stage right."

Violet turned to see who belonged to the French-accented voice. It was quite possibly one of the ugliest men she had ever encountered, with long hair, parted to one side and not recently washed. His beard was unkempt, there were ashy gray pouches under his eyes, and his belly strained mightily against his jacket. She estimated him to be around sixty years of age, and the predatory years seemed to have settled on him like an ancient shroud, patiently waiting to claim their victim.

However, he grinned broadly at Violet and Sam, and it removed at least a decade from his lined face. "It is theater, is it not?" he asked. "They are the performers; we are the spectators."

It was an interesting way to put it. "I do not believe we have met," Sam said, extending a hand. "You are . . . ?"

"I am many men, *mes amis*. An author, a playwright, a poet. Most consider me an art critic." The man put a hand over his chest, as if humbling himself while letting them in on the joke that he had no humility at all.

"I am Sam Harper; this is my wife, Violet. We are with the British delegation, although I'm afraid our only reason for acclaim is that my wife has provided undertaking services to the queen." The two men shook hands firmly.

"You also saved Her Majesty's life from a madman intent on killing her at Windsor," Violet reminded Sam pointedly.

"You sound like most distinguished guests to me. I am Théophile Gautier," the other man said, sweeping low like a courtier. "My friends know me as *le bon Théo*."

"How do you do, Monsieur Gautier—" Violet began.

"*Non*, you must call me Théo, I insist." He took her hand and pressed his rough, chapped lips to it. "You will allow me to observe the unfolding of this great drama with you, *oui?*"

The ceremony began with an opening from the Muslim platform, where prayers were offered that Violet did not understand. However, listening to these prayers made her realize something very curious about the proceedings.

"Monsieur Gau— I mean, Théo, have you also noticed that there seem to be no Muslim dignitaries present today? In fact, I have not noticed any since our arrival yesterday."

Sam nodded in agreement. "You're right. Except for Egyptians and Orientals serving and performing, I see no Easterners onstage, no Mussulmen."

"And now we come to act one, scene two. Scene heading: Port Ismailia, opening speeches," Gautier intoned. "The character named Isma'il Pasha says, 'Friends, I would have invited such illustrious personages as the sultan of Morocco, the Persian shah, and the bey of Tunis, but no accommodations were available.'" The author/playwright/poet/art critic did a fair impression of the khedive. " 'With the best intentions on earth, and opening all of my residences, I could not possibly have had more than eighty palaces ready for all of the princes who would have wished to honor me with their presence. Knowing, though, that I desire European approval above all else, including approval from God Almighty, I had to exclude anyone not from a country north of the Mediterranean Sea.' "

Violet couldn't help it. She burst into merry laughter, and Gautier inclined his head and flourished his hand like a Shakespearean actor accepting accolades.

As the *ulema* finished his practiced delivery of kneeling, bowing, and praying, the attention then switched to the Catholic stage. A man announcing himself as the archbishop of Jerusalem conducted a mass, replete with Latin readings, incense, and prayers. When he was finished and had stepped aside, the balding, clean-shaven Monsignor Bauer—Eugénie's confessor—approached the center of the stage. Appareled in a cheap brown robe and sandals—incongruent beside the pomp and color of every other creature and object surrounding him—he commenced speaking. His speech was a short yet lofty proclamation of de Lesseps's worthiness: a greatness not seen since Christopher Columbus himself sailed to the Americas, though de Lesseps might in fact be remembered in history as even greater than the Genoese explorer.

"Hmm," Gautier observed dubiously. "I shall have to inform the Spanish ambassador to France that Ferdinand and Isabella can no longer be credited with financing one of the world's greatest expeditions; *non*, instead it is France." Gautier rocked back and forth on his heels, no easy feat for a man his size. "Yes, that should sit well with His Excellency. Act one, scene—"

Gautier ceased his acerbic comments as de Lesseps took the stage, to the now oft-chanted *De Lesseps! De Lesseps! De Lesseps!*

De Lesseps reveled in the accolades for several moments before motioning to the crowd that he would like to speak. They quieted and listened attentively as he began. "As anticipated to happen, and has now been proved successful, the Suez Canal reveals itself to be of sufficient depth. We have upwards of forty—forty!— seaworthy ships here in the harbor, the largest being the Russian frigate *Alexandrite*, which *ees* drawing seventeen feet, two inches of water. *Remarquable!*"

The crowd cheered, its enthusiasm like a thunderclap of approval from the heavens above.

"The canal has just opened, yet the world knew of her importance, for only the greatest sovereigns in the world are here." De Lesseps swept a magnanimous hand to indicate everyone onstage with him.

"Except we know the ones who are missing, eh, Madame Harper?" Gautier said in a stage whisper.

"Not only sovereigns, but the world's greatest artists, poets, and writers are here, ready to paint and scribble their impressions of the unfolding events here, if it *ees* even possible to capture it at the tip of a brush or pen."

Another deafening roar of approval.

As if Gautier simply could not help injecting his own colorful commentary at every possible point, he held out his hands, palms up, and, gazing at them in wonder, said mockingly, "Now I see that to report upon the proceedings here is the culmination of all of my dreams. What rapturous effusions will flow from my fingertips tonight in my tent! What acclaimed scripts I can create so that the world will know what has happened here. Yes, I can now die a happy man in my wife, Ernestina's, arms."

Violet tried to control her amusement at the man's tart

observations. It would be most rude to laugh while de Lesseps spoke, yet she couldn't help thinking that Monsieur Gautier must be a brilliant satirist.

De Lesseps continued his speech, extolling the Empress Eugénie's virtues, followed by those of Franz-Josef, Crown Prince Frederick, Grand Duke Michael, and so forth.

"What are you telling these pitiful victims of your wit, Théo?" asked a middle-aged man. He had a wild shock of hair that stood up on end as if lightning had struck him, and it was both silver and dark in large patches, rather than a subtle threading of gray through his natural hair color. His features were grave, and his lips set in a firm, colorless line. Tiny beads of perspiration dotted his forehead.

"Henrik!" Gautier exclaimed with delight. "Monsieur and Madame Harper, this is Henrik Ibsen. He and I are both members of the little artist colony that Pasha and de Lesseps have formed here. You have heard of him?"

Violet vaguely recognized Ibsen's name. Also a writer of some sort from somewhere on the Continent?

The four of them now stood as their own oddly matched group, half listening to de Lesseps's seemingly tireless enthusiasm for his project and for those who had come to pay him homage.

Ibsen ran the flat of his hand upward against his forehead and into his mane of hair. "*Min Gud*, but it is hot here. Nothing like Norway. Are all of you not perspiring?"

"Poor Henrik," Gautier observed. He removed a handkerchief from a pocket and offered it with pronounced chivalry to the other man. "He is used to ice caves and snow castles. No, Henrik, it is quite balmy and comfortable here. Do not dehydrate yourself before we have an opportunity to experience what an Egyptian feast is like. I'm thinking there might be roasted crocodile, or maybe even fricasseed cobra. You wouldn't wish to miss that."

Ibsen made a strangled noise. "Perhaps the khedive has taken all sensibilities into account, and I might be able to find some *gravlaks*, although I hardly see that salmon could survive a trip from Norway to this place of hellish torment."

De Lesseps was concluding his speech. "Tonight there shall be a grand banquet, which I call the Dinner of the Sovereigns, which will allow the world to see these illustrious leaders, once facing one another across the various chessboards of Europe, strategizing and plotting against one another, now seated side by side, sharing delicacies and dipping their crystal glasses into fountains flowing with the wines *magnifiques* as candelabras burn brightly overhead in illumination of a new world."

The Frenchman was a dreamer, without question, but Violet couldn't deny that he had an effect on the crowd, which oohed and aahed over his rich descriptions. The crowds went wild when he was done, their cheers blotting out even the blowing horns of the ships in the harbor, whose crews also demonstrated their zeal for de Lesseps's words.

Now Pasha took to the center of the stage, and he and de Lesseps locked arms and kissed each other on the cheeks. De Lesseps then stepped aside so Pasha could speak.

"Today I announce a great surprise, one unknown even to Monsieur de Lesseps, that there has been an opera conceived by my nation's great Egyptologist, who shares his homeland with Ferdinand de Lesseps. Yes, I mean Auguste Mariette."

Violet started at the sound of the name. That was the third time she had heard the man's name in the past day.

Pasha continued. "I offer the opera, entitled *Aida*, as yet another way to keep the memory of what has happened here alive forever, much as our great pharaohs and kings have remained eternal in the hearts and minds of people. It will tell the story of an Ethiopian princess's love for an Egyptian king's general, and her willingness to die with him when he is executed. Thus is the relationship between Egypt and France that our friendship will extend beyond death."

Pasha! Pasha! Pasha!

The khedive's gratification at the crowd's unchecked acclaim was visible even at Violet's distance. "In true keeping with the international cooperation magnified here, the opera with an Egyptian setting and the scenario written by a Frenchman . . .

will be composed by no less than the great Italian Giuseppe Verdi and performed in the new opera house in Cairo."

There were scattered gasps at this, followed by enthused clapping.

"So Verdi has come out of his storage bin, eh?" Gautier said. "I thought he was busy walking the fields of his estate and playing the great landowner. Ah, well, whatever he does with it should prove interesting. I should think, though, that the Egyptians themselves are not quite as in love with Europe as Pasha is. I hope he does not have cause to regret so much importation of the Continent. Of course, all of it works mostly in France's favor, so I have no cause to complain."

Something in Gautier's tone put Violet on alert. "Do you worry for the khedive's safety?" she asked.

He smiled, once again transforming his frightful features into those of a kindly old bear. "I exaggerate, I assure you, Madame Harper. Act one, final scene: In a great tragedy, all of the Egyptian natives turn on the khedive and murder him in his sleep, thus turning the production into a one-act play. A little joke, a *blague*, yes?"

Violet nodded. She had promised herself she would relax for just a short while, and here she was, already feeling tense again about the entire theater production, as Gautier would likely put it, that was the grand opening of the Suez Canal.

Probably sensing her discomfort, Gautier changed the subject. "Where do you live in Great Britain, Madame Harper?"

"London. I have a shop there. My husband is—" She stopped, realizing that Sam's attention had returned to the stage. Sam was what? The poor man had left his homeland to join her back in England when her mother had been ailing, and then agreed to stay. Since then, he had been unsuccessful in two ventures, one involving dynamite manufacture and another with a coal mine. Tentative offers had been dangled before him, but it had been impossible to confirm anything, given that he had now followed Violet to Egypt. He had been ecstatic to help his old comrades put out the fire last night, and had avidly watched their demonstration today with a puppylike longing.

She glanced at her husband through fresh eyes. Was Sam miserable, and Violet blind to it? A lump the size of a chunk of black coal formed in her throat, and she quickly blinked back tears.

"My husband is—was—a lawyer by trade back in America, where he is from, and has been involved in several investments here," she finished vaguely.

It was good enough for Gautier, who probably didn't care about the activities of anyone who wasn't part of the current art movement. "Will you be staying for all of the canal events? I believe they will go on for days."

"Yes, we are committed to staying with *Newport* for as long as she's here. We are most indebted to our queen for extending this invitation to us," Violet said, happy to stop thinking about her husband's contentment—or lack thereof—for the moment. "We plan to stop in Pompeii on our return to London," she added. "An extra holiday for just the two of us."

"Ah!" Gautier dramatically put a hand over his heart. "You will be instantly transported to ancient Rome. I was so moved by my own visit there, so overwhelmed, that I wrote a story about it, 'Arria Marcella.' You have heard of it?"

Violet shook her head. She knew almost nothing about great artists, composers, and writers. Her tastes ran more along the lines of the entertaining Mr. Dickens.

Ibsen rolled his eyes. "They haven't heard of it because it is such drivel. I will tell you what it is, monsieur and madame. Three friends visit a museum in Napoli. One of the friends, Octavien, is taken with a Pompeiian cast of a beautiful young woman. Because the young man is an idiot, his friends go on to visit Pompeii while he remains to daydream about the pile of ash. After his friends return, Octavien visits Pompeii himself, and is somehow transported back to AD 79, attending the theater, listening to Latin in the streets, and then, lo! He finds the beautiful woman from the museum, alive. What rot."

"It is immersion, Henrik. One must *feel*—" Gautier attempted to explain his beloved tale of love.

"Even worse is his vampire tale, 'La Morte Amoureuse,' about a priest who falls in love with a female vampire who drinks drops of his blood at night while he sleeps so that she can survive. Vampires, can you imagine? What a canker for the brain."

At this, Gautier laughed aloud. He seemed to be taking his fellow author's mockery with good-natured aplomb. "Ibsen takes himself far too seriously. He writes plays, but ah, the constant moralizing with you Germanics. The man is scathing in his commentary. Have you seen *Brand*?"

Violet once more shook her head no, beginning to feel quite intellectually inadequate.

Ibsen sniffed, temperamentally interrupting Gautier. "First, I am Norwegian, and only reside in Dresden for the moment. I'll thank you not to refer to me as German again."

Now it was Gautier's turn to roll his eyes. "You understand what I mean?" he said to Violet.

Ibsen frowned and concentrated his intense gaze at the French playwright. "Second, the problem with you, Théo, is that you do not take your work seriously enough. You have a great power to influence, to right wrongs, within your grasp. But you believe that art should be 'impersonal,' and free of any moral lesson. I say you are wrong, and that the aim of the artist is not just to create a perfect form, but to create something that is divinely *good*."

The men were arguing, but Violet was beginning to see the affection they held for each other. It seemed as though the two had actually struck up an unlikely friendship here among the Egyptian palm trees. Actually, they were the first two genuine personalities she had encountered since landing. Everyone else was so concerned with their stature, their importance . . . their *dignitas*, as the ancient Romans would say. All of a sudden she was grateful that she and Sam were to be seated with writers at the Dinner of the Sovereigns.

☙❧

With the speeches finally over, the delegation members were escorted by Egyptian servants to the various tents assigned to them along what was interestingly marked as the Avenue of Victoria. The avenue was lined with exotic carpets so that guests did not have to step on exposed ground. The tents—there must have been more than a thousand of them—were arranged along either side of this makeshift street located near the red-roofed villa that Violet had noticed when they first arrived in Ismailia.

"This is yours, my lord and lady," their escort said, parting the curtained doorway before one of the tents. Potted palms stood on either side of the entry like sentries, and there was a rope-pulled bell on a post to the left of the doorway. The interior was surprisingly spacious, and outfitted with an opulently covered bed, a writing desk, and two tall chests with drawers, all in the very masculine Renaissance Revival style that was currently the rage in England. On top of one of the chests was a vase bursting with jasmine blooms, the sweet perfume filling every square inch of the space. The luxury of this tent town made it appear to be a palace turned inside out, with all of the decor gracing the outdoors.

Sam stood in the middle of their private tent, which was at least ten feet tall, and shook his head in amazement. "Do you imagine the French delegates have tents full of tortoiseshell and ivory?"

Violet laughed as she approached the framed tabletop mirror sitting next to the floral arrangement and took a quick glance to ensure that her bonnet sat properly on her head. "And I would wager that *le bon Théo* and Mr. Ibsen have sheaves of writing paper and dozens of ink pots in theirs."

Sam shrugged out of his jacket, tossed it carelessly over the bedpost, then sat on the bed. Within moments he was reclining, making himself comfortable against the pillows, his hands in their usual resting position, clasped on his chest. Violet opened a chest drawer to find that her garments were already here and folded neatly inside the drawer. Since every possible detail had been taken care of for lowly delegation members like her and

Sam, she could only imagine what sort of luxurious tents the royalty enjoyed. To think that the empress had her own villa constructed for just these few days was an astonishing thought.

The servant cleared his throat from just outside. "If there will be nothing else, my lord and lady, His Highness Isma'il Pasha requests your presence at tonight's dinner, in the Literary Corner."

Violet stepped out of the tent to speak to the servant, leaving Sam to what was apparently becoming a nap. "Yes, my husband and I will be in attendance. May I ask, who lives in the villa there?"

The servant looked at her as if she were the stupidest human alive. "That is Monsieur de Lesseps's villa, of course."

"I see," she said. "And so that . . ." She pointed in the direction of the palace.

"Is the khedive's palace," her escort finished for her.

Violet wondered where Eugénie's villa was, and how close it was to that of de Lesseps. Well, it was none of Violet's business. She returned to the interior of the tent, where Sam was watching her with a quizzical expression. "Is something wrong, wife? You look unsettled."

His innocent observation rushed her previous insecurities about Sam's contentment to the surface. "Now that you mention it, I was wondering . . . wondering if . . ." She wasn't even sure how to phrase it.

Sam sat up on the edge of the bed and patted the space next to him. "Sit with me."

She did so willingly, and he said, "Are you troubled about the bodies you found?"

"No. I mean yes, of course that weighs on my mind, but there are other things that worry me a little." Just sitting up against her husband's warmth was reassuring. Maybe she was embracing foolishness to think there was anything wrong. Nevertheless . . .

"It has occurred to me that your time since we returned from Colorado has been less than . . . engaging . . . for you, and I wonder if you are perhaps bored. Or dissatisfied. Or even . . . unhappy."

Violet cringed at hearing herself utter a word that had never even crossed her mind in their four years of marriage.

To make it worse, Sam did not immediately rush to console her as he usually did. Instead, he deliberated for several moments, as if forming his thoughts. Then he took one of her hands carefully in his. "A man has to be useful, Violet," he explained slowly. "Not just his wife's appendage. I am proud of you, and the fact that you have royal notice and a flourishing undertaking trade, but I must have my own trade. I have been as unsuccessful in Britain as I can possibly imagine, and left a good law practice in our son-in-law's hands to be here."

Violet felt the pinpricks of tears again, but was determined not to dissolve into a bout of uncontrolled weeping in front of him. "So you *are* miserable," she accused gently.

Sam flashed a smile and released her hand. "Not miserable, wife, as long as I have you."

It was a cryptic answer, and it left Violet feeling even further unsettled. She simply wasn't used to any discord whatsoever between her and Sam, and the idea that he had been harboring a sense of despondency without her even having an inkling of it made her stomach roil. The worst part of it was that there was nothing she could do to fix Sam's situation.

They were interrupted by the ringing of the bell outside their tent. Sam rose and admitted Sir Henry Elliot. Violet also stood and greeted him.

"Mr. and Mrs. Harper, we have a most unusual invitation." The ambassador held up an open letter. "His Highness Franz-Josef wishes to receive the British delegation aboard his ship to discuss what he terms 'important matters of state.' "

"What matters are these?" Sam asked.

Sir Henry shrugged. "I don't know. Austria is in the midst of bitter arguments with Prussia, what with their continued attempts to unify Germany under the House of Habsburg, but it has nothing to do with Great Britain and we have no quarrel with them."

"But surely His Highness is seeking to meet with you and the Prince of Wales, and not lowly members like us," Violet said.

"That is probably quite true. But since he gives no reason for this summons, the prince believes that arriving in full strength will prevent the emperor from being too demanding. Besides, you *are* an official part of the delegation."

Their audience with the emperor of Austria would prove to be one of the strangest encounters with a royal Violet had ever had.

chapter 16

THE BRITISH DELEGATION BOARDED SMS *Viribus Unitis* a half hour later. They were escorted into Franz-Josef's reception quarters by Karl Dorn, the emperor's chamberlain, who bowed stiffly before showing them down a wide staircase. Lining the center of each stairway tread was a uniformed, expressionless servant standing ramrod straight. The delegation passed down either side, holding the polished wood rails.

A strange choreography commenced at the enormous double doors leading to the emperor's presence. Rather than throwing open both doors for the entire delegation to enter at once, or at least to process in a line one at a time, Dorn instead maintained tight control of the opening and closing of the door in a bizarre routine. Both doors were opened to welcome in the Prince of Wales, with several of the servants who had been positioned on the stairs surrounding him as if they were escorting a precious transport of gold bars.

The doors clicked shut behind the prince; then, moments later, only one door opened in its entirety and the ambassador was admitted. When the turn came for the Harpers, Asa Brooks, and even Commander Nares—for he had also been conscripted for the duty—the single door opened only wide enough to permit one of them at a time, and even then Violet's skirts just passed through without crumpling.

Inside was yet another miracle of wealth to which Violet

should have been accustomed, having witnessed so much luxury in the past day, yet she found she was still breathless at the sight of it. The interior of what could hardly be termed a cabin, for surely it extended half the length and width of the entire ship, was awash in gilding, crystal, and priceless artwork. At one end stood Emperor Franz-Josef himself, resplendent in his red-striped trousers, with medals bedecking his chest.

Sam, handsome in his own uniform, Captain Nares, and Asa Brooks were presented first to the emperor, and all bowed stiffly before the foreign sovereign. Violet was presented last, and she took her turn with a deep curtsy. Was it her imagination, or did Franz-Josef's eyes narrow suspiciously at her?

Except for Bertie, the other delegation members then unashamedly soaked in the opulence, Violet included. It was difficult to remember that they were on a ship, docked at least a thousand miles away from the nearest European palace.

Franz-Josef came directly to the point. "I requested the British delegation's presence for a specific purpose," he stated. "One of great import that must be addressed right away prior to this evening's dinner, and I—"

"Have you nothing to smoke?" Bertie interrupted.

The emperor's eyes narrowed again, but he signaled to Dorn, and from some magical place a box of thin cigarettes was produced. Franz-Josef's movements were controlled, but Violet could see him mentally tapping his foot with impatience as the Prince of Wales took his time in selecting one. After it was lit, Bertie drew deeply from the wrapped tobacco and slowly exhaled in pleasure. "As you were saying?" he said casually.

"Yes, there is a grievous situation at hand."

"I do not know how Great Britain can assist you. We are not involved in your affairs, nor do they interest us," Bertie said, verbally dismissing the emperor's concerns.

"Even if the very future of Europe is at stake?" Franz-Josef challenged coolly. He had hardly moved from his rigid military stance since they had entered the room.

This finally piqued interest, and Bertie waited expectantly

for Franz-Josef's next words, but Sir Henry abruptly broke in. "Are you Germanic states on the brink of war again, as we have suspected?" the ambassador said.

Franz-Josef nodded once, the movement quick and clipped. "Thus *vhat* happens in the next few hours is critical."

"What is the trouble, Your Highness?" Sir Henry asked, in far more solicitous tones than Bertie had used.

The emperor gave the ambassador an appreciative nod. "I have the seating chart for tonight's dinner. It is unacceptable. I am seated below Frederick."

The only sound that could be heard was the distant screeching and cawing of red-throated loons outside. Inside the room, no one even dared breathe.

Finally, Bertie broke the tense silence. "Pardon, I'm not sure I understand. You are seated below me and the Empress Eugénie, as well."

"Yes, I am *villing* to concede a lesser place to Great Britain, but I *vill* not do so for the Prussians."

Violet could hardly believe her ears. *This* was the matter of international import? A seating chart? How absurd!

The Prince of Wales must have thought so also, as Bertie started to laugh heartily. Sir Henry dove in and tried to steer the moment diplomatically. "Your Highness, I believe the Prince of Wales shares your disbelief at the great dishonor done to you, but isn't this simply a matter for the khedive's own chamberlain? Surely he could rearrange chairs to suit you."

Franz-Josef compressed his lips in great displeasure. He really was the most humorless man . . . until he was in Eugénie's bewitching presence. Violet began to suspect he was far less concerned with the indignity of placement vis-à-vis Prussia and much more worried about having an opportunity to brush up against Eugénie and feed her from his plate all evening.

"I have sent my man to see the khedive's man, and Dorn *vas* told there could be no changes at this late date."

Sir Henry spread his hands helplessly. "I do not see how adding our own request to change the seating assignments can be of any help. Perhaps you need to supplicate directly to the khedive himself or de Les—"

"Supplicate!" Franz-Josef barked. "Austria does no such thing. Frederick is but a crown prince, whereas I am *emperor*. He is much lower than I, and must not be given precedence over me. It is unacceptable. The Habsburgs *vill* not be humiliated. *Nein*, you *vill* help me."

Sir Henry cleared his throat. "Ahem, Your Highness, even if we were inclined to do this, Monsieur de Lesseps and the khedive are already angered that our queen is not here herself. I hardly think we are in a position to—"

Bertie stopped the ambassador with an airy wave of his hand that held the cigarette, which resulted in a hot stub of ash dropping onto the finely woven carpet beneath their collective feet.

Violet winced at Franz-Josef's expression as he watched the ash sprinkle on top of the floor covering. She imagined Mount Vesuvius had looked like this nearly two millennia ago, venting smoke and spitting fire.

Bertie took no notice of his fellow prince's smoldering, though. "Afraid we can't help you with this. Pasha and de Lesseps have been quite hospitable to me on both of my trips to Egypt, especially this one. I will not upset them with such a request. It is not in Great Britain's interest to do so."

"I tell you it is," Franz-Josef insisted, his eyes practically afire in rage but his body remaining perfectly still. "Be assured that there will be great trouble ahead if this outrage is not repaired. Then Great Britain *vill* realize her mistake."

As usual, no expense had been spared for the evening's dinner. For every event the level of luxury surpassed the ostentation of all the previous events, and the Dinner of the Sovereigns was no exception. Knowing that there were a picnic and a ball to come, Violet could hardly imagine how the khedive would surpass what overwhelmed the senses and mind right now.

Along what was heralded as the Avenue of Empress Eugénie was the most enormous tent Violet had ever beheld. It contained different sections, including a large square center section with lower wings that extended out and wandered in several directions. Yet they were all connected under one contiguous roof, which was topped with the flags of various nations.

Violet and Sam waited in line to enter through the center tent, from where they were to be escorted to the "Literary Corner," according to the gold embossed seating cards they were handed. She immediately understood why all guests were filtered through the main tent, as it was an opportunity for all of the guests to view the elevated pomp reserved for the sovereigns alone.

Already this tent was filled with seated rulers, who happily quaffed ruby-red liquid from crystal glasses that reflected the shimmering light of dozens of ornate multibranched candelabras. The imposing candelabras were splendid to behold, reaching upward of five feet in precisely measured distances along the table. The banquet table, so long it probably would not fit in most dining halls in the palaces of Europe, was draped in snowy white linens, accenting the multitude of silver salvers and monogrammed plates set before the guests. The guests sat on tufted chairs, with the ladies' dresses spilling elegantly onto a thick rose-patterned carpet that covered the entire tent floor. Violet felt as if she were walking on the finest English fescue grass. A string quartet struggled to make chamber music heard over the clinking and chattering inside this affluent, self-contained world.

Lining the inner perimeter of the tent, tall potted palm trees, their tops bent along the curve of the tent's roof, created a canopy of lacy fronds. They dangled lushly over the diners, who were laughing and joking, *sans souci*, and being graciously attended by liveried servants.

All except Emperor Franz-Josef, who was seated midway down the table and was glowering into his empty glass while snapping his fingers in the air. A servant immediately materialized with a silver pitcher and refilled it halfway. Franz-Josef snapped his fingers again and pointed down at the glass. The servant poured again and quickly moved away, as if avoiding another summons to that particular glass.

The khedive sat at the head of the table, with de Lesseps to his left and Eugénie to his right. Violet was glad to see Louise-Hélène had been given a place of prominence next to her fiancé. She recognized Bertie, of course, seated next to Eugénie—who was opulently draped in pearls and feathers—as well as Crown Prince Frederick and both General Ignatiev and Grand Duke Michael from Russia. There were other sovereigns she vaguely recalled from either last night's festivities or those from earlier in the day. Interestingly, near the end of the table was a round-faced young man with heavy eyelids. He was not yet an adult, but looked weary beyond his years already.

They were escorted through makeshift hallways constructed in the tenting to their dining section. This outer tent had a lower roof, fewer decorations, and merely a flutist accompanied by a piano for musical pleasure. But the food was still palace-worthy, gauging by the tureens and bowls heaped with all manner of delicacies. All was waiting to be served, and there could be no danger of any guest leaving the table dissatisfied. Violet was relieved to see that she and Sam were to be seated across from Gautier. Not that it mattered, for it appeared that guests moved around as they wished in the smoke-filled tent, and were milling about, forming their own little cliques.

Sir Henry had also been placed in here, as had Eugénie's maid, Julie, who nodded stiffly at Violet when she caught the maid's eye.

Gautier looked up from his deep conversation with both Ibsen and a man whose bleary eyes and loose cravat suggested he had already imbibed far too much. "Ah, Monsieur and Madame Harper, you will save me from this wretch, *non?*" Gautier said, rising but clapping the muddled man on the shoulder in a friendly way. "He loves the burgundy, but it despises him. We must pity the poor maid who will attend to his lodgings tomorrow, especially since he is a mathematician wandered in from another tent and cannot stop describing formulas used for digging the canal. She will go insane from listening to him before she finishes tucking in one corner of his stinking, sweat-soaked, vomit-splattered bedcoverings."

The man grumbled good-naturedly, but espied a group passing around a silver pitcher, and so lifted his glass, saluted Sam and Violet, and stumbled off to join the group for a refill and presumably more appreciative company.

"Could you not have arrived sooner?" Ibsen said. "Good Lord, the man kept asking me to quiz him with algebraic equations. I believe I need another glass of *la fée verte* to recover." He held up two fingers to a waiter, who presented both Ibsen and Gautier with glasses partially filled with a green liquid that had a nearly phosphorescent quality to it, then a carafe of water, a crystal container full of sugar cubes, and two flat, slotted utensils. Ibsen signaled again, and the waiter retrieved two more utensils and glasses of liquid, setting them before Violet and Sam.

"What is this?" Sam asked, frowning.

Gautier smiled enigmatically. "You must try it for yourself, monsieur. It is absinthe, all the rage in Paris, despite the best efforts of those humorless prohibitionists, who could probably use a glass themselves. Do as I do."

The writer, as well as Ibsen, took a utensil, which reminded Violet of a cake server except that it was embellished with several open swirls at the center of it. They balanced it across the top of the glass, so that the slots were directly above the apple-green liquid.

Sam shook his head. "What is the purpose of—"

Gautier held up a finger in patient tutelage. "You shall see. Place your absinthe spoon across your glass, *s'il vous plaît.*" Violet also picked up her spoon and placed it carefully across the top of her glass.

"Now, you must put a sugar cube on top of the spoon, like this. Madame Harper, you may wish to use two cubes, as you have the female constitution *délicat.*"

Violet was happy to do so, worried that what they were about to imbibe was worse than drinking straight from the Thames. She surreptitiously sniffed at the glass, and was surprised at the odor of anise and . . . fennel and . . . something sweet, like basil.

"Now," Gautier instructed further, picking up the carafe of water, "you will pour water over the sugar cube, about three times as much water as absinthe, like this." He courteously poured over Violet's sugar cubes first, then poured for Sam, Ibsen, and himself. The cubes dissolved through the slots and into the glasses as the pours were finished.

"Now what?" Violet asked.

"We wait." Gautier and Ibsen stared at their glasses expectantly. Were they hoping for a frog or rabbit to leap out of it?

Sam and Violet exchanged looks, then imitated the two writers. Violet felt foolish waiting for a glass of liqueur to perform a task. But, lo, the drink had completely changed consistency, and there were now rolling clouds inside the glass, which then settled into layers.

"Incredible," Sam said.

Gautier picked up his own glass and peered in through the side, as if examining a diamond against the light. "What do you think, Madame Harper?"

"It has become milky," she said, the words sounding simplistic and foolish in her own ears.

"Yes, that is the *louche*. The anise and fennel release their essences and blossom into the glass. You must smell the aroma now."

Violet sniffed again. All of her earlier impressions of the spicy fragrance were magnified. Far more intoxicating than the jasmine blooms outside, this was so much more . . . more . . . Violet had no words.

"Drink, *mes amis*," Gautier said. He and Ibsen tipped their glasses.

"Tarnation, but this is good," Sam said.

"Tarnation?" Ibsen asked, frowning.

"He is an American," Gautier said, as though that explained it all.

Violet's tongue was too numb for her to offer her own thoughts. The absinthe was strong and overwhelming, yes, but it was also sweet and candylike at the same time. She must have been making strange facial expressions, for the usually stern-faced Ibsen actually offered a smile. "The anise troubling you, madame? It requires a bit of getting used to, eh, Théo?"

Violet drank more, and found that the absinthe was smoother and sweeter the farther she got into the glass. By the end of it, she felt as though she were floating above the guests inside the folds of some iridescent silk fabric being held aloft by the cigar smoke in the room. Ibsen's hair grew into taller spikes before her eyes, while Sam's eyes grew so large they seemed to absorb his face. It required several minutes for her to regain cognizance, once more grounded in her seat, by which point Ibsen was arguing with someone else about the respective theatrical merits of the naturalism and realism movements. The two men were arguing in French, with excessive hand gestures. The other man helped himself to his own glass of absinthe, while Violet pushed her own away.

Perhaps Gautier was correct about her having a delicate constitution, at least where this overpowering drink was involved.

Violet realized that Gautier was gazing at her with concern. "Too much, Madame Harper? Act two, scene one. We open upon the khedive of Egypt, having met his goal of transcending national barriers, with representatives of all the European nations imbibing themselves into oblivion without regard to profession, sitting contentedly at dinner, knowing that bankrupting his country to make Egypt look far wealthier than she is has been completely worth it. 'After all,' the khedive says to no one in particular, 'a peasant is just a peasant, but to have *le bon Théo* at the same table as Auguste Mariette, now that is an accomplishment.' "

That name again.

"Have you met this man Mariette?" Violet asked.

"Of course," Gautier replied, lighting a cigar, drawing on it, then fixing it in the right corner of his mouth. "You have, as well. He sits there now with my grumpy friend Henrik, pretending to be an expert on opera now that the khedive has selected his *Aida* plot for production. Never mind that Mariette is not writing the script, nor composing the music, nor involving himself in any aspect of producing it. He simply had the idea for it. Most impressive." In a very interesting trick, Gautier managed to tilt his glass of absinthe back while keeping the lit cigar in his mouth, so that the muted green liquid flowed past the wrapped stick of tobacco without either the cigar or the drink dropping in his lap.

Violet hardly had time to give any thought to Mariette, for a commotion near the entry of the tent caused her to look up. It was Thaddeus Mott and his American Civil War crew, who had all clearly been enjoying the free-flowing wine and were singing, if the slurred caterwauling could be termed that. It was quickly drawing the attention of everyone else in the tent. The men had their arms linked about one another's shoulders, and were laughable in their attempt at some sort of marching-and-kicking routine together. Together they drunkenly sang:

> *When Johnny comes marching home again*
> *Hurrah! Hurrah!*
> *We'll give him a hearty welcome then*
> *Hurrah! Hurrah!*
> *The men will cheer and the boys will shout*
> *The ladies they will all turn out*
> *And we'll all feel gay*
> *When Johnny comes marching home.*

Next to her, Sam had that same expression of longing again. Violet realized in that moment that, in addition to needing to be useful, what Sam needed most of all was male camaraderie. "Go," she whispered to him, and Sam was off in an instant to join his friends again. With a sigh, Violet turned back to the table and found that Gautier had disappeared, but Mariette had taken his seat and was staring at her intently.

"Is your husband an American?" he asked.

"He is."

"And you are one of these bohemian women, writing romantic novels at outdoor cafés and such?" Mariette gazed at Violet curiously, as if she were a new artifact he'd never seen before.

"No," she replied as blandly as she could. "I am an undertaker. Have you a corpse that requires care?"

Mariette's jaw dropped and he quickly shut it. "*Mon Dieu*, I have never encountered a woman who does this work. Your husband—he is an undertaker, too?"

She shook her head, but it made her wonder if Sam would be interested in it. So few people could stomach the work, much less enjoy it as she did. But he had witnessed his share of death and carnage in his life, and if he learned her routines and methods, then maybe . . .

"What group are you here with, then?" Mariette persisted.

"Just the British delegation, monsieur. I am aboard the Prince of Wales's ship."

His face registered surprise again. "An undertaker is a member of the British delegation? *Je ne comprends pas.*"

Violet sighed. "Most people do not. I have performed services for the queen, and she has granted me this boon of attendance at the opening festivities."

"So you are not just an undertaker, you are the royal undertaker."

"No, not especially. I am just—" Violet held her hands palms up, unable to find the right words. "I am just the queen's acquaintance."

"Curious indeed." There was that examining stare again. "And your husband . . . was he in the American war? I see he disguises a limp."

"Yes, he was injured at a place called Fredericksburg, Virginia."

Mariette nodded and casually pointed to Sam standing next to Thaddeus Mott, where it appeared that they were trying to teach new lyrics to the other men. "His friends are most . . . interesting. Earlier I saw one of them berate an Egyptian soldier he was training. Perhaps the Egyptians were also planning a military display and it was the American's job to quickly prepare them? It was a tongue-lashing of a nature most *sauvage*."

Violet remembered Mott having reprimanded one of his own men. What caused such a choleric temper? Sam certainly didn't have one, and presumably had similar experiences to Mott.

"I trust the poor man recovered," she said.

"I trust so, as well. The American war created great stress upon Egypt, and I would hate to think that your husband's *compatriotes* are continuing to exert undue pressure on innocent Egyptians."

That was a curious statement. "How did the war affect a country six thousand miles away?" she asked.

A waiter appeared and offered Mariette a complement of absinthe materials, but Mariette waved the man away, instead focusing his attention on Violet. "Their Civil War put a premium on Egyptian cotton, since theirs could not be exported from the Confederacy. Egypt enjoyed a great boom in trade, and the price of Egyptian cotton increased. When the war ended, so did the increased prices. The *fellahin* who had expanded their cotton fields went seriously into debt, which resulted in the usual, inevitable consequences: large mortgages, foreclosures, and usurious moneylending. Meanwhile, the village headmen and great estate owners were able to purchase land abandoned by the peasants for mere centimes. There is still great suffering in Egypt, but here you have . . . this." He held up a hand, indicating the opulent space around them.

It had never occurred to Violet that the United States's struggles had affected any other countries except Great Britain and France, and now she wondered about all of the Egyptians lining the banks of the canal as they sailed, cheering and waving. Were these members of the peasant class to which Mariette had referred? She remembered something else.

"I understand that the khedive has laid thousands of miles of railroad track for his country."

Mariette nodded. "I can only imagine how much borrowing he must have done to pay for it all. But Pasha has great dreams for his country, imagining it to one day be part of the Europe he so admires, with himself the equivalent of a king. This is why he has a Frenchman leading his antiquities department and a Frenchman taking credit for every aspect of the canal, even though it is likely to be what completely bankrupts Egypt. Pasha is *l'enfant terrible*, outrageous and irresponsible in his behavior, yet he manages to have success with it."

"That success being this internationally renowned canal," Violet said.

She was surprised that Mariette casually brushed the achievement aside. "Among other things. He has grander plans than merely directing the shipping of the world. He plans to extend Egypt's rule throughout Africa—with himself, not the sultan, as ruler—as well as to build more palaces per kilometer than any other sovereign, living or dead. You have visited the palace here on Lake Timsah, *oui?*"

"I'm afraid not. But the ball is to be there tomorrow evening."

"Yes, of course. You will see it then. You will be amazed to know that the palace is nearly twenty thousand square feet and was completed in just six months, in time for the celebrations. Naturally, it is populated with some of the finest statuary and relics to be found in Egypt."

So the khedive *would* be able to top this evening and everything that had gone before tonight's dinner.

"It is most impressive," Violet murmured, also declining a waiter's offer of absinthe.

"What is not impressive is that Pasha has spent nearly a million francs on these celebrations, on top of the nearly unimaginable amount spent on the canal itself. And that was with using slave labor—at least, until you British put an end to that. Your country's bellowing over it, when you are so recently disengaged from true slavery yourselves, demonstrated that you did not understand the principle of it."

"What do you mean?" Violet asked, uncomfortable on the topic. Slavery had been outlawed in Britain since 1833, the year she was born. Her experiences with workhouse inmates had been bad enough; she couldn't comprehend outright slavery.

"Many nations have used corvée labor. It is not slavery; they are merely conscripted for a period of time to work on projects that benefit the nation as a whole. Eventually, the *fellahin* return to their homes and fields. They are not chained up in cellars for their lifetimes. I admit that one thing I cannot fault Pasha for is using a system that has been in place for thousands of years."

Perhaps it was time to change the subject. "You are the director of antiquities, are you not, monsieur, and have provided the story for *Aida* to the khedive?"

Mariette flushed with self-admiration, nodding in acceptance of the recognition. "Yes to both of these, madame. My time in Egypt has been mostly worthwhile, and the khedive is not *l'enfant terrible* in all ways."

"You are thus responsible for excavations in this country?"

He nodded proudly. "I have overseen dozens, and have published a little treatise about them that can be purchased at the book stalls here in Ismailia." He then frowned. "At least, I intend to have more digs. You British are frightful with your tomb raiding and interferences. You must be watched like dogs around the kitchen."

"I do hope, monsieur, that you do not blame me personally, and that we can be friends?" Violet asked.

"*Non*, madame, it is not you I blame for what is wrong with antiquity preservation in Egypt, but the khedive. He has an unfortunate tendency to take antiquities for himself that belong in the museum, having servants spiriting away treasures faster than I can lift them out of the ground. It is despotic and wrong, but I intend to resolve it. Very soon."

Mariette's tone was overtly menacing, and Violet involuntarily shivered at it. How did he intend to resolve his dispute?

The dinner progressed, with hours of dining, drinking, card playing, and impromptu speeches throughout the tents. Sam and Violet spent time in the Philosophers' Tent, although their conversation was far too profound for her, and they also visited the Tent of Artists, where an impromptu painting competition had started. There was great laughter here, as the free-flowing liquor ensured that every brushstroke resulted in messy drips. The artists all heartily congratulated themselves on their fine work.

Shaking their heads, Violet and Sam returned to the Literary Corner tent. She was about to recommend to her husband that they consider retiring to their own quarters, as she was tired from the absinthe, the heavy cloud of smoke, and the din of voices that grew louder with each passing minute. She also wanted to contemplate some very interesting statements that had been made to her during the evening.

However, Sam wanted to spend more time with Mott, and she didn't have the heart to press her desire to leave. Noticing that Eugénie's maid was seated alone at a far end of the long table, Violet joined her. "Mademoiselle Lesage, are you enjoying yourself?"

Julie's eyes were narrowed as she stared at the group of Americans that Sam had rejoined. "I suppose it could be said so," she said indifferently, not looking in Violet's direction.

Violet tried again with tactful flattery. "Your mistress is certainly the most celebrated of the sovereigns here."

Julie's attention was finally torn from the soldiers and focused on Violet. "And why should she not be? She is the empress of France, a princess of Spain, and a renowned beauty besides. It is only proper that she be made preeminent. This is as much a French celebration as an Egyptian celebration."

They were interrupted by the Austrian emperor's chamberlain, Karl Dorn, who came up behind Julie and across from Violet. "Pardon me, Frau Harper and Fräulein Lesage, you will permit me to sit?"

Julie shrugged and motioned at the empty seat next to her, her attention fixated back upon the soldiers.

"Herr Dorn," Violet began, "how do you find—"

Dorn swayed unsteadily as he grabbed the back of his velvet

chair, then slumped down into it. Was this lurching fellow the same man as the precise, clipped manservant of yesterday evening?

"How do you find the festivities?" she concluded cautiously.

"What?" Dorn said, stumbling over the simple word. He appeared disoriented, and the man's complexion was ashy as he stared at Violet, no longer seeming to recognize her. His pupils were pinpoints, and his hands, which were now placed upon the table as if to continue to steady him, began to spasm.

"Herr Dorn," Violet cried in alarm, truly anxious about the man. "Is something wrong? How can I help you?"

In response, Dorn crashed down face-first onto the table, eliciting a nervous titter from Julie. "Too much absinthe, I think," she said airily. "It is surprising that most men in here have retained their faculties."

Violet jumped up, grabbed her skirts, and ran around the corner of the table to the other side where Dorn was. She knelt down and put a hand to the man's shoulder, shaking him gently. "Herr Dorn? Can you hear me?"

"Hmmm?" he slurred, barely opening his eyes. He was no longer spasming but had become oddly still. Dear Lord, what was happening to the man? Violet wondered fleetingly if there was a Tent of Medicine. From the other side of the incapacitated Dorn came Julie's indifferent voice. "Has he gone to sleep?"

"Hardly," Violet said. "Help me lift him to an upright position so I can look at him." She had no idea what she thought she would discover. She was an undertaker and dealt only in corpses, not a physician who cared for the sickly.

With difficulty, she and Julie maneuvered the heavy Karl Dorn so that he was vertical in the chair. As his head slumped strangely to one side, Violet let out a gasp, realizing with a start that, indeed, she was once again dealing with a corpse.

chapter 17

"WHY WON'T HE WAKE UP?" Julie asked as she patted Dorn on the hands and face to rouse him.

"Julie," Violet said in a low tone, "go and ask my husband and his friends to come assist me. Quickly."

But Julie bristled, drawing herself up indignantly to her full height. "I am lady's maid to the Empress Eugénie. You cannot order me about as if I am—"

Violet had had enough of her arrogance. "Do it now, you brainless little nitwit, or I shall grab you by the ear, drag you to the canal, and joyfully drown you. *Go!*"

Julie opened and closed her mouth several times, pop-eyed like a goldfish, then turned and flounced off. Sam and Thaddeus Mott were at her side in moments, but Julie did not return. Out of the corner of her eye, Violet thought she saw Julie talking with one of Mott's men. In fact, it appeared to be Caleb Purdy, whom Mott had dressed down during the demonstration earlier. Was she actually over there flirting?

Thank heavens Violet's own daughter, an undertaker in her own right, wasn't as silly and self-absorbed as this ninny of a girl.

"What has happened?" Sam asked.

Keeping her voice low, she said to both men, "Herr Dorn here is dead, I am afraid."

"What?" Mott exclaimed, surprise flashing across his face.

"Shh," Violet instructed forcefully, forgetting that she was talking to a US lieutenant colonel. "I'm not sure what happened to him. Perhaps he had some sort of medical condition," Violet said, not really believing that to be a real possibility.

As if he had been coached by Julie, Mott said, "He probably couldn't tolerate the absinthe." At least his voice was lower.

"Perhaps," she replied, not really thinking that possible, either. Dorn seemed no more likely to allow himself to get carried away by absinthe than his master was to permit his dignity to be impugned. His symptoms were also not those of someone who had overimbibed alcohol. It was more as if he had been—dare she say it?—poisoned.

She didn't dare utter it aloud. Not yet.

"Gentlemen, can you help me get him out of here? Pretend he is insensible from drink so that no one bothers us." Violet glanced around as casually as possible under the circumstances. Good, thus far no one was paying any attention to them.

"I know where we can take him," Mott said, giving a low whistle, which no one but Ross Keating and one other man seemed to hear. With no questions asked, they instantly obeyed Mott's instruction to move Dorn. Four men carried him to a corner of the tent, while Keating figured out how to detach that section of the fabric wall so that they could all slip out with the body.

Outside the confines of the smoking, music, and laughter, it was as though they were in a different world. The noise receded into the background, leaving only the men's heavy breathing as they struggled with their unfortunate load and the guttural braying of camels somewhere in the distance.

Mott led them to a small outlying tent. Keating had managed to find a lantern along the way, illuminating an interior containing open chests overflowing with costumes and props, undoubtedly for future entertainments. By the look of it, there would be jugglers and acrobats later.

The men put Dorn down in the center of the tent, and Violet examined him as best she could. His waxy skin, his constricted pupils, his slurring, the spasms . . . what in the world did they mean?

"Do you think it was an excess of drink?" Mott asked. "I don't think he has any marks to suggest foul play with weaponry, which is good. It means he was not in any fights with locals."

Violet knelt next to the dead man's now gaping mouth and sniffed. The men in the room recoiled as she did it, and she rolled her eyes at these battle-hardened soldiers becoming squeamish at her actions. She didn't notice anything unusual other than a faint, vaguely flowerlike odor, which suggested he might have had some hibiscus tea earlier. He definitely had not had any spirits, and most certainly had not been drinking absinthe just prior to his death. She began a minimal disrobing of his jacket and shirt.

"Mebbe he killed himself," offered one of Mott's men. "Wouldn't be the first soldier to do it."

Violet frowned. "Why do you say he's a soldier, sir?"

The man shrugged. "I'm Sergeant Owen Morris, ma'am." He eyed the dead man. "And you can just tell."

Sam put a hand to her shoulder. "I agree with Owen. The man had an air of soldiering around him. And look there, along his rib cage. I'd say that looks jagged and misshapen enough to be battle related. In fact, it looks as though he endured something quite painful."

Sergeant Morris and Colonel Mott nodded in agreement.

Was that possible? That Karl Dorn had seen the horrors of war and attempted to do away with himself? He had seemed so very controlled, though. It was difficult to believe that the man she had met was someone intent on killing himself in short order. It was even more difficult to think that he would do so in this public place.

"He may have done so," she said slowly, rising up with Sam's assistance. "But he didn't do it with liquor, and I haven't any idea how he might have done so. I believe he may have been pois—"

The flaps of the tent were rudely yanked apart, and General Ignatiev of the Russian delegation entered, bearing his own lantern. He held it up and surveyed the occupants of the tent. Espying Dorn on the ground, the general grunted. There was no shock in the grunt, just an odd sort of acceptance. "Sorry for disturbance," he mumbled. "I saw you carrying man out, and I think I will see what has happened. This man is dead," he concluded.

As it was impossible to hide that fact, Violet said, "Yes, he has met with some sort of accident."

"Yes, some sort of accident." Ignatiev stroked his mustache while contemplating the body. "What will happen with dead man?"

"Herr Dorn will need to be properly attended to," Violet said, wondering how to forestall the body being removed in a moment of distraction. "I must inform the emperor."

"Good for him to know," the general said simply, and lumbered out of the tent.

Now Violet's curiosity was thoroughly piqued. Turning to Mott, she asked him to watch over Dorn's body while she slipped out of the tent to follow the Russian, who appeared to be headed in the direction of the main tent entrance. Sam was right on her heels, and she was just about to suggest that they run after Ignatiev to talk to him before he reached the sovereigns' dining area when her husband stopped her. Pointing to the exit that Mott's man had made in the tent, Sam showed Violet that Julie Lesage was making her way out, stumbling in her skirts through the rough opening. However, she finally freed herself and dashed across the grounds, directly toward Ignatiev.

Violet and Sam watched as the maid spoke in urgent undertones to the hefty general. It was difficult to see exactly what was going on in the intermittently flaring torchlight, but it seemed as if she was relaying information. Or perhaps a message.

Ignatiev finally nodded and followed Julie back inside the Literary Corner tent.

Why was the behavior of every single person on this journey so puzzling? How did Julie even know Ignatiev? Regardless, Violet sensed that it was imperative that she reach the emperor quickly to inform him of his manservant's unexpected death.

"Will you stay with Herr Dorn's body to make sure no one

removes him?" she asked Sam.

"Yes, but return quickly. If you aren't back in fifteen minutes, I shall send the troops to find you." Sam kissed her forehead. "I can make that happen literally, you know."

Violet smiled gratefully and dashed around to the main tent. The glow, the music, and raucous laughter told her that the party was still proceeding with abandon. The servant guarding the entry recognized her and let her pass.

In her determination to immediately find Franz-Josef and pull him aside, Violet paid little attention to her surroundings and nearly ran straight into Gautier, who put out both hands to stop her. "Why the rush, Madame Harper? Did you also hear that they had turned on the wine fountain spigots in here?"

Violet apologized for coming so close to colliding with him. "I must talk to the emperor."

Gautier chuckled. "The emperor? Which one? There are many to choose from here this evening."

"Franz-Josef. I must tell him something important." Violet looked past Gautier, searching for the emperor. Ah, he was brightly illuminated to her left, where he had managed to leave his assigned seat and find his way next to Eugénie, who was laughing at whatever he was saying as he bent his head closely to hers.

Gautier looked at her knowingly. "Act two, scene two. The undertaker enters the room with sensational news. The world is shaken by it. International cable messages are sent with dizzying speed, and the earth rumbles and quakes."

Violet hoped that he merely was being absurdly dramatic, and that he didn't actually know why she was here.

∽

"Your Imperial Highness," Violet said, dropping into a curtsy behind the chairs of Franz-Josef and Eugénie. They both turned, clearly irritated at the intrusion.

"*Ja?*" he asked. The aggravation was not only in his eyes but also in his voice.

"Your Highness, I am sorry to intrude, but I must speak to you privately. It is a matter of great urgency."

"How urgent can it be that I must be interrupted from my international fellowship by a lowly member of the British delegation, which has been most uncooperative?"

"*Please*," Violet said, attempting to guide him outside.

With a huff of impatience, he made to follow Violet, but took two large steps to ensure that he was physically in front of her. He led her down the red carpet a distance away from the tent, practically marching instead of strolling.

He stopped abruptly and turned to face Violet, lightly clicking his heels together. "And now, Frau Harper, *vhat* is it you have to tell me?"

In a rush, Violet explained what had happened to his servant. Franz-Josef remained utterly impassive at the news. He did not gasp. He did not put a hand to his chest. He did not say, "Impossible!" Violet might as well have told him that a stray cat had disappeared from Schönbrunn Palace's gardens for all of his lack of emotion.

"Would you like to see him before I tell Monsieur de Lesseps, Your Highness?" Violet asked gently.

Franz-Josef stood ramrod straight. "*Ja*, I suppose de Lesseps must know. You *vill* tell him now?"

"I can wait until you have visited Herr Dorn. My husband and his friends are standing guard with his body."

Still no reaction from the emperor. He simply stood there for several moments, during which a horn blew and an announcement was given that fireworks were to commence shortly. Almost immediately the occupants of the main tent began tumbling out, joking and singing with wineglasses in their hands, with servants stumbling behind them to keep up with carafes and lanterns.

Eugénie came out on the arm of Crown Prince Frederick. Franz-Josef's eyes narrowed. "*Nein*, I *vill* not go. You *vill* tell de Lesseps and take care of the matter." With that, he strode off to join Eugénie and Frederick.

Violet was flabbergasted beyond measure. Wasn't Dorn a valued servant of the Austrian Crown? Well, she couldn't worry about it now. Once the fireworks began, it might be impossible to find de Lesseps in the crowds, and she needed to return to Dorn's body before Sam got concerned and came searching for her.

∞

Violet eventually found de Lesseps once again seated upon his pavilion, surrounded by Louise-Hélène, Pasha, and a regally dressed couple. Fighting her way through the other dignitaries standing on the stage, Violet arrived at de Lesseps's side, breathless. Once more, she begged a private audience with someone clearly irritated to grant it to her. "This *ees* my first opportunity to greet Prince Henry and Princess Sophie of Holland in days. We have barely spoken since the Nile cruise, and now you wish to create a disturbance. Very well." He threw up his hands. "You will excuse me," he said to the others, who graciously nodded.

Prince Henry's face was as long and sharp as Princess Sophie's was small and squashed, an incongruity given that they were siblings. "*Groeten*," the prince said. "We will enjoy fireworks now."

As if in response to Prince Henry's comment, the first shower of color exploded in the air, in stripes of blue, white, and red, resembling the French tricolor flag.

As the crowds oohed and aahed their appreciation, Violet led de Lesseps to a far corner of the stage away from the direction of the fireworks, and once more explained what happened. Where Franz-Josef was impassive, de Lesseps was outraged, only not for the reason Violet would have expected.

"The audacity!" he exploded as though he were his own fireworks barrage. "How dare this man attempt to ruin my canal opening by dying like this! It *ees* most inconsiderate. I will talk to Franz-Josef about the quality of his servants. I find it highly unacceptable that he would bring along someone so ill as to create this *ravage* to my time of celebration. I will have—"

"Monsieur, I do not believe the man was ill," Violet said, getting irritated herself with his callous response. Was no one involved in the canal opening capable of the slightest bit of grief? She dropped her voice. "I think he may have been murdered. Poisoned."

"Again with this, madame? You are nearly hysterical, finding criminals behind every palm tree and sand dune. Perhaps you are also interested in seeing the celebrations ruined. Why else would you continue to suggest such things?"

Another round of fireworks exploded, this time in the red and white of the Ottoman Empire. With de Lesseps's attitude, Violet was starting to see red herself. "What you suggest is perfectly ridiculous, monsieur. There have now been three suspicious deaths in less than two days and I—"

"None of them have been suspicious except in your own mind, madame. Besides, everyone knows that the Austrians are drug addicts and that *ees* undoubtedly how he died." Thus having reached his own conclusion, de Lesseps held up his hands as if to ask if there were anything further to discuss.

Perhaps Violet should have been used to this by now, but it chafed badly, especially since de Lesseps had given her nominal permission to conduct an investigation. Best to do what she could for Karl Dorn. "We must discuss what is to be done with the body."

"Have you spoken to Franz-Josef?"

"Yes, and he wanted me to speak with you and take care of the matter. I recommend—" But there was to be no sympathy from de Lesseps.

"I will have Pasha provide some servants to pick up the body and dispose of it so that this episode can be quickly forgotten. I have bigger things to worry about than this, Madame Harper. The future of the world rests on my shoulders."

As if to emphasize his words, another burst of fireworks plumed into the air, this time erupting in an ironic pattern of three bands: one red, one white, then another red one; the same as the Austrian flag that flew above Franz-Josef's ship. Distracted by it, Violet's gaze took in the pavilion in which she stood, and she noticed that Eugénie and Franz-Josef seemed to be in a cozy tête-à-tête onstage.

Except they weren't. In fact, at second glance they appeared to be arguing. Arguing so violently that Eugénie pulled away from the emperor and walked to where Prince Henry and Princess Sophie were standing. Eugénie presented her back to Franz-Josef, and with sagging shoulders he disappeared among the other royal onlookers.

The distraction, though, did not diminish Violet's outrage. The utter callousness of these privileged people was causing her temper to heat up rapidly. "Monsieur, I shall not permit this. Herr Dorn is an Austrian who should be returned to his homeland, not tossed in some unmarked grave like an unwanted stray dog. I insist that he be preserved for the duration of the ceremonies so that he can be taken home and properly buried in a Christian manner wherever his family so dictates."

De Lesseps shook his head with outright disgust. "Madame Harper, you try my very soul. Bah, do as you will, just leave me in peace so that I can bask in my moment of recognition."

The Frenchman returned to Louise-Hélène, Eugénie, and the prince and princess of Holland, not once looking back at Violet. She would have happily left him in peace through the entire festivities were it not for the fact that no one seemed to care that men were dying at an alarming rate here.

At least she had permission to take care of Karl Dorn, which would set her mind at ease, knowing she was doing all she could for the man. Unfortunately, it wouldn't be enough.

Violet retrieved her new undertaking bag—now full with its transferred supplies from *Newport*—then directed Sam and the other Americans to move Dorn to *Viribus Unitis*. Sailors on the Austrian ship guided them down to Dorn's quarters, which were near the emperor's but of course much smaller and less ostentatious. Sailors hurried to place multiple lanterns in the room for illumination. Violet then requested a bucket of clean water, some soap, and a few rags, which were promptly produced for her.

Meanwhile, the Americans started to unceremoniously drop Dorn onto the floor of his tidy cabin, but Violet intercepted them and instructed them to lay the Austrian on his bed. Mott and his men departed to watch what remained of the fireworks show, leaving Violet and Sam together with the corpse.

"I've never actually seen you at work," Sam said. "I admit I'm rather curious."

This gave Violet a quick flash of inspiration. "Would you like to help me?"

"Help you? How so?"

Sam hadn't recoiled at the idea, which she took as a good sign.

"Well, first, I need Herr Dorn to be comfortable." She knelt down next to the body, and Sam followed suit. With a light touch, Violet began smoothing out Dorn's clothing, which had become rumpled, and she lowered her voice to talk to him.

"Is it true that you wanted to kill yourself, sir? I can't believe it to be so. You would have done such a thing here, in the privacy of your cabin, wouldn't you?"

Sam stopped her as if she were losing her wits. "My dear, you are speaking to a corpse."

She nodded. "Yes, it calms me for the work ahead. I think it is also respectful of the dead. Perhaps part of his spirit remains, hovering and watching, until he is successfully interred." Violet had never before uttered that tiny concern she always kept locked away in the back of her mind. "I need him to feel confident that I will competently care for him until the moment his body is committed to the ground."

"I see." Sam grew very quiet as he watched Violet proceed with her work of disrobing and washing Dorn, then redressing him, working against time in case rigor mortis should set in soon. For her part, she became absorbed in the task and nearly forgot that her husband was present until it was time to embalm the body. She rose and went to her large, new tapestry satchel, nearly tripping over a small chest that must have slipped out from its resting place beneath Dorn's bed. Violet shoved it back under with her foot and opened her bag. She was disappointed to remember that she had purposely not packed any of her embalming fluid, a concoction of ingredients known only to herself, as she didn't want to risk the bottle breaking on the journey.

However was she to preserve Dorn's body until he could be returned home? It might be weeks before he was reunited with his family and buried properly. She frowned, thinking, and then suddenly remembered what she had seen aboard *Newport*.

"Sam, do you think you could go topside and find me some pitch?" she asked.

"You mean . . . what they use on rope?"

"Yes. It preserves the rope against rain and salt, and it is sometimes used as a preservative for bodies," Violet said.

He nodded. "I'll be back in a moment."

True to his word, Sam returned in a few minutes with a small bucket of the pine tar oil while she set out her implements. The potent odor quickly filled the tiny room. "I recommend that we work quickly," Violet said as she positioned Dorn's limbs into what resembled a comfortable resting pose.

Over the next hour, Violet silently led her husband through the embalming process, first having him pour the pitch into her pump canister, then demonstrating how she made incisions at the femoral artery in the upper thigh and the carotid artery in the neck. Into each incision site, she inserted nozzles attached to long tubes connected to the pump canister. Violet worked the pump to begin flowing the pitch through it and into Dorn's body. Once it was streaming adequately, she had Sam hold the embalming substance high in the air so that gravity would maintain the flow. She moved Dorn's chamber pot next to the bed to serve as a collection receptacle for the man's blood, which coursed out from his leg, pushed out by the pitch.

"Good Lord, this stinks to high heaven," Sam grumbled.

"Yes, my own preparation isn't nearly this bad. I'm worried

that it will make his complexion an odd color, too, but I have a good blend of cosmetic massage that hopefully will improve his skin tone." She looked down at Dorn and promised, "I will do my best for you."

Once he was embalmed, Sam took the chamber pot from the room without being asked, and returned with it rinsed out. Violet didn't want to know how he explained that to the crew.

With Sam observing and handing her implements, Violet completed the process, using a little more pitch in Dorn's mouth and pressing it closed to prevent it falling open. She used a few drops of her own fish glue, which was an exceptionally clear adhesive, to seal his eyes shut. A hair combing, the application of Medium Taupe No. 6 on his hands, face, and neck, and Herr Dorn almost looked as if he were sleeping.

Again considerate, Sam helped her with putting away her tools. Her work thus concluded, Violet thought to issue some instructions to the sailors for leaving the body undisturbed for the remainder of the journey in Egypt and back to Austria. But she remembered that sailors were a superstitious lot and so there was little danger of them entering Dorn's cabin.

She was more worried about someone climbing aboard and removing the body, but perhaps that was just nerves after what had happened to the bodies of the lumberyard owner's son and the Egyptian ship captain. Surely no one would touch the valued servant of a royal delegation member.

Violet remained quiet as she and Sam returned to their tent. They agreed not to return to the dwindling festivities so they could rest for the next day, which would feature a daylong picnic and a fancy ball in the evening. Lying in their new, luxurious tent, though, did not bring Violet sleep any more easily than she had obtained it last night aboard *Newport*. Her mind whirled with questions about the three dead men, whether their deaths were related or just a trio of completely coincidental accidents.

Herr Dorn's death might be explained away rationally, but the others . . . ? No, with one man stabbed and another violently struck, all within a single day, it was difficult to come to any conclusion beyond what she knew in her heart to be true.

There was a murderer rampaging through the festivities, and his motive was unfathomable.

chapter 18

November 18, 1869

THE NEW DAWN BROUGHT FOG and a misty rain with it, which perfectly complemented Violet's mood and her muted gown of drab green. However, there were still more festivities scheduled for this afternoon and evening before the flotilla headed down to the terminus of the canal at the Red Sea tomorrow. She and Sam—who was in uniform again today, his ceremonial saber at his side—learned that the London-like weather was not an unusual occurrence in Egypt in November. Nevertheless, the visitors who had been in Egypt for several weeks said that it would all soon burn off, so at the recommendation of someone from the Italian delegation, she and Sam decided to stroll among the merrily striped, Ottoman-crescent-topped tents of the Arab chieftains. They were located along the Avenue of Franz-Josef between Lake Timsah and the canal, with the khedive's palace as a backdrop.

Apparently, the chieftains had been relegated to this area to greet delegation members, instead of holding honored positions themselves in the ceremonies.

With their umbrellas in hand, Sam and Violet entered the makeshift street, and it appeared that all of the delegation had had the same idea, for the area was flooded with visitors carrying black umbrellas, all determined to lose themselves in revelry despite the gloom of the morning.

Violet could easily see that the chieftains' tents, unlike their own private tent with fabric walls, were merely tall canopies hastily staked to the ground. Despite their rudimentary design, though, many of them were variously festooned with green garlands, fluttering multihued ribbons, and dangling, clinking strings of colorful beads.

Inside the tents, the chiefs, in their customary cultural garb of simple white garments topped with wide belts and fur-trimmed robes, called out eager invitations to passersby to come in for coffee, sherbet, and other appetizing treats. Some did so while stretched out on divans with attentive servants surrounding them. Others stood in the doorways of the tents, hawking their exotic wares in broken English and French to the many European visitors.

Toiling horses and plodding donkeys shared the street with the throng of pedestrians. Not even the valiant efforts of certain workers, whose sole purpose was to push carts up and down the street and scoop up the fresh dung, could keep up with the ever-increasing number of droppings. Violet found herself time and time again swiftly sidestepping piles of fresh manure, steaming and rank in the warm, drizzly morning.

Spotting someone he recognized, Sam led her to a gaily striped tent where a bearded chieftain lay inelegantly sprawled on a cerulean-blue divan set low on a gold-patterned carpet. Violet imagined he neither sat down nor rose without the help of several people.

The chieftain laughed throatily as Sam ushered Violet into the tent. With a wave of casual salutation, he indicated that they should find a seat among the other occupied divans that surrounded his like palm trees about an oasis.

They folded their dripping umbrellas and handed them to servants, who already were holding their hands out expectantly. They settled on a red-and-gold-striped divan, with Violet sitting at one corner that abutted the corner of another sofa.

On the far end of the neighboring divan was Sergeant Purdy,

who greeted Sam enthusiastically. In the center of the sofa was Théophile Gautier, who was passing a long, thin carved pipe with a jewel-encrusted bowl to the man who sat on the corner adjoining Violet's seat. A sweet aroma wafted up from the pipe, mercifully masking the stench of the street dung.

Purdy had cleaned up considerably since Violet initially met him two nights ago. He had trimmed his hair, and his lean frame and handsome but weather-beaten face marked him as someone who had spent many a day in the saddle.

Introductions were made. The chieftain's name was Yamlik, and the unfamiliar man on the divan next to Violet's was a Prussian named Richard Lepsius.

Lepsius, with flowing white hair and mustache and tiny round glasses perched on the end of his nose, held an air of gentleness around him like a soft blanket. He was an Egyptologist who had led a scientific expedition to Egypt in the early 1840s, and then returned to teach at the University of Berlin. Three years ago, he had come back to Egypt for another expedition, whereupon he had discovered the Decree of Canopus.

"What was this decree?" she asked. Violet was woefully ignorant of Egyptian time periods, rulers, and accomplishments, despite the Egyptomania that had been sweeping over her country in waves since Napoléon's failed campaign here against Ottoman-British forces seventy years ago. Certainly she knew that the entrance to the Egyptian Avenue path within Highgate Cemetery in London was constructed to evoke ancient Egypt, with its bold columns decorated at the base with plaster palm fronds, but such was the extent of any contact she had had on the subject outside of shallow travel booklets.

"It is an inscription on stone, Frau Harper, written in three languages: Egyptian hieroglyphs, Greek, and ancient Egyptian script. Obviously, the Greek on it helped us decipher the Egyptian parts, and we learned that it was the record of a great assembly of priests held at Canopus in 238 BC, which honored the pharaoh Ptolemy III Euergetes and his queen, Berenice. You have perhaps heard of the Rosetta stone that Napoléon's men discovered? That dates to about 196 BC, making the Canopus Decree older." Lepsius sucked on the pipe several times, then leaned back against the divan and blew a column of smoke up into the air. "I do not claim, however, that Canopus is more important than Rosetta, you understand. All of our finds are critical in the understanding of ancient Egyptian culture."

"You must know Monsieur Mariette, then," Violet said. "He has written a book on the digs under his auspices."

"Yes. Mariette is renowned for what he has done in discovering the ancient sites. As for me, my work has been largely in cataloging papyri, drawings, and other archaeological remains, as well as a small attempt in establishing a chronology of Egyptian history. I am honored that the prince asked me to be a member of his delegation."

Yamlik laughed heartily at what was obviously genuine modesty on Lepsius's part. Violet suspected Lepsius had done much in the field of Egyptology, even if Mariette was the acknowledged master.

"Would you like to try the *chibouque*?" Lepsius politely offered the pipe to Violet, but she declined. She had had enough from last night's absinthe and two days' worth of murders, and had no stomach for anything else new. He passed it on to Sam, who smoked appreciatively from it.

"How have you enjoyed your experience in Egypt thus far?" Lepsius inquired. "Beyond what the khedive has provided, which is to make you think you never stepped foot off Europe's shores."

Unwilling to speak of the three deaths, Violet found herself at a loss as to what to say about Egypt. Sam deftly stepped in and told the story of their time in the Arab shopping stalls and of the wonderful treasures they had seen, then shared the incident of the young boy stealing Violet's fan, giving a comical description of their futile and breathless chase after the urchin.

With the group in high spirits and the pipe passing freely among the men, Lepsius said, "Your tale reminds me of the legend that our friend Yamlik here told me yesterday. Highness, tell again the story of the treasure thief."

But Yamlik begged off, encouraging Lepsius to retell the tale. As Lepsius did so, Yamlik chattered at his servants, who disappeared and returned with plates of pastries stuffed with custard and covered in a sweet syrup.

Leaning back and closing her eyes to more fully appreciate both the treats and the story, Violet became entranced by Lepsius's words.

"Long ago," the Egyptologist began, his accented voice low and warm, "Rameses III became pharaoh. Egypt grew prosperous under his reign, and Rameses began to gather his treasures together in the form of gold, silver, and priceless gems. As his hoard grew, Rameses became very anxious about someone stealing his treasure."

"When I build up my treasure one day, I'll protect it with my Schofield revolver," Purdy interrupted.

Sam laughed. "Any plug-ugly with a slingshot and a pebble could knock you from your guard post."

"You're an idiot," Purdy retorted good-naturedly.

Lepsius continued skillfully, evoking images of Egypt several millennia ago. "So Rameses asked his master builder, Horemheb, to build him a mighty treasure-house made of stone, one so thick and strong that no man could ever force his way into it. Horemheb did *zis*, erecting a pyramid over the new building, with a great treasure chamber at the center of the building. Pharaoh's valuables could only be accessed through three sets of doors: one of stone, one of iron, and one of bronze. The doors were locked and secured with Pharaoh's great seal, and Rameses rewarded Horemheb richly for his work, which set Pharaoh's mind at ease."

"I wish I had pen and paper," Gautier said. "For I sense a great tragedy coming which could be reproduced onstage." He said no more, for the pipe passed back to him.

"But Horemheb had played his master false, having constructed a secret passage inside the thick wall of the treasure-house, accessible only to the one who knew where the secret spring was that would open the entrance to the passage."

Gautier slid the pipe to Purdy. "Ah, act two, scene four. Pharaoh catches servant stealing treasure and has him sealed away alive inside the pyramid, where only the intervention of Horus can save him," the playwright guessed.

Lepsius shook his head and pushed his glasses farther up onto his nose. "Nothing so simple. Horemheb stole unnoticeable little bits and pieces of the treasure for several years, but before he died of an illness, he told his two sons about the secret entrance to the treasure room. Horemheb's sons were stupid and greedy, and began to plunder the valuables to the point that Pharaoh soon noticed his treasure's depletion."

"The sons must be in your employ, Harper, since they are so brainless," Purdy said, needling Sam.

"*Non*, the sons are the great comic relief to my play," Gautier said.

"Gentlemen, *please*," Violet admonished as she picked up another square of pastry. "Let us have the rest of the story."

Lepsius picked up the thread of his broken narrative. "Since the seals were never broken and the doors never opened, Rameses was at a loss to figure out how the treasure was being stolen. He had traps and snares set inside the treasure-house, and sure enough, one night the brothers went in and one of them was caught inside a trap from which there was no escape.

"He begged the second brother to kill him, strike off his head to make him unidentifiable, and sneak back out of the treasure-house with the head. 'For,' the first brother said. 'I cannot get out of *zis* snare, and when Pharaoh's men find me in the morning, I shall be tortured and killed anyway, and then they will come for you and possibly our mother.'

"The second brother did as requested, decapitating his brother and fleeing from the treasure-house. The next morning, Pharaoh's men found a headless man caught in their trap, more treasure gone, and still none of the seals into the treasure-house had been broken. Outraged at the cleverness of the thief, Rameses had the first brother's body hung from the walls of the palace, instructing his guards to keep watch for anyone who might come along to claim the body or to weep over it.

"But determined to retrieve his brother's body and reunite it with the head so that it could be properly buried—lest it wander the world as a ghost lost upon the earth—the second brother was more clever still."

Lepsius paused for dramatic effect. He had no need to do so, for the group around him was enraptured. "He pretended to be a wine merchant, carrying loads of wine skins on a donkey, and managed to position himself to pass by the soldiers' encampment near the palace wall, causing his donkey to bump up against one of theirs. In the distraction of braying and jostling, the brother secretly slashed holes in several of the wine skins he carried, sending the precious fluid splashing out, and set up a loud wailing, lamenting the fact that his cargo of excellent wine was being lost. The soldiers greedily rushed over, saying they would help the false merchant, and instead put their mouths to the wine skins and drank themselves insensible. Once they were snoring on the ground with their mouths open, the brother cut down his brother's body, put it over the back of his donkey, and left with it.

"The next morning, Rameses was furious, and after punishing the incompetent soldiers, Pharaoh set his own trap, by setting up one of his daughters near the city gate, offering her own hand to the man who could tell her the cleverest tale of the most wicked deed he had ever committed in his life."

The pipe passed back to Lepsius once more, and he drew deeply from it, then coughed. "Needs more," he said, and a servant removed the pipe from his hands to tamp out the ashes and refill it with fresh leaves. Once Lepsius had a newly lit pipe in his hands, he resumed the story.

"The treasure thief knew at once who the maiden was and her purpose in asking the question. Determined to outwit Pharaoh once more, he went to visit the princess at twilight. Under his robes he carried the arm of a man who had just been executed for treason. 'Fair princess, I would have you as my wife, and will therefore tell you the story of the most wicked act I have ever committed.' As the sun went down behind the hills that hid the Valley of the Kings, the brother told all, concluding, '. . . and so, the wickedest thing I ever did was to cut off my brother's head when he was caught in Pharaoh's trap in the treasure-house, then hid it, and later stole his body out from beneath the noses of Pharaoh's guard.'

"Pharaoh's daughter grabbed the thief by the arm and called out to the guards that she had finally captured her father's prey. But she discovered that all she had in her hand was the arm of the executed criminal, and the thief had escaped into the darkness; thus had Pharaoh been tricked a final time.

"When Pharaoh Rameses heard about what happened, he said, 'Zis man is too wily to be punished! Go, and tell the thief that I will pardon him and give him my daughter in marriage, as promised. If he serves me well and faithfully, I will reward him in an even greater manner.' So in the end, the treasure thief married the royal princess, became the loyal servant of Rameses, and never had need to enter the treasure-house again."

As if to raise the curtain on the story, the fog began dissipating and the sun's rays tentatively peered out from behind the clouds. Inside the tent, there was silence except for the crackling of tobacco as the pipe was passed among the men.

"Is this story true?" Violet asked.

The chieftain spread his hands. "How could it not be true?" he said.

Violet was reminded of Auguste Mariette, who felt that the khedive was the equivalent of a treasure thief of Egypt's ancient artifacts. Of course, in the khedive's version of the story, Mariette would be Rameses, who was gathering all of the treasure into a secure location.

There was no more time to contemplate the legend, for horns began to blow, summoning guests to the picnic now commencing on the grounds near de Lesseps's villa. There were the usual decorations—streamers, flags, garlands, and arches—and somehow statues of both de Lesseps and Pasha had been transported in to stand proudly next to each other in the middle of it all. Small stages set up around the enormous picnicking area suggested there were to be multiple entertainments, but there were no royal-sized pavilions here.

Violet and Sam had hardly found spots at one of the hundreds of tables scattered around in ordered chaos. The tables, with their fluttering cloths and white wood chairs—apparently there was to be no reuse of last night's velvet stuffed seats—seated anywhere from four to twelve people. This time it appeared there was to be no special section for the sovereigns: they mingled with all levels of the delegation. Sam and Violet found themselves with Prince Henry and Princess Sophie of Holland, whom she had just met the previous day onstage.

There was little time to get to know either of Their Majesties, however, for Julie Lesage came to their table, insistent that she speak to Violet, *immédiatement!*

CHAPTER 19

LEAVING POOR SAM TO MAKE entertaining talk with the royal personages, Violet followed Eugénie's maid as she wove her way through the haphazardly placed picnic tables and beyond the earshot of anyone attending the event.

"Please, Madame Harper, a little farther," Julie urged as Violet began to hesitate. Why did they need to move so far away from the festivities for Julie to make a comment to Violet?

Julie slowed down, and Violet realized they were now on the outskirts of some tiny local village. The undertaker's discomfort with being this distance away from Sam and the others was making her stomach do somersaults. She was about to insist that they turn back when Julie stopped.

"I believe this is private enough for us," Eugénie's maid said, at last turning to face Violet.

They were in the shadow of a small tiled building, and Violet instantly recognized it for what it was, another mausoleum. "You wish to speak to me *here*, mademoiselle?" she said.

"Yes, this is comfortable enough, isn't it? This little house gives us shade."

Violet bit her lip against revealing the truth about the "little house." "As you wish," she replied.

"Madame Harper, I did not see you again after Monsieur Dorn's unfortunate demise." Julie readjusted her hat as she said this, tucking up loose strands of hair.

"No, I had responsibilities for caring for his body, and then I returned to my tent for the evening." Why was the girl so interested in Violet's whereabouts?

"Of course, that makes sense, yes." Julie stood there, tapping her hands together as if contemplating what to say next.

"Mademoiselle, you could have asked me this question at my table. Is there something else you wish to know?" If Violet hadn't known better, she would have said that Julie Lesage was downright nervous.

Julie opened and closed her mouth several times, then finally blurted, "I believe I am in danger."

Of the many things she had thought the girl might confide, Violet certainly hadn't expected *that*.

"In danger? How could this possibly be?"

"Monsieur Dorn, he was a servant of His Highness Franz-Josef. Captain Naser, he was a servant of the khe—"

"How do you know about the ship's captain and what his name was?" Violet demanded.

Julie looked at Violet as if she were a simpleton. "Madame, I float aboard *L'Aigle*, and Her Highness and Monsieur de Lesseps speak freely in front of me, since I am, after all, a lady's maid with no ears and no mind, *non?* There is little that happens that I do not know about."

Violet wondered exactly how much Julie knew about her mistress, but said nothing, waiting to see what more the maid had to say.

"There was also the death at the lumberyard, the owner's son. He, too, was like a servant to the khedive." Julie looked at Violet expectantly. What did she want Violet to say?

"I suppose we might look at it that way, but—"

"*Exactement!*" Julie cried, reaching out a hand to grab Violet's, as though they had come to an understanding together. "I have given this great consideration, and I believe that the servants of the sovereigns in attendance are dying." Julie dropped her voice into a theatrical whisper that would have made Gautier proud. "That they are being *murdered*, Madame Harper."

Violet froze. She and Julie shared a similar conclusion, although it had not occurred to Violet that all of those killed could be classified as servants. Was that the commonality across them all? "We do not know that they were murdered," she began, in order to calm the girl. "That is merely speculation. Herr Dorn may have overimbibed, and the ship's captain, he was known to—"

"You do not believe that any more than I do," Julie stated flatly.

Violet was silent, unable to argue with Eugénie's maid.

"You see then that I am in danger?" Julie said, squeezing Violet's hand.

"I'm afraid I do not," Violet said to comfort her. "The deceased were all men who had responsibilities away from their masters during the festivities, whereas you—" A thought was occurring to Violet, but she had no time to contemplate it because Julie was determined to be hysterical in her theory.

"How can you not understand? I, too, am the servant of a great and powerful sovereign! In fact, I travel with both de Lesseps and the empress, making me doubly in peril. *Mon Dieu*, I shall lose my mind if the murderer is not caught soon. That is, if I am not *morte* before then. Madame Harper, you must help me."

Violet felt helpless as she removed her hand from Julie's firm clutch. "Mademoiselle, first, we must avoid being overly distraught and think this through. If it comforts you, remember that—if your theory is true, that these servants have been murdered—it has only happened when they have been far away from their masters. You are almost always with the empress and her entourage, so there is little danger to you."

Julie frowned, clearly having not considered this. "So you are saying that as long as I stay close to my mistress, I will be safe?"

"I believe so, yes."

Julie tapped her hands together again. "There is more. I believe there is something—how do you English say it?—*fishy* with Isabelle Dumont."

"The future Madame de Lesseps's maid? What do you mean?"

Once again, Violet's stomach turned somersaults, reflecting on the strange actions she had witnessed herself.

"She is not what she seems to be, Madame Harper, of this I am certain. She has not the skill to be a lady's maid. Mademoiselle de Bragard's hair is disastrous, and her dresses are never adjusted properly."

"She may simply not have your own excellent skill, Julie," Violet said soothingly.

The maid shook her head. "No, it is more than that. She is incompetent, and it makes no sense that the future wife of Ferdinand de Lesseps should have her. Any *femme de chambre* would be happy to have such an exalted position. It is not as exalted as mine, you understand, but it is highly respectable nonetheless. Why does she choose a girl who doesn't know the difference between eau de cologne and perfume? *Non.*" Julie shook her head again. "There is something very wrong with Isabelle Dumont."

Of what, exactly, was Julie accusing Isabelle? Was she merely jealous of her fellow maid, who seemed to have more freedom than she did? Was there a secret rivalry between the two that Julie was not revealing?

With assurances that she would contemplate all that Julie had told her, Violet was finally able to lead the woman back to the picnic area, and Julie went on to reunite with her mistress. Violet returned to her own table, where she was gratified to see that Sam had the Dutch royalty doubled over in hearty laughter, since it gave her an opportunity to be alone with her own thoughts. Those thoughts were cascading in a terrible direction. Was it really possible that servants *were* being targeted for some particular reason? Perhaps their work behind the scenes on behalf of their rulers caused them to witness deeds that were better left unseen. But what could those doings possibly be?

Moreover, if Julie's theory were true, it was quite likely that another servant would be attacked. Worse yet, it was completely impossible to know who it would be or how soon it would happen.

The picnic featured staggering entertainments, leaving Violet to wonder why she continued to be amazed. Today there was an extraordinary demonstration of Bedouin horsemen. They were clad in robes and complicated head scarves, galloping to and fro on their horses bedecked in fringed cloths, shouting and firing off their muskets, to the great amusement of the guests. This was followed by another demonstration by Thaddeus Mott's soldiers, who fired their rifles in precision as their horses stepped in time to a drummed tattoo. It was a different sort of showmanship altogether, one that sent whispers rippling through the crowd about American military expertise.

Naturally, the smaller stages were occupied at various times by desert orchestras playing raucous music. High-pitched singers and other performers offered every last drop of their energies to please the crowds, and they were rewarded with cheers, clapping, and even the occasional tossing of coins.

The most enthusiastic reception was saved for the female dancers announced as *ghawazee*. Scantily clad in long transparent gowns, they performed quick, hypnotically sinuous dances to beating drums and castanets. Sparkling ornaments adorned their hair, their eyes were bordered with thick lines of kohl, and their hands and feet were stained with henna. It was difficult to look away from them as they gyrated sensuously about the stage.

Violet eventually excused herself to visit one of the many necessary buildings constructed to suit European sensibilities. Princess Sophie had earlier told her that she had accidentally wandered into one of the necessaries meant for locals and that the primitive holes in the ground were shocking. The specially constructed tents for the delegations were, naturally, quite a distance away to keep offending odors away from the revelers; therefore, Violet found herself walking beyond the khedive's palace to reach them.

She saw that quick progress was being made on preparation for the evening's ball. Workers swarmed all over the grounds, erecting a long entry canopy as well as gazebos on either side of its starting point. There were the usual hangings of garlands and streamers on torchère posts, fencing, and any other nonmoving object. Scenic backdrops were also constructed, evocative of stage settings. Violet wondered what they were for.

The workers chattered, joked, and sang as they continued their work. After Violet visited the toilets, she returned to the outer edge of the construction area to watch the work being conducted. Would this hive of activity really be complete in just a few hours, ready for what was sure to be the glittering spectacle of gem-encrusted gowns and medal-laden jackets?

Her doubts were allayed, though, as in a matter of just a few minutes an extraordinary amount of work was completed. Already there were men stretching out the fabric to be laid atop the entry tent poles.

Violet's attention was distracted by a perspiring man working on one of the gazebos. He looked familiar. She watched as he cleaned up scattered scraps of wood and used nails; then she realized who he was and approached him.

"Pardon me," she said, but jumped back when he looked up in irritation and growled at her. Then recognition dawned in his own eyes, and he stood and bowed.

"Good afternoon, my lady." His English was very carefully spoken, as if he were having to focus on getting each word right.

"Good day, Rashad. I am Violet Harper."

He nodded as he tossed a handful of bent nails into a bucket. "Undertaker."

"Yes. What are the gazebos intended for?" she asked.

He frowned and shook his head, puzzled.

Violet indicated the structure he was working in. "Yes," he said. "For music." He imitated the playing of a violin, which made Violet laugh aloud. Pleased, he finally relaxed and offered a toothy grin himself.

"So you do this work in addition to being a porter for the khedive?" she asked.

"Everyone works at what they are told, my lady. Except for men like my brother, Hassan, who must be at khedive's side at all times."

If Hassan was by the khedive at all times, he was likely in little danger, but what about Rashad and all of the other workers here? Had any of them witnessed anything whatsoever that might put them in danger? Who might be next?

"You should be careful," Violet said on impulse.

He looked at her quizzically again. "Of what, my lady?"

"Of . . . of . . . dangerous people who might harm you." *What a ridiculous cautionary statement, Violet Harper,* she admonished herself.

"I am strong, my lady, and do not need protection," Rashad assured her. "But do need to work."

Another thought struck her. "Do you remember both the ship's captain, Captain Naser, and the lumberyard owner's son, Yusef Halabi? You and your brother removed their bodies."

Rashad wrinkled his nose in obvious distaste of the memory. "Yes, had to remove bodies. Very bad."

"Yes. Where did you take them?" she pressed.

"To proper Egyptian burial, my lady," he said patiently.

"Did you bury them yourself?" Violet wondered if the men had been reunited with their families.

But at this, Rashad bristled. "You are British woman, why do you need to know? You do not think Rashad does proper job? Pasha will tell you that Rashad is very good, very loyal."

Violet realized she had completely overstepped her bounds with the Egyptian. "Forgive me, of course you are. I'm afraid my curiosity is always ahead of my manners. Thank you for your time."

He bowed politely and went back to his work.

Violet returned to the picnic, her mind whirling. Was Julie Lesage correct in her notion that servants were being targeted? If so, was Violet overlooking an entire pool of servants at risk of death? But with no definite proof that it was true, or what the motive could be, or even an inkling as to who might be committing the crimes, what could Violet possibly do to protect anybody?

Fortunately, Violet had not been missed during her long absence. Sir Henry Elliot and Asa Brooks had joined the prince and princess, and a deck of cards and piles of coins were spread on the table. According to Sir Henry, who was serving as the game's banker, Sam had disappeared to join his American friends.

Violet sighed, wondering if she should search for Sam or just let him be.

She spent some time watching the faro game, declining to join in the play as her thoughts would never have permitted her to focus on the rapid flipping of cards.

Brooks eventually engaged Violet in conversation as the game continued. "So, Mrs. Harper, have you been interacting with the locals?"

Had he witnessed her discussion with Rashad? "Why do you ask me this?" she said, more sharply than she intended. Everyone lowered their cards to look at her, and Violet found herself apologizing for the second time in less than an hour.

"I mean, yes, I have met several Egyptians. A very friendly people. I met an Arab chieftain this morning, as well," she said.

Brooks nodded as everyone returned to laying bets on cards. "I offer you caution. Many of Pasha's servants are former corvée labor, and are reputed to be stealing valuables directly off the delegates as they walk by. The Prince of Wales himself nearly had a pearl cufflink stripped directly from his person."

Sir Henry nodded in agreement. "The *fellahin* are also enjoying the easy finds. You remember the child who stole your fan at the Arab market?"

Princess Sophie gasped, making a wheezing sound as she did so. She and her brother immediately searched their persons and were satisfied that all of their accoutrements were in place. Violet self-consciously reached up to where she had pinned her ankh this morning, relieved to find it was still there. "I shall be careful," she assured Brooks.

But inside, she was confused. Were the servants truly at risk from some malevolent force? Or was it the delegation in peril?

Or was it both?

Eventually tiring of watching the card game, at which Mr. Brooks was winning quite a hoard of coins, Violet decided to find Sam. As Sir Henry had said, he was with his American friends. The horses had already been stabled again somewhere, and the men were showing off their sabers to one another. Sam had his own ceremonial sword out, and had just laid the blade across Mott's hand. Mott balanced the blade in his palm and nodded approvingly.

Mott was the first to notice Violet's arrival. He handed the sword back to Sam and greeted her with, "The fetching Mrs. Harper has graced us again with her presence. Surely you do us honor." He swept his hat off his head, while Sam came and cupped Violet protectively by the elbow.

"Sweetheart, are you feeling well?" he asked. "You look plumb worn out."

This was no time to explain her dread and confusion over what might be happening at the ceremonies. "Fear not, I'm well. Just a little overwhelmed."

Caleb Purdy, who had been with them earlier in the chieftain's tent, laughed. "And Harper calls *me* names. That's no way to talk to your wife. Tell her she's comely and a vision in green."

The other Americans hooted at Sam, who rolled his eyes. Violet felt that she was intruding in the men's sacred space. She was about to say her good-byes to perhaps find Louise-Hélène, but she noticed that Purdy's expression suddenly seemed odd. "Sir, are you quite all right?" she asked.

"Never better," he said, but his assurances seemed feeble. His pupils were constricted and his hands began to shake. The hairs on the back of Violet's neck began to prickle as she realized whom else she had seen in this condition.

"Perhaps you should sit down, sir," she suggested calmly, approaching him.

"I'm truly fine, ma'am. I'm just—just—" Purdy held out an arm, and two of his comrades helped him find a seat on the ground. He was sweating profusely now.

Violet knelt down in front of him. "Mr. Purdy, what did you do after we left the chieftain's tent this morning?"

"What did I do? What do you mean?" His color was distinctly ashen now. "I suppose I wandered about, had a bowl of *kushari*, watched the *ghawazee*. Spent time with this bunch of simpletons." He laughed again, but this time it was weak and he swayed a little with the effort.

His mates surrounded him, clapping him on the back and attempting to revive him with ribald jokes. Violet saw no use in it, but surprisingly, within a few minutes Purdy's color began to return. Within another few minutes, he had risen from his seated position on the ground, pretending that nothing had happened.

Whatever had poisoned Dorn had poisoned Purdy, of this Violet was sure, except that Purdy had not ingested as much and was therefore most fortunate to be alive right now. What Dorn and Purdy had in common, she had no idea.

Especially since Caleb Purdy was no servant.

chapter 20

L ATER, AS VIOLET AND HER husband rested in their tent prior to the evening's planned extravaganza, Sam could talk of nothing but what had happened to Purdy. In fact, Sam was not resting at all, but was instead pacing across the floor of the tent. He, too, had realized that Purdy had nearly died and that his death would have been much like Dorn's.

Violet told Sam of Julie's opinion that servants were being targeted for murder.

"That woman is foolish," Sam said, dismissing the maid's dread. "Purdy was hardly a servant, nor was the ship's captain, nor the lumberyard man."

Sam's words echoed her own thoughts. "Right. But perhaps in Egyptian eyes, all workers who perform services for the khedive are servants."

Sam paused thoughtfully, resting his elbow against a chest of drawers. Some servant had removed the jasmine blooms in the vase and replaced them with palm fronds. In an analytical tone he began, "Let's assume that is true. What difference does it make? What impact do a bunch of servants have on the politics at play in the opening of the canal?" He crossed his feet as he contemplated it further. "If some varmint was determined to ruin the festivities, why not poison the emperor himself? The death of his chamberlain, while a tragedy, does nothing to bring a cloud over de Lesseps or Pasha."

Violet, sitting on their bed, held up both hands, palms facing upward in supplication. "Excellent questions. Is it possible that in the course of their work they witnessed something that required the murderer to silence them?"

Sam contemplated this as he fingered the edges of the palm fronds. "Perhaps. But never in my born days could I imagine what the three men would have all witnessed. None of them associate with the same people, nor do they perform remotely the same work, nor do they all have the same master. I am at a loss to come up with an answer."

So was Violet. However, it was a relief to discuss it with Sam, and to know that he was now viewing the deaths as seriously as she did.

With no warning, Sam abruptly changed subjects. "What will happen with Dorn's body?"

"Presumably he will be left in peace until *Viribus Unitis* returns to Austria."

"It doesn't seem right that he should be left exposed like that for what might be a week or more. We should have put a winding sheet on him."

Violet was impressed by Sam's instinctive funerary acumen. "You know, you're right. We could have wrapped him in his own bed linens. I'm afraid I was so distracted by everything else that it didn't occur to me that I should consider covering him."

Their conversation was interrupted by a messenger delivering a note to Violet from Louise-Hélène, requesting that Violet come to her quarters at de Lesseps's villa so that they could prepare together for the evening's festivities.

"That's rather an odd request, don't you think?" Sam asked as he read the missive over her shoulder.

Violet folded the note and tossed it next to the vase. "Perhaps, but it could be that she is just seeking friendship. I feel pity for her, so young and naive, and now set to marry a much older man who is the toast of the world. She must be overwhelmed."

As she began putting together a bag of items for clothing herself that evening, Sam said, "Since I will obviously not be able to accompany you to the ball tonight—a fact I find most distressing since I looked forward to making a grand entry with you—I suggest that while you are with the future Madame de Lesseps that I return to the Austrian ship and wrap Dorn's body. Then I'll meet you at the palace later."

Violet bit down on the *No!* that immediately bubbled up. After all, *she* was the undertaker and should supervise any funerary activities. Sam was experienced in death as it related to war, but he had not properly managed a corpse on his own, and—

She stopped. All Sam was asking to do was to wrap a corpse. Women did it for their relatives all the time. What he proposed to do was rational and easily accomplished and did not require Violet's presence. Moreover, the sailors aboard *Viribus Unitis* already recognized Sam and surely would not stop him, even if the emperor was back on board and preparing for the evening himself.

"I think that is a perfect idea, and I thank you for doing it, but don't let Harry know that you're instructing me or I'll never hear the end of it," she said, referring to her business partner at Morgan Undertaking, Harry Blundell.

When Violet left their tent to head up to de Lesseps's villa, Sam was whistling a contented tune softly to himself. At least there was one thing to be happy about on this trip.

☾☽

Louise-Hélène's quarters inside the villa were befitting of a queen. Commanding a full half of the villa's second floor, with the other half occupied by de Lesseps, her suite of rooms boasted herringboned olive wood floors and gilded moldings. Exquisite crystal chandeliers hung from the ceilings, fringed floor-to-ceiling draperies blocked out what were surely blistering summer suns, and illusionary paintings on the walls and ceiling stunned the eye. The furniture looked to be exact copies from Versailles. Dominating the sleeping chamber was a massive carved poster bed, awash in embroidered coverings and hangings.

Louise-Hélène seemed very tiny and insignificant surrounded

by such grandeur.

"Ah, Madame Harper, you are most welcome." The young woman made her way across the large expanse of floor in her receiving room, and took both of Violet's hands eagerly in hers. She was in the beginning stages of preparation, and wore a long, flowing robe, while her presumably wild mass of hair was bundled up under a turban. "We shall enjoy each other's company, and Isabelle will help us both."

Isabelle held a silk taffeta gown of muted teal. A vision of loveliness, the gown featured a lace panel inset and flared sleeves with matching black lace encircling the elbows and frothing at the ends. It was spectacular, and would be lovely with Louise-Hélène's coloring. Violet's own dress, of emerald green with a pale green overlay drawn up along the hem and edged in simple cream lace, did not compare in the least to the sheer, stunning beauty of Louise-Hélène's gown. Violet was happy to see that the other woman would be able to make a grand entrance dressed so magnificently.

Of course, who knew what Eugénie would be wearing this evening to dwarf every other minor planet to her brilliantly blazing sun?

While Violet unpacked her things, Isabelle went to work on her mistress. The undertaker became painfully aware that Julie had a point about Isabelle's incompetence, for in short order the young woman dropped a set of combs, stuck her mistress with a pin, and dumped talc on the floor.

Louise-Hélène seemed oblivious to Isabelle's shortcomings, though. As Violet waited her turn and watched the proceedings, she realized that Isabelle didn't seem incompetent as much as she seemed nervous. Certainly tonight's culminating event would be enough to set any lady's maid on edge as she attempted to make her mistress the most glittering woman in attendance, but Julie had observed Isabelle's stumblings prior to this evening.

"Do you know what would be a lovely amusement, Madame Harper? Some Turkish sand coffee. Have you had it yet? *Non?* I have developed a taste for it very quickly—ah! oh!—since my arrival in Egypt." Isabelle was tugging mercilessly on a knot in her mistress's hair.

Momentarily breaking free from her maid's ministrations, Louise-Hélène pulled a bell rope dangling nearby. After a few minutes, no servant had shown up, so Louise-Hélène rang again. When that didn't produce the desired result, either, she looked wistfully at Violet. "Might I intrude upon your good nature . . ." She let the request dangle.

Violet nodded. "Of course, mademoiselle." Violet would happily seek out a tray of coffee in order to avoid watching any more of Isabelle's torments.

As Violet walked down the staircase to the lower level to seek out a house servant, she heard arguing voices beneath her. One of them sounded like Pasha. She looked around and saw no one anywhere.

Did she dare?

The argument was increasing in volume, so Violet was able to reach the bottom of the staircase without her footsteps being heard. She glanced around again, feeling for all the world like a guilty little child trying to sneak candy away from the kitchen. On tiptoe, she crept up to the door from which the voices were emanating and put her ear up to it, wondering what she would say if a servant happened to enter the passageway at this very moment.

"You are unreasonable . . . No, I have never said that . . . Tewfik, I—" Pasha's voice was very distinct now, although she still couldn't hear everything being said.

The other man, presumably this Tewfik to whom Pasha referred, had a much higher-pitched voice. ". . . sultan will never allow . . . Orabi says . . . future good of Egypt."

"Tewfik, what you suggest is foolish . . . If the French . . . I cannot allow—"

Tewfik shouted even louder. "You cannot betray the sultan!"

Violet wondered whether de Lesseps and Pasha each provided the other rooms in their respective residences. Guilty over eavesdropping and certain that the volume was going to draw servants any moment, Violet slipped away as quietly as she could, finding a servants' staircase and taking it down into the kitchens. There, she found an Egyptian man who was stacking plates according to size inside a glass cabinet.

After first ensuring that the servant spoke English, Violet made the request for Louise-Hélène's Turkish sand coffee.

He made an odd clucking noise, shaking his head in disapproval. "All of the time she wants the coffee. And she takes it with too much sugar. I make it sweet enough, it does not need so much sugar. Too much risk of burning with adding so much." As he complained, he opened another cabinet and removed a brass-handled copper pot with two spouts, a metal spoon, several sealed jars, a metal cylinder with a brass crank at the top of it, a coffee pot, and a half dozen small, nearly square cups and saucers. He added all of the items to a copper tray.

"You will come?" he said before disappearing through a door at the back of the room.

It was more of a command than a question, and Violet obeyed. She found herself in a tiny courtyard, at the center of which was a little sand pit edged in stones. Chunks of coal were centered in the sand pit, and the Egyptian servant crouched down on the other side of the stones, his worn sandals exposing yellowed toenails. His position looked very uncomfortable, and Violet didn't dare imitate it, lest she not be able to rise again. Instead, she gingerly knelt down on the courtyard tiles, as if she were attending to a corpse.

Violet now realized that the lumps of coal were already heated, glowing red with thin tendrils of smoke rising up from the grains of sand. The servant actually stuck his hand in the sand and stirred up the coals, causing Violet to cringe at the action, but he seemed completely undisturbed by touching the hot chunks.

His first step was to nestle the spouted pot into the hottest part of the pit, so that it was half submerged in sand and coals. He then opened one of the sealed jars and poured in water nearly to the top, then added some sugar from a second jar. As that heated, he removed the crank from the top of the metal cylinder; then, from another of the sealed containers, he poured coffee beans into the cylinder and reattached the crank. Now he operated the crank over the heating pot as finely ground coffee came sprinkling out of the grinder like the coal smuts that forever floated through the London air. When he was satisfied with the amount, he put down the grinder and waited. As the water began to simmer, he stirred the coffee so that the grounds were evenly distributed. As it grew closer to boiling, foam formed on top of the pot, which the servant deftly scooped off with his long-handled spoon. Next he tossed spices in, the fragrant odor suggesting at least clove and cinnamon, plus something aromatic she didn't recognize.

Then he grabbed the brass handle of the pot, which was surely as hot as the pot itself, and tipped the spout into one of the cups, placed it on a saucer, and handed it to Violet. How kind that he was going to have her try it first. She began to lift the cup, and he said "No!" very sternly, motioning for her to put the cup back down into the saucer.

"You must wait," he instructed.

"For how long?" she asked.

"Wait," was all he said, as he poured the remainder of the pot into another cup, then began the process all over again. As he concluded the second grinding of the beans, he said, "You may drink."

Violet raised the cup to her lips, and was surprised by how thick and flavorful it was, so unlike the overboiled coffee she was used to in London shops. And still hot, even after waiting a few minutes. As she finished the cup, she realized that the waiting was to allow the grounds and spices to settle to the bottom of the cup. By this time, the servant was working on his third pot, and he poured it fresh into her cup.

"I will bring all to the lady's rooms," he said.

"No, I can manage it," Violet told him, rising and dusting off her skirts. She allowed him to hand her the tray, from which he removed all of his supplies, just leaving the fragrant cups of coffee. "Thank you," she said, and received a grunt in return, as he was already concentrating on stoking the smoldering embers to keep them lit.

As she walked back in through the kitchens and into the passageway that led upstairs, Violet observed that the tray itself was beautiful. She decided she would take the main staircase when she reached the ground floor, as she was certainly not going to attempt some narrow, winding set of steps to reach Louise-Hélène's rooms and risk tripping over her skirts while carrying these steaming cups.

As Violet reached the bottom of the staircase, she noticed that the coffee cups were decorated with gilded handles and were painted in the bright, bold fashion that she had already become accustomed to here in Egypt. They reminded her of—

She was no longer sure what the painted cups reminded her of, as all she was cognizant of was the loud crack that preceded an intense pain in the back of her head, so acute that she felt both dizzy and numb at the same time. Her last conscious thought was of the tray full of beautiful cups flying out of her hands and up the staircase, the coffee sluicing out of the fragile cups as they smashed against the treads. She crashed against the stairs herself, her forehead receiving the same profound blow as her crown, and she knew nothing else.

chapter 21

VIOLET AWOKE SLOWLY, HER FIRST sense being that of overwhelming pain. Her head hurt so badly it was difficult to even open her eyes. Wherever she was, it was quiet. Utterly silent, in fact. She strained to listen for any noise: the distant braying of a camel, the bellow of a steamship, or even the wailing of Egyptian singers. Anything that Violet had become accustomed to over the past few days.

Nothing.

She attempted once more to open her eyes and take a deep breath, and was rewarded with more blackness and the feeling of something soft against her face, flattening against her lips as she drew air in.

Heavens, how her head throbbed, as though her brain were pushing and pulsing in an attempt to escape through her skull. She was lying on her back, and struggled to lift an arm to press it against her forehead in an attempt to contain the pain, but found that she couldn't move it. Was she paralyzed? No, she could feel her arm and hand straining. In fact—

She moved her hand around and felt sand beneath it. Where was she? This was Egypt, so lying on sand could mean that she was anywhere in the country. A horrific thought struck her: She *was* still in Egypt, wasn't she?

Gradually her senses were coming back, and with them came increased thirst. She licked her parched lips, and tasted both blood and gritty sand as her tongue found the gauzy fabric that seemed to be lightly draped over her face. It was almost as if she were in a . . . a . . . shroud.

The thought stilled her feeble movements. Was she dead? Was she passing into the afterlife? Was this sense of confusion what preceded the great meeting with the Almighty?

Get hold of your senses, Violet Harper, she told herself sternly. *The dead do not have violently clanging headaches, nor are they thirsty.*

No, she definitely was not dead.

But where was she? Was she lying along the canal bank somewhere? If so, why weren't there any stars above her?

Violet wriggled a little, and then she realized that she wasn't just lying on top of sand, but was loosely buried in it. The realization of what must have happened set her heart to pounding, and she stopped moving once more as she fit together the random puzzle pieces.

Someone had struck her while she carried the tray and, believing she was dead, had carried her off and buried her. And *that* awareness gave rise to the certainty of exactly where she was.

She continued her slow but steady squirming, shaking the sand off of her body, until she was finally freed enough to remove the cloth that had been tossed on top of her before some shovelfuls of sand had been added. The effort left her exhausted and panting, but at least she no longer had fabric impairing her breathing.

After a few more minutes, Violet was finally able to rise to one elbow, propping herself up and slowly easing into a seated position. Once upright, she spent a few moments gathering herself together, willing her head to cease its incessant drumbeat. She knew she had to confirm what she believed to be true, so she put out an arm in the inky blackness and began feeling her way around.

As expected, Violet's arm connected with a stiff form. Absentmindedly apologizing to it, she crawled over to it and ran both hands over it. It was the form of a woman.

Violet laughed, the sound reverberating in the silent tomb and piercing back into her ears. She knew she sounded deranged, and it wasn't far from the truth to think that she might be entering a state of hysteria.

Better to laugh, though, than to focus on her predicament. She was a living corpse, stuck in a mausoleum, and no one knew where she was. Including herself.

Another bubble of delirious laughter caught in her throat as she realized something new. Had she actually died, she would have simply been labeled an unfortunate disappearance. There would have been no hearse ride for Violet Harper. No offer of prayers by the minister, no offer of condolences to Sam.

Ah, Sam. The thought of what her vanishing into thin air would do to Sam was overwhelming and a little nauseating.

As it was, she had no idea what time it was, nor even what day it was.

Violet Harper, you must rescue yourself.

But how? She had toured a mausoleum. She knew that she was now underground, and that even if she could reach the upstairs, there were no windows and the door would be locked from the outside. And if the criminal were clever enough, she was in some mausoleum miles from Ismailia to ensure that no one would ever find her, much less hear her cries for help. That thought caused panic to well up in her chest.

Calm yourself. Solve one problem at a time.

Violet crawled around in the pitch-blackness until she found the edge of the wall. From there, she arose and, using her hand on the wall as a guide, she followed it until she reached the opening of the women's burial room. She was sickened by having to drag her skirts over bodies attempting to rest in peace, and she apologized to every woman upon whom she trod, making a promise to find whoever had desecrated their sacred spot by burying a living person in it, particularly a living person who did not belong to whatever family owned the mausoleum.

She finally reached the entry, and made a wholly inelegant job of climbing out, simply lying on the floor for several minutes to recover now that she was out of the sand pit. Mercifully, her head no longer felt as if it were about to explode like a catapulting firework, and the pain was receding to a dull roar. Once more, she crawled along the passage, feeling her way until she reached the end and her hand grasped the bottom of an angled ladder. Not as easy as the staircase of the previous mausoleum, but at least a way out.

Praise the Almighty.

It took every bit of Violet's will and strength to make it up the ladder without losing consciousness and falling. She accomplished it by pausing at every step, clinging to the rail with both hands, and pressing her cheek against the next tread in front of her. It was an inexorable climb; it must have been like this for the poor ancient Egyptian slaves to climb up the pyramids during their construction.

But Violet was determined to reach her destination. She was thwarted again, though, by the door at the top of the steps, which wouldn't budge as she pressed against it. She remembered that it would be covered above by dirt and sand. Once again her heart began to pound with dread.

She took deep breaths to calm herself. *Do not panic. Think of something else.*

As Violet stood perched at the top of the steps, her thoughts wandered back to the last moments she remembered. Louise-Hélène had requested Violet seek out some Turkish sand coffee, and the surly servant had made it at Violet's request. The servant was going to take it to his mistress, but Violet had insisted that she do it, and she had been carrying the tray of coffee up the staircase when she was struck from behind.

Carrying the tray. Like a servant.

No, it was quite impossible to think that anyone would mistake Violet for a servant. She had obviously been part of the delegation, and she wasn't wearing a servant's uniform.

But lady's maids frequently wore the cast-off clothing of their mistresses, and they could be fine dresses only a season old. With a tray in hand, was it possible that Violet looked like a maid?

But she had witnessed nothing that she considered nefarious. Why was someone attempting to kill her?

She decided that she was through speculating on her attempted murder for the moment. It was time to determine how to at least get to the ground floor of the mausoleum, where hopefully there might be slivers of light getting through, and then she could take the next step of freeing herself.

When Samir Basara had opened the panel that led to the lower staircase of his family's mausoleum, hadn't he pulled on a large iron ring? Would there perhaps be a corresponding ring below? Violet felt around on the solid piece of wood, hoping to avoid splinters. Ah, there it was. Now she prayed silently that it would give her the leverage she needed.

With a click that was deafening inside the confines of the mausoleum's silence, the door's latch released. Violet sobbed quietly in relief. Pushing it against the earth she knew was piled atop her was difficult, but with short bursts up and down she was able to shake off enough of it that eventually she opened the door completely. Once more she found herself crawling inelegantly out of an opening.

Twilight poked through tiny slits in the upper walls of the mausoleum. Whatever day it was, the sun had not yet gone completely down. Violet went to the entry door and banged on it, crying out for help. Her pounding was feeble, though, and she doubted it could be heard very much past the exterior of the thick wood door.

Had she come this far only to be thwarted by a door?

She turned her back to the door and sank down to the ground against it, thinking idly that her dress was completely ruined. Even without a mirror, she knew that no one would think she was a servant now, but they might consider her to be deranged. She even laughed out loud at the thought, a little too hysterically, which made her think that perhaps she *was* going mad in this dark place.

Then another thought struck her. Perhaps the door mechanism was the same as the one leading down into the crypt, and she could simply open it from inside. With renewed hope, she clambered back up again, trying the iron handle. It refused to open. However, it did make a great creaking noise as she twisted it back and forth, piercing the air as her cries could not do. Violet determined that she would maneuver the door handle until someone, anyone, heard it and realized that someone was trapped behind it.

After several minutes of this exhausting work, her shoulders were now shrieking torturously in pain and her head had resumed its previous internal cacophony. But at last Violet was greeted with a muffled *"Excusez-moi*, is there someone in there?"

It was a familiar voice, French and male.

"Yes, please help me," she gasped.

"Who are you?" The voice was curious, not realizing there was a nearly stark-raving mad woman inches away, pining for release.

Violet took a deep breath. "I am Violet Harper, a member of the British delegation to the Suez Canal."

Silence. Then, "Ah, Madame Harper the undertaker. It is I, Auguste Mariette. How did you manage to get yourself locked inside a mausoleum?"

This was not a moment for explanation of all that had happened to her. "Can you help me?"

From outside came the sound of the man attempting to work the handle from the other side. "It is locked," he said.

"Yes, of course it is," she said impatiently. "Have you ever picked one before?" Not that Violet herself had, but perhaps a renowned Egyptologist would have had occasion to do so on ancient artifacts.

"Hmm." His voice came from below, as though he were kneeling before the handle. "This is a Chubb & Son's lock, the Detector model."

"How in the world do you know that?"

"I visited your country's Great Exhibition back in '51, and witnessed that American—Hobbs, I believe was his name?—pick this very lock, which was deemed impenetrable until that time. Caused quite a stir. Were you there? A very interesting fair, but of course no match for France's Expositions Universelles, which are much larger and more impressive."

Was she now to discuss which country held the best world's fairs? Violet put her hand to the door for balance, as she was beginning to feel dizzy again. "Monsieur, do you remember how Mr. Hobbs was able to break into the lock?"

"I think perhaps I do. Madame, have you any hairpins?"

Violet reached up. Her hair was in such disarray that even Louise-Hélène's coiffure would look like a smooth length of silk by comparison. She did have pins, though, many of them hanging on for their very lives.

"Yes." She found a tiny crevice beneath the door and pushed several pins through it.

"I'm afraid I will destroy them and won't be able to return them to you," Mariette said.

"I don't think hairpins would help my appearance at the moment anyway, monsieur," she said, attempting to be lighthearted about it.

After what seemed an eternity of clicking, muttering, and cursing, the lock's latch finally released and Violet stepped back, allowing the door to open. Mariette's expression upon seeing her was all the indication she needed as to how dreadful her appearance was. He offered an arm and helped her step outside. "What day is this?" she demanded, her only thought whether Sam was aware of her absence.

"It's Thursday, of course. The ball has started." Mariette pointed off in the distance, where Pasha's villa dominated the skyline. Violet exhaled in relief. Only hours had passed.

She looked back at the building in which she had been temporarily entombed. It was the same mausoleum where Julie had dragged Violet earlier in the day to share her concerns about Isabelle and her worry that servants were being targeted.

Violet was more confused than ever, but remembered something that had happened before her attack.

"Monsieur, do you know who someone named Tewfik is?"

"Tewfik Pasha? Of course, he is the khedive's son, although not his favorite. Pasha went to great lengths to secure a younger son as his heir, but the sultan wouldn't permit it. Why do you ask?"

Violet ignored his question. "And what of Orabi? Do you know who that is?"

Mariette frowned. "I do not believe I know this name, madame. Where did you hear of it?"

"From the khedive," Violet said, hoping her vague answer was enough to avoid further inquiry.

The Frenchman didn't seem curious about her questions and instead presented his own. "Madame Harper, may I escort you somewhere? To your husband, perhaps? You do not look well at all, and your forehead—" He clucked almost disapprovingly. "I still do not understand how you managed to get yourself trapped inside this building which was locked from the outside."

Violet deftly sidestepped his question and observations with a query of her own. "I might ask how you happened upon my distressing situation."

Mariette shrugged. "I like to walk by myself late in the day, and now I'm glad that I do so, for otherwise I would not have found you. I have been preparing myself for this evening's event, which I confess I dread. I have much to accomplish in my time here, and I prefer to be studying in my tent this evening, instead of smiling and partaking in the grand waste of francs that tonight will prove to be. Ah, speaking of francs, I have something of value to give you."

He dug into a pocket inside his cream-colored linen jacket. With a flourish, he produced a book.

Violet took it and studied the gold-embossed titling on the burgundy leather cover:

Mariette-Bey
Itinéraire des Invités de S. A. le Khédive aux Fêtes de
l'Inauguration du Canal de Suez

"I mentioned this to you at dinner last night. It gives details about all of the digs in this part of Egypt, and is intended as a souvenir of the opening celebrations, as well as an itinerary that can be followed for anyone who wants to visit the archaeological sites," Mariette said.

How very coincidental that he happened to have this volume on him as he chanced upon Violet's dire situation. "Thank you, sir, I shall look forward to perusing it. Tomorrow, of course, as I must still change my clothes and get to the ball."

"If you are certain you are well enough . . . ?"

Violet nodded. "I am well enough."

"Then I insist that I be permitted to escort you to your quarters to ensure no further harm comes to you." He offered her his arm, and despite Violet's fright that whoever her attacker was might have returned to de Lesseps's villa, she allowed him to walk with her back there.

The villa was deserted except for a few servants who permitted her upstairs to get ready. Interestingly, not a single one of them inquired about her appearance, pretending that a fright of a woman was simply an everyday occurrence. The coffee tray had been cleaned up so that there was no trace of what had happened there: no dregs, no china shards, not even a stain on the wood.

Violet went to Louise-Hélène's darkened rooms and turned up the gas in several lamps before preparing herself for the evening. A glance in a mirror gave her pause. Perhaps Mariette was right about her condition. She straightened her shoulders. Violet Harper was not going to permit some madman to cow her into submission. If he was at tonight's ball, he was going to witness her entry and quake with fear that she had literally risen from among the dead.

She was finally dressed and presentable, with her hair pinned dramatically around her forehead to cover the bruising. Violet took one last look in the mirror before leaving. It might not be perfect, but it was a definite improvement over what she had looked like a short time ago. Before departing, though, she picked up Mariette's book and quickly flipped through the pages, which featured descriptions and line drawings of his various digs. Names like Luxor, Thebes, and Karnak flashed before her.

But what stopped her was the inscription to her in the front of the book.

To Madame Harper,
For where your treasure is, there will your heart be also.
Auguste Mariette
17th November 1869

An innocuous Biblical inscription. Certainly Mariette's life—and heart—had been with his famous digs, and this was probably how he inscribed all copies of his book. And yet . . . there was something odd about it. Violet tucked the book in with her other things, which she would pick up later. For now, it was time to get to the ball.

As Violet walked to the palace, which rose like a beacon from the ground, with thousands of shining lights beckoning the distinguished guests to come and mingle inside, she couldn't help but contemplate her rescue from the mausoleum.

Had Mariette truly just been walking about and stumbled upon Violet? Maybe Violet's suspicions were reaching the point of derangement. After all, if Mariette had bashed her head and then buried her in the mausoleum, he certainly wouldn't have come by to rescue her.

Unless this had all been merely a warning to her.

Chapter 22

THE GROUNDS OF PASHA'S PALACE were even more impressive than what Violet had witnessed earlier that very morning. Enough torches were lit so that one probably could have read a book outside if one so desired. As Rashad had indicated, musicians filled both of the gazebos at the start of the long entry tent. As she and other straggling guests waited to enter, they were entertained by costumed performers inside each painted tableau Violet had seen earlier, striking poses and sometimes comical expressions. One contained men pantomiming the digging of the canal, with their backdrop painted realistically like the shore of the canal, even including the sight of a mechanical dredge to one side. Another tableau was painted to look like one of the grand pavilions, and in front of it two actors dressed like de Lesseps and Pasha shook hands, waved, and clapped each other on the back.

The many tableaux, though, were nothing compared to the interior of Pasha's palace, which was even grander than what Mariette had described at last night's dinner. The main reception hall was lined with sofas against Moorish-tiled walls in a fascinating array of cobalt, cocoa, mustard, lime, and burnt umber. In fact, every square inch of the immense space was either tiled or painted decoratively, including the columns under rounded archways that marked entries into other parts of the palace. The ceiling must have been thirty feet high, and from the center of it, inside a rounded floral design, hung a great gas chandelier, hissing with so many jets that the entire space was brightly lit.

Combined with the crush of guests milling about, their voices drowning out the musicians who sat on a balcony overlooking one end of the reception hall, it was all enough to overwhelm Violet, who had had quite enough for one day. It was incredible to think that, once again, Pasha had topped his previous extravaganza.

She stood on the outskirts of the grand fête, scanning the immense crowd for any sign of Sam or his fellow Americans. As she mulled over how to most efficiently look for Sam, the khedive's cultural attaché, Hassan Salib, approached the rails of the musicians' balcony. He clapped his hands together to get the audience's attention.

"We now begin the introduction of the most esteemed and honored dignitaries," he said loudly, his voice echoing around the room. By instinct, Violet and everyone else turned to face the doors through which they had come, which had been closed at some point. Liveried servants threw the doors open, and Hassan began announcing the guests singly and in pairs.

"Her Highness Eugénie, Empress of France, and the man above nearly all other men, Monsieur Ferdinand de Lesseps."

To great applause, de Lesseps entered with Eugénie on his arm. Eugénie's gown, as Violet suspected, eclipsed the gown Louise-Hélène had planned for the evening. The empress wore a scarlet silk gown so bright that it practically flashed in the gaslight. It contained magnificent folds, revealing white silk panels in the front and blue stripes slashed down the side of the skirt, with a large bustle in the back and a train that did not permit anyone to get too close to her. Eugénie looked as though she were completely wrapped in the French flag, which was undoubtedly her intent. Poor Louise-Hélène.

"His Highness Isma'il Pasha and his beloved son Tewfik."

To further applause, in walked the khedive and his son, the young man she had seen seated morosely at the sovereign's table last night. Despite his youth and dour expression, the boy carried himself like a far more mature man. He did not wear all of the medals and decoration his father did, but was finely groomed nonetheless. Were these really the two men she had overheard arguing a few hours ago?

Pasha and Tewfik stood to one side, as if waiting for someone or something.

The presentations went on, with the musicians striking up the chords of whatever national anthem was associated with that particular representative. His Imperial Highness Franz-Josef entered alone, as did Crown Prince Frederick and the Prince of Wales. Grand Duke Michael of Russia marched in with General Ignatiev. Prince Henry and Princess Sophie of Holland stumbled in, laughing, perhaps already a little tipsy. Other rulers followed in suit upon their names being announced, and the stirring patriotic music filled the room.

"And so the *shawabtis* spring to life," came a deep intoning from behind her.

Another man's voice, again familiar. She whirled around. "*Le bon Théo!*" she exclaimed, happy to see him. "What is a *shab*— What did you say?"

"*Shawabti.* They are part of old Egyptian lore. The *shawabtis* were figurines placed in ancient tombs to serve as slaves for departed souls, or as substitutes for souls who might be required to perform forced labor. Romantic, isn't it, to think of any of them serving others in the afterlife?" Gautier lifted a glass toward the assembly in a mock toast. He was probably well on his way to inebriation, too.

Despite her lingering headache and concern about what criminal might be prowling the party, Violet couldn't help laughing. "Yes, terribly romantic, Théo. Shall I undertake you one day and put a *shawabti* upon your coffin to write plays for you?"

He put a hand to his chest. "*Mon Dieu, non,* Madame Harper. I need a *shawabti* specifically to keep away the critics, as mine is the only worthwhile opinion, of course. You will see to it, won't you?"

"I promise," she replied solemnly in the spirit of the exchange. "But you may need two of them for such an important job."

Now that all of the primary dignitaries had made their grand entries, Rashad clapped his hands together twice to obtain everyone's attention. "Now we will have the presentation of the medals."

To Violet's surprise, a ceremony was now held whereby each of the sovereigns awarded Pasha an important medal of honor, adding to his already-decorated chest. Franz-Josef presented him with the Grand Cross of the Order of Leopold, consisting of a red-and-white-striped sash and an ornate cross that Franz-Josef pinned to Pasha's chest. From Greece came the Grand Cross of the Order of the Redeemer, and the Italians presented him with the Grand Cross of the Order of the Crown of Italy. On it went, and Pasha beamed proudly at the array of glittering metal now hanging haphazardly from him.

His son, though, scowled, seeming less than pleased at his father's honors.

"Act three, scene one," Gautier said. "Guests are suffocating at a party that has no absinthe. A madman formerly known as an art critic takes out his rage on the assembly, and they are no match for his extraordinary strength due to the disgusting lack of liquor to lull him to a peaceable state. No, wait, I may have to rewrite that scene." A server passed by with a tray of filled wineglasses, and Gautier followed him, leaving Violet alone in the crowd once more.

Where in heaven's name was Sam?

A vision of teal and black approached her. "Madame Harper, where have you been?" Louise-Hélène said, her face flushed as she came rushing up to Violet. "I waited and waited for your return until I could wait no more."

"I, er, ran into a little trouble with the coffee. I apologize that I was unable to bring it to you," Violet said, hoping to avoid further discussion of where she had been.

"Well, I did so miss your company."

"Your dress is simply lovely," Violet said, changing the subject completely.

"Oh, this," the girl said carelessly, then cast a covert glance at where Eugénie stood with de Lesseps. "It is nothing. De Lesseps purchased it for me as an early wedding gift, but I am sure he will shower me with others even grander. More colorful."

This wasn't a good subject, either. "Where is Isabelle?"

"A separate party is being held for the more important staff, in a tent in the back gardens."

Violet wondered if that was where Sam was. There had been no grand entrance for the Americans, as the soldiers were performing a service for the khedive, not representing President Grant. If Mott and his men were in the outdoor tent, Sam was surely with them.

"*Ma louloute*, here you are." De Lesseps had arrived, the glittering Eugénie still on his arm. "This is the pinnacle of the festivities, is it not?"

"Yes, of course," Louise-Hélène agreed meekly. It was remarkable how Eugénie could cause the girl to wither, like a rose suffering from a lack of water.

Eugénie snapped open a fan whose leaves were elaborately painted with a pastoral scene. She raked Louise-Hélène over in a single complacent glance. "You look lovely, my dear. Very elegant." The empress's insincerity toward Louise-Hélène settled like a heavy cloak around the girl's shoulders, and Violet could have sworn she saw Louise-Hélène's shoulders sag.

Eugénie seemed oblivious. "Will the dancing start soon?" she said, her gaze flitting about distractedly. That gaze caught Franz-Josef stoically enduring the chattering of some minor noblewoman, and Eugénie quickly excused herself.

Louise-Hélène immediately revived, as if her blooms had been offered a midsummer shower.

Violet knew she had to quit worrying about Louise-Hélène, as there were far more pressing matters at hand. "Monsieur de Lesseps, this is indeed a remarkable gathering of the world's leaders. I had not realized before that that young man was Pasha's son."

De Lesseps glanced back to where Tewfik still stood sullenly with his father while Pasha continued collecting handshakes, cheek kisses, and congratulations on his multiple awards. "Pasha has many wives and many children, but Tewfik *ees* his heir. I don't believe either of them is happy with the prospect."

"That is very sad," Violet murmured. "May I ask, have you heard of someone named Orabi?"

De Lesseps turned his attentions back sharply. "You mean Colonel Ahmed Orabi? He *ees* the radical, madame, and best forgotten. He is a member of the *fellahin*, but the first to rise up in the military ranks of the Egyptian army. Orabi believes that non-Egyptians should be evicted from the country because they prevent the peasant class from earning a living. Imagine how the canal building would have been impacted if I had been unable to import Greeks and Turks and other nationalities to finish it. There wouldn't have been enough Egyptians available if Pasha himself had agreed to work on it."

Violet wondered why Tewfik would have brought Orabi up to his father in an argument.

"Where *ees* your husband, Madame Harper?" de Lesseps asked.

"I'm afraid I don't know. We came separately as your fiancée invited me to get dressed with her—"

"Except that she ran off from me, Ferdinand." Louise-Hélène attempted this coyly, as Eugénie might have done, but she wasn't experienced enough at witty banter, so her statement dropped to the ground like an anchor.

Violet attempted to tug at the anchor. "Your fiancée is quite correct, monsieur. I was so overtaken by your magnificent villa that I found myself in too much awe to even remain in Mademoiselle de Bragard's rooms. She has graciously forgiven me, and I hope that you will forgive me also, as I am eager to locate my husband."

Good Lord, she was turning into a courtier. Violet shook her head at the thought as she quietly moved away, and the motion reminded her that she was still suffering the throbbing effects of the earlier blow to her head.

She hadn't made it very far before she was accosted by General Ignatiev, who for once was not in the duke's company. "Violet Rose, you have discovered cause of death for the Austrian?" he asked without preamble.

Violet wondered at the man's deep interest in Dorn, but said politely, "It was not completely clear. However, there were wine and absinthe flowing freely during the dinner, and perhaps the two do not mix well."

Ignatiev grunted. "You look in wrong direction. These Egyptians, they like opium."

Violet shook her head. "But Herr Dorn is—was—not an Egyptian." Nor was Purdy.

"Of no matter. He probably die of opium." He said the words with finality, as though, now that he had declared the truth of the matter, there was nothing more to be said. What was the source of his interest in the fallen Austrian? Was it merely concern for a fellow delegate, or was there something darker in it?

Violet wanted to know more about Ignatiev.

"General, I noticed that you are friendly with the Empress Eugénie's maid, Julie," she said.

He stared at Violet as if she were touched by madness. "I do not know this Julie."

Why was he lying to her?

"I am certain that you do, sir," she insisted.

"I am not here for love affairs, Violet Rose. I am here for diplomatic purposes, and then I return to post in Constantinople. Dorn is dead from opium. Act or do not act, I do not care."

With that, the enigmatic Russian diplomat bowed stiffly to her and disappeared into the crowd, presumably to rejoin Grand Duke Michael.

How peculiar all of these delegates were. Was there not one of them who was not hiding a secret, or trying to settle a score, or—

"Finally! Where the devil have you been?" It was Sam, once more dressed in his uniform, his saber at his left side, his cane in his right hand. He stood proud and erect, the buttons of his jacket gleaming like brass jewels. Before she had a chance to respond, he peered searchingly into her eyes. "Something has happened."

Violet shook her head. "I have a great deal to tell you, but it will have to wait, I'm afraid. How is Herr Dorn?"

"Safely cocooned. I think you would be pleased. By the way, Thaddeus and the others are in the party tent for the servants, and I was thinking . . ."

She smiled. "Yes, we will be much more comfortable there."

Thus far, no one inside the palace had expressed even subtle surprise that Violet was alive. Either the attacker was at the servants' party, or was far shrewder and more deceitful than she could have ever imagined. It would be interesting to note the reactions of those attending the other par—

But before the couple could head out of doors, a piercing shriek tore through the reception hall as if a banshee had been let loose and was streaking through the air above them.

Everything—the chatting, the music, the dancing, the drinking—stopped in a single instant. Violet's heart nearly did, too, but Sam was already on the move. He grabbed Violet's hand and began running toward the sound of the screaming, which was rending the air with its unceasing high pitch, while the other party guests remained frozen. Before she knew it, she and Sam were at the open front door, where she saw Eugénie's maid, Julie Lesage, standing outside, holding a bloody shawl and managing to cry and screech at the same time.

chapter 23

VIOLET ATTEMPTED TO QUICKLY ABSORB the scene before her. Julie was clad in what was surely a cast-off dress of Eugénie's, but the off-the-shoulder taupe-and-lavender gown had been expertly retailored, and if not for her hysterics, Julie might have looked like a member of the nobility herself.

She clutched a floral-patterned fringed shawl that clearly did not belong with her dress. Julie held it up and shook it at Violet, expressing an emotion Violet could not understand.

As the other party guests began to crowd around them to see what was the matter, Violet stepped outside and took Julie a short distance away, wrapping an arm around her and removing the woman's fingers from the offending garment.

"What happened?" she whispered, which had the desired effect of calming the maid down.

"I—I— It is too *horrible* to describe, madame." Julie sniffed, pulling a handkerchief from her sleeve now that her hands were free and dabbing at her eyes.

"Try your best," Violet said patiently. Sam had now joined them but stood with his back to the gathering crowd to give the two women privacy.

"I was at the other party, there in the tent." Julie waved at the house to indicate the festivities set up behind it. "It was very hot inside, so many people, you see . . ."

"Yes," Violet said. "The palace is the same, as well."

Julie sniffed again, but was now dry-eyed. "So I walked outside for a breath of the cool night air. As I wandered around to the front of the house, I saw the most dreadful thing . . ."

Violet waited, but Julie clearly wanted to be coaxed along. "What did you see?"

"I saw a man stabbed."

Violet blinked in astonishment. "Pardon me, are you sure of this? It is dark outside."

"Yes, madame, but you see how well lit the grounds are. I am certain of what I saw. Furthermore, I am certain I saw the man stabbed by a woman. I hid behind the house momentarily, frightened out of my mind. After all, what if this madwoman came after me? When I emerged, she was gone and I ran to the place where she had stabbed him and found . . . that." Julie nodded at the shawl now in Violet's possession. "I'm afraid my fear came out in a bit of the *hystériques*."

Sam spoke up now. "Were you alone in your walk?"

Julie frowned. "What are you suggesting, monsieur? I was not having a tête-à-tête with a gentleman, if that is what you mean to imply. I am the lady's maid to the Empress Eugénie of France."

As if that explained everything, including Julie's avowal of her own virtue.

Sam was not to be put off by her statement, though. "Where is the man's body?"

Julie turned and pointed at the tableau that represented the grand pavilion. The actors portraying de Lesseps and the khedive, as well as the musicians from the gazebo, were of course long gone now that there was no one to entertain in the entry line.

While they waited, Sam went to inspect the location. Guests were beginning to spill out of the palace, catching the scent that what was happening outside was far more interesting than Pasha's medals and the endless rounds of drinks and mindless chitchat.

Violet wasn't sure how long she could protect Julie, especially once Pasha—or, worse, de Lesseps—discovered what had happened.

Sam returned quickly, his face thunderous. "Now tell me what *actually* occurred."

"What?" Julie said, confused. "What do you mean?"

"You said a man was stabbed out there by a woman," Sam said. "Yet there is no body there. Given that corpses have little mobility on their own, I ask you, where is his body?"

"I—I—I cannot explain it," Julie stammered. "I hid around the side of the house, and when I emerged, the woman was gone. I came to the house to report it, and as I neared the house, I found the shawl. That is all."

Sam wasn't done with his accusations. "And after witnessing a murder, fearing for your life, and then traipsing across the grounds, it was only once you found the shawl that you set up your wailing alarm?"

Violet's husband had a point. She looked at the shawl in her hand. Did it belong to one of the women now crowding them, or had it been intentionally placed out here for some reason?

Sam's interrogation was interrupted by Eugénie's arrival, this time on Franz-Josef's arm, with de Lesseps close on their heels. "Julie, what is this?" Eugénie said.

"Your Highness, it is a tragedy. I witnessed a murder!" Julie put a hand to her chest.

"No, that is not possible." Eugénie gasped, her eyelashes fluttering prettily as she grasped Franz-Josef's arm for support. The emperor stood there stoically, although a look of confusion crossed his face.

"*Oui*, I saw a man stabbed." Julie dropped her voice. "By a *woman.*"

Why did Violet feel as though she were in the middle of a play? Perhaps the whole affair could be moved over to one of the tableaux for better effect. Sam passed her a glance that told her he thought the same thing. "Wait here, I will go to the other party and investigate," he whispered to her and slipped away.

The drama continued to unfold between mistress and servant, but Violet should have known she could rely on de Lesseps to inject himself into the proceedings. "What is wrong with you, mademoiselle?" he demanded crossly of Julie. "Have you no thought for what your delirium does to my reputation? Was it impossible for you to report this quietly instead of heralding it to the world? Must the greatest project in history be discredited?" He threw up his hands. "Silly little strumpet, you are determined to ruin me."

These were shocking words against the maid of the woman whom de Lesseps had been lavishing attention on—a sign of how exasperated he really was. More importantly, though, the Frenchman once more had no concern for a man who had died as a result of being in attendance at the canal celebrations. Violet's immense irritation at this rose to the surface again, as de Lesseps began shooing everyone inside, insisting that they return to the dancing and merriment.

As everyone else filed in, Violet examined the shawl in her hands. The blood on it was already dried, and it had stiffened the patches of material where it had adhered. There was so much blood that it was difficult to tell whether the shawl had been used to mop it up, or if the shawl was just a casualty in the stabbing incident. Perhaps she would try to find the woman to whom it belonged.

A ridiculous idea, really, because the woman who had lost that shawl had probably long ago departed the party and discarded the clothing that went with the bloody item.

Violet folded the crusty shawl as best she could. She, too, should go back to the party until Sam returned with news. As she looked up, she noticed that Pasha and his son stood together nearby, as they had inside the palace, observing her closely but not saying anything. A short distance away from them, General Ignatiev stood behind a pillar, his attention focused on Pasha and Tewfik.

Violet felt chills run up her spine as she scurried back into the party.

chapter 24

THE ORCHESTRA HAD RESUMED ITS joyful tunes, and the partygoers, disappointed that there had been no actual murdered body to view, returned to their self-absorbed dancing. Violet knew she couldn't walk around carrying the grisly piece of evidence in her hands, and so determined to find a place to tuck it away until after the party was over. Surely there was some sort of cloakroom in one of the halls near the reception room.

She avoided meeting anyone's curious glance as she made her way through the crowd and down a promising corridor. Unfortunately, all she found were a few bedchambers, presumably in use by certain dignitaries whose status was such that they would not be relegated to tents, no matter how luxurious the outdoor accommodations were. Violet retraced her steps back to the reception hall and followed another arched corridor, her heels echoing against the tiles beneath her feet. She quietly poked her nose into another room, which was clearly a makeshift cloakroom. It was furnished with ornate floor mirrors, clothing trunks, and a variety of plush ottomans where weary attendees could rest in private. There were also hooks on the walls and multiple clothing racks consisting of brass pipes set into oak feet atop wheels.

Gaslight sizzled from a chandelier in the ceiling, illuminating the mass of shawls and men's jackets that had been shed in here as the night had gone on. The cloakroom was a jumbled mess, yet it felt very cozy, and so, after hanging the shawl on a hook dangling from a clothing rack, Violet succumbed to the temptation to take a rest herself. She headed for a tufted fainting chair, carved to resemble a swan, the imagery further enhanced by its snowy white upholstery. Violet leaned back with only the gaslight as her immediate company, with the distant rumble of the party barely registering with her.

With her eyes closed, she reviewed the facts of the deaths that now stood before her.

Yusef Halabi had died the first day here, during the fireworks or just prior. Stabbed.

Captain Naser had been killed while en route to— Where, exactly, had the captain been heading? He had suffered blows to his chest.

Karl Dorn had died from some kind of poisoning. Perhaps it was absinthe. General Ignatiev stated that it was opium. Franz-Josef seemed little perturbed by his servant's death.

De Lesseps was greatly perturbed by all of the deaths, but mostly for what it did to his *dignitas*.

The general had spoken with Julie in secret during the Dinner of the Sovereigns and lied about it. Was that relevant to anything, or had Violet simply witnessed an amorous assignation?

Julie claimed to have witnessed a murder, but there was no body to support her claim, just a bloodied shawl.

Julie had also sought Violet out with suspicions about servants being targeted for death. Was it a reasonable theory?

Violet had nearly become a corpse herself.

There were certainly grudges abounding here in Ismailia. Mariette resented de Lesseps. Tewfik Pasha was angry at his father. General Ignatiev seemed to harbor suspicions toward Pasha and had also been humiliated by the British. De Lesseps was outraged by the British perfidy at slipping *Newport* to the head of the flotilla. Louise-Hélène was intimidated by Eugénie. Julie despised Isabelle.

Violet put a hand to her head. This was the first time she could recall in her role as an amateur detective that she had literally no suspects. Or perhaps everyone she had encountered was suspect. There was certainly enough malice to go around.

What was she missing? What had she forgotten?

She opened her eyes once more. There was very little of this puzzle in which she could form connections or relationships. Perhaps some ancient Egyptian curse had settled over her. She yawned and swung her legs back around to the floor. Surely Sam was back now, and perhaps he had discovered something important.

As Violet started to rise, she noticed what she had not seen when she first entered the room. At first, she froze, unwilling to believe it. No, it had to be a mistake. Willing her feet to transport her to a large ebony trunk, she closed its open lid for a full view of what lay partially obscured behind the storage box.

Not again.

Violet didn't know whether to become as hysterical as Julie or as stoic as Franz-Josef. She took a deep breath and shoved the trunk aside, dropping to her knees at the body that lay before her.

It was Caleb Purdy.

He looked like a rag doll that had been tossed upon its back, his arms and legs askew, his fists tightly bundled together as if he had wished to strike whoever had come after him.

What was worse was the manner in which he had been killed. A gorgeously engraved saber had been driven deep into his midsection, the blade now spattered with blood almost up to the brass hilt. The poor man had survived the savage carnage of war, only to be brutally murdered like this. His expression was twisted in agony, and Violet could only imagine how excruciating his last moments had been.

Dear God, a fourth body. Was this who Julie had witnessed being murdered a short while ago? He could have been brought here through a rear entrance while everyone was distracted out front. It seemed a foolish burial place, but none of the killings thus far had reflected much cunning in terms of body disposal.

Other than the attempt on her own life.

She hardly knew what to do with Purdy's body. Remove the saber? But it might look terribly suspicious if, after all of her grousing about the deaths that had already occurred, she strolled back into the ballroom dragging a bloodstained sword behind her as though she herself were the murderess. No, she would have to leave him in his unfortunate position until witnesses were brought in.

Violet took one of his clenched hands in both of hers. "Mr. Purdy, you cannot tell me who did this to you, but I promise I will find out on your behalf and will bring justice to you. To you and the captain and Karl Dorn and Yusef Halabi." She squeezed his hand, knowing he couldn't feel a thing, and that was when she noticed a rough object sticking out of his fist. It brushed against her skin.

She put his fist in her lap, ignoring the incongruence of a dead man's pale limb resting against her fancy green dress. Rigor mortis had not set in yet, informing Violet that the death was fairly recent despite the dried blood, and she carefully uncurled his palm to find a small paper-wrapped package, tied off at both ends, much like a Christmas cracker. Curious.

"I hope you will not mind if I take a look at the little present in your hand," she said as she removed it and untied one end.

She stared at the sticky brown mass inside, which looked like a failed cooking experiment. She sniffed at. It was familiar, with a faint floral—oh! Violet reared back as her heart skipped a beat. She had caught this same aroma on Herr Dorn after he died. Was this opium?

How had Dorn and Purdy both managed to obtain this substance? To Violet's knowledge, the two men had never even met each other. Although Dorn might have died from it, clearly Purdy had not, given that the bloody mess on his chest meant he had been alive when he was stabbed. Had the opium not worked to kill Purdy, leading his murderer to resort to more . . . guaranteed . . . means?

How interesting that General Ignatiev might have guessed right about Dorn. Or perhaps he had been leading Violet down the path upon which he wanted her to tread. Regardless, she now had even more questions to be answered.

Violet sighed heavily and rose to her feet. She had to find de Lesseps and Pasha to inform them of yet another death.

"Who did this to you, Mr. Purdy? And what I do not understand is why would he want both you and me killed. Is there simply a madman on the loose, or do you and I know something that we don't realize we know?"

Violet shuddered to think of how much danger she might still be in at this very moment from a stranger. Or, worse, from someone at the canal celebrations who had smiled at her and pretended to be a friend.

chapter 25

VIOLET, DE LESSEPS, PASHA, AND Hassan Salib stood together in the cloakroom, staring at Caleb Purdy's dead body. Sam had not yet returned to the palace, so she faced the situation on her own.

De Lesseps reacted as explosively as Violet had imagined he would. "I have been treated with treachery yet again. Yet again! These Americans are liars and cheats! You, Pasha, you hired them to form your military, but you hired criminals. One can only imagine that they had too much liquor and began brawling with one another, resulting in this—this—*mort*. Or maybe you have a different contrivance, eh? Perhaps you planned to use these soldiers to intimidate all of the other delegates, even killing unimportant people. You think, 'I will make the world bend the knee to Pasha.' But they are so wild they begin killing each other!"

De Lesseps's accusations were obviously without merit and born out of some feral place in his soul, but Pasha blanched at the Frenchman's anger.

"I assure you, I know nothing of this situation, and had no idea that the Americans were such swine. My only desire is for the canal celebrations to be joyful, and if you are unhappy, there is no joy for anyone." Pasha snapped his fingers at Hassan. "I want the Americans brought in now."

Hassan bowed obediently and silently left. Soon Sam,

Thaddeus Mott, Ross Keating, and Owen Morris had been escorted to the cloakroom under the guard of several ferocious-looking Egyptians. They looked thoroughly mystified—and then horrified, particularly at the sight of their friend lying so pitifully on the floor. Violet cringed, both at their discomfort and at the fact that poor Purdy was now being treated like a zoo animal on display.

"Your Highness," Hassan said with another bow to Pasha, "these are all of the Americans in attendance at the servants' party." This was only a small contingent, so the others must not have been in attendance at all.

With everyone's gaze now upon him, the khedive puffed up and became commanding.

"Show us your sabers," he said.

The soldiers cautiously unsheathed their curved-tip weapons and presented them to Pasha's guards. Except for Sam, whose scabbard was empty.

He reacted in speechless shock at the realization that his saber was not on his person. Violet knew exactly what he was thinking, and she shared his thought. How could someone have been stealthy enough to remove it without his knowing?

"Is my point not proved, Pasha?" De Lesseps said with satisfaction. "Undoubtedly the sword belonging to the undertaker's husband is the one now buried in the other man."

"What reason would I have to kill my comrade?" Sam demanded, finding his voice again.

Pasha glared at Sam's daring claim of innocence. "That is not for me to figure out. How can *you* prove that you were not the wielder of *your* sword against that man, thus embarrassing Egypt?"

Thaddeus Mott rose in Sam's defense. "I have been diligent in training your troops, Your Highness," he said, anger flickering in those once-teasing eyes. "My men have behaved with honor, and they are all friends. Harper is not part of my contingent, but I served with him and know that he is also a man of honor. It was someone else who did this, not Samuel Harper."

But Pasha seemed more concerned with impressing de Lesseps than with reaching the truth. He tried to imitate the delicate shrug that de Lesseps and every Frenchman performed so fluidly, except on Pasha's frame it seemed like a nervous tic. "It is not for you to decide. You are no more than a paid servant in my employ, and as such, you are subject to *my* judgment."

Mott opened his mouth again, and Violet knew that a diplomatic inferno was about to erupt if she didn't defuse it.

"Your Highness," Violet said, gently but firmly, "it is apparent by the deaths of not only Caleb Purdy but also Karl Dorn, Captain Naser, and Yusef Halabi that we are dealing with a far greater issue than a few brawling Americans, not that there is any evidence that they were ever fighting with one another."

Pasha stared at her as if she were a babbling idiot. "Those other deaths were unfortunate accidents. This man here is the only murder, which we see is obvious, *madaam*, by the sword protruding from his chest."

Violet's head began to ache again, but now it was the khedive's obtuseness causing it. "Men are not always killed in obvious ways. Murderers frequently seek clever ways of taking their victims so that others believe it to be an accident," she said with as much patience as she could muster.

But Pasha was determined to ignore her.

"You are an obedient wife, concerned for your husband. Therefore, all of these men will be put in the dungeon until we return from the Red Sea, instead of just your husband. Then I will try them. If I find them guilty of various offenses"—he glanced pointedly at Mott—"I will have them all executed." Pasha nodded his head with satisfaction at his tidy solution.

"*What?*" Violet said, panicked. How had they tumbled so quickly into an abyss of words like "dungeon" and "execution"? "What do you mean? They've done nothing wrong. Your Highness, there is no justice in this, there is no—"

Pasha flicked his hand at her, his decision made.

She appealed to de Lesseps. "Monsieur, surely you do not mean to permit these innocent men to be condemned like this!"

"We do not know that they are innocent, madame. One of them has an American sword lodged in his chest, which would suggest that one of his friends did this to him, even if it *ees* not your husband. Pasha has spoken. We will continue on and see about the men when the canal celebrations are over."

As if Pasha's opinion had been the final word on any matter thus far.

Violet tried again, using a different approach. "You must realize that my husband is a member of the delegation."

De Lesseps shrugged. "Not a particularly important one. His government did not send their president or anyone in a high position, did they? I doubt they will miss a few grizzly soldiers."

Violet was so mortified and outraged all at once that she could hardly form words in response. The entire trip had been a swirling sandstorm of events stained in red, culminating in this absolute travesty. She couldn't even contemplate what Pasha's "trial" might look like in this foreign land. What was she to do? She had to find Sir Henry Elliot so he could attempt to reach a diplomatic solution to this. Maybe even the Prince of Wales himself would intercede. Perhaps—

Her mind went blank as she watched the group of four men led away, their shoulders slumped. All of a sudden the room grew fuzzy and distant, and she thought she might faint.

Stop it, she admonished herself. *You must help Sam.* She reached out a hand and found herself grabbing one of the rolling clothes racks for support. Taking a few deep breaths, Violet contemplated what she would say to Sir Henry, and her energy was marginally renewed. Until she overheard the Frenchman speaking in low undertones to Pasha near Purdy's body.

"See to it that the American body *ees* taken out to one of the canal boats during the night. We do not want the guests to know about this and become agitated. He can be dumped into the Red Sea when we reach Suez."

"No!" Pasha whispered back urgently. "Egyptian waters must not be sullied like that. I will have him removed and buried immediately. I can pay some *fellahin* to take care of it."

De Lesseps was unmoved. "If we take him out on a boat, he will soon be a meal for the sea creatures and your waters will not be defiled for long."

"I have done all as you wish," Pasha shot back. "But this must be done according to our customs."

De Lesseps continued pressing his point with vehemence. Now Violet was more agitated than ever. Purdy should be preserved and sent home to his family in America, not tossed overboard like rotten fish. The evil that seemed to permeate this place like a thick—

"*Madaam?*" Violet felt a light touch at her elbow. She turned to find Hassan standing there. He glanced over at Pasha, who was absorbed in assuaging de Lesseps's anger and not paying attention to anything else.

"I regret what has happened here," he said quietly. "You must understand that I must obey Pasha, although I do not think your husband—or any of the Americans—guilty of anything."

Violet wanted to burst into tears at his kindness, but merely nodded.

He handed her a slip of paper. "You will meet me at this address tomorrow morning, before we head on to Suez. I will personally ensure that you are able to see your husband. Tell no one, for if Pasha were to find out . . ."

Violet gratefully accepted the folded piece of parchment. "Why do you extend me this courtesy? Surely Pasha will punish you if he finds out."

Hassan sighed. "Sometimes, my lady, it is important to do that which creates proper order, not merely that which is given by order. You are a woman of an orderly mind, I think. Now, you must go to the rear of the building at this location to meet me. It is where de Lesseps arranged for a prison during the canal building, as there were many troubles among the different nationalities. The cells were cleared out for the celebrations and the prisoners sent elsewhere, so be comforted that the Americans will be the only inmates. I will do what I can for them until they are brought before Pasha."

Hassan bowed and slipped away, leaving Violet to decide whether to intercede once more for Purdy. Did she dare antagonize de Lesseps and Pasha one more time to crusade for the proper treatment of the dead man's body? She thought about how it might affect Sam's treatment and that of the other veterans. She bit her lip, her insides churning at the impossible choice it was, her concern for her husband at war with her ingrained principles on undertaking rituals.

However, she knew what she had to do, for although the dead deserved the utmost respect, the living must come first. She followed in Hassan's footsteps, fleeing the room with the bloody shawl while Pasha and de Lesseps were still busy arguing over Purdy's disposition.

Violet stepped into the ballroom, which was now deserted. Undoubtedly everyone had gone outside to witness yet another night of fireworks, which burst happily in the air as if another man had not been killed and Violet's husband had not been hauled off to some pestilent hole. She couldn't even imagine what this prison would be like. She shut her mind to it, hurrying back to her tent while fireworks transformed the streets of Ismailia into rivers of fire, her own injuries completely forgotten in light of Sam's captivity.

chapter 26

November 19, 1869

VIOLET WAS TENSE TO THE point of shaking after the previous day's ordeal and a night without a moment's sleep. Although her first instinct had been to locate Sir Henry and Bertie and demand that they do something about the situation right away, she decided that, with Hassan's help, she might be able to secure the Civil War veterans' release on her own. She would try almost anything to avoid a diplomatic incident.

She arrived at the prison building early, but Hassan was already waiting for her. The cultural attaché obviously had influence, for the prison guards offered no resistance to him escorting Violet in. Hassan carried a lantern as they walked down a narrow set of endless stone steps that would lead them to the cells, and explained to her that the rooms above were actually Canal Authority offices, occupied by workers from various countries.

Violet could not have cared less about what the pencil-sharpening men upstairs were doing.

Seeing that his words had no effect at relaxing her, Hassan said, "My lady, I wish to apologize for my master's behavior yesterday. He is under tremendous strain to ensure that the canal celebrations go well and that de Lesseps is pleased. Sometimes it causes him to behave a bit rashly. I know it is not helpful to you in this moment, but perhaps one day you will forgive him?"

The cultural attaché was convincing, but Violet was still pent up with fear and anger, and in no mood to absolve Pasha of his sin.

When they reached the bottom of the stairs and she saw the condition of the cells, her fear and anger transformed themselves into unreserved fury.

The men were locked away in a stone cell whose walls were broken only by a door with a small rectangular viewing area—not that a larger hole would have done them much good, given how little light there was from the weak candlelight in the passageway. Hassan had the guard open the cell, then handed Violet his lantern while he waited outside.

Given the condition of their cell, the men were in remarkably good—if still baffled—spirits. They had rough wood benches to sit on, and a barrel in the corner of the cell whose stench made clear its purpose.

"Sweetheart, how did you get in here?" Sam said as he and the other men attempted to stand at her presence. She noticed that Sam no longer had his cane.

"Please, do sit. I'm not sure how long I will be permitted to visit you. I must ask you some questions." Violet set the lantern down in the middle of the floor, illuminating just how grim their confines were. There shouldn't have been four men in this space, although it was at least dry. They all sank back down on the benches, which creaked under their weight.

"First, have you eaten?" She would see to their physical needs before questioning them about last night.

"Yes," Mott said on everyone's behalf. "That one Egyptian fellow had some sort of bean gruel sent in. It wasn't quite what we've become accustomed to over the past few days, of course, but it filled us. I don't believe Harper will be asking your cook to make it again any time soon." Mott's vitality sparked and flickered.

"I confess to you, gentlemen, that I am not quite sure how to achieve a diplomatic release for you other than seeking help from the British ambassador and the Prince of Wales. But that

may not be a viable solution. The political situation here . . ."
Violet knew she probably didn't have to explain it all to them.

Sam laughed mirthlessly. "We know all about how governments and politics tend to get men killed. Ironic, isn't it, that we would survive the politics of the war, only to be victims of it in this foreign place."

She couldn't let them succumb to dark thoughts. "I do have another thought, though. If I could prove your innocence, then Pasha would have to release you."

"How would you do that, ma'am?" Ross Keating asked, the raw hope unmistakable in his voice.

"By proving who the guilty party actually is."

"You believe you can do this?" Now Keating didn't sound so hopeful.

"Son," Sam said, "if anyone can do it, it's my wife. She has proved the guilt of more than one man."

The other men stared silently at Violet, who now represented their only prospect of freedom. Could she manage to deliver it to them? She steeled herself for the task ahead, knowing she would do near anything to see Sam out of this dark, crowded cell. "Now, you must answer my next question very truthfully. Where were all of you prior to the party?" Violet inquired.

"I was mucking and feeding our horses like the colonel asked," Owen Morris volunteered.

Mott nodded. "I want my own men taking care of our horses, not foreigners who know nothing about our Morgans."

Violet wanted no part of a competitive discussion over Morgan versus Arabian horses. "And you, Colonel, where were you before attending the party?"

"I was in my tent, writing out lessons on camp layouts for Pasha's recruits. But somehow I found myself indisposed and unable to work with them before Pasha granted me leave. Perhaps you will have to take over for me, Mrs. Harper, and show the men the proper manner in which to arrange tents and huts. Remember, dear woman, kitchens and latrines on opposite ends of the camp, with latrines running downhill."

Violet smiled at Mott's continued easiness in light of his uncertain situation.

"You will be back at your post in no time, Colonel, I promise you," Violet said with a confidence she wasn't sure was real. "And you, sir, Mr. Keating, isn't it? How did you spend your time leading up to the party?"

Violet expected a similar answer to that of Mott or Morris, and was surprised when the man hesitated. "I, er, I was engaged socially."

This obviously came as a surprise to the other men. "What does that mean?" Mott demanded.

Even in the lantern light, Violet could tell the man was reddening.

"I had a— I had been invited— You see, sir . . ."

"What were you doing?" Mott was practically shouting.

"There is this young miss with the French delegation. Very pretty, she is, and an accent to charm the saddle off a horse. She asked me to escort her through the Arab tents, and that's where I was."

Various women were running through Violet's mind, and certainly she didn't know every single one attached to the French delegation, particularly not the servants. "What was her name?" she said.

"Ah, well, I'm not sure I should—"

"Damnation, man!" Sam exploded. "I'm not going to be shot or hanged because you won't reveal the name of your doxy."

"She's not a doxy! She is a sweet girl, a lady. I won't have you speak of her that way."

"Mr. Keating," Violet broke in, impatient with the man's obliviousness over the gravity of the situation, "I understand that you wish to protect the reputation of your lady friend, to ensure no one thinks ill of her for spending private time with you. However, I remind you that all of you are under suspicion, not just Sam, and not only do you require an alibi, but I need every possible scrap of information to enable me to find out who did this to Mr. Purdy."

But now Keating was resolute, stubbornly jutting his chin forward, as though Violet were some enemy interrogator. She remembered that Julie spent considerable time with the soldiers during last night's Dinner of the Sovereigns before her clandestine meeting with General Ignatiev. There must be a connection.

Violet's next visit would be with Julie Lesage.

"Gentlemen, I have just two more questions. One, did any of you see the moment Sam lost his sword?"

"Violet, I didn't lose it. My sword was taken from me," Sam insisted.

"I'm sorry. Of course. Presumably none of you saw his sword being taken?"

They all shook their heads.

"And yet someone must have done so, and used it to kill Caleb Purdy sometime between Sam's arrival at the party and my discovery of the body. Sam, when did you notice it was missing?"

"Truthfully, not until I was asked to present it. So much had happened, what with the maid screaming, the search for the body . . ."

Yes, someone had been quite successful working under the cover of total bedlam, a bedlam created by Julie Lesage.

"I will ask you a final question. Have any of you been eating opium since you arrived in Egypt?"

They all glanced around at one another, shaking their heads. "No, ma'am," said Ross Keating. "We are whiskey men. Can't say as I've ever tried opium myself." The others shook their heads in agreement that they, too, had never tried it.

"Were you aware that Caleb Purdy was ingesting it?"

Understanding dawned in Mott's eyes. "That what happened to him at the picnic?"

"I believe so. There was a package of it in his hand when I found him in the cloakroom."

"What's that got to do with us, Mrs. Harper?" Keating asked. She had no idea.

As she exited the cell, Violet had another idea. Obtaining Hassan's cooperation, she secured a private meeting with Sam in another cell. Hassan promised the guards that he would offer his own life if Sam attempted an escape with Violet.

Still clutching the lantern, Violet set it on the ground and flew against her husband as soon as the door clanked shut on them. Sam's arms folded around her as he pulled her close.

"All will be well, sweetheart," Sam said, kissing the top of her head.

Violet pulled back and looked up at him. "*You* are comforting *me*? Very ironic."

He shrugged. "I have every confidence that you will quickly find out who the devil is in our midst." He kissed her forehead and then pressed the fingers of her right hand to his mouth. "Then we will leave this pestilent place and sit along the edge of Mount Vesuvius. I'm beginning to think a volcano in Pompeii is safer than this shallow canal."

Violet couldn't agree more.

Knowing they probably had only a few minutes together, she quickly apprised him of what had happened at the villa, her harrowing experience in the mausoleum, and her suspicions of Julie Lesage.

Sam had an immediate understanding of the twists and turns of the situation, no doubt a reflection of his clandestine work in Great Britain.

"I agree with you that there is probably not a diplomatic solution to be had," he said. "I know you want to confront Mademoiselle Lesage, but I believe you should also attempt to speak to de Lesseps privately. He and Pasha are the strangest combination of friends and competitors I've ever seen. They're like a bobcat and a coyote working together to hunt a jackrabbit. They will probably secure a good meal, but will also likely kill each other in the process."

"So you are saying the bobcat and the coyote might each behave differently if I speak to them separately."

Sam nodded. "Try to meet de Lesseps in a safe public place."

Violet knew her expression was one of misery. "Sam, there is no longer a safe place for me here. I will stay on my guard as much as I can."

"I suppose I must be satisfied with that, although I'm not. Meanwhile, I will find out who Keating's paramour is if I have to . . . Well, never mind what I will do. Be assured that he will tell me."

Violet nodded. Sam had persuasion skills, both diplomatic and those of a more . . . direct . . . kind.

"Poor Sergeant Keating is better off telling you than facing Colonel Mott's wrath, I imagine," she said. "The colonel seems to suffer from a volatile temper, doesn't he?"

Sam laughed gently. "Thaddeus acts as he does to keep men off balance and paying attention. It is part of his great stage act and is how he gets such good results from men beneath him. Enough about him; when can you return?"

Could she come back? Violet didn't want to impose upon Hassan's generosity again, as he was putting himself at great risk in enabling this one visit. "The moment I can," she promised.

He pulled her to him one more time. "Be safe, wife. To lose you would be far worse than my own death."

Violet nodded mutely, her eyes filling with tears at the mere thought of Sam's death becoming a reality. She simply couldn't allow it to happen.

chapter 27

DESPITE SAM'S ADMONISHMENT THAT SHE find de Lesseps in a public location, Violet knew that his villa was the one spot where she could speak privately with him. She returned with the stained shawl tucked inside her reticule, not willing to leave it out of her sight for a moment. She was surprised by her confidence in entering this place where she had been brutally attacked the previous day. Her blood was racing with the driven notion that she would not stop until Sam was released, and it propelled her across the villa's front garden and through its front door, where a servant escorted her to de Lesseps's study.

To her chagrin, though, she discovered that de Lesseps was not alone. Pasha and Tewfik were with him, and the three appeared to be reviewing plans and diagrams spread out on a large table. With its brass surface resting atop at least a dozen carved legs set in a complicated pattern, this piece of furniture was like nothing Violet had ever seen.

Smoke hung in the air like a wafting shroud as the three smoked cigars. They pointed and made notes about what Violet quickly realized was tomorrow's event at Bitter Lakes, the last waypoint before the flotilla reached Suez, turned around, and returned to Port Said, with an intermediate stop back in Ismailia.

Violet gently cleared her throat, and the three looked up at her in unison.

"Madame Harper," de Lesseps said flatly, with as much

welcome in his voice as a patient for a saw-wielding surgeon.

Now that she was here, Violet wasn't exactly sure what to do. With de Lesseps and Pasha together, she wasn't going to get far. How could she get the Frenchman to speak with her in private?

"Monsieur de Lesseps, I—"

A look passed between de Lesseps and Pasha that she didn't understand; then Pasha interrupted her. "You have not met my son Tewfik. My son, this is the British woman who is also the undertaker."

Recognition dawned in Tewfik's eyes, as though he hadn't remembered Violet from last night outside the palace but all of a sudden knew her by reputation. She exchanged brief pleasantries with the young man, then turned her attention back to de Lesseps.

"Monsieur de Lesseps, if I might have a moment of—"

"Again, Madame Harper? You have become like the blood-sucking *moustique*, flying about, whining shrilly, then biting the unsuspecting to satisfy your temper." De Lesseps looked at his company for approval, and received it in polite chuckles from Pasha and Tewfik.

Clearly the Frenchman was not going to grant her a private audience. Well, that certainly wasn't going to stop Violet Harper.

"Monsieur, I plead on behalf of my husband and the other Americans. Surely you realize that they are not deserving of the rough treatment they are receiving."

"What rough treatment is that, *madaam?*" Pasha asked her suspiciously, and she realized that she was dangerously close to revealing that she had visited the men.

"The fact that they are being unjustly held, while we know that it is very likely that someone else is behind the murder of Caleb Purdy and the others."

"Like the mosquito that bites the wrist, then continues to drone around looking for an opportunity to bite the neck," de Lesseps said, clearly pleased with his ability to drag out a metaphor. Soon Violet would hear that she was responsible for a malaria outbreak.

Pasha, too, expressed his irritation with Violet. "*Madaam*, you do not understand that there is more at stake here than the lives of a few foreign soldiers. Besides, they did not help to build the canal."

Violet tamped down her impatience. What difference did it make whether or not Sam's friends had operated a dredge or hauled away dirt?

With bitter words on her tongue aching to be set free, Violet swallowed them with great difficulty and said as pleasantly as she could, "I shall remain behind, as well, then, to wait for my husband's release."

Pasha's expression was one of amusement. "No, *madaam*, you will continue on with the flotilla where you can be watched. If I let you stay behind, who will make sure you don't seduce my guards and help your friends escape?"

De Lesseps nodded in agreement, and Violet knew she had made a huge mistake in attempting to intervene on Sam's behalf while in the presence of both of these men. Pasha had essentially just told her she would be a prisoner for the remainder of the journey. How would she be able to assist Sam now?

"Tewfik will escort you out." Pasha turned back to de Lesseps, and together they went back to their papers.

Violet had just been summarily dismissed.

Blinking back her rage and frustration, she did not expect kindness from Pasha's son. "My lady, if you will . . . ?" He gestured toward the door and followed her out, then indicated that she should follow him. Violet's heels clicked along on the white marble flooring, which had a fleur-de-lis pattern scattered on various tiles. She assumed it must be the latest Parisian rage. Stylish or not, it was clearly taking her farther into the villa, not out.

"Tewfik, this is not the correct way," she said.

"Please, into here," he said, holding open a door for her.

Now Violet was suspicious. She crossed her arms. "I'm perfectly well here in the corridor," she insisted.

Tewfik smiled, and it struck Violet that this young man—a

boy, really—might have an infusion of charm that was not apparent when he was busy sulking next to his father.

Still, she refused to move. Charm did not make a man innocent.

"You believe you will come to harm with me, lady? This is not so. I merely wish to ask you questions."

Violet considered this. If he could ask her questions, then perhaps she could ask him questions, as well. She followed him into some sort of sitting room, which had a feminine look to it, done in pastel blues, creams, and pinks.

Now she and Tewfik Pasha sat across from each other on matching settees with a low, marble-topped table between them and a romantic scene painted above them on the ceiling. Tewfik jumped in without preamble or the offer of refreshment. "My father said you are an undertaker in your home country."

"This is true," she replied. Most people were morbidly fascinated and repulsed at the same time by her profession.

"How does a woman do this? It is not seemly." Tewfik's question was genuine, and Violet took no offense, for it was commonly asked of her.

"It is not always easily done," she said, "for it can be difficult for me to move literal dead weight. But I manage." An image flitted through her mind of Sam helping her with Karl Dorn's body, along with the question of whether he might want to be more involved with her business. Of course, that could only happen if she saw him freed, which wasn't looking likely at the moment.

One step at a time.

"You speak English well," she said to Pasha's son.

He brushed aside the compliment. "My father insists that I be tutored in both English and French, as he believes I cannot be the future khedive without easy communication with our European counterparts. I should like to know about your burial rites. Do you bury bodies or burn them?"

"Heavens!" Violet said, taken aback by his bluntness. "We do not burn bodies in Britain. We bury them."

"In mausoleums like ours? In sand?" Tewfik was like an eager schoolboy in his curiosity.

"Not exactly," Violet said carefully, not wishing to insult his country's customs. "Our crypts hold multiple bodies, but they are more . . . separate . . . from each other." She cringed inwardly, thinking about yesterday's inadvertent and inconsiderate crawling over bodies inside the mausoleum. "And there is not this much sand in Great Britain. We bury people in soil."

Tewfik frowned, as if that were a strange notion. "But sand preserves the bodies; dirt decomposes them, does it not?"

True. But they decomposed *privately*, and with markers to denote the soul's previous existence, not loosely commingled with other bodies.

"Tewfik, I am baffled as to your interest in my work. Is this a sudden passion you have for the dead?"

Pasha's son seemed genuinely surprised by her question. "You are not pleased that I am interested in you? Do not all women like attention?"

"Well, certainly, but—"

"You are very unusual. I like it that you are so strange. Egyptians used to ritualistically embalm bodies, now it is just sand. But you say you do not do any preservation." What was strange to Violet was how interested a young man was in funerary customs.

"Not usually, no. The Americans have become very fond of embalming"—her heart skipped a beat to think of any American she knew being embalmed anytime soon—"but in Great Britain there is great resistance to it. I confess that I approve of it myself, but only rarely have the opportunity to do it."

Tewfik nodded. "Well, we don't embalm anymore because it is against Islamic custom. But the way we bury today in mausoleums is not so different from burials in pyramids from thousands of years ago. This has been most interesting, my lady, thank you. I trust I will see you again, but for now I have to return to my father and his grand plans."

Tewfik stood and departed abruptly, leaving Violet alone in the room. She hardly noticed his absence, for her mind was whirling over what he had said about mausoleum burials being quite similar to those in pyramids. Something clicked in Violet's mind, but she wasn't sure exactly what it was, almost as if she had just heard a door unlocking in a distant room of a house.

She needed to go to her tent and think. As she made to leave the villa, Violet noticed a flash of lavender dress furtively scurrying down a hallway and was certain that it was the retreating figure of Julie Lesage. What was she doing in the villa? Violet stopped at the grand entry door that a servant was opening to see her out.

Mademoiselle Lesage had many questions to answer, and she was going to answer them now.

Violet turned on her heel and went down the hall to find Julie, leaving the servant shouting at her in Arabic, undoubtedly an admonishment that she wasn't permitted in other parts of the villa. De Lesseps could bellow and rage all he wanted about her intrusiveness; Violet was determined to have satisfaction in this matter.

Violet found Julie in a storage room, pretending to arrange a variety of women's hats and gloves on shelves. As if Violet was to believe that Julie would actually perform such a task for Louise-Hélène.

"Mademoiselle, I wish to speak with you," Violet said to her.

Julie looked up in feigned surprise. "Why, Madame Harper, I did not know you were here."

"Indeed. I should like to ask you about the American soldiers that Pasha hired to train his own army."

Now the surprise was real. "Why should I know anything about them?" She slapped a pair of ivory gloves against one hand and placed them next to a matching hat with layers of lace wrapped around the brim.

"Surely you realize that I noticed you speaking with them during the Dinner of the Sovereigns. I am wondering if you have formed a liaison with one of them."

"With an *American*?" she squeaked. "You must be the *imbécile*, to suggest such a thing. I will marry a Frenchman, and my mistress will see to it that he is of a good family."

Violet pressed further. "Those may be your marriage plans, but perhaps your heart has led you down a different path."

Julie straightened out the trailing ribbons of another hat, avoiding Violet's gaze. "Madame, I did know these rough, slovenly soldiers prior to our canal journey, and it is *absurde* to believe I would sully myself with one of them. You should ask Isabelle about them. It is much more likely that she would engage in a flirtation with some common American."

Violet put a hand to her hip. "I'll thank you to remember that I am married to one of those rough, slovenly Americans."

Julie reddened. "Of course, madame. Perhaps I should have said that Isabelle is not likely to make as good a marriage as I am, so she would be more likely to engage in the *liaison amoureuse*. In fact, I have been wondering if it wasn't she whom I saw outside last night."

Violet couldn't believe what she was hearing. "Are you suggesting that Isabelle stabbed a man?"

Julie shrugged and clasped her hands together, finally facing Violet. "Perhaps you should ask her yourself, madame."

∞

Violet considered what Julie had said. Although she suspected the maid was either deflecting attention from herself or merely attempting to cast suspicion on another woman she despised, it wouldn't hurt to ask Isabelle a few questions while she was here.

Violet quietly crept up to Louise-Hélène's quarters to seek out the lady's maid, and fortunately did not encounter any servants on her way. To her surprise, she found that Louise-Hélène and Eugénie were taking tea together.

The empress was the first one to notice her. "Madame Harper is here. *Ma louloute*, you must chastise the servants here. No one announced the undertaker's presence."

Louise-Hélène turned to see Violet standing there and quickly stood, her linen napkin edged in gold embroidery slipping to the ground. "M-madame Harper, what are you doing here?"

"I apologize for my intrusion. I have come to see Isabelle. Is she here?" Violet had hoped she might be able to simply find the maid without incurring the curiosity of these two women, but that was a foolish notion.

"*Ma louloute*'s maid? You wish to talk to her maid?" Eugénie said. "Whatever for? Do you plan to hire her away?"

"No, Your Highness. I would like to ask her some questions regarding last night's party."

"Ahhh," Eugénie said knowingly. "The little incident with the soldiers. De Lesseps told me all about it. You must be aware of it, too," she said to Louise-Hélène.

De Lesseps's fiancée was still standing, and looked about awkwardly. "I— Well, I turned in most early last night, and so I—"

"Oh, my dear, there was apparently quite the fuss. The soldiers had some sort of *désaccord*, and one stabbed the other. Rough, wild men, you know. No breeding. So Pasha locked them all up." Eugénie snapped her fingers to emphasize Pasha's decisive action.

Louise-Hélène's cheeks burned brightly. "This is terrible news."

Violet's stomach churned with acid at the casual way the empress spoke of the matter, but she also realized that de Lesseps had almost certainly given her a skewed version of events. "I do not believe there was a disagreement, as you say, Your Highness. Rather, I believe someone intentionally killed Sergeant Purdy, making it look like it was one of the other soldiers by using one of their sabers for it. In fact, it was my husband's that was used."

"*Mon Dieu*," the empress breathed, ostensibly in sympathy, but Violet heard the fascination in her tone.

Louise-Hélène's reaction was unexpected. "Pardon, who did you say was killed?"

"Caleb Purdy."

Violet could have sworn a look of relief swiftly crossed the girl's face. "That is very sad indeed," Louise-Hélène said, composed once more. "What does this have to do with Isabelle?"

"Nothing, I hope. I would just like to ask her whether she noticed anyone or anything suspicious on the grounds of the villa during the party."

Louise-Hélène shook her head, the dark mass of curls shuddering. "I'm sure she saw nothing. She was at the servants' party for the evening."

"Don't be silly, *ma louloute*," Eugénie interjected. "It would be most interesting to witness Madame Harper's interview. You must ring for Isabelle at once."

Violet was frustrated that she had to conduct another interview in front of an audience, but waited patiently while Louise-Hélène reluctantly pulled the bell cord to summon her servant.

Eugénie was not yet done with Violet. "Madame Harper, I have the most wonderful idea. You must sail with us aboard *L'Aigle* this afternoon down to Bitter Lakes so that you can tell me all about your little investigations."

Violet hardly thought this could be termed a "little investigation." "Your Highness, my husband is among those who have been imprisoned," she said through gritted teeth.

How did the people who tiptoed around royal thrones endure it when their monarchs made such utterly oblivious statements, knowing they were unable to dress down their superiors by pointing out how thoughtless they were?

"Of course, of course. Well, we will take your mind off it for the day, won't we? I think we can convince de Lesseps to have Pasha put on another picnic before we turn around and return. Wouldn't that be lovely? Oh, perhaps Pasha could provide some of those Arabian horses for us to ride. We could shoot rifles in the air like the Bedouin." Eugénie was already consumed with the next entertainment.

Violet nodded her head, knowing it would be impolitic not to accept the empress's invitation.

Isabelle arrived, carrying a stack of folded chemises. "I am sorry for taking so long, mademoiselle, I was in the laund—" Isabelle halted as she realized that Eugénie and Violet were both there.

Violet gently took the clothing from the maid and set it upon a side table. "It is I who have requested your presence, Mademoiselle Dumont. I must ask you a few questions."

"Regarding what? I am—I am very busy serving my mistress." Isabelle's eyes were wide with fear.

"This shall only take mere moments. Do you know Ross Keating?" Violet asked. The direct approach was probably best.

"Keating? Ross Keating? I do not think so. Mademoiselle? Do I know him?" she asked of Louise-Hélène, who shook her head no.

Violet thought a well-aimed barb might help improve the maid's memory.

"Sergeant Keating admits to a relationship with a Frenchwoman whom he will not identify. Julie Lesage believes she saw you on the palace grounds last night, with this." Violet pulled the bloodied shawl from her reticule. "Do you know this item?"

Isabelle blanched and shot her mistress a questioning look before saying, "I— No, I've never seen it before."

"So you are not seeing Keating?" Violet said.

"Hasn't this become most fascinating?" Eugénie said to no one in particular.

"Of course I am not." Isabelle now glanced at Eugénie before finding her courage and speaking boldly. "I am not surprised that Julie would accuse me of such a thing since she hated me the moment we met. Her accusation is probably an attempt to cover her own wrongdoings. Undoubtedly she herself is the one carrying on the liaison."

The room went silent, with everyone realizing that Isabelle had just tossed an incendiary explosive in front of Eugénie. Insulting the empress's personal maid was no casual matter. Even Violet found that she was holding her breath, waiting for a reaction.

To her great relief, Eugénie simply filled the room with her tinkling laughter. "Oh, *ma louloute*, our maids fight like the *chats* who live in the slums." Eugénie held up a hand and imitated a curled paw swiping at the air. "What grand entertainment."

Could the empress think of nothing else?

Louise-Hélène laughed weakly, and Isabelle seemed torn between pride in her response and a great desire to go scrambling underneath a bed in hiding.

Violet was not to be put off. "Julie says she saw someone, and if it was not you, it was someone else. Did you notice anyone on the palace grounds during the party?"

"I did see someone, actually," Isabelle said, again darting a nervous look at her mistress. "That ferocious man from the Russian delegation."

"General Ignatiev?" Violet said.

"Yes, that's him. He was leaping about with a sword, as if practicing fencing moves. I thought he was merely intoxicated. Intoxicated men do the most foolish things, and—and . . ."

Louise-Hélène took up where her maid was faltering. "I've noticed this Russian for myself. He is very gruff and *intimidant*. Someone so large and strong—and inebriated—would be likely to run another man through with a sword, wouldn't he?"

There was something evasive occurring between Louise-Hélène and her maid. With a sinking heart, Violet wondered if perhaps Julie was right that there was a *liaison amoureuse* in progress, only her jealousy made her too blind to realize that it was actually Louise-Hélène herself engaged in some sort of affair with one of the soldiers—an affair that Isabelle was trying to shroud in secrecy for her mistress.

Would Louise-Hélène really do such a thing, though? Violet could think of a hundred reasons why she might be drawn to a dashing soldier closer to her own age, yet she could also think of a hundred reasons why Louise-Hélène's best prospects lay with Ferdinand de Lesseps.

A cold chill settled over Violet as she drew that thought out further and played with it. Perhaps de Lesseps had discovered Louise-Hélène's affair, hence his insistence that all of the Americans be punished. It would explain de Lesseps's refusal to even consider their innocence.

Moreover, what if de Lesseps himself had something to do with Purdy's death? But that was simply unthinkable. He was, after all, Ferdinand de Lesseps, who had just completed the world's greatest feat since the pyramids. Some might sarcastically call him the Ditchdigger, but it was undeniable that he was currently the most famous man in the world. Surely he was above jealousies and lovers' revenges?

The evidence suggested he might not be. Regardless, she had no proof of anything and she was constantly coming up empty-handed.

Would no one tell Violet the truth?

chapter 28

DESPITE HER INITIAL MISGIVINGS, VIOLET actually didn't mind being aboard *L'Aigle* with Empress Eugénie and under de Lesseps's custody. The empress took great pains to make Violet comfortable, and she soon realized that Eugénie was more concerned about Violet's anxiety over Sam than she had let on inside Louise-Hélène's rooms.

Still, it was like having her heart ripped from her chest to watch Ismailia fade into the distance, not knowing what was happening to Sam.

"Madame Harper, you must try this pastry," the empress urged, handing her a tray full of confections. She was remarkably more serious now that the two of them sat on chairs on *L'Aigle's* deck. Violet almost wondered if the lighthearted persona the empress typically wore was merely a facade for the public.

That impression was confirmed as the sailing continued. Louise-Hélène and Isabelle remained scarce, and de Lesseps made a single perfunctory visit, obviously displeased and uncomfortable with Violet's presence.

As they glided through the water at the front of the flotilla, with Eugénie periodically waving to small groups of people positioned on the shore, the empress shared some of her own worries.

"These celebrations are very important to my husband, Madame Harper. They demonstrate France's power and strength at a time when it is sorely needed." Eugénie fanned herself lazily with the exquisitely painted fan she had held the day they arrived in Ismailia. It wasn't particularly hot, and Violet suspected that using the fan was merely a habit the empress affected.

"Needed, Your Highness?" Violet asked. She knew little of France's politics. The average Briton had stopped caring about France after Napoléon was defeated at Waterloo, leaving the minor political skirmishes to the elected officials.

"Yes." Eugénie sighed and took a bite of a tart that was bursting with apples and almonds, then leaned back quietly against her chair. Violet had almost decided the empress was asleep when suddenly Eugénie sat up straight again and continued fanning herself. "I am from Spain by birth, but have adopted France as my homeland. It is distressing to see that our—France's—power has weakened in the ascent of Prussia's military power. My husband believes that if he could defeat Prussia in a war, it would stave off the current Republican opposition to our dynasty, thus strengthening us both politically at home and militarily in the world. As such, he is at Tuileries right now, concocting an excuse to attack Prussia. I fear what will happen if he goes through with it."

Violet could at least understand all of the implications in this. "Your Highness, there is a general in my husband's country named Lee. He once said that it was well that war is so terrible— 'Otherwise we would grow too fond of it.' "

Eugénie nodded. "I believe I have heard of this general. His saying is wise. I think Napoléon wants the glory that would accompany his being a conquering hero, much like his namesake uncle. I have my doubts, though, about his ability to win against Prussia. Why indulge in so much loss of life in order to feel proud of himself? If only he recognized the canal as a crown of glory. De Lesseps would no doubt share the crown with the emperor of his own country. Alas, I am trying my best to achieve diplomatic peace with Austria, anyway. I accept Franz-Josef's attentions and his tedious stories. His little love notes, too, which he has had rowed over, secretly placed in my belongings, or sent to me by every other method except the carrier pigeon. All so that he might view France favorably in light of my husband's actions against Prussia, and so that Franz-Josef will not believe Napoléon will come after Austria, as well."

So the note that Violet had witnessed Julie pass to her mistress in Ismailia had been a love note.

Eugénie leaned toward Violet, speaking quietly and confidentially. "Sometimes, Madame Harper, I even start little fights with Franz-Josef so that he believes us to be in lovers' quarrels. This at least makes it a little interesting for me. I wonder sometimes if my husband has these quarrels with his mistresses. There are so many of them, though, that he probably discards them the moment they express any *colère, non?*"

The empress sat back. "Anyway, Frederick is like a walnut shell. Very hard to crack through to see the meat inside, although it is rumored he does not wish war under any circumstances. I cling to that hope."

"It must be a difficult balancing act for you," Violet murmured.

"This is the life I was born to, madame, and so I live it as best I can. Ah, look!" Eugénie pointed ahead to where Violet saw that yet another crowd was awaiting them on the banks of their next stop.

"Do you know why this place is called Bitter Lakes, Your Highness?" Violet asked. "It seems a most unhappy name."

"De Lesseps says these weren't really lakes at all prior to the canal, but dry salt valleys. The canal made them actual lakes. Seawater now flows freely into this lake from both the Mediterranean and the Red Sea. De Lesseps also says the current flowing north of Bitter Lakes is different from that on the south side, but I do not understand why."

Violet couldn't hazard a guess, either. Her limits of scientific application were the principles of rigor mortis and bodily decomposition.

They sailed along in silence for some time, each woman leaning back against her chair, lost in her own thoughts, until a feminine voice broke the hypnotic sounds of the craft slicing through the water and the gulls squawking overhead.

"Your Highness, do you wish to change for supper?" It was Julie. It appeared that court etiquette was to be obeyed even on a casual sailing trip.

"I suppose I must. Bring me a couple of choices to look at." Eugénie had already returned to a reclined position, waving the fan gently below her chin.

"Yes, Your Highness." Julie curtsied even though Eugénie was not watching her, and then she nodded to Violet. Violet thought it a little onerous for the maid to have to lug two heavy outfits to the deck, only to haul them back down to the empress's cabin again for the actual changing, but then, royalty probably did this all the time.

Forming an idea, Violet told Eugénie that she was going to seek out the necessary room and would return shortly. With the empress's permission to leave, Violet followed Julie belowdecks. "Mademoiselle," she said before Julie could open the door to a cabin. "I would speak with you, please."

Julie frowned. "Again?"

"Yes. I wish to ask you more about what you saw with Mademoiselle Isabelle Dumont."

"Oh. That." Julie entered the empress's quarters while Violet remained in the doorway, certain that she shouldn't enter this domain without permission. She stood quietly while Julie sifted through gowns separated by tissue inside large leather trunks. She found one, then another, and took a horsehair brush to each of them to ready them for presentation to her mistress.

When she was done and the two dresses lay across the back of a sofa, Julie turned back to Violet. "I must tell you, madame, that I did not actually see anyone being murdered during the party. I found the bloody shawl, and it gave me the idea to claim I had witnessed a murder and hopefully throw a shadow upon Isabelle."

Violet stared in disbelief. "Why would you wish to commit so heinous an act?"

Julie shrugged. "I do not like her," she said simply. "She is not trustworthy, and it's just a matter of time before she exposes her real self."

"She is hardly the only one with an integrity problem," Violet snapped, causing Julie to stare openmouthed in return. Violet softened, as it would do no good to alienate the empress's maid. Besides, whether or not Julie had lied about witnessing the murder, there had indeed actually been a body.

Did the shawl belong to Louise-Hélène, or to someone else in the delegation? Even if she found the owner, would it actually lead her to a murderess, or just send her down another complicated badger's burrow? Time was quickly running out for Sam and his friends, and Violet was no closer to an answer.

chapter 29

November 21, 1869

AFTER TRAVELING ANOTHER DAY TO reach Suez for an overnight stay and more fireworks, during which she saw little of Louise-Hélène and Isabelle, Violet obtained permission to return to *Newport* while the ships realigned themselves in the port. Fortunately, Captain Nares must have decided he had fully made his point to the French, and did not attempt to maneuver *Newport* overnight to the head of the flotilla. *L'Aigle* proudly sailed ahead of everyone else for the day's return trip to Ismailia, accompanied by great fanfare on shore and from the deck of *Viribus Unitis*. The journey left Violet nearly a nervous wreck in her anxiety to return, to ensure Sam was still safe.

When everyone had disembarked from their respective ships, they headed toward the great pavilion. There were more tedious speeches, among them one by the Prince of Wales, waxing on about having ceremoniously opened the dam of the first section of the canal back in March with his wife, Princess Alexandra. Included in his oration was a non sequitur of having acquired a fabulous mummy from Egypt's Twenty-Sixth Dynasty.

Violet left the self-congratulatory proceedings, thinking she might attempt to see Sam again. She was truly down to hours now to figure out who had committed this crime in order to see the Americans freed. If the canal celebrations ended without uncovering who killed Caleb Purdy, there was no question in Violet's mind that Pasha would simply declare Sam and his friends guilty and dispose of them. And sadly, no one in the dispersed delegation would give much thought to the citizens of a country that had no real representation at the festivities.

Violet was desperate.

She tried to find Hassan in the crowds, but instead managed to bump into Tewfik, who was not with his father onstage. "Lady, why the hurry?" he asked.

Seeing the boy made Violet realize that perhaps she could win him to her side. Tewfik could influence his father or, at the very least, could get her back inside the prison so she didn't have to ask Hassan to risk his own life again.

"Ah, I am very sad," she said, clinging to his arm.

He smiled and led her away from the throng of people. "You must tell me all."

Tewfik led her out to the chieftains' tents, which were doing a sorry business with all of the populace off to the speeches. They all clamored and barked for Tewfik's attention, particularly upon recognizing who he was.

The khedive's son paused at a tent to purchase a cup of Turkish sand coffee for Violet. She watched as the servant inside made it precisely as de Lesseps's servant had done, and gladly accepted the cup. Tewfik smiled to see that Violet liked the taste of it.

"Now, my lady, it is not possible to be sad after having this nectar, but you must tell me what upset you previously." He led her away, toward the outskirts of the Arab tents.

"I am sad because my husband is imprisoned here, most unjustly," she said.

Tewfik frowned. "It is not unjust if he has killed another man. He will be put to death for it."

Tewfik might as well have run Violet through with a sword for how badly his words cut her. "But he did not do it," she insisted. "My husband had no motive for it, nor did any of the others he is with."

"Then who did do it?"

"I don't know." Violet's unhappiness rode on the wave of those three perpetual words rolling off her tongue.

Tewfik shrugged. "Then this subject no longer interests me. Come, I have a treat for you."

Violet was still grappling with his dismissal of her situation when he led her to a grove of palm trees, which had large bundles of finger-shaped, molasses-colored fruit dangling from their branches, too high to be reached by hand. "Here," he said, pointing to a large urn that was attached to one of the trees. A tap was inserted into the tree, and thick juice from the tree was slowly dripping into the urn.

They approached the urn, where Tewfik dipped his finger inside and pulled it out, sucking the amber juice that dripped from it. "You must try."

Violet obediently followed suit, and found the sap to be sweet and delicious.

"You like?" Tewfik asked, his delighted expression revealing that he already knew the answer.

"It is very good," Violet admitted.

"We cannot reach the dates, but the sap is in some ways even better. In the Qur'an, Allah instructs Maryim to eat dates when she gives birth to Isa. Therefore, in Egypt we always recommend them for pregnant women." Tewfik's gaze was suggestive.

Oh dear.

Violet thought quickly, and decided to appeal to his pride as heir to the khedive. "Which means you should have plenty of dates on hand when your father arranges what will surely be a brilliant marriage for you."

"My father." He said this flatly. "He cannot die soon enough."

The words made Violet shiver. Was she safe here with this boy about to become a man?

"Why are you at odds with him?" she asked.

Tewfik offered the typical woes of son versus father, which apparently changed neither from generation to generation, nor from culture to culture. Pasha was controlling, vindictive, and condescending; Tewfik was smart, honorable, and visionary.

Pasha's view of Egypt's future was brainless; Tewfik's made sense.

"What is your view for Egypt?" Violet asked.

"Egypt must be for Egyptians, of course. My father has permitted far too many foreigners to come in, not only to work on the canal but to set up permanent encampments. Not even the *fellahin* have the opportunity to do the lowliest jobs because of them."

Violet was reminded of what de Lesseps had told her after she had overheard Tewfik's argument with his father. "There is a Colonel Orabi who agrees with you, isn't there?"

Tewfik seemed pleased that she knew this. "Yes. He tries to carry this message of nationalism about, but he needs money to build his enterprise, which is hard to accumulate with the waste my father has brought upon the country."

"Waste of money is better than waste of life, is it not?" she said.

"Is this about your husband again, my lady? I can find you another one. In fact, once I am married to an Ottoman princess, I can add you to my harem of women. You would be well cared for. It would please me to have an exotic woman like yourself. I have my eye on a few others, too."

Violet was aghast at what he was suggesting. This required tact. "I'm afraid I would be a poor companion to you, as I would mourn my husband too much. As I mourn him now."

"Why do you mourn him now?" Tewfik reached into the urn for another fingerful of sap.

This was her final opportunity. "Because he is being held in terrible conditions. All of the men are heaped into one cell with no light and the most unsanitary conditions and little food," she said in a rush.

He considered this as he wiped his finger across the front of his jacket. "How do you know about their conditions, my lady?"

In her anxiety over Sam, Violet realized she had made a foolish, foolish mistake. "I—ah, I overheard some men talking about it."

Fortunately, Tewfik was still young enough that he couldn't quickly think through the unlikelihood of Violet's statement, and he accepted it as is. However, his next statement nearly made Violet slap him, no matter that he was the khedive's son.

"I don't see that their circumstances are poor at all. My father has not given any order for torture or beatings, so their treatment has been exceedingly gentle. Besides, I would be a half-wit to want him released, wouldn't I?" Tewfik's smile was almost wolfish. "Enough of this talk about your husband. Would you like to see my collection of stuffed gorillas at the palace? I am thinking of expanding into antelopes, although they are a little harder to obtain."

What Violet wanted was a place away from this silly, spoiled boy. Presumably he would mature in the coming years, but right now the thought of him taking his father's place as khedive over Egypt was nauseating.

"I'm afraid I must see to some things before the flotilla leaves again for Port Said. I am grateful to you for offering to show me what I'm sure is a fascinating array of animals." Violet couldn't get away from Tewfik quickly enough.

He was yet another failure in her effort to see Sam released.

Violet managed to find Hassan again and begged him to escort her to Sam once more. The cultural attaché was hesitant.

"My lady, you know that this could mean great trouble for me."

"I promise that I will only be moments with my husband. Please, sir. I cannot leave Ismailia without having seen him again." If Hassan denied her, Violet swore to herself that she would dig a tunnel into the jail with her own two hands.

Hassan sighed. "Very well, but quickly, my lady."

She followed him down the staircase of the prison building once more. All of the men looked as if they had aged ten years in two days, and Violet's heart broke in pity, but she tried to maintain a hearty outlook. "I believe we will have a resolution soon," she told them before she once again went with Sam to a private cell to talk.

Once there, Sam spoke first. "Keating confessed to me that it was Louise-Hélène's maid, Isabelle, that he has been seeing in private. He didn't want anyone to know because he had promised to take her with him back to America. She is an old friend of Louise-Hélène's, who hired Isabelle to help her escape an abusive husband. Keating plans to make her escape permanent."

So Julie wasn't completely wrong about Isabelle, and Louise-Hélène had been helping her friend in this. That explained a little, anyway, but told Violet nothing about who had killed Caleb Purdy or the other men.

She told Sam what precious little she had gleaned from de Lesseps, Eugénie, and Tewfik, leaving out Tewfik's boorish behavior.

"What now?" Sam asked, his eyes bleary and his unshaven cheeks scraggly.

"I will solve this, I promise," Violet assured her husband with a confidence she didn't feel.

"My lady, it is time to go." Hassan stood in the cell's doorway. "I have been notified that the khedive is nearby. I cannot risk this. If he should decide to visit these men . . ."

Violet nodded, embracing Sam for what she prayed was not the last time, and followed Hassan quickly out of the building.

Fortunately, Pasha had instead decided to attend a shadow-puppet play on the other side of the canal, and was hopefully too busy with de Lesseps, Eugénie, Franz-Josef, and the rest to remember that he was planning to issue judgment on the Americans. Violet breathed a sigh of relief when Hassan translated Pasha's whereabouts to her from one of the guards.

"Tomorrow the flotilla returns to Port Said," Hassan said, stating the obvious. "What shall you do?"

"I will know who did this before the flotilla sails. What more is there?" Violet then thanked Hassan for his assistance, but as she turned to leave, she remembered something. "Do you know what happened to the dead American, Sergeant Purdy?"

"No, my lady. The khedive handled it without me. I am sorry." He bowed formally to her.

Violet returned to the festivities, furious about Purdy, in agony over Sam, and thoroughly bewildered about the evil activities occurring along the Suez Canal.

◯◯

Violet made her way back to the edge of the pavilion area, where she saw that most of the delegation was focused on the puppet show, while others were drifting toward a stage that had been set for a play. She stayed a distance away, simply observing, for she had no heart for any festivities. Eventually, the puppet show finished to great applause, and everyone attending it made their way to the stage, as well.

Pasha was providing entertainment until the very last minute, to ensure that no guest would have a single moment to consider anything other than personal pleasure. It truly was sheer genius.

Pasha stood on the stage now, and announced that he had a surprise for the audience. Instead of being performed at a future date in the Cairo opera house, Mariette's opera, *Aida*, was to be premiered here in Ismailia. Now. Performers and musicians had been working day and night to ensure that the delegation would be the first to see it.

The crowd went wild. Auguste Mariette took to the stage to receive his due, as well.

As everyone else was distracted by the presentation, Violet noticed that workers were actively dismantling the pomp and splendor of Ismailia in the background. She watched idly as several men stripped jasmine garlands from gazebos, fencing, and tent posts.

This is it, then. After the performance, everyone will return to the tents for a final night of sleep in the sweet Egyptian air; then they will board their ships and depart tomorrow morning for a final farewell at Port Said.

Two men carried a trunk that must have been full of bricks based on how much they struggled with it.

The delegation members will then return to their home countries, with no one caring at all about four men in a prison cell.

She turned to one side. More men were tearing down fencing, stacking the pieces in piles, and Violet could only assume they would be used elsewhere.

Pasha, when he finally remembers Sam, Thaddeus, Ross, and Owen, will simply go and pronounce them guilty.

A half dozen workers watched another one knock down tentpoles, while they stood by to capture sections of fabric in their hands and roll them up.

Once they are pronounced guilty, they will be taken to a place of execution. How are executions conducted in Egypt?

Something clicked again in Violet's mind, like another door opening somewhere in a house. Then another door opened, and another.

She whirled around once more to watch the two men with the trunk, now hefting it onto a cart attached to a patiently waiting horse. *Click. Click. Click.* All of the doors were opening, revealing to her an answer that was so breathtakingly malevolent that she nearly staggered from the weight of the revelation as various statements and events meshed together in her mind like the gears and wheels of a finely made clock.

The condition of the ship captain's body . . .

The observation of the American Colonel Mott that the Austrian Dorn had not been in a fight . . .

The playwright Richard Lepsius's tale of ancient Egypt . . .

The Museum of Cairo director Mariette's witnessing Mott berate an Egyptian soldier . . .

The hysterical demonstration by Eugénie's maid, Julie, outside the party at Pasha's palace . . .

There was only one answer as to who had attempted to kill Violet, as well. Yes, Violet knew what had happened, but she needed to verify one simple thing to be sure.

Sam, keep faith, I have the truth now, and the truth will set you free.

chapter 30

VIOLET LOCATED FRANZ-JOSEF. HE SAT ramrod straight in his chair next to Eugénie, looking positively bored with Mariette's story of ancient Egypt. When Violet demanded that she be taken aboard his ship, his expression was one of relief as he stood to escort her himself, when in ordinary circumstances Violet knew he would have been insulted and cold, leaving such a petty task to a servant.

As she and the emperor boarded, the trumpeters started up again. Violet was so agitated by what she had to do that as she was helped down to the deck she snapped, "For heaven's sake, will you please stop that infernal racket!"

The horn blasts faded into sputters as the shocked musicians actually obeyed her.

Not caring whether Franz-Josef, or anyone else, was behind her, she made her way down to Karl Dorn's cabin, murmuring prayers that his body would still be there and not whisked away overnight to some watery grave.

To Violet's relief, Dorn was still there. So was the lingering odor of the makeshift embalming fluid, although it wasn't nearly as overpowering as it had initially been. She intentionally cleared her mind of its jumble of thoughts to concentrate on Dorn, adopting her usual kneeling pose next to the body and whispering, "Herr Dorn, I see that my husband has done his job most satisfactorily. You have been well wrapped by him, and I believe you are in perfect shape for the remainder of your journey home. Forgive my intrusion on your temporary resting place, but I must check something."

She dropped down farther to look under his bedstead. The trunk she had tripped over and shoved under the bed when caring for Dorn's body was no longer there. Violet returned to her kneeling position next to Dorn. "I believe I know why you died, sir, and I am sorry for it. Be assured, though, that I am preparing to accuse a murderer in our midst, and your death was not in vain."

She patted the man's shoulder and rose to leave.

"Did you find what you wanted, Frau Harper?" Franz-Josef said from outside the doorway. He hadn't entered, but then most monarchs, by superstitious custom, were not permitted to be in the presence of death, lest it come and visit the throne itself.

"I did *not*, actually, Your Highness, and therefore everything I suspected I now know to be true."

There had been so many liars in Violet's presence. Some of their lies were irrelevant, meant to cover up love affairs and other foolish activities. But the other lies—the cleverest of the lies— had been intended to throw Violet's suspicion in every direction except where it belonged.

She had to give credit to the murderer's calculating flair.

chapter 31

VIOLET HAD NEVER BEEN ONE for dramatics, leaving that
sort of thing to family members who were crazed with grief.
Violet's role was more that of a mere stage manager, ensuring that
all went well and that the staging of the funeral was executed
flawlessly, while the actors and actresses carried out the sometimes
genuine, sometimes affected histrionics that accompanied the
mourning play.

On this day, however, Violet mounted the stage where the
actors were in their final scene of Mariette's story. A man and a
woman in ancient Egyptian dress sat huddled together in a set
that resembled a temple. No, wait, it was meant to be a crypt.

Well, that was certainly an appropriate backdrop for what
Violet had to say.

Someone—probably the director—was hissing at Violet from
somewhere to depart from his stage, as the musicians slowly
ended their playing and the two people onstage trailed off in
their singing of the sweet and beautiful death they were about to
experience together.

What an ignoramus Mariette was in this story line, Violet
thought, even as she was barging in on the sorrowful scene. The
dead deserved honor, respect, and sentimental remembrances by
those who remained behind and grieved, but death itself was
a messy business, and not to be sung of as some alluring and
desirable release.

The audience, by now well used to constant entertainments and stunning spectacles, viewed Violet's intrusion as some interesting new development in the play—despite her modern dress against the ancient Egyptian sets and costumes—and applauded her appearance politely.

"I apologize for my trespass upon this last of the festivities," she began, amazed at how the set construction was such that her voice reverberated around her and projected out over the crowds.

"My name is Violet Harper, and I am a member of the British delegation. Queen Victoria honored my husband and me with an invitation to attend the Suez Canal celebrations, and although Monsieur de Lesseps and the khedive have provided unending pageantry and delights, to which most of you have been happy spectators, I have witnessed death and ruin and devastation during our journey along the canal.

"*Aida* presents the death of two lovers as romantic, but what has been occurring over the past week has been the extreme of evil." Violet paused, gathering her thoughts and her nerve for the accusations to come.

Hushed whispering rippled through the audience, but at least the likes of de Lesseps and Pasha had not attempted to stop her. In fact, the two men were seated close to the stage, openmouthed in shock.

Tewfik sat two rows back from his father, naked admiration for Violet in his expression.

As Violet continued to speak, she saw more delegation members she recognized. Eugénie sat with Franz-Josef, naturally. What remarkable, almost animal instincts he had for finding Eugénie and placing himself in her orbit.

Crown Prince Frederick sat with a group of other Prussians who were pointing at Violet as they gossiped, but he stared straight at her, smiling enigmatically.

The Russians, Grand Duke Michael and General Ignatiev, looked so bored they might have been corpses themselves in their seats.

Sir Henry Elliot, Asa Brooks, and the Prince of Wales seemed delighted by Violet's bold interruption of the proceedings. It was as if she were once more *Newport* bullying ahead of *L'Aigle*.

Except that Violet was playing no game of cunning subterfuge. She was here for justice.

Prince Henry and Princess Sophie of Holland seemed confused as to whether Violet was a planned part of what must have been the most unusual opera ever or if she was a genuine interruption.

The various royal servants were scattered about, the more important ones tending to their masters and mistresses, others helping in the background with the dismantling of Ismailia, and still others likely beginning to pack up sleeping tents.

Violet caught the eye of Théophile Gautier, who nodded his head and pantomimed three slow claps. Encouragement to continue, or merely an acknowledgment of her boldness? She could almost hear him saying, "Act three, scene four. Deranged undertaker mounts stage and makes wild allegations."

She continued on. "Many of you do not know that upon our arrival in Port Said a few days ago, there was a death in the lumberyard, which burned down during the fireworks display. The death was that of the lumberyard owner's son, Yusef Halabi, and although he had ostensibly perished in the flames, it was quickly obvious to me that he had been stabbed prior to the fire."

Several people in the audience gasped, while de Lesseps's expression turned thunderous.

Violet couldn't worry about the Frenchman's anger at this point. Sam had to be publicly declared innocent and freed, and there was no better way to do this than to explain the story to every single delegate present, who could then exert pressure upon Pasha to release the Americans or risk an international crisis.

"Later in the evening, while most of you had rejoined the festivities or were boarded back on your ships to prepare for the next day's sailing, another murder occurred, this time of a ship's captain who had been hired to carry certain items to Ismailia.

His death was made to look as if he had piloted his ship into a canal embankment while completely in his cups, but I knew from his injuries that this could not be true. Captain Naser had also been murdered."

Violet started to pace onstage, a habit of hers when sorting out a knotty problem. The two "dying" actors, spooked by her own performance, held hands and quietly exited the stage, leaving her alone inside the "crypt" walls to make her earth-shattering denunciations.

"Although I understood that both men had been murdered, it was difficult to see what they had in common. Why would someone wish to do away with a man working in a lumberyard and also a man who pilots a ship? It made no sense. Perhaps they had nothing to do with each other." Violet paused and held up a hand to the audience. "But they *were* related."

"The undertaker undertakes a great mystery!" Asa Brooks shouted from his seat, eliciting nervous laughter from the audience.

Violet ignored him as she readied for what she had to divulge. "First we witnessed local Egyptians being killed, then the deaths moved into the delegations. Herr Karl Dorn, chamberlain to His Imperial Highness Franz-Josef, died during the Dinner of the Sovereigns. As with the captain, most people believed that it was due to an overabundance of liquor. But the chamberlain struck me as very devoted to his duties. Would he truly lose control of himself in this way, shaming not only himself, but also the Austrian emperor? I did not think so.

"It was too much to be hoped that all of the death would cease with Dorn, for then there was a final, most heinous death among the American soldiers, who were not here as delegation members but as a special team training the khedive's own army. We all watched the Americans and their military displays at the picnic. That night, one of them, Sergeant Caleb Purdy, was killed, run through with a cavalry saber. But not just any saber . . . it was the one belonging to my husband."

This set the chattering apace, which was no surprise to Violet.

She waited for the audience to calm down.

"The Americans were hauled off to a jail here, and were it not for the kindness of one of the khedive's men, I may have never seen my husband again." Violet sighed. "Of course, Sam had not killed Purdy, any more than he had killed any of the other victims. But had a single person killed all four men, or were there multiple killers at work? And what could these men possibly have in common?

"It was the Empress Eugénie's lady's maid, Mademoiselle Julie Lesage, who convinced me that it was one killer, and that that one killer was targeting servants attached to the canal celebrations. Mademoiselle Lesage was an excellent actress, worthy of the greatest Parisian stage—or Cairo opera house— for her performance as a frightened domestic. Her intent was to throw my suspicions upon poor Isabelle Dumont, lady's maid to Louise-Hélène Autard de Bragard, fiancée to the great Ferdinand de Lesseps, of whom she felt great jealousy because she did not believe Mademoiselle Dumont to be her equal. Mademoiselle Lesage is also petty and spiteful. She tried her best to portray Mademoiselle Dumont as deficient, even going so far as to seek out a member of the Russian delegation for help—which fortunately was not provided—as well as to use a bloodied shawl to imply that the other maid might have had something to do with Purdy's murder."

Violet shook her head in disgust at how she had been duped. There was no sound whatsoever coming from the audience now. Braying camels and their shouting drivers could be heard in the distance, but inside the hastily erected playhouse there was complete silence. Violet glanced out over the audience, and noticed that Eugénie was pale. She was about to become paler.

"As it turned out, Mademoiselle Lesage was partially correct. Isabelle Dumont was not truly a proper lady's maid, but a mere friend of Louise-Hélène's, one whom Louise-Hélène was attempting to help escape a bad marriage. They did not know that Isabelle would meet one of the American soldiers during this trip, and that the two would become enamored with each other.

A happy occurrence, but a complicating one for Mademoiselle Lesage.

"The empress's maid probably felt emboldened in her actions because of Eugénie's unintentional condescension toward the common Louise-Hélène." Violet turned to squarely face de Lesseps. "Monsieur, you must not permit other women—no matter how great they are—to occupy the space that rightfully belongs to Louise-Hélène. Do not humiliate her, and I believe she will be the most precious of wives."

De Lesseps was practically sputtering in rage over Violet's public chastisement, but she didn't care. That poor girl deserved more than to be a dusty old piece of luggage stored away in a closet.

"Although I understood this about the two maids, it still did not resolve the great mystery surrounding the deaths of four men. But during the past week, I have gathered some crucial pieces of information, most of which I had no idea were important until everything came to me about an hour ago.

"First, I extend my compliments to General Nikolay Ignatiev, whose recognition of Herr Dorn's death by overeating opium was brilliant. Had I immediately acted upon that idea, I might have reached the answer sooner. You were also wise to avoid Mademoiselle Lesage, who accosted you during the Dinner of the Sovereigns."

Ignatiev inclined his head graciously at her. "I did not know who she was, but I do know beautiful women not usually wish to talk to Nikolay," he said.

Le bon Théo was becoming impatient. "Dear lady, we, too, would like to reach the final scene of your dramatic piece before the next century arrives," he called out. "Or, if it will take that long, at least let us have some drinks."

There was nervous laughter in the audience, but no one seemed inclined to leave or worry about refreshments. Violet was more than happy to allow the murderer to continue to suffer in suspense, unable to bolt from the proceedings because guilt would be apparent without Violet's words of condemnation.

She took a deep breath. "I spent so much time focused on the discordance between the two maids that I missed the true nature of the situation, how ruthless and determined and, yes, how *motivated* the killer was. These attributes are why three men had to be murdered."

"Four, Mrs. Harper. There were four men killed," Sir Henry said.

She shook her head. "No, just three. Karl Dorn really did die simply by overeating opium. I did not initially recognize the symptoms, but now I believe he was a man who suffered great physical pain, and probably sought relief in many substances. He did not understand the power of opium, which he found in a chest aboard his ship. I am certain the opium had been secretly stashed aboard *Viribus Unitis* by the murderer, who intended to retrieve it at a later point. No one would have suspected that the chest, which contained much more than mere opium, would be hidden upon the Austrian emperor's boat, making it a convenient transport vessel to Ismailia and beyond.

"It was the most unlikely person attending the canal celebrations who actually revealed to me the truth of the matter. My husband and I visited the Arab tents, and while there, we met the Egyptologist Richard Lepsius. He retold the legend of the treasure thief, about a trusted servant of Pharaoh who proceeds to deceive his ruler by building a pyramid to hold Pharaoh's riches, but leaving a secret entrance for himself to steal gradually from Pharaoh's stores.

"The story was amusing but meaningless to me, until I received from Auguste Mariette a copy of his book, in which he inscribed, 'For where your treasure is, there will your heart be also.' It caused me to consider what Mariette had said to me one evening at dinner, that the khedive had the unfortunate tendency to . . . select antiquities for himself that would . . . otherwise find their way to the national museum. It was the story of the treasure thief, but in reverse, since the equivalent to the pharaoh—the khedive—was the one spiriting away national treasures."

Pasha shouted an obscenity to Mariette, who ignored him but looked at Violet in utter shock at her betrayal. She silently hoped Mariette would forgive a distraught wife doing everything in her power to free her husband, especially with what else she had to say.

"If so, had Mariette orchestrated a series of deaths to cast a pall upon the canal celebrations, to discredit Pasha's rule and possibly even dethrone him, thus stopping the great pillaging of antiquities? It would have been a bold move for the Frenchman.

"However, this was not the case, although Mariette did witness something important. He told me that he saw one of the American soldiers berating an Egyptian soldier. I do not think this was what he saw at all. He witnessed the murderer arguing with Caleb Purdy, but because Mariette does not know military uniforms, he was confused about what he had witnessed."

Gautier lolled his head back against his chair dramatically and once more called out to her. "Please, Madame Harper. My grandchildren are becoming old men while we wait for the *dénouement* of your very interesting, but most complicated, story."

Very well. Perhaps it was time to move the murderer into custody.

"As every participant here knows, Pasha's most ardent goal is to modernize Egypt. He has been most successful in his efforts, as the world now sees. Unfortunately for the men who were murdered, Pasha also desires to turn Egypt into a European-style nation. This does not sit well with many, including his own son Tewfik."

Even Gautier was openmouthed at the implication of this.

"Tewfik revealed to me that there is a burgeoning nationalist movement in Egypt, one that seeks to expel all foreigners who have been relocated here as a result of the canal construction."

Pasha jumped up and turned to face his son. "Who is behind this?" he exclaimed furiously. "I will have this traitorous idea crushed immediately!"

Tewfik stared stonily ahead, ignoring his father.

For her part, Violet took no delight in participating in internal political squabbles between Pasha and Colonel Orabi.

"Your Highness," she said, returning his attention back to her, "I believe you already know who that is. However, we have a worse man in our midst. Someone whom you trust but who does not deserve your trust. Someone whom you might believe has the best interests of the canal in mind, but actually desires its destruction."

"Who would dare betray this great achievement, Mrs. Harper? Dare to betray me?"

Violet paused, hating to deliver the news to a man who had poured his entire reputation, his country's fortune, his very *life* into this enterprise. She moved to the edge of the stage and looked directly at Pasha. "It is your cultural attaché, Hassan Salib."

A crypt-like silence descended over the audience, with probably half the audience wondering what Pasha would do and the other half wondering who Hassan even was.

Pasha was as stunned as Violet had expected he would be. He signaled a servant standing nearby, who immediately ran off to do his master's bidding.

"*Madaam*, you cannot possibly know what you are talking about," Pasha protested.

"I know that you are distressed, but it is true."

"I do not believe it. Hassan has been my most valued man for many years."

Clearly certain members of the audience—those who had seen Hassan at Pasha's side, who had seen Hassan serve as the respectful announcer of guests at the Ismailia party—did not believe Violet, either, for there was a low rumble of discontent.

"Your valued man is devoted to Colonel Orabi, sir. It is the only explanation. He has always sought to serve him, and working under you as cultural attaché gave him plenty of opportunity."

"But he was trained in European countries. He is fluent in several languages. He would not associate with a risen *fellah* like Orabi."

"I cannot account for Hassan's loyalties; I can only tell you what he did. It began with the antiquities that you have intercepted on their way to the Cairo Museum."

"What of them? They belong to me."

At that moment, Pasha's servant reappeared with several soldiers and Hassan himself, whose calm and placid exterior infuriated Violet.

Pasha pointed at Violet. "Now you must prove it in front of Hassan himself, *madaam*."

But Pasha was sadly mistaken if he thought Violet was fearful to do so, particularly when Sam's life hung in the balance. "As I said, Hassan is an Orabi loyalist. More so, he is actively supporting him through the sale of artifacts and opium."

Only a brief tic in Hassan's eyes revealed to Violet that she was correct.

"As Your Highness would go through the artifacts and select those you wished to keep, Hassan would set them aside as instructed, but instead of sending all of the remaining pieces to the museum, he would select certain ones into which he could stuff opium packets, which he believed would add to their value, to sell them in order to raise money for Orabi's movement. Thus Mariette was seeing nearly all of the museum's treasures vanishing before they ever arrived. But for Hassan, this theft was legitimate, as he was helping to save his country from the foreign invasion that had resulted when de Lesseps started his canal and imported workers from all over the world with Pasha's blessing. No longer would Egypt be in submission to the international community."

Mariette stood and pointed a finger at Pasha. "I knew that you were responsible for the decimation of my museum! It will take years for me to rebuild the collections, which have probably been sent to the ends of the earth by now. No doubt the British have taken the lion's share of them."

This caused Bertie to jump up, too. "Good Britons pay handsomely and honestly for artifacts, which are offered by every stall vendor and street urchin in this country. It is not wrong if we have a deeper appreciation and care for antiquities of other cultures."

Now de Lesseps interjected to defend his countryman, shouting at Pasha, "I knew that there were forces seeking to undermine me. Now I know that those forces were coming from *you*, and that they sought to undermine *all* French interests in Egypt."

Hassan's lips curved up smugly at the argument, which Violet saw was carrying attention away from him. She knew this was spiraling out of control, like a funeral service full of inebriated mourners, but she also knew exactly how to manage such a situation. She clapped her hands together several times. The cracking noise echoed sharply over the proceedings and caused everyone's attention to turn back to her.

"I should like to finish this story before you all establish your battle lines," she said. Everyone sat once more, except for Hassan, who had soldiers on either side of him, holding his elbows.

"Hassan's plan worked very well for quite some time, I cannot imagine how long, until it came to the canal celebrations, where his misfortunes began. First, Pasha intercepted a load of treasures that he wanted to examine while on his ship, which meant that Hassan would have to risk moving them in front of thousands of people. So he came up with a distraction in Port Said that provided him an opportunity to slip away with his current load of treasures and hide them near the khedive's palace in Ismailia, then return to Port Said before the flotilla set out the following morning. I believe his brother, Rashad, was Hassan's partner in everything, for the events executed would have been difficult for one man to accomplish, and the two of them were frequently together."

Hassan, still confident, said calmly, "This is a terrible slander against my brother and me, my lady. I am no criminal."

"No." Violet shook her head. "In your mind, you are not, as you believe you are performing a patriotic duty. However, murder is a crime in nearly every society, and you are guilty of *that*.

"You and Rashad decided to set fire to the lumberyard, which would cause great commotion and require significant manpower to extinguish. Its proximity to the fireworks stand would only make it that much more distracting. But the lumberyard owner's son Yusef Halabi caught you as you were placing the tools for your evil deed, and so you easily killed him, believing that the murder would be disguised inside the fire. You did not count on an undertaker being a part of the proceedings, but you managed well by also being in a position to be directed to spirit the man's body off before I could establish my point about his death." Violet hated to think how much might have been covered up had she not been there.

"Great conjecture on your part, but it is only that," Hassan said, then appealed to his master. "Your Highness, this woman is clearly insane. We should see her off right away with the rest of the British delegation."

By now Pasha was vacillating in his defense of Hassan, and it was obvious that he was interested in Violet's retelling of the events.

"While all attention was on the fire, you and your brother boarded the ship commanded by Captain Naser, whom you undoubtedly told that you were on important business for the khedive in order to convince him to ferry you and your artifacts to Ismailia right away."

Now the khedive regained his balance. "But I told Hassan to take my artifacts to my palace in Ismailia and have the rest sent on to Cairo via the Fresh Water Canal. He was acting on my behalf."

Violet corrected Pasha again. "No, Hassan and Rashad were worried only about their own contraband that night. I believe the captain suspected they were up to no good. Maybe he threatened to report them. Maybe he attempted to blackmail them. Perhaps he even wanted to be part of their scheme. In any case," she said, turning back to Hassan, "you killed Captain Naser, and when the ship became grounded as a result, you fled back to Port Said with your trunk of goods, probably by some passing caravan. When we went down to dislodge Naser's ship, you intentionally dumped his body in the water right in front of me to disguise the cause of his death, and, just as with Yusef Halabi, you whisked him away before I could properly report on him.

"You told me then that Pasha had no regard for the captain, and would only seek to please de Lesseps. I did not realize that you were hinting your great displeasure at the khedive's eagerness to be associated with Europe.

"Frustrated in your attempt to get the trunk down to Port Ismailia ahead of the flotilla sailing, you decided to hide the trunk aboard one of the delegation ships while everyone was still preoccupied with the aftermath of the fire, along with the renewed fireworks. You thought that if the trunk were discovered, that country would be blamed, and if you were later caught removing it, you could claim that you had uncovered the country's plot to steal antiquities from the khedive and were only trying to get them back for your master.

"*Viribus Unitis* was probably the nearest ship you found. Stowing the trunk aboard, you thought you were safe in your intrigues. Unfortunately, Karl Dorn stumbled upon your treasure chest. I noticed that he was a man in great physical pain, and without question he would have found the opium stuffed in the trunk to be a good temporary solution to his problem. Alas, it was a deadly solution, and he accidentally killed himself with it.

"His death was of no import to you, other than a realization that he must have found the trunk. So you removed it from the ship, and, knowing that there was a contingent of American Civil War soldiers in attendance, you decided to try your hand at negotiating the trade of the valuable opium-laden artifacts for some of their weapons, which you could transfer directly to Orabi."

Hassan shrugged, apparently no longer willing to protest his innocence. "They are a lowly lot, but a lowly lot with excellent access to a cache of weapons."

"This would also serve a secondary purpose for you, which was to manipulate the very men the khedive had hired to

Westernize his army into cooperating in the destruction of all of Pasha's plans for Egypt."

"How could you possibly know this?" Asa Brooks spoke up for the first time.

"Colonel Mott told me, although I did not understand it at the time. He said that he was glad that Dorn hadn't been killed by any weapons, and at the time I thought he was making reference to the earlier deaths, but by that point Hassan had attempted to work a deal with him."

"And to think that Her Majesty had asked me to keep a watchful eye over you on this trip. You were instead watching over all of us!" The ambassador's man was joined in bemused laughter by Bertie, but Violet was determined not to be distracted from her allegations.

"You must have opened negotiations with the veterans, attempting to convince them that they could become instantly rich and sail for home without having to continue troubling themselves with training Pasha's army, if only they would agree to an ongoing weapons deal with Colonel Orabi. How could Pasha's meager payments compare to the infinitely more valuable treasure you would give them?

"But you assumed wrongly that they would all be interested. In fact, Thaddeus Mott rebuffed you, and you were about to give up when Caleb Purdy approached you, seeking to try some opium. We witnessed the aftereffects of it in Purdy during the picnic. You may have even negotiated an exchange of weapons for just opium, enabling you to return the artifacts to the museum, an ideal solution.

"Purdy agreed to steal some rifles and swords, and to do the exchange with you and Rashad during the palace party a few nights ago. However, he showed up without the agreed-upon cache of weapons. He accepted the artifact stuffed with packets of opium, but said he was having second thoughts about the bargain he had struck. An argument ensued, perhaps, and you walked away from each other.

"Rashad went to the servants' tent party, where you knew the rest of the soldiers were, and managed to remove Sam's saber from him while you were still in attendance on the party in the palace. You coaxed Purdy out of the servants' tent, threatened him more, but when he insisted that he was no longer interested in selling you weapons, you killed him and dumped his body in the cloakroom, then skulked out through some side entrance. Back outside, you nearly ran into Isabelle Dumont and Ross Keating together in one of the tableaux. They fled, and you picked up her dropped shawl, using it to wipe Purdy's blood off yourself. Julie Lesage found the shawl and created a fuss around it."

"This is very dramatic, my lady Harper," Hassan said. "Almost worthy of Mariette's story. Perhaps Pasha will have Verdi put it to music, as well? If I were responsible for Purdy's death, why would I help you to have contact with those men, and why wouldn't Colonel Mott report on me to you?"

Violet ignored the taunt. "That was what made you so clever. I imagine Mott was scared into silence by your presence, at both the discovery of Purdy's body and then, when you escorted me to the dungeon, the false belief that *you* were responsible for the men's imprisonment and that a further word of accusation from you could mean a secret execution in the night.

"You made me believe you were assisting me, but in reality you were letting Colonel Mott know how much power you held over the veterans' lives . . . as well as my own. However, of all the deaths you caused, whether intentional or inadvertent, there was one in which you were not successful, and that was your attempt on my own life. But you played this bad card perfectly, as being in your trust in the prison spoke volumes to Mott, namely that you held sway over my life, too. Unbeknownst to me at the time, I was your hostage to quiet Mott."

She turned to Pasha. "Your Highness, Hassan must have been inside de Lesseps's villa the day of the party, waiting upon you."

Pasha nodded.

"I was there also, at Louise-Hélène's request. I overheard you arguing with Tewfik, and shortly thereafter I was attacked and buried alive inside a mausoleum."

"Yes," Hassan growled. "The lady would be surprised by how difficult it was to break into the mausoleum and relock it, as well as by how heavy she is as dead weight."

"As surprised as you must have been to find me walking after burying me alive," she shot back.

"I told Rashad to make sure you were—" He stopped, realizing his mistake, even as a pair of soldiers went off in search of Hassan's brother without needing instruction from Pasha.

Violet now addressed the crowd at large. "Hassan Salib is the worst sort of villain, for he extended great kindness to me . . . a kindness meant to disguise his evil deeds, for why would I ever suspect the man who had helped me secretly meet with my imprisoned husband, at great risk to his own personal welfare? It clouded my judgment, and prevented me from understanding the truth as soon as I should have."

"I should have simply drowned you like the pestilent little rat you are, my lady Harper, once I knew you had survived Rashad's burial. He is of very bad temper, and that temper makes him hasty and clumsy. I, however, am neither rash nor oafish like my brother. No, I am very polished, and it is what has made me very successful in my life. In fact—"

Only now did Violet realize that Hassan had been slowly relaxing his arms in such a manner that the guards next to him hadn't noticed, and had in fact released him. Before anyone could properly react, Hassan had slipped away and stormed up the stage steps to where Violet stood. In an instant, his hands were around her throat as he shook her head violently. She attempted to push him away from her, but it was no use against the man whose calculated veneer had melted away like wax and was replaced with the feral growling and loathing stare of a jungle cat.

If he was the calm and sophisticated brother, what must have Rashad's victims endured?

Violet couldn't breathe, and the pain of Hassan's fingers against her windpipe was unbearable. She beat uselessly against his chest, but knew that it was as effective as the beating of a butterfly's wings. From somewhere far in the distance, she heard chairs being overturned and the din of people shouting; then everything went as black as the inside of a mausoleum.

∞

As Violet came to, she realized she was lying on the floor of the stage, and once again began laughing hysterically to herself to think that she had almost died inside a stage set to look like a crypt.

Multiple faces peered down at her: the Prince of Wales, Sir Henry, Eugénie, General Ignatiev, and Théophile Gautier, who pursed his lips and said, "Madame Harper, I am at a loss as to describing this scene, but I think we can agree that it is the final scene of the play, *oui?*"

It was the Empress Eugénie who helped her up and rearranged her skirts, fluttering over Violet as if she herself were a lady's maid. Violet was enveloped in the bizarre irony of it all.

However, she was quickly regaining her senses, and pushed through the assembly around her to find Pasha, who was still offstage, overseeing the arrest of the brothers.

"Your Highness," Violet said, clutching her bruised throat with one hand and raising her voice to ensure every single person heard her, "I beg you to release my husband and his friends straightaway." Her voice croaked, but he turned to her and offered a curt nod.

With Hassan and Rashad in the custody of some Egyptian soldiers who probably had been trained by Mott and his men, the Americans were freed in mere minutes. There was, of course, no apology from Pasha or de Lesseps, who deemed this a trivial matter next to the international opening of the canal, but it didn't matter to Violet. Sam was at liberty, and his condition was nothing a night of sleep, a good meal, and some time at the washbasin couldn't repair.

Nevertheless, Violet Harper was most desperate to leave

Egypt—a land full of exotic spices, intoxicating drinks, enthralling recreations, beautiful jewelry . . . and far, far too many badly handled corpses.

chapter 32

November 22, 1869
Port Said

AFTER A LAVISH FAREWELL BREAKFAST on the shores of Port Said, the delegation members began drifting off to their respective ships for their return journeys. Violet and Sam waited for the Prince of Wales and Sir Henry to complete their own boarding before joining them on *Newport*.

Captain Nares had agreed to pilot Sam and Violet to the Italian coastline, where they would spend a peaceful week in Pompeii before making their own way back to London. Violet looked forward to Italy's reputedly beautiful museums, artwork, and cathedrals, in addition to the Pompeii ruins. It was almost as if she and Sam would be on the grand tour together.

As they stood watching the glorious array of flotilla ships for the last time, they were visited by other delegation members who also had not yet boarded. Violet was touched that Crown Prince Frederick came to her.

"A performance *vell* done, Frau Harper," Frederick said, taking her hand and offering a courteous bow over it, a high honor to her.

"It was only what any wife would do for her husband, Your Highness," she replied. "I must remind you again that we are stopping in Pompeii on our return to London. Are you certain you would not wish to have this letter taken to Her Majesty by another courier so that it arrives more quickly?"

Frederick smiled as he dropped her hand. "I do not believe I *vould* trust any other courier as much as I now trust you."

Eugénie swept up to her after Frederick moved on and clasped one of her hands in both of hers. "Ah, Madame Harper, you missed the most melodious of breakfasts. Pasha invited me aboard *El Mahrousa* because the piano arrived, and we had a little performance during our eggs with fava beans. The instrument holds a place of honor on the yacht." She frowned, turning more serious. "I confess I will miss your strange presence. You became my little confidante, *oui*? And now I return to France to face my husband and *le chaos* in his foreign policy. Pray that we will not be at war by this time next year. My *félicitations* on your release, Monsieur Harper."

Sam took Eugénie's proffered hand and bowed over it.

Julie was with Eugénie, but studiously avoided Violet's gaze as she waited for her mistress to conclude with the undertaker before scurrying away behind her, never saying a word or even acknowledging Violet's presence.

Isabelle Dumont also did not meet Violet's gaze, but only because she and Ross Keating were so completely engrossed in each other as they whispered, giggled, and made cow eyes at each other.

"Good Lord," Sam said, shaking his head. "I wonder if he means to have her right here on the wharf."

"Sam!" Violet said, laughing. "I'm sure they are quite disconcerted at having to be separated from each other, since for some reason Sergeant Keating has chosen to stay here with Colonel Mott and Sergeant Morris and won't be ready to leave here for quite some time. I imagine Isabelle will wish to return to France with her mistress."

"Actually, this is not the case," came a voice from behind Violet. It was Louise-Hélène.

"Isabelle plans to remain behind with Sergeant Keating until his work with training Pasha's army is complete. Then they will return to the United States together, although Keating has no family and they are not sure where to go."

"Hmm." Sam's look was pensive. "Maybe we should offer to put them in touch with Susanna and Ben, if they wouldn't mind the rather rough wilds of Colorado." He went to talk to the lovebirds, whistling as he tapped his cane along the ground.

"I must thank you, Madame Harper," Louise-Hélène said warmly, "for ensuring Sergeant Keating's freedom. She was nearly *dérangé* over his imprisonment, as I'm sure you were over that of your husband."

Violet nodded but did not respond, unable to dwell upon the horror of what might have been had she not figured out what had happened.

"I think then," Louise-Hélène continued, "that Isabelle will be very happy in her new homeland, and that you, too, will be happy with your husband when you return to Britain. I, too, intend to have a very happy and blessed marriage with de Lesseps."

At this pronouncement, all thoughts of the disaster that might have been fled from Violet's mind. She impulsively hugged the young woman and found her face buried in that wild thundercloud of dark hair.

"I, too, believe you will have a most contented life, mademoiselle," she said, stepping back and taking Louise-Hélène's hand in her own.

Louise-Hélène smiled. "Actually, I have a secret. De Lesseps says we will marry as soon as all of you have gone. Just *la cérémonie* private here with the khedive and a few attendants. De Lesseps says—" And now Louise-Hélène blushed prettily. "He says that he can no longer wait for me."

At this, Violet felt more happiness than she had at any point during this fateful trip to Egypt.

"Ah, there is de Lesseps now," Louise-Hélène said. "If you will excuse me . . ." She ran to meet her fiancé, who looked up with a broad smile at Louise-Hélène's arrival. He caught Violet's gaze from behind his intended, and although he did not stop smiling, for a moment it did not quite reach his eyes.

Violet was certain that she would remain forever in de Lesseps's mind as the woman who nearly ruined the opening of the Suez Canal.

Sam was still conversing with Isabelle and Ross Keating, and based on Isabelle's hand fluttering and Keating's thumping of Sam's back, they were quite receptive to Sam's idea. Violet herself noticed Richard Lepsius and Auguste Mariette in a heated conversation next to a tent selling gold cartouches to the departing travelers.

"Gentlemen, is all well?" she asked as she approached them.

"What?" Mariette said, startled out of his discourse by Violet's arrival. "Ah, Madame Harper, you have arrived to settle an argument for us. We know that both sexes wore wigs in ancient Egypt. But women who kept their own hair were told they could bring back its natural color by rubbing in a mixture of oil and the boiled blood of a black cat or bull. Would women do this with their human-hair wigs, as well? Lepsius says yes, but I say the color of the wigs would not fade, so there would be no point to it."

"You are the *Dummkopf*," Lepsius said. "Of course the hair would change. Without question it would fade."

"No, no, no," Mariette retorted. "It is you who is the *Dum*—"

"Gentlemen," Violet interrupted, hoping to stave off an international incident resulting from two scientists mauling each other over ancient hair care. "I'm sure that both of you are correct in your assertions. Some women probably did, and others didn't."

The men grumbled at Violet's compromise, undoubtedly preferring to carry on their argument. She suspected the two would end up good friends.

"Thank you again for the book, Monsieur Mariette," she said. "I shall always treasure it."

Lepsius frowned. "You gave her a gift? Wait a moment." He went to the cartouche seller and returned shortly, handing Violet a small packet made of felt. Inside was a gold amulet in the shape of an oval with some hieroglyphics inside.

"This is very generous, Herr Lepsius, but I do not understand it," she said.

He grinned broadly. "*Zis* is a cartouche bearing the name of Rameses III, the pharaoh spoken of in the tale of the treasure thief. Since it was my telling of that tale that inspired you to solve the murders, it only makes sense that you should have *zis* to remind you of your time in Egypt . . . and me."

"Braggart," Mariette declared. "Madame Harper, since you rescued my museum's pieces from further theft, I will purchase for you—"

"Gentlemen," she demurred. "Please, I wish for peace between you. Your energies are much better put to finding—and preserving—this nation's antiquities. However, I shall always hold my gifts from you in high esteem."

With that, the two men bowed and went back to arguing, this time about irrigation projects during the Twelfth Dynasty.

Théophile Gautier stood a short distance away, his expression thoroughly bemused at what had transpired between Violet and the two men. "You have two admirers," he said generously as Violet approached him.

"Not admirers, but competitors trying to best each other," she said, shaking her head. "However, the khedive is fortunate to have such passionate Egyptologists working on his behalf."

"They have the same passion for dead ancients as you do for the dead moderns, eh?" Gautier said with his customary wittiness. "I believe I shall write a play for you entitled *Death Conquers All*. Clever, *non?* I'm sure it will play in opera houses all over Europe and lead me to even further greatness. I must find that *imbécile* Ibsen and tell him that I have beat him to the idea. It has been a pleasure, madame."

Violet smiled at Gautier's retreating figure, finding it comical that he did not realize that he and Ibsen were just as competitive as Mariette and Lepsius.

Surely by now the prince was finished settling in aboard *Newport*. Violet decided she would retrieve Sam so they could board themselves and get under way. Before she reached him, though, she was once more thwarted as the Russian duke stepped into her path.

"I watched you at opera *Aida*, Violet Rose. Very entertaining. Now you have your husband back, this is good. You fortunate to have your husband with you. I have been away from wife far too long. She will be anxious to have me home."

"Thank you, Your Highness," Violet said. "I wish for you safe travels until you can be reunited with your family."

Behind the duke, General Ignatiev shook his head, mumbling in Russian, but did approach Violet when the duke became interested in the argument between Lepsius and Mariette and wandered away.

"You must know, Violet Rose, that Dorn's death almost ruined my work with Pasha. It was why I wanted truth known about him quickly so I could turn Pasha's attentions back to discussions for liberating Bulgaria from Ottoman domination, where it has been for centuries. The Ottomans treat Orthodox Church with terrible oppression that we have been unable to break, so I think to myself that we will have diplomatic solution during canal ceremonies. I think we have accord now, and Bulgaria will be free country soon when Pasha goes to sultan."

Violet hoped that Pasha still had that much influence with the sultan, and felt an inexplicable sadness for the retreating general, who seemed to carry an almost visible weight upon his shoulders.

Franz-Josef was already standing aboard the deck of *Viribus Unitis*, in position to acknowledge the crowds once the ships began to depart from port. His musicians were also in position, trumpets to their lips and hands to drumsticks. The Austrian emperor caught Violet's eye and held a hand up in deferential greeting—an enormous concession of protocol, she thought in surprise, one that he did not even offer to Eugénie.

Poor Franz-Josef. He had realized nothing of his goals in this trip. Eugénie had ultimately rebuffed him, despite his best efforts, and his grand plan for establishing Austria's diplomatic preeminence had crumbled into grains of sand and washed away.

Who knew what would happen next to his country?

Violet returned the wave.

"You don't plan to leave with him instead of me, do you?" Sam asked, coming up beside her and cupping a hand over her elbow.

"No. Not today, at least," Violet teased, putting a hand to his face and running it over his now neatly trimmed facial hair. Sam had shaved off his beard after the war, but perhaps he intended to grow it again. He laughed and grabbed her hand, kissing her open palm.

"A-sailing we will go," he said, leading her to the ship. Violet was intercepted one final time by Pasha and his son.

"I cannot say thank you, I do not think," Pasha said without preamble. "You nearly ruined the ceremonies, and now my favorite servant is in the dungeon. I am not happy with what happened. What I will say, though, is that, well . . . I will say that if you return to Egypt you will not be unwelcome. You, as well," he said, nodding to Sam.

Violet knew that was the closest they would get to an apology for all of the hardship they had experienced, and it was good enough.

Pasha moved on to speak with de Lesseps and Louise-Hélène, but Tewfik remained behind for just a moment.

"You missed a great opportunity with me, my lady," Tewfik said, his voice full of regret as he bowed and walked away.

"What opportunity is this?" Sam asked, frowning at Tewfik's retreating figure.

"Nothing. Nothing at all," Violet said, relieved to be out of the young man's sights and whatever his designs were for her.

Thaddeus Mott and Owen Morris also bade farewell to Sam, with much joking and insults. Mott made a solemn promise to have a new saber forged for Sam that he would personally drop off in London on his way back to the United States.

"As regards you, Mrs. Harper," he said, doing his best courtier imitation, "I shall go to my grave with thanks to you on my lips, although I trust you will not have to suffer the indignity of caring for my broken-down old body."

Mott bowed almost to the ground in his false modesty.

"Colonel, you do me honor," Violet said lightly, then turned serious. "But I must ask you, why did you choose to remain behind with Pasha's troops, given all that has happened?"

Mott's grin was wide. "Ah, because I learned that Pasha is not in so much debt that he couldn't borrow more in order to triple the fee for training his troops. It was an especial coup for me once I learned that the sultan is demanding more tribute from Pasha in order to choke off the khedive's grand plans for himself. I like to think I am part of the sultan's efforts to drain the khedive of power.

"I've also secured quite comfortable accommodations in Pasha's palace for me and my men, so it was an easy decision to remain behind." Mott winked at her with his natural impudence.

Violet had no doubt that Pasha's men would end up being well trained and efficient, if Mott's flashes of temper didn't get him into trouble.

They were handed fresh glasses of *karkadé* as they boarded *Newport* for a final time. As the ship pulled out of Port Said and into the waters of the Mediterranean, Bertie waved from one side of the deck, while Violet and Sam stood inseparably to the other side. Violet didn't think she would let her husband out of her sight ever again, and it made her realize that she herself had given him many sleepless nights during the dangers she had encountered in the uninvited investigations that had fallen into her lap.

Sam's gaze was pensive as he stared forward toward Europe. Imagining him to be preoccupied with thoughts of the Pompeiian ruins, she said lightly, "Can't wait to see some plaster casts of ash-covered bodies?"

Her husband turned to her, his tone sober. "Perhaps. You know, I've been close to dying twice. Once as a prisoner of war, and then as a prisoner here. This was worse because of the uncertainty and because I was thousands of miles from home, as well as because I knew that my situation was putting you through such agony. I spent quite a bit of time thinking about death, wife, and what it means to the person who is experiencing it. I found it terrible to imagine that my body might be abandoned to vultures or carelessly tossed into a grave when I was gone. I see now why you take such interest in the proper care of corpses. There is something rather . . . holy, I suppose, in being the guardian of the dead as they transition to the afterlife." He paused, gazing out at the sea again as he formed his next words. The ship was picking up speed, and the wind ruffled his auburn hair, which was showing some strands of silver at the roots, much like Violet's.

He turned to her once more. "What I mean to say is that I have always *respected* your work, but I wouldn't mind also *understanding* it."

Violet nodded, elated at the thought. What a different sort of colleague Sam would make from her long-dead first husband, Graham. There was much Sam could learn from both her and her business partner, Harry. "When we return to London, I will teach you everything I know. For the next two weeks, though, let's just enjoy the peace and serenity of Pompeii."

Sam affectionately slung an arm about her shoulders and drew her closer. "Do you think I haven't been married to you long enough to know that, with you around, there is never peace and serenity? Trouble seems to lie in wait for you like a prowling cougar."

"Not this time," Violet said resolutely. "This time there will be complete repose and contentment."

I hope . . .

THE END

AUTHOR'S NOTE

FERDINAND DE LESSEPS AND THE Suez Canal appeared in one of my previous novels, *Stolen Remains*, but I knew that I wanted to explore this world-changing event a little further, particularly from the perspective of the dignitaries attending the extravagant festivities of the canal's inauguration.

The canal's opening ceremonies were prefaced with a weeks-long trip down the Nile for many of the elite participants, and overall the festivities went on for weeks. It was a fitting end for a project that went on for a decade, and had actually been first conceived in ancient times, then unsuccessfully taken up by Napoléon Bonaparte in 1799. It was only through de Lesseps, formerly French consul to Cairo, that an agreement was secured with Isma'il Pasha's predecessor and uncle, Muhammad Sa'id Pasha, to build the hundred-mile canal across the Isthmus of Suez.

In 1856 the Suez Canal Company was formed, construction plans were drawn, and digging began in 1859, primarily by corvée labor using picks and shovels. Later, because of British pressure to stop the use of this nearly slave labor and the fact that a vast number of workers were needed, Europeans were imported, aided by dredgers and steam shovels.

As might be expected with a project of such immense scale, there were many holdups related to labor disputes and even a cholera epidemic, delaying completion until 1869, four years behind schedule. The canal officially opened on November 17, 1869, during ceremonies in Port Ismailia.

The initial canal was only twenty-five feet deep, seventy-two feet wide at the bottom, and a maximum of three hundred feet wide at the surface. As a result, fewer than five hundred ships navigated it during its first full year of operations. Major improvements began in 1876, culminating in a major $8.5 billion expansion of the canal in August 2015, deepening the main waterway and providing ships with a twenty-two-mile channel parallel to it. Egypt's hope is that the expansion will increase traffic handled by the canal and thus improve the country's economy.

There have been struggles as well as improvements during the past 147 years of the canal's existence, though. Because of Egypt's ongoing debts, Great Britain was able to purchase Egypt's shares in the canal for the paltry sum of 400,000 pounds in 1875. The canal was thus controlled by France and Great Britain until 1954, when a treaty was signed that provided for the gradual withdrawal of all British troops from the zone.

In July 1956, Egyptian president Gamal Abdel Nasser moved to nationalize the canal, intending to charge tolls large enough to pay for construction of a massive dam on the Nile River. Israel, Great Britain, and France landed troops in early November but, under pressure from the United Nations, withdrew. Egypt took permanent control of the canal.

Ten years later, Egypt shut the canal down following the Six-Day War and Israel's occupation of the Sinai Peninsula, and for the next eight years the Suez Canal became the front line between the Egyptian and Israeli armies. In 1975, Egyptian president Anwar Sadat reopened the canal as a gesture of goodwill toward Israel.

Today, the Suez Canal handles 8 percent of global sea trade, with fifty ships per day carrying more than three hundred million tons of goods per year.

Many of the dignitaries that I mention were actually in attendance. All had their own goals and motivations for being there as political chess pieces were being moved across the European chessboard. One can only imagine what turmoil it was, despite all of the pretty speeches made that claimed the canal would bring all countries together.

However, there is no question that **Ferdinand de Lesseps (1805–1894)** was the star of it all. His early years were spent in Italy, where his father was involved in diplomatic duties. Following in his father's footsteps, de Lesseps was assistant vice-consul at Lisbon by age eighteen, and rose through various positions until he became consul to Cairo in 1833. A two-year outbreak of plague cemented de Lesseps's sterling reputation in the hearts and minds of Egyptians, as he continued to go back and forth between Alexandria and Cairo in his efforts to combat the disease.

In 1837, de Lesseps returned to France, was married, and became the father of five sons. He was given more diplomatic posts, now in Rotterdam, Barcelona, Madrid, and the Vatican. In 1851, he was awarded the Portuguese Grand Cross of the Order of the Tower and Sword. He retired from diplomatic service, and tragedy struck in 1853, when he lost his wife, Agathe, and one of his sons within days of each other.

In 1854, the accession of Sa'id Pasha inspired de Lesseps to make the Suez Canal a reality.

Louise-Hélène Autard de Bragard (1848–1909) was born on the island of Mauritius. She married Ferdinand de Lesseps on November 25, 1869, and together they had twelve children, eleven of whom survived their father. Between Louise-Hélène and his first wife, de Lesseps had a total of seventeen children. She died January 29, 1909, at Château de la Chesnaie in France. Little is known of her, but I find her to be fascinating. She was decades younger than her famous, flamboyant husband, and I imagine that she was quite overshadowed by him, yet the marriage seemed to bring her peace and contentment. I would note that she and de Lesseps were not married in Egypt, but in Paris shortly after the conclusion of the canal ceremonies.

Other than Louise-Hélène, the most influential person in de Lesseps's life had to be **Isma'il Pasha (1830–1895)**, the khedive of Egypt from 1863 to 1879.

Pasha was ambitious for his country, stating once, "My country is no longer in Africa; we are now part of Europe. It is therefore natural for us to abandon our former ways and to adopt a new system adapted to our social conditions."

He was also ambitious for himself, successfully petitioning the sultan for the title of khedive, or viceroy, instead of the title of *wāli*, or governor, which had been used by his predecessors.

Unfortunately, achieving his aims of the Europeanization of Egypt came at a steep price, as the nation couldn't afford endless miles of railroads, an improved postal system, and other modernizations on top of satisfying de Lesseps's demands for financing the canal. Pasha borrowed as much and as fast as he could, resulting in tremendous debt. By 1875, he was forced to sell Egypt's shares of the great canal, thus toppling his power—and his person—into the hands of the British, who forced his removal from the khedivate in 1879 in favor of his son Tewfik, who was considered more pliable.

Pasha's removal was quite an irony, given that Great Britain was opposed to the entire project from the beginning because they felt it would decrease British influence in shipping . . . and give France too much influence.

Pasha was exiled first to Naples, and then to Constantinople (modern-day Istanbul), where he reputedly died while trying to guzzle two bottles of champagne at once.

Pasha's eldest son, **Tewfik Pasha (1852–1892)**, grew up in Egypt and was not sent to Europe to be educated like his younger brothers. He lived a generally placid country life in his palace near Cairo until the sudden deposal of his father. The new khedive was reportedly so displeased by the announcement of his hurried accession that he soundly boxed the ears of the servant who brought the news to him.

Life for Tewfik would continue to be displeasing for him, as Egypt united behind **Colonel Ahmed Orabi (1841–1911)**, who is mentioned but never seen in the story. Orabi was a disaffected member of the *fellah*, or peasant, class who was the head of the nationalist movement in Egypt and led an 1879 revolt against Tewfik's administration, a government that was under Anglo-French control. Ironically, Orabi's movement through the ranks would never have been possible without Isma'il Pasha's reforms and modernizations. It is almost a parody that Orabi would eventually suffer the same fate as Isma'il Pasha: exile, with the further insult of the British once more dominating the government of Egypt.

It should be noted, however, that Orabi's nationalist movement was actually just in its infancy during the time of this story.

Speaking of the British, **Sir Henry Elliot (1817–1907)** was the ambassador to Constantinople for a decade beginning in 1867. He and General Ignatiev, the ambassador to Constantinople for Russia, were frequently at odds with each other. He retired in 1884, his health broken from a long diplomatic career that began in 1841.

Commander George Nares (1831–1915) was highly respected as a leader and scientific explorer. He led the British Arctic Expedition, a failed attempt to reach the North Pole that nonetheless resulted in the collection of huge amounts of scientific data.

He also maneuvered HMS *Newport* to the head of the flotilla line during the canal ceremonies, earning him an official reprimand from the Royal Navy . . . and a promotion to the rank of captain.

France's most celebrated delegate was, naturally, **Empress Eugénie (1826–1920)**, consort of Napoléon III. A devout Catholic woman from Spain renowned for her beauty, Eugénie was considered glamorous and charming, and her fascination with Marie Antoinette sparked a revival for the clothing, architecture, and decor of King Louis XVI.

Although theirs was a love match, Louis-Napoléon was never particularly faithful to her, but this did not stop Eugénie from being perfectly devoted to her husband. He came to trust her implicitly, and she served as regent of France in his absence in 1859, 1865, and 1870. Unfortunately, she could not stop Napoléon's antagonisms against Austria and Prussia, and in 1871 the French Empire collapsed, with the French royal family fleeing into exile in Kent, England.

Eugénie maintained good relations with Great Britain after her husband's death in 1873, and was named godmother to Princess Beatrice's daughter, Victoria Eugenie of Battenberg.

Eugénie died while visiting Spain in 1920, age ninety-four,

and was buried in the Imperial Crypt at St. Michael's Abbey in Farnborough, Hampshire, England, with her husband and son.

It is rather sad to think that, despite all of the outward show of international friendship and cooperation during the Suez Canal ceremonies, Eugénie's husband would be surrendering his army to Crown Prince Frederick of Prussia in a mere ten months' time, and that her son would eventually die in British uniform during the Zulu War of 1879.

Another French luminary in Egypt was **Auguste Mariette (1821–1881)**, a brilliant scholar and Egyptologist who worked tirelessly to explore ancient sites and to prevent their destruction and pilfering.

In 1860 alone, Mariette set up thirty-five new dig sites, while attempting to conserve existing sites. To the great consternation of the British as well as the Prussians (who were allied with the Ottoman sultan), Mariette had a virtual monopoly on digs in the country, thanks to his good relationship with Isma'il Pasha.

Unfortunately, that relationship was not always smooth.

Pasha assumed that all discoveries ranked as royal treasure and were his to dispose of, choosing what went to the museum and what remained in his personal possession. Mariette was constantly rushing to confiscate boatloads of antiquities that had been raided from dig sites for the khedive's perusal.

In 1878, Mariette's museum was ravaged by a flooding of the Nile. Already broken in health and nearly blind, Mariette handpicked his successor to ensure the French would retain the directorship, rather than allow the powerful position to end up in the hands of an Englishman, as by then the British comprised the majority of Egyptologists in Egypt.

Mariette died in Cairo just shy of his sixtieth birthday. Fittingly, he was interred in a sarcophagus, which is on display in the garden of the Museum in Cairo.

Crown Prince Frederick of Prussia (1831–1888), later Frederick III, was greatly celebrated in his youth for leadership and successes during the Second Schleswig, Austro-Prussian, and Franco-Prussian wars—an irony given that he professed a hatred of warfare, and was roundly praised by both friends and enemies for his extremely humane conduct.

He and his wife, Princess Victoria, eldest daughter of Queen Victoria, were well matched, as they were both admirers of Prince Albert's attitude toward greater representation for commoners in the government. During the twenty-seven years that he spent as crown prince, it was always Frederick's intent that he and Vicky should rule as consorts as his in-laws had in Great Britain.

Frederick became emperor on March 9, 1888, and reigned a mere ninety-nine days before succumbing to throat cancer, which had been diagnosed in 1887. Not only was Frederick never able to institute the reforms he had planned for the good of his people, he was succeeded by his son Wilhelm II, a colorless and unpopular leader who led Prussia straight into World War I, with catastrophic and tragic results.

Another prominent Prussian was **Richard Lepsius (1810– 1884)**. An Egyptologist like Mariette, Lepsius is today known as the father of the modern scientific discipline of Egyptology.

In perhaps his greatest achievement, Lepsius led an expedition, modeled on an earlier Napoleonic mission, to Egypt and Sudan in November 1842 to record the remains of ancient Egyptian civilization. He and his team spent six months at their scientific study, discovering over sixty pyramids and more than 130 tombs.

The expedition resulted in the publication of a twelve-volume compendium containing nearly nine hundred plates of ancient Egyptian inscriptions, plans, maps, and drawings of temple and tomb walls.

In 1846 Lepsius was rewarded for his work with a professorship at the Berlin University, and in 1865 was named keeper of the Egyptian antiquities department in the Berlin Museum. He returned to Egypt for a final time in 1869 to witness the inauguration of the Suez Canal, before returning to Berlin and publishing many more works prior to his death on July 10, 1884.

The story of the treasure thief that Lepsius tells Violet is an actual Egyptian myth.

One cannot speak of theft without mentioning the Russian

diplomat **Nikolay Pavlovich Ignatiev (1832–1908)**, who did indeed run into some trouble when he pocketed (inadvertently, he claimed) a newly developed cartridge while inspecting the British army's ordnance works. However, most of his military career was stellar.

Ignatiev was a major by the time of the Crimean War, after which he began his diplomatic career when he participated in negotiations over the demarcation of the border between Russia and the Ottoman empire on the lower Danube River, at the Congress of Paris in 1856.

He was then military attaché at the Russian embassy in London, where the cartridge incident occurred, making the posting a very short one before he was sent back to Russia. He also served as plenipotentiary to the court of Peking (modern-day Beijing). He managed Chinese fears regarding Anglo-French advances so smoothly and coolly that he ended up obtaining Outer Manchuria for Russia.

With his success in China, he was made ambassador at Constantinople, a position he occupied from 1864 to 1877. His chief aim was to liberate Christians—chiefly Bulgarians—from Ottoman domination, which he worked mostly through secret channels. He was largely unsuccessful and fell out of favor with Alexander II, but unsurprisingly, he remained immensely popular in Bulgaria, and was at one point even considered for the Bulgarian throne.

Ignatiev later served under Alexander III as minister of the interior, but was accused of fomenting pogroms against, and suppressing protections for, the Jewish population. He was also suspected of extortion.

He retired from office in June 1882, and held no influence in public affairs from that point until his death on July 3, 1908. Although I give him the honorific of "General" in the story, Ignatiev was not actually promoted to this rank—specifically, General of the Infantry—until 1878.

Grand Duke Michael of Russia (1832–1909) was the fourth son and seventh child of Tsar Nicholas I and Charlotte of Prussia. His placement in the succession line virtually assured that he would never be tsar, but he was made governor general of Caucasia, located at the crossroads of Western Asia and Eastern Europe, and bordered on the west by the Black Sea and the east by the Caspian Sea. He remained there for twenty years, from 1862 to 1882, with his wife, Cecily Auguste of Baden (who adopted the name Olga Feodorovna), and their seven children. In fact, four of their children were born there.

In the course of Michael's life, four members of his family ruled as emperors of Russia: his father, Nicholas I; his brother, Alexander II; his nephew, Alexander III; and his grandnephew, Nicholas II.

Michael died in Cannes, France, on December 18, 1909.

Franz-Josef I of Austria (1830–1916) was emperor of Austria and apostolic king of Hungary from 1848 until his death in 1916. As a young man, he was described as handsome, charming, and courteous. In his later years, he became sober, unimaginative, and withdrawn, particularly in his understanding of royalty and his role as undisputed head of the House of Habsburg. In that role, he would brook no opposition to his royal will.

The emperor was not a particularly deep thinker, and he dismissed the philosophizing views of his wife, Elisabeth—or Sisi, as she was nicknamed—who was a breathtaking beauty ill-prepared for her life with Franz-Josef when she married him at only sixteen years of age.

Mocked as the "red-trousered lieutenant" for his love of all things military in his youth, he regarded the army as the most important pillar of the monarchy. Unfortunately, he was not gifted with an aptitude for strategy, and was more suited to the peacetime activities of military exercises and parades. He adopted military wear as his daily attire and considered punctuality and orderliness to be the highest virtues.

However, Franz-Josef was also known as a man of integrity and decency, who responded stoically to numerous political and military defeats, as well as to the early death of his daughter Sophie; the execution of his brother Maximilian, the failed emperor of Mexico; the scandalous suicide of his only son, Rudolf; and the 1898 assassination of his wife.

Franz-Josef's main foreign policy goal had been the unification of the Germanic states under the House of Habsburg. Unfortunately, his goal proved unattainable on the great European chessboard, and after several conflicts and the machinations of Otto von Bismarck, he found himself losing out on his grand vision to Prussia.

Interestingly, after Rudolf's suicide in 1889, Franz-Josef's heir was Archduke Franz Ferdinand, the son of Archduke Karl Ludwig of Austria. Franz-Josef was unimpressed with Franz Ferdinand, and fought him bitterly over his desire to marry a countess, when established rules stated that only members of reigning or formerly reigning dynasties of Europe could marry into the Imperial House of Habsburg.

Franz Ferdinand and his wife visited England in the autumn of 1913, spending a week with George V and Queen Mary at Windsor before going to stay for another week with the 6th Duke of Portland at Welbeck Abbey in Nottinghamshire. The 5th Duke of Portland's strange story features in my previous novel, *Death at the Abbey*.

When Franz Ferdinand and his wife were assassinated in Sarajevo in 1914, thus sparking World War I, Franz-Josef was reputed to have told his daughter that he had far greater confidence in his new heir presumptive, his great-nephew Archduke Ferdinand Karl, and that for him, the assassination was "a relief from a great worry."

Franz-Josef died of pneumonia at Schönbrunn Palace on November 21, 1916.

The United States was virtually a nonplayer in the opening of the Suez Canal, although she would become very influential in the twentieth century. However, **Thaddeus Mott (1831–1894)**, a former Union Army officer, was indeed enlisted by Isma'il Pasha to reorganize and train Egypt's military forces. Because Pasha was subject to the sultan, he had no real authority, nor the right, to request this sort of assistance, and did so through independent agents.

Mott was an intriguer and adventurer by nature, and thus a perfect fit to help Pasha. He had served in revolutionary Italy under Giuseppe Garibaldi at the tender age of seventeen, was a shipmate on various clipper ships, spent a year in the Mexican Army, and eventually returned to the United States and enlisted in the Union Army. He served in the infantry as well as the cavalry, where he reached the rank of lieutenant colonel.

Most of the men whom Mott recruited to help him rebuild the Egyptian army and navy had fought on one side or the other during the Civil War, and were graduates of West Point and the Naval Academy. In 1870, Pasha made Mott his first aide-de-camp, and two years later Mott became a Grand Officer of the Imperial Order of the Osmanieh, an Ottoman military decoration.

However, once his contract with Pasha expired, he left Egypt for Turkey, where he took part in the wars between Serbia, Russia, and the Ottoman Empire.

By 1876 Mott was in ill health, and by 1879 was forced to retire from military service. He settled with his family in Toulon, France, as an American consular agent, and lived there until his death on November 23, 1894.

Numerous brilliant and famous figures of the art and literary world were in attendance at the opening ceremonies, including the French writer **Théophile Gautier (1811–1872)** and Norwegian playwright **Henrik Ibsen (1828–1906)**.

Other real figures that feature in the story include **Monsignor Bauer (1829–1898)**, Eugénie's confessor and deliverer of a dedicatory address at the Suez Canal, as well as **Albert Edward, the Prince of Wales (1841–1910)**, whom I have covered extensively in other novels, and **Prince Henry of Holland (1820–1879)** along with his sister, **Princess Sophie (1824–1897)**.

Many of the locations referred to in the story are real. There were separate European and Arab shopping districts set up at Port Said for the opening ceremony attendees. Pasha did have a twenty-thousand-square-foot palace in Ismailia (among many others in Egypt). De Lesseps's villa in Ismailia is today a guesthouse for visitors of the Suez Canal Authority. Pasha did build a villa just for Empress Eugénie's use during the ceremonies, while most other visitors stayed in elegantly appointed tents along streets named for various sovereigns.

Most of the ships referred to are also historically accurate. HMS *Newport*, as mentioned, was the flagship for the British team, whereas *L'Aigle* held the French diplomats, and SMS *Viribus Unitis* was indeed Franz-Josef's favorite ship. I could not find record of the name of the Russian ship in attendance, but they did frequently name their seacraft for precious gems, hence the name *Alexandrite*, which seemed appropriate given that the tsar of the time was Alexander II.

El Mahrousa was personally ordered by Isma'il Pasha and designed by the same British shipbuilding team that designed Queen Victoria's first steam yacht. Completed in August 1865, the 411-foot, five-floor, ocean worthy vessel was sailed from the River Thames to Alexandria. Empress Eugénie did indeed give a piano to the khedive, which is still on the ship today.

Interestingly, during the August 2015 inauguration ceremonies, also held in Ismailia, for a major expansion of the Suez Canal, the president of Egypt appeared aboard *El Mahrousa*.

I took several liberties with history in creating the plot of this story and making the pieces fit to my satisfaction. First, there is debate as to whether Mariette's plotting of the opera *Aida* was actually done to celebrate the opening of the Suez Canal. However, Giuseppe Verdi served as composer for the opera, and the world premiere was finally held at Cairo's Khedivial Opera House in December 1871, to great acclaim. It has become a standard in opera houses around the world. The modern musical version, with music by Elton John, is also based on Mariette's original scenario.

The lumberyard fire next to the fireworks stand at Port Said actually happened, though it occurred a few days earlier than November 16. It suited my purposes more to have it occur during the first night of festivities at Port Said.

Also, each member country of the delegation, particularly the larger and wealthier nations, typically had more than one ship involved in the flotilla. For example, Great Britain brought along *Psyche*, *Newport*, *Deerhound*, and *Rapid*. However, for simplicity's sake, I limited the action to just a few ships. In addition, the ships entered the canal as two different convoys from its southern- and northernmost points, then met at Ismailia. This was too complicated for the plot I was creating, so I have the entire flotilla moving as a single entity from Port Said down to Ismailia. I trust that the astute naval history reader will forgive this compression of details.

SELECTED BIBLIOGRAPHY

De Lesseps, Ferdinand. *The History of the Suez Canal: A Personal Narrative*. Edinburgh: William Blackwood and Sons, 1876.

Egerton, Francis, C. M. Norwood, and William Rathbone. *Great Britain, Egypt, and the Suez Canal*. London: Chapman and Hall Ltd., 1884.

Fitzgerald, Percy. *The Great Canal at Suez: Its Political, Engineering, and Financial History*. London: Tinsley Brothers, 1876.

Hennebert, E. *The English in Egypt: England and the Mahdi, Arabi and the Suez Canal*. London: W. H. Allen & Co., 1884.

Jenkins, Henry Davenport. *Instructions for Sailing through the Suez Canal, with Notes on the Navigation of the Gulf of Suez and Red Sea*. London: James Imray & Son, 1893.

Lynch, T. K. *A Visit to the Suez Canal*. London: Day and Son, Ltd., 1866.

Mariette-Bey, Auguste. *Monuments of Upper Egypt*. Translated by Alphonse Mariette. Boston: J.H. Mansfield & J.W. Dearborn, 1890.

McCoan, J. C. *Nations of the World: Egypt*. New York: Peter Fenelon Collier & Son, 1900.

Mitchell, Henry. *The Coast of Egypt and the Suez Canal*. Boston: Fields, Osgood, & Co., 1869.

Nourse, Joseph Everett. *The Maritime Canal of Suez: From its Inauguration, November 17, 1869, to the Year 1884*. Washington, DC: Government Printing Office, 1884.

Pakula, Hannah. *An Uncommon Woman: Empress Frederick, Daughter of Queen Victoria, Wife of the Crown Prince of Prussia, Mother of Kaiser Wilhelm*. New York: Touchstone, 1995.

Payne, Robert. *The Canal Builders: The Story of Canal Engineers Through the Ages*. New York: MacMillan Company, 1959.

ACKNOWLEDGMENTS

I lost my mother while in the middle of forming the plot for this, Violet's sixth adventure. Mom and I were always connected by books. She taught me to read for myself before I even started school because I pestered her so much to read to me. Every Saturday during my childhood, Mom would bundle me up in the car and off we would go to the library, parting ways at the circulation desk so I could get lost in the children's section and she could visit her beloved mystery section.

As I grew older, I developed a book collection to rival her own, and of course we were always lending each other books. Many were the times we laughed over having purchased books we already owned, or high-fived about finding a rare volume to complete some particular series.

Even as Mom's health waned and her eyesight betrayed her, I would drive her to the library each week, no longer to get physical books but to pick out audiobooks. When she could no longer go to the library, I downloaded audiobooks to her tablet. When she made what would unexpectedly be her final trip to the hospital, I bundled up the tablet and several books for her to have beside her. She couldn't really read anymore, but she liked having the physical presence of books with her.

As you can imagine, Mom was very tickled when I decided to embark on a writing career, and when my interests turned to historical mystery, she was nearly beside herself. She enthusiastically accepted copies of my draft manuscripts to go through with her magnifying glass, correcting my numerous mistakes and lecturing me about splitting infinitives and other crimes against grammar.

Mom also joined the Mystery Guild Book Club, and would excitedly rip open each month's offering to see if my latest book was being featured.

As my mother's various illnesses grew worse and she required more time at the hospital, I learned how to write there. It required a lot of mental discipline, as hospitals are very chaotic places. Mom continued helping out, sitting up in bed and keeping track of my hourly word count with a chart in order to make sure I met my deadlines.

When talking to others, she frequently referred to me as "my daughter, the author." I will, of course, never hear those words again.

And so, I would like to extend an appreciation that is difficult to express in mere words to those who were there during my mother's final months, either to support her or to comfort me, or to make sure life continued on as normally as possible. I will simply mention them all by name: Tammy Brindley, Lynn Buonviri, Dennis Dougan, Misha Hash, Michelle Holso, Nancy Jackson, Sarah Jean Kemp, April Mattedi, Carolyn McHugh, Mary Oldham, Mary Russell, Faye Snyder, Diane Townsend, Christopher Trent, Petra Utara, and Marian Wheeler. Thank you all for your various kindnesses to me and Mom.

My brother, Tony Papadakis, was right there suffering with me while trying to minister to me at the same time. I'm sure it wasn't always easy for him to do, yet I don't know what I would have done without him.

When I consider my husband, Jon, I wonder what I did to deserve such blessings. He spent many sleepless nights at the hospital, and many weekends taking care of my mother's house. No pyramid could hold enough treasure to equal his worth.

Once more, I extend my arms out to the nurses and staff of MedStar St. Mary's Hospital Cancer Care and Infusion Services: Dr. Amir Khan, Mary Abell, Cathy Fenwick, Teresa Gould, Rose Jupiter, Diane Loftus, Rachel Louden, Gloria Nelson, Joan Popielski, Patty Svecz, and Sherry Wolfe. You all know why.

Domino Optimo Maximo.

ABOUT THE AUTHOR

Photo: Jax Photography

CHRISTINE TRENT IS THE AUTHOR of the Lady of Ashes historical mystery series as well as three other historical novels. Her books have been translated into Turkish, Polish, and Czech. She writes from her two-story home library, where she lives with her wonderful bookshelf-building husband, five precocious cats, a large doll collection, entirely too many fountain pens, and over four thousand books. Learn more about Christine at www.christinetrent.com.